Do As I Say

This book is a work of fiction. Any names, places, characters, and incidents are either products of the author's imagination or used fictitiously. Any resemblance to locales or events or persons, living or dead, is entirely coincidental.

Do As I Say

David A Sterling

Dedication

This book is dedicated to my brother-in-law Mark. Although he lost his two and a half year battle with Lymphoma, during his battle he inspired all that knew him with his fortitude and determination to make every day one worth living. He taught me that there truly was no day but today. Thanks to his inspiration and the support of my family, my wife Mary Ann, my daughters Keri and Amanda, and my son Austin, I am happy to present to you, "Do As I Say".

A special acknowledgment to the men and women of our armed forces

Daniel Webster once said, "God grants liberty only to those who love it, and are always ready to guard and defend it."

Thank you for the sacrifices you have made and continue to make for us in order to preserve our liberty. If we told you how grateful we were a million times over, it wouldn't be enough. May God bless you and keep you safe.

Chapter 1

A Rude Awakening

We've all had those days when the alarm goes off, and as we try to pull ourselves out of the bed, we realize that it just isn't going to happen. Today was one of those days. I woke up feeling like crap. I'm not sure if it was related to the heavy drinking I had done at the party I attended last night, or if it was the onset of the flu. My choices were to watch over the old man during a lunch speech at a DC hotel, or I could take one of those days off that I never take and just stay in bed. It didn't sound like me. But the way I felt, I was more than happy to listen to whoever it was. I took my advice along with some cold medicine, called in sick, pulled the covers over my head, and the lights went out.

I remember it seeming like only a few minutes had passed before there was a knock at my door. Scratch that, it was more like a pounding. I pulled myself out of bed and as I worked my way to the door, I caught a glance of the moon hanging in the night sky. Could I have actually slept the day away? It didn't seem possible, but you can't argue the evidence. I could hear a familiar voice bellowing my name "Bennett, Bennett are you in there?" As I peered through the peephole of the door, I was surprised to see my friend and fellow agent, Bill Rich, standing there still in his FBI work standard issue black suit and white shirt. Many people when they first met Bill and I would assume we were related because we shared so many of the same physical traits. We both had a thick head of brown hair combed to the side and deep brown eyes. Although Bill at six-foot three, two-hundred and fifty pounds had a couple of inches and about forty pounds on me, our general builds were very similar. There are a couple of features that kept people from assuming we were brothers. Bill has a roman nose and a fair complexion. I remember playing basketball with him for a couple of hours last summer. The next day, he was so pissed off at me because I was sporting a great tan while he was so badly burnt that he could hardly move without wincing from the pain.

At the moment, he appeared haggard and even more pale than usual. The look on his face was one that I had seen before, and I knew at that moment that it wasn't going to be good news. I opened the door, and after telling him that he looked like crap, asked him what was wrong. Bill proceeded to tell me Senator Billings, aka "the old man" that I was supposed to follow around today had been assassinated. My heart jumped into my throat and I nearly fell off my feet. I managed to make my way to the couch where I dropped onto it so hard that I thought I had broken it. Bill sat down next to me still in shock himself. You always know that something like this could happen. Otherwise there would be no need for a security detail. But when it does occur, it hits you like a ton of bricks. After all, you and your team are expected to prevent this sort of thing. There were three regular members on our security team and a fourth standby agent that would be rotated in if any of us were unable to perform our duties. With my calling in sick, Bill was that fourth agent having the unfortunate privilege of filling in for me today.

I asked Bill for more details on what happened. The event was supposed to be a celebration lunch followed by a thank you speech for those that supported the Senator in another successful reelection bid. It should have been simple, an enclosed room, security checks, metal detectors at the door. Basically, there was no way that a gunman could have gotten into that room. Bill explained that when the hotel workers entered the room this morning to prepare for the event, they found the room was flooded and there was a partial collapse of the ceiling. Apparently, the damage occurred when some water pipes in the ceiling mysteriously broke. As hard as the security detail tried to convince the Senator to postpone the event, he and his daughter Hope believed the show should go on. Hope made arrangements with the hotel and they ended up relocating the event to their outdoor space. One thing about the Senator was that he could seldom be convinced to make changes to his schedule. About ten minutes into his thank you speech, a single shot to the head fired from one of the rooms on the fifth floor ended the Senator's life. He was dead before his body hit the floor. One of the hotel guests on the fifth floor reported to hotel security that after hearing two gun shots, they heard the sound of something falling hard to the floor in the adjacent room. By the time our people were informed and were able to reach the room, the shooter's body was completely surrounded by hotel security. He was lying in a puddle of his own blood with his brains splattered half way across the room. Although the crime scene was quickly vacated by our security team, the damage had already been done. Any evidence that we might have hoped to acquire from the room had been irrevocably compromised by the incursion of hotel security. The forensic team tried to salvage what they could, but it was clear that it would be a challenge for them to come up with anything useful. Bill, along with the other two regular members of the team, spent the rest of the day filling out reports and dealing with the aftermath of the events that had ensued. And all of this happened while I was sound asleep in my bed.

I had always used the expression "old man" as a term of endearment, not as an insult to the Senator; after all, he was in his 70's. Once, he had even overheard me use the term while talking to Bill. I am not sure how he heard it, but he came over to me, patted me on the back said "young man" and started laughing. He knew by my tone that I meant no disrespect. In fact, it was an honor to be assigned to his detail even though I had no idea how an FBI rookie at the time would have been fortunate enough to draw such a coveted position. Maybe it helped that I was from his home state of Arizona. The Senator was a true patriot serving in two wars and having received enough metals to make him one of the most highly decorated Veterans alive. Although he was a man of great power within the senate, he never looked down on anyone and treated others with the same level of respect that was accorded to him. He was known for being an even tempered man with a good sense of humor. However, during the last couple of months he seemed a bit on edge and his humor had evaded him. We would have chalked it up to the tension that a candidate usually experiences during a re-election bid, but in his case he had no reason to worry. He was too well loved by his constituents for anyone to mount a serious challenge for his seat. The Senator held one of the highest approval ratings ever attained by a member of congress.

I had been on his detail for two years and was looking forward to another six after his successful re-election bid, but an assassin's bullet put an end to that. There were two things that were unusual about our security detail assignment. Normally the secret service would handle those responsibilities, but the senator requested his detail come from the Bureau. Bill once told me that Senator Billing's first government job was with the FBI and it gave him a feeling of nostalgia being around Bureau agents. Initially this odd request was balked at, but the senator had enough clout to get his way. It was also very unusual for a senator to be assigned a security detail. But based on his stature and his hardline stance against corruption, he was considered a high profile target. I guess you can't be considered a senator of the people and still be a friend to elements that have made Washington politics so corrupt. Other men of his means would have retired and enjoyed their golden years, but he had a commitment that is rarely found these days. He wanted to make a difference. He wanted to leave the world a better place. Unfortunately, he left too soon and I wasn't there to do my job, I wasn't there to protect him. I will always wonder if the outcome might have been different had I been there. That question will plague me for the rest of my life.

Since my abrupt awakening, I had failed to take note of the fact that besides the sick feeling in the pit of my stomach brought on by the tragic news, I was otherwise feeling pretty good. After giving it some thought, I couldn't come up with a good reason why I shouldn't immediately head over to the office to see what I could do to help in the investigation. Even though the perpetrator was dead by his own hand, I needed to find some answers and clearly Bill was still too frazzled to give them to me. I told Bill of my plans and suggested he head home to get some sleep. He looked like he had been through a war, but it was clear that sleep was the last thing on his mind. He offered to drive us to the office. Based on his condition I saw no reason to put either of our lives at risk and decided that I would do the driving.

"Give me ten minutes to pull myself together and then we'll head out" I said.

"Okay, do you have anything with caffeine in it?" he asked.

"Check the fridge" I replied, "I think I have some soda in there."

While Bill headed for the kitchen, I went into the bathroom to grab a quick shave, brush my teeth, and comb my hair. I suspected that my boss might be there and didn't want to show up at the office looking like grunge. Before walking away from the mirror, I did a double take to make sure my eyes were not bloodshot from drinking last night. I threw on my freshly pressed suit and then Bill and I took the elevator down to my car. As soon as I entered the garage, I panicked when I noticed that my car wasn't in its usual parking space. My first thought was that someone had stolen the new car that I had purchased as a birthday present for myself.

Bill pointed over to the corner and said "it's over there".

"How did my car get over there?" I asked in a puzzled tone.

"You weren't in any condition to drive yourself home last night, so I volunteered," he replied. "I didn't want to leave your new car at the bar, so I left mine there. I had to take your car home after I got you up to your apartment."

"It wasn't easy," he said, "getting you to your apartment was like dragging a six-foot, two-hundred and fifty pound sack of potatoes around".

"You're the one that is two-fifty; I'm only two-ten," I replied, "but I get the idea."

I did not recall drinking that much, but then again I didn't remember most of the evening so I guess I would have to take Bill's word for it. We walked over to the car and I reached into my pocket which was empty and then looked towards Bill as he dangled the keys from his left hand. He tossed me the keys, I unlocked the doors, and we hopped into the car. It still had that new car smell as of last night, and I was relieved not to find it replaced with the smell of alcohol and vomit. As we pulled out of the parking lot, I had a strong feeling that it was going to be a long night followed by an even longer week.

We took the beltway which was always a nightmare to travel on. As a regular commuter, I found it was hard for me to recall the last time that I didn't run into traffic here, even when it was late at night. If it wasn't rush hour volume, it was construction delays, and you could never discount the stupidity of other motorists slowing down to watch some poor slob changing a flat tire. Personally I never saw any entertainment value in someone stuck on the side of the road, but I guess I was unique since just about everyone else seemed to enjoy the show.

While Bill sat silently for the duration of the drive, my mind wandered to thinking about Hope, the Senator's daughter and only child. I wondered how she was dealing with this tragedy and wanted to give her a call, but the earliest that I would be able to reach her, if she took my call, would be in the morning. It was no secret amongst the other guys in the detail that we had been romantically involved at one time, but once I was assigned to protect her father she broke it off to avoid any complications. Or so she told me. I wasn't sure what problems our relationship might have caused, but asking to be reassigned after drawing such a coveted position would have been tantamount to professional suicide. I would have thought that she was just using it as a more compassionate reason to end our relationship rather than just out right dumping me. But Hope wasn't the type of person that would worry herself about hurting the feelings of other people. She was a pretty straight shooter and didn't usually mince words. That was probably one of the biggest reasons why our relationship was doomed to fail regardless of my assignment to her father's detail. It appeared to me that she was a little bit offended that when she broke the news to me I didn't make an effort to try change her mind. The truth was that part of me was actually relieved that I wasn't the one that had to do the breaking up, especially since I would be working for her father. Earlier in our relationship, it might have been a different story. The first time we met was at a bar where many of the Bureau newbies would congregate after hours. A few of the guys after noticing a cute blonde sitting at the bar bet me that I couldn't get her to have a drink with me. I knew that it wasn't the first time that she had been hit on as the result of a bet by the way she reacted to my offer. She didn't even turn around before flat out rejecting me. As I started to head back to my friends with my tail between my legs she turned around and looked at me with her big blue eyes. She told me that after I paid off my bet that, if still wanted to buy her a drink I was welcome to come back to the bar and ask again. I did and she said yes…we started dating regularly a couple of weeks later. When she broke up with me it was awkward at first—at least for me—when we would cross paths at the senator's events. It took a while, but eventually the awkwardness seemed to disappear. Now, there would be a different type of uneasiness when I had to explain why I wasn't there to protect her father. Not that any rational person would blame me for being sick, but it is hard to think rationally when you just lost your father.

It took just over an hour before we finally arrived at the DC head-quarters and although most nights it was relatively quiet at this hour, it was anything but quiet tonight. The President was looking for answers and the press was on one of their usual feeding frenzies. So far, the few answers that were provided satisfied neither the President nor the press. As we walked up the stairs to enter the building, we were intercepted by a group of reporters.

One of them had recognized Bill as being on the Senator's security de-tail when he was killed and made the mistake of asking the question "How do you feel about having failed to protect the Senator?"

Bill responded, "How does it feel to be an asshole?" and started moving in the direction of the reporter.

I put my hand on his shoulder, not to restrain him, because it would have taken two of me to do that since he had four inches and forty pounds on me, but to just remind him that the last thing we needed at the moment was to get into a confrontation with the press. All we would have needed was to have a skirmish with the press show up on the Eleven O'clock News and our collective gooses would all be cooked if they weren't already. Bill recognized that it was a bad idea and stopped himself, altering his direction back towards the entrance of the building. I could never figure out the press. They would spend the entire night sitting around waiting to get information knowing full well that the only words they would hear are "no comment." Hell, they probably knew as much as we did at that moment anyway.

Bill and I had barely cleared security when I heard a familiar voice calling my name. It was the voice of the one person that I was trying to avoid tonight, but it appeared that I had failed in my attempt. It was Matt Web, one of the head investigators, and he happened to be my boss. Back at the apartment Bill had mentioned that Web was overseeing the investigation and he also intimated that he was looking for some heads to roll. We were hoping it wasn't going to be ours. It looked like there was going to be a slight detour before I could get to work and hopefully find some answers. While I started my less than happy journey towards Web's office, Bill turned and headed in the direction of the conference room where two of my regular team members were already sitting and waiting for our arrival, Fred Dean and Mike Smith. Fred and Mike may have been old timers, but losing the person you were assigned to protect was just as new to them as it was to Bill and me. On a normal day, one might say they appeared to be haggard by the years. Being in this business long enough could do that to you, but tonight they looked near death. It had been a long day for them and it was obvious that they had been getting a lot of grief from above. From working with them every day we had become friends, so seeing them in that condition was kind of rough. When I first joined the detail, they used to give me a hard time which I guess was their way of welcoming the newbie into the fold. Most people would have considered it an initiation ceremony, but after a few months they treated me like a son teaching me everything they knew. They were thought of in such high esteem that they could have easily been transferred to the Secret Service and assigned to the Presidential detail, but for some reason they never sought the position. I am sure that the prevailing thought amongst other agents was that if Fred and Mike with all their years of experience couldn't protect the Senator, then nobody could.

Web was in his mid-fifties, a hulking six-three and built like a tank. Even though I worked out regularly and considered myself to be in pretty good physical condition, I felt puny by comparison as I followed him to his office. We walked through the door and before it closed he yelled, "Where the hell were you all day?"

It caught me off guard, but I quickly responded, "I called in sick this morning didn't you get the message?"

"If you were home sick, then why the hell didn't you pick up the damn phone?" He yelled. "We must have called you a dozen times. I finally gave up and sent Bill to get you."

I told him that I didn't recall doing it, but I must have either pulled the phone out or turned off the volume so I could get some undisturbed rest. Web played college football for my alma mater Arizona State. I'll bet that the opposition was just as intimidated on the field being stared down by those piercing blue eyes as most people that sat on the opposite side of his desk.

"I guess you lucked out being out sick today," he said, "it probably saved your ass." He responded in a somewhat calmer tone.

Apparently, Fred and Mike were going through one final debriefing before being sent home on paid leave pending further investigation. My guess is that since they were the senior members of the team and Bill was just standing in for me today that it made sense that they would be the fall guys. They were already fully vested in their retirement, so from a financial perspective they wouldn't be hurt by the loss of their jobs, but I knew that they loved what they were doing and they would be devastated if they were cut loose. By all indications, it was a foregone conclusion that their departure from the bureau was inevitable. Since I wasn't involved, Web did not have much of a reason to continue the conversation so he told me to get briefed on the details and see if I could help figure out what went wrong today.

As I entered the conference room, Fred and Mike simultaneously stated that they couldn't stop the Senator from moving the celebration lunch outside. It was clear that they knew they were being setup as the fall guys. Bill made a noble effort to draw the heat off of Mike and Fred trying to assume responsibility for the security failure himself. While I'm sure the guys appreciated him risking his own career to save theirs, as a last minute fill-in, nobody would ever think of holding him responsible. The truth was that there was no way that anyone could have stopped the Senator and certainly no way they could have known that some nut would be waiting on the fifth floor of the hotel with a sniper rifle. One thing I've learned from being around Washington politics over the last four years is that the DC bureaucrats didn't need a good reason to hang you out to dry. They were quite adept at fabricating one when necessary. Part of me felt like I had let down the team, and part of me was relieved that I wasn't sitting in the proverbial hot seat myself. I asked them to fill me in on every detail they could remember. It was clear that they were all shaken, but between the three of them I hoped I would get the complete picture of what had transpired in my absence.

After a couple of hours of debriefing them, I had the full story. It was clear that there was nothing to be gained by keeping them any longer so I told them they should go home and get some rest. I promised them that I would do everything I could to help them. Even though they knew they were getting a raw deal they wanted to be kept informed and offered to help in any way possible. They understandably did not like what was going down, but they did like the Senator. I would have bet my career that either one of them would have taken the bullet in his place if they had the chance. While I was with his detail for only two years, they had been assigned to him for twelve years. You can't be around someone for that long a time without having a significant connection.

As they walked out the door I found myself alone in the conference room with too many unanswered questions. According to the information obtained so far, we had an Iraq-Afghanistan war Vet. He returns home and takes a job as a cab driver and then becomes an assassin. We had the mystery of how he could have known that the event would be moved to the outside in clear view of his balcony, and a motive that still hadn't been established. It was clear that there would be some long and difficult days ahead, but there was nothing left to do tonight. It was time to go home. I dropped by Web's office on the way out leaving him with my notes from the debriefing and a promise to hit the ground running in the morning.

I got home just before midnight, dropped my case and immediately went into the kitchen to check my phone. It was still plugged in, the volume wasn't muted, but there were several new messages from Web waiting to be played back on my machine. I must have really been out of it I thought to myself. After sleeping the day away I figured I wouldn't be able to go to sleep, but I guess the evening had taken its toll because as soon as my head hit the pillow…lights out.

Chapter 2
Something Is Not Right

By the time I got to my desk the next morning, a profile of our killer—pulled together by the night staff—was waiting for me. Our killer's name was Brian Rodney. He was a career military man serving in two wars with enough medals to demonstrate that he had seen some serious action. He was honorably discharged after an incident where several men in his unit were killed by a road side bomb. Apparently the loss hit him hard, but who wouldn't be affected by the death of so many men that he considered as friends. If not for a flat tire on his jeep he might have been a casualty of the explosion himself. After speaking with the brigade shrinks, they realized he was probably more of a detriment to his outfit in his current condition than they could afford and sent him stateside. Upon arriving home, he went through several months of psychiatric therapy to help him re-assimilate into society. After his release, he spent almost a year trying to find regular employment in his area of expertise before taking a job as a cab driver. According to the interviews with his friends and neighbors, he had a beautiful and loving wife and a baby on the way. With all he had to live for, it was incomprehensible to me. What might drive someone to do what Rodney had done. As I sat there pondering what had happened, Bill walked through the door.

"It doesn't make sense, does it?" he said.

"No, no it doesn't," I replied.

Anyone that had taken the time to listen to the Senator over the years, knew him to be as staunch an advocate of the military and returning vets as one could be. Being an ex-vet from an unpopular war, he was aware of how hard it was for our vets and did everything he could legislatively and charitably to help them when they returned from battle. With that said, the Senator was dead when Brian Rodney pulled the trigger the first time and when he pulled the trigger the second time he destroyed any chance we might have had to find out why. It was curious that Rodney being in top physical condition did not try to escape after he killed the Senator. His military background certainly would have afforded him a distinct advantage over the hotel security team. How could someone be intelligent enough to plan the assassination of a Senator and not have planned an escape route? What would he have lost by at least trying to get away? He had already proven his willingness to give up his life. Maybe he would have gotten away and maybe not, but why didn't he at least try? He had broken into the room that he used, so there was no clear way of tying it to him. The security cameras were down the entire morning which is either a huge coincidence or more likely Rodney or someone working with him took the system down. If he knew the camera system was down, he could have easily disappeared back into his life and the name of the assassin might have never been known. Could he have had such little regard for his own life? According to interviews with Rodney's friends, he was looking forward to the birth of his child and even with the overwhelming evidence against him they still couldn't believe he was the killer. Many might argue that these types of crimes never make sense, but usually the perpetrator in some delusional fashion feels justified in their actions. In this case, I hadn't read or heard anything yet that would even come close to a motive.

Bill had come to let me know that Rodney's wife was in the hospital and being sedated to protect their unborn child. Her doctors were extremely concerned that the emotional distress that she was suffering might put her into premature labor. Web wanted us to go down and talk to her in hopes that she could shed some light on things. Neither Bill nor I were looking forward to that conversation, but we didn't have much of a choice. On the way out, we stopped by forensics to see if they had any new information for us.

Dr. Bob Rush was the head of the forensic team in the Washington HQ. He had been there for over thirty years and although he was short in stature, he was a giant in the area of forensics. Rush was charged with the responsibility of identifying all of the fingerprints found in Rodney's hotel room. Not an easy task considering he needed to check all of the members of hotel security, the maids, and even previous guests of the room. It was obvious what he was looking for; another set of prints that might indicate that Rodney had an accomplice. To add to the coincidental failure of the hotel cameras the day of the assassination, we had the pipes breaking in the event room leaving Rodney in the perfect position to kill his prey. Certainly all of these so called coincidences would make it appear that someone else might be involved, but for the moment there was no hard evidence to prove this theory.

Dr. Rush had already verified the bullet that killed the Senator came from the sniper rifle that was covered with Rodney's fingerprints. He also verified that the handgun that Rodney used to kill himself also had only Rodney's prints on it. If there was an accomplice, he was only an observer at the time.

After leaving we made one last stop before heading over to the hospital to interview Rodney's wife. We dropped by the coroner's office to get an update on Rodney's autopsy. The coroner was still examining the body when we arrived. Although I had seen many dead bodies during my career, I had never grown comfortable with observing one during the autopsy. I made an unsuccessful effort to catch the eye of the coroner to draw him away from the table. After realizing my failed attempt, I reluctantly made my way over to where the coroner was working. Before I could get the first question out of my mouth, he began to blurt out his findings.

"No great surprises here boys," he said as he pointed to Rodney's body. "The bullet was fired at point blank range into his head and based on the powder burns on his hands and around the entry wound it seems clear that he pulled the trigger."

Neither Bill nor I were surprised to hear that.

"Anything else?" I asked.

"It looks like an open and shut case," he said and then paused for a minute. "One thing that you might be interested in, your guy was an insomniac."

"Do you mind me asking how you were able to come to that conclusion?" I asked.

"We did a blood work up and found a drug called Imovane in his system," he responded.

Although I wasn't familiar with the drug, Bill had heard of it before. He had a friend that had a sleeping disorder and was prescribed Imovane.

"I've heard of cases where soldiers returning home from battle were diagnosed with sleep disorders," I said, "but how can a guy that is taking sleeping pills function well enough to plan out, and execute a hit like this?"

"Habituation," he said, "if you are on the drug long enough your body becomes accustomed to it, thus weakening its effect on the individual taken the drug."

The coroner informed us that Imovane was a prescription drug and it was illegal to possess it without it being prescribed. But according to Rodney's medical records there were not any prescriptions on file. Bill and I stood there for a minute absorbing what we had heard when the coroner asked if we had any additional questions. When we told him no, he then politely excused himself. Apparently, he had "some body" to get back to. I didn't recall reading that Rodney had been under the care of any physician since he ended his treatment with the military psychiatrists. After leaving the hospital, I stopped by the bureau office to confirm that I hadn't missed anything in Rodney's files. According to the records, there were no entries of any recent psychiatric care. I presumed that if you can get cocaine and heroin on the streets, why not Imovane?

While leaving the building we passed the same group of reporters that we had the run in with the previous night, but after that encounter, they were keeping a safe distance from us.

"Nice display of restraint," I said to Bill as we reached the street.

"You have no idea," Bill responded as he stared back towards the group of reporters.

If looks could kill, I'd be arresting Bill for multiple homicides after that one. Bill was typically a calm guy that rarely exhibited a temper, but the events of yesterday had clearly shortened his fuse. We made our way to the parking garage, got in the car, and drove off to George Washington University Hospital. It was mid-day, so the traffic was heavy as usual. Ordinarily all of the stop and go would frustrate me, but today I didn't mind the delay at all. It was actually a blessing in disguise giving me some time to listen to music and clear my mind. Bill would always rib me because I enjoyed listening to music of different genres. I could be playing rock one minute and show tunes the next. The team nick-named me the Renaissance man suggesting that I was a bit more cultured than the rest of the crew. I didn't mind taking a few jabs now and again, and I certainly didn't mind dishing a few out either. While I drove, Bill closed his eyes and his head tilted off to one side. It was the middle of the day, but I knew that when he got home last night he probably didn't get much sleep. If it was me, I would have been recapping everything that happened leading up to the senator's assassination.

Chapter 3
More Questions, No Answers

We arrived at the hospital and found that there were several reporters camped out by the entrance. They were like buzzards looking for their next meal. We decided to pull the car around to the emergency room parking area so we could make a more discreet entrance. We were fortunate enough to have skated by one group of reporters today without incident. I was not looking to tempt fate with another encounter. We walked up one floor to the main desk, flipped our badges to the attendant, and asked for the room number of Rodney's wife. The woman at the desk must have been in her eighties, but she was sharp as a tack. She knew that we were there to question Mrs. Rodney and didn't seem too keen on the idea. It seemed like she instinctively felt the need to be protective of her. I could understand how she was feeling. This woman's entire life just got turned upside down. She wakes up one morning happy about her marriage, her life, and the birth of her child only a couple of months away. Before the sun sets, her husband is dead, accused of assassinating a prominent Senator, and now her baby is in jeopardy of delivering prematurely. With all that she had been put through over the past two days, here we were about to put salt in the wounds by questioning her. It was not one of our proudest moments. If our actions caused any harm to her unborn child, I'd have a hard time looking myself in the mirror.

Ironically her room was on the fifth floor. It was the same floor number that this time yesterday her husband camped out on waiting for a clear shot at the Senator. As I got off of the elevator, I could see a police officer standing in front of a room at the end of the corridor. I guess there was no need to check the room numbers. There were several people of varying ages standing on the path to the room, and all of them looked very upset by our appearance. I assumed it was Rodney's friends and/or family. It felt like we were about to walk a gauntlet in order to get to her room. We were only about a third of the way down the hall when we were approached by a middle aged couple. They introduced themselves as Mrs. Rodney's parents. Although I expected this would be an ugly encounter, I couldn't have been more wrong.

Even though they appeared to be both upset and bewildered at the events that had unfolded, their primary concern at the moment was the health and safety of their daughter and their unborn grandchild. I assured them that while it seemed insensitive at the moment, our questioning of their daughter was necessary. Before continuing on our way, I promised them that we'd do our best to keep things short and take extra care not to add to the trauma their daughter had already experienced.

They thanked us, and as we continued down the hall her mother yelled out, "Brian couldn't have done this", before breaking down in tears in her husband's arms.

I turned briefly to acknowledge her and could see in her eyes that in spite of the overwhelming evidence, she truly believed what she was saying. One would think they would be angry with their son-in-law for bringing this tragedy upon their family, for leaving their daughter to deal with the cowardice of his actions, but if there was any anger, they kept it well hidden from us. Rodney's parents were not at the hospital. They had to be moved to a safe location to protect them from retribution from the supporters of the Senator. There were a lot of people that had strong feelings for the old man and you never knew when someone might take those feelings one step too far.

It was only a hundred feet from the elevator to the room, but it seemed like a mile. When we finally arrived at the door, Bill and I paused for a minute before pulling out our badges and showing them to the cop stationed outside the room. As soon as we entered the room we were immediately confronted by a woman who introduced herself as Dr. Kruse.

"This is not a good time for you to be upsetting my patient by asking her a bunch of questions," she said, "Couldn't this be done at another time?"

I motioned for her to walk with me to the far corner of the room. I wanted to put some distance between Mrs. Rodney and our conversation. I spoke to her in a whisper to keep what was being said private. "We have two men that are dead, and we need to try and make sense out of the senseless. I don't want to question your patient any more than you want me to, but I don't get to make that choice. Her husband killed one of the greatest senators that this country has ever known and people are demanding answers. I'll do my best to make this quick, but like it or not it's going to happen and happen now."

"It looks like I have no choice," she responded, "but I must insist that I be present to monitor my two patients."

"No need to insist," I replied, "I wouldn't have it any other way, but understand that whatever you hear in this room does not leave this room."

"Agreed," she said.

Janice Rodney was clearly sedated, but conscious and willing to speak with us. Her voice was weak as a result of the medication she was on, making it hard to understand what she was saying at times. She was clearly surprised at what her husband was accused of doing and refused to believe that he could have done something so horrible. I knew that arguing the point with her wasn't going to get me anywhere. I decided to take a different tact and instead engaged her in a conversation about her husband in hopes that she might provide some insight into what led to these tragic events. She talked about how he was proud of his time in the military and how upset he was at the loss of his fellow platoon members and friends in the road side bombing. She told us how that tragic incident ultimately led to his release from the military. I asked her how her husband felt about the war and if he blamed anybody for his involvement and the deaths of his friends.

"He was proud of his contributions in helping to liberate the oppressed people of Iraq and Afghanistan," she insisted.

The only person that she was aware of that he blamed was himself for not being there to either help or die alongside his friends. This was all consistent with what we had read in his psychiatric records when he returned to stateside. We asked if he had any political views and if there was anything going on in Washington that was particularly upsetting to him. We all know what goes on in Washington, and it wouldn't be unusual for any of us to have a list a mile long of things that pissed us off about the partisanship and the corruption that was prevalent in politics. I wasn't interested in getting a list I just needed the one item that would provide a motive as to why he decided to kill this particular Senator. You can imagine how shocked we were when she told us that her husband had voted for Senator Billings in the last two elections. Seeing how he was just re-elected that eliminated the possibility that Billings had done something that betrayed Rodney's trust. She continued explaining that when her husband couldn't find a job after his discharge, he ran into a friend that drove a cab and connected him with the supervisor—who was also an ex-vet—who offered her husband a job on the spot.

Although he had strong political views, he was told that if he engaged in any political conversations with a fare, he'd get better tips if he made believe that he shared their political views. It bothered him that he had to play this game, but he knew that by capitulating to the views of his patrons, he could triple his income. With a baby on the way, they needed every dime they could get. He had gotten very good at the game and was quite convincing, but there were days when he would come home furious about what he had to endure just to make a buck. The more I heard, the more confused I became. At one point Bill and I looked at each other and without him saying a word I knew that we were both thinking the same thing. This just didn't make any sense.

It was now time to start asking the more difficult questions. We asked her about her husband's use of drugs.

"When Brian came back to the states, he was treated at the VA hospital," she told us. "He was having problems coping with what happened over there, including nightmares that would keep him from getting a good night's sleep. When he was released, he seemed fine for almost two years."

"What happened then?" I asked.

"The nightmares started to come back a few months ago," she replied.

"Is that when he started taking medication?" Bill asked.

"Yes," she responded.

She went on to tell us how fortunate he was to pick up a fare that happen to be a psychiatrist.

"He told the psychiatrist that he was an ex-vet and had a relapse of nightmares that would disrupt his sleep. The psychiatrist arranged to meet him the next day giving him a bag of pills that he said would help him sleep better at night."

"Do you know the doctor's name?" I asked.

"No," she replied, "He didn't give Brian his name. He just told him he wanted to remain an anonymous Good Samaritan."

"Was there a pharmacy name or doctor's name on the prescription?" I asked.

"He never got a prescription," she responded, "but whenever Brian was running low on pills, more pills would show up in the mail in a plastic bag. We just figured they were from him."

It was just what we needed, another mystery. A Good Samaritan doctor that wanted to remain anonymous. It wasn't unusual to see someone pick-up the check of a soldier now and then as a way of thanking them for their service, but providing a regular supply of prescription drugs was a new one for me. I would have liked to talk to our Good Samaritan, but with all of the politicians and lobbyists in this town, I couldn't begin to imagine how many psychiatrists there might be in the DC area. Unless we were able to uncover some additional information on this doctor, or he was to show up on our doorsteps, the odds are he would continue to remain the anonymous Good Samaritan. Even if by some miracle we were able to locate him, under the circumstances, he would probably deny knowing Rodney in order to avoid some culpability for what had happened.

While I was monetarily lost in my thoughts, I failed to notice that Mrs. Rodney had started to cry. I looked at Bill, and then turned towards the doctor. She was sitting in the corner keeping a vigilant eye out for her patient. Even though the corner where she had been sitting was not well illuminated, I could see that she was crying as well. They were tears of sympathy for her patient and the tragedy that had befallen her. I saw no reason for us to continue our questioning. She was clearly as surprised as everyone else at the actions of her husband. She was not a conspirator, just another victim. I turned back to Bill to see if he had anything else to ask. As I did I saw him wipe his eyes on his sleeve. In all the years that we'd known each other, I could not recall a single time that I'd seen Bill shed a tear. We'd done what we were asked to do, now we needed to do what was right and leave this poor woman alone. I reached my hand out putting it on top of Mrs. Rodney's and gave it a little squeeze.

"I'm sorry for your loss," I said. "Thank you for your time."

As Bill and I got up and started walking out of the room, I realized that we were probably leaving with more questions than we had when we arrived. Agent Web would be waiting for us to file our report. I was sure he would find it to be as underwhelming as we knew it to be. We were anxious to get back to the office and get our report in so we could attend the Senator's wake. Tomorrow, there would be a private morning service for family and close friends. The Senator's body would then be moved to the church for a public ceremony before being laid to rest in Arlington.

I wasn't looking forward to facing his daughter Hope, but it was inevitable that our paths would cross at the funeral. Her father had only been dead for two days, not even buried, yet there were rumors that the Governor was considering Hope to replace her father's vacated senate seat. It would have been in bad taste for him to publicly approach her while she was still in mourning. But considering the senator's popularity, the governor knew that Hope would be a good political choice.

We made excellent time getting back to the office. I went to report to Web, while Bill went back to his desk to log our conversations with Mrs. Rodney into the Bureau system. I was just about to knock on the door when I heard Web call me into the office by name. After entering and closing the door I asked "How did you know I was there?"

"Don't worry, I'm not clairvoyant," he said as he pointed to the monitor setup at the corner of his desk. "I'm assuming you didn't notice the video camera I have above my door."

"I guess not," I replied.

We were both anxious to get to the wake so we dispensed with the idle chatter and got right down to business. I filled him in regarding the results of my questioning of Mrs. Rodney. I told him that I thought there were still some questions that needed to be answered. The more I talked, the more agitated he seemed to become.

"This is a waste of time!" He barked. "You can't argue the facts, the evidence is indisputable!"

He had made himself clear, as far as he was concerned it was homicide, case closed. I was surprised that as good as he was at his job that he would let so many questions go unanswered. I guess the pressure from above to put this case to rest must have been too overwhelming, even for Web. So after a quick dog and pony show of an investigation, they decided that they wanted this one in the history books. There was nothing I was going to say or do that would change things.

"Why don't you and Bill take some vacation time?" Web suggested. "Let things quiet down a bit. When you return, we can look into getting you into a new detail."

"What about Mike and Fred?" I asked.

"They were through as soon as Billing's body hit the floor," he replied. "Don't worry about them they're going to retire with full pension."

"You mean they're being retired," I responded.

"Just consider yourself fortunate you were out sick, or this conversation would be going differently," he quipped.

After having to endure the stench of this investigation, I was more than ready to accept the vacation time. I needed to get out of town and breathe some fresh air, but not before I paid my respects to the old man and Hope. I had tried calling her a couple of times, but she never answered my calls. Could she have just been overwhelmed with the funeral arrangements, or was she was just avoiding my calls? I couldn't see how she could be holding me responsible for her father's death, but with Hope, you could never tell.

Chapter 4
Funeral For A Friend

As one could imagine, being a member of the Senator's security team and attending his wake after he was assassinated was uncomfortable to say the least. While there were some that were sympathetic to our part in all this, there were those that clearly believed we were to blame for the Senator's untimely demise. Bill and I were obligated to partake in the wake, procession, and services, although we would have attended whether we were required to or not. Mike and Fred on the other hand were stripped of that obligation as they were being forced into retirement, but they planned on attending nevertheless. After twelve years of service, the Senator and Hope were like family to them. I doubt that anyone could have kept them away. After paying our respects we congregated at one side of the hall just trying to blend into the crowd of dignitaries in attendance. It was an event so grand in scale that if one didn't know, they would have thought this assembly was a sendoff for a President. If you didn't love the old man, and few didn't, you had to respect him. He never minced words and his motives were as pure as I have ever known a politician's motives to be. I am sure there are a few lobbyists and organizations that won't miss him, but you can't be a true servant of the people and be friends with the special interest groups.

We stayed for an hour and when we felt like we'd paid our dues, we escaped to a local bar that we frequented when we were off duty. It felt strange not being able to fill Mike and Fred in on how the investigation ended, but being retired it would be a violation of the rules for that information to be shared with civilians. However, there were no rules that would keep us from being able to talk about old times. Having spent only two years with the detail, I hadn't racked up too many old times to speak of. Mike and Fred on the other hand had some whoppers to tell. My guess was that with the passing of the years, these stories had become more fiction than fact, but Mike and Fred both enjoyed telling them. Even though Bill & I had heard them several times before, out of respect we would still laugh as if it was the first time. Many of them had to do with the Senator's first and second wives. His first wife came from a simple life. She was born in the same small town as the Senator. When she first came to Washington, she tried to act all high society and mingle with the more sophisticated crowd. As much as she would spend on her wardrobe, you could take the girl out of the small town, but you can't take the small town out of the girl. She was like a fish out of water. She came to hate the life of a Senator's wife so much that she gave him an ultimatum of her or his career. Unfortunately for her, the old man loved politics a bit more than he loved her. He gave up most of his wealth to keep things civil and she disappeared back to her small town life. It wasn't long before he met his second wife. They were married within a year and divorced before their second anniversary. She saw big money and perhaps a future life in the White House. After six months of marriage, she started to realize that he wasn't in this for the money. She knew that unless you got into bed with the special interest groups, your odds of making it into the White House were slim to none. It wasn't long after that realization that the marriage became intolerable and they went their separate ways. Long before the divorce, she had already found a replacement and consummated that relationship, if you know what I mean. That little indiscretion on her part made the divorce a fairly quick and inexpensive one for the Senator. I hardly knew his third wife since she died shortly before I was assigned to his detail, but according to Mike and Fred she was a real lady. I guess what they say about the third time being the charm must be true. They were married for three years when Hope was born. Mike and Fred joined the Senator's detail when Hope had just turned sixteen. She was a rambunctious teenager that loved the notoriety of being the daughter of a prestigious Senator. Hope knew that as an only child, she could get away with anything and regularly took advantage of that. There was a time when there was a standing bet on how long she could go without getting into trouble. Fortunately for the Senator, one day Hope had a miraculous and inexplicable turn around, deciding that she wanted to follow in her father's footsteps. From that time forward, she became very active in her father's political life and even gave introduction speeches for him at various events.

As much fun as it was sharing a few drinks with Mike and Fred, Bill and I had to get up early to prepare for the funeral procession. Mike and Fred voiced their intentions of attending the services, but under the circumstances, planned on keeping their distance. I said my goodbyes to the boys and left the bar. I was pretty sure that I had exceeded the legal drinking limit, so I decided to grab a cab home. I slipped the cabby a healthy tip in advance to make it a quiet ride. Thankfully, I was in better shape than the night before the Senator was killed and was able to make it up to my apartment on my own. I dropped the clothes I had worn onto the floor and climbed into bed. Unlike Rodney, I had no problems going to sleep. I was unconscious before I could count to ten.

The alarm clock sounded like Big Ben chiming under my pillow. I'm not sure why I never invested in an alarm that played music, but it was now going to be on my short list of things to buy. My first stop was the medicine cabinet for some aspirin, and then off to the kitchen to make a strong pot of coffee. The funeral service was only couple hours away and I needed to pull myself together. As one of the few remaining members of the Senator's detail, I would be included in the procession from the hearse to his final resting place. After reaching the grave, I anticipated being one of hundreds to offer my condolences to his family. The only difference is that to my knowledge I would be the only person on line that was romantically involved with his only daughter.

I pulled my suit from the closet. Not much of a selection since they were all standard issue for the security details. After recalling that I had abandoned my car in the parking garage of the bar last night, I realized that the only way I was going to make it on time was to grab a cab to the office. The funny thing is that cabbies have a reputation for driving like lunatics, but for some reason it takes twice as long to get anywhere. During the drive I had an opportunity to think about what I might say to Hope when we came face to face for the first time since this tragic event, but all I could come up with was I'm sorry.

By the time I arrived, most of the other agents attending the funeral were waiting outside for final instructions. We all piled into cars and started our drive to The National Cathedral for the service. As much as I wanted to be inside the church for the service, congressmen, senators and the President filled out the church, leaving many of us standing on the steps and the grounds surrounding the church. Many dignitaries that wanted to attend were not allowed because of security reasons. The Vice President was actually very close friends with the Senator, but because the President was in attendance he had to view the ceremony remotely. The rest of us were stuck outside in the hot sun waiting for the procession to the cemetery. As one might imagine, with so many blowhards in one place, this wasn't going to be a short service. We would get occasional updates as the service progressed. By all accounts a total of thirty eulogies were given before people started filing into their cars. I guess the good news was that with everyone speaking their peace inside the church, the only one left to talk at graveside would be the priest.

We arrived at the cemetery in just under an hour, it was usually a two hour trip in traffic, but that is what a police escort will do for you. The President couldn't be part of the cavalcade because he had to prepare for a meeting with the French President later that evening. While many of the Senators and Congressman decided to skip the graveside service to avoid the heat and humidity, many of his closer friends in the Senate and his former staff attended. Hope was seated about ten feet from the grave when the hearse pulled in. Bill and I, along with a few of his upper staff members were given the honor of being pallbearers. Considering the Senator was a pretty frail guy, the coffin must have been filled with bricks because it weighed a ton. Bill and I worked out three to four times a week, so we were in pretty good shape. His staffers on the other hand looked like they were being crushed by the weight of the casket. There was no question that Bill and I were carrying more than our fair share.

As we approached the grave, I noticed Fred and Mike up on the hill keeping their distance as they had suggested they would. When we set the coffin down on the platform above the grave, you could hear a sigh of relief coming from the other pallbearers. We had barely settled back in with the rest of the crowd when the priest started reading a scripture followed by a prayer. Once the ceremony had completed, we lined up to pay our final respects. After walking past the Senator's casket, we continued on to pay our condolences to his family and friends. When I reached Hope, our eyes met for a second, she shook my hand and, looked to the next person in the procession. Her reaction to seeing me seemed very aloof, but considering the situation I tried not to take it personally. Any romantic feelings I had for her were long gone and I'm assuming it was no different for her. I was surprised at how well she held up through the reading of the scripture and prayer. I did not see her shed a single tear. I knew she was a strong person, but I did not anticipate that kind of strength. I guess I did not know her as well as I had thought.

After paying our final respects, Bill and I worked our way up the hill to where Fred and Mike were standing. They were being protected from the harsh sun by a shady tree. It must have been fifteen degrees cooler once we stepped into its shadow. We talked for a while during which time Fred and Mike revealed their plans of becoming PI's to keep themselves occupied. It wasn't unusual for people retiring from jobs like ours to try and pick up some additional cash working in the security industry. Becoming a PI was not a typical next step, but it was not huge stretch either. I told them that Web had suggested that Bill and I take some vacation time while our future assignments were being worked out. The death of the Senator hit Bill harder than I would have expected, but then again he was on the front lines when the Senator was shot. It was clear that he needed, and deserved, his getaway more than I did. Bill planned on doing some touring of the states to take in some historical sites. His vacation plans would unquestionably be more fun than mine. My vacation plans, if you would call it a vacation, was to head home to Arizona to see my parents. It seemed like forever since I had been there last, but that was for a very good reason.

"Just make sure you keep me informed about your whereabouts," I said in an emphatic tone.

"How many days do you think it will be this time?" Bill asked.

"With my father," I responded, "a couple of days at best before I check into a motel. Just make sure you keep your phone on."

It was getting late and I needed to get back to the apartment to pack my bags. I had a morning flight and I wanted to catch as much sleep as possible before heading for the airport.

"Enjoy your vacation," I said as I reached out to shake Bill's hand.

"Do you need a ride to your car?" he asked.

It had slipped my mind that my car was still parked in the bar garage.

"Thanks, but I don't want to put you out again," I replied.

"Not a bother, what if you get there and your car was towed?" he asked as he motioned for me to follow him to his car.

"If you insist," I said as I patted him on the back and thanked him.

Chapter 5

A Chance Meeting

It had been a while since I'd gotten out of DC and it was way overdue. The past week had taken its toll on me. I had lost the Senator, a couple of partners, and had been ignored by an old flame. But as much as the first two bothered me, I was even more disturbed that I still couldn't come up with an explanation for Rodney's actions. I really had to stop thinking about it, or it would probably drive me mad. Web said the case was closed and I wasn't going to be the one to argue the point with him. If I did, my next job might be on security detail for the President's daughter. Although it was my understanding that her teacher was a real looker, I had no interest in relearning fifth grade math. As the song goes, my bags were packed and I was ready to go. Right on cue, the cabbie started hitting the horn.

It wasn't long after the cab started moving that the cabbie tried to engage me in conversation. I wondered if he wanted to talk politics to increase his tip. For the moment, I was leaving politics behind so I threw a twenty into the front seat and told him to just drive. Fortunately traffic was light and we got to Dulles with plenty of time to spare to catch my flight. I felt naked traveling without my gun, but since this was a vacation, I felt the hardware was optional. The gate seemed rather crowded considering the early flight, but I guess I wasn't the only one in a rush to get out of town.

I was fortunate enough to get an exit row seat so I had some room to stretch. I don't begrudge a fellow passenger from being able to recline their seat, but I hated when it was in my lap, especially for a long flight. A tall, thin, silver haired man with a Texas-sized moustache who appeared to be in his mid-fifties excused himself past me seating himself in the window seat. I noticed as he squeezed by me that he was carrying what appeared to be a standard police issued gun. When I asked him if he had a badge to go with the hardware he smiled and pulled out an Arizona PD detective's badge.

"How did you know?" he asked.

"I used to be a cop myself," I replied, "the gun seemed all too familiar."

I told him I was with the FBI on security detail. He held up the Washington Post—with a picture of the Senator and an inset picture of his coffin—joking that I hope you weren't on his detail. He could tell by the look on my face that he had just inserted his cowboy boot in his mouth. He apologized, but there was obviously no harm intended.

"Special Agent Bennett Mills," I said as I extended my hand to show that there were no hard feelings.

"Detective Ed Lynch," he said as he shook my hand.

It only took a few seconds before he put two and two together asking me if I was any relation to a retired police chief in the Arizona area named George Mills. My father was pretty well known in Arizona. He led one of the biggest drug busts in state history, making the cover of every major newspaper the next day. Based on that and his other successes, he was considered somewhat of a hero in the state.

"Yep, that would be my dad," I responded, "Since I had some unexpected and unwanted down time I figured I would drop in for a surprise visit."

Speaking of surprises, while we were chatting, I hadn't realized that the flight had taken off, and on time too.

He rolled the paper up in his hand like he was getting ready to hit a dog on the nose for peeing on the carpet.

Instead he slapped it into his other hand and said, "this just didn't make any sense to me".

I assumed Lynch was referring the Senator's death. If he was, he would have known that I wouldn't be at liberty to provide any details that were not already disclosed to the public. Being a detective I am sure the look on my face and the subconscious nod of the head told him all he needed to know.

"You know," he said, "we had a case down in Phoenix that was very similar to this one just over a year ago. It wasn't quite as high profile as the assassination of a Senator, but pretty high profile for our local business community."

There are times when you find yourself sitting next to someone on a flight that wants to exchange idle chatter and you just can't get them to shut up, this wasn't one of those times. He knew that he had my curiosity peeked by the way I shifted my body in the seat to be in a better position to listen. He didn't skip a beat before continuing on with the story. Another Vet by the name of Dan Stone, came back from Iraq and took a job with building security for a pharmaceutical company. According to his supervisor, he is doing a great job taking on extra hours when needed, working an extra shift now and then. One day as the president of the company is walking through the lobby of the building he draws his revolver and puts a bullet in the president's chest. Before the guy even hits the ground, the guard puts the gun in his own mouth and pulls the trigger. Besides the parallels that they were both Vets and both killed themselves after killing their prey, at the moment I was still considering it a coincidence. But he wasn't finished yet. As he continued the story, any thoughts I had about it being a coincidence came into question. It seems that the Vet had just gotten married a year prior to the incident. When the police interviewed his wife, she was insistent that there were no warning signs that her spouse was on the verge of being involved in a murder-suicide. Like Mrs. Rodney, the shooter's wife couldn't provide any reasons why he would have singled out his victim. The wife did note one thing about her husband; he recently started to suffer from insomnia and was taking some type of medication to help him sleep. He could see in my eyes that he had just struck a nerve. Not only were there too many coincidences in the story, but I started to get the feeling that this chance meeting wasn't by chance at all. At this point, I bluntly asked him if this seating arrangement had been pre-arranged. He smiled and intimated that he might have had something to do with it.

"Why?" I asked.

"The vet that I was telling you about wasn't a stranger, it was one of my best friend's son," he replied.

When details started to be released regarding the Senator's assassination, he had hopped a plane to DC hoping that some professional courtesy might allow him to get some inside information regarding the case.

"Unfortunately," he told me, "the FBI did not believe in professional courtesy unless they were the ones needing the information".

"I apologize for the deception," he said," but I needed to see your face when I brought up the sleeping medication to prove my theory."

He didn't have to say it; I knew what he was thinking, because I was thinking the same thing. Somehow these two cases were connected. One question remained and at this point I was willing to step over the line in order to get the answer we both needed.

"Who prescribed the drugs?" I asked.

"I'll tell you," he said, "but my gut tells me you already know."

"Why don't you tell me anyway," I replied.

"Some doctor that was trying to help him out, and we have no clue who he is or where to find him," he told me.

I paused for a moment, turned towards Lynch and said "I guess this will be a working vacation."

He broke out into a shit eating grin and said, "We still have a couple of hours before we land." as he pulled out a pad and pen to make some notes.

I pulled out my I-Pad and pointed to the wireless symbol on the back of the plane seat and said, "How about joining me in the 21st century?"

He smiled again and said "I'd love to".

I knew that I was violating more than a few rules by allowing Lynch to see what we had in our database, but sometimes you just have to say to hell with the rules. Within a few minutes I was connected to the FBI system and couldn't help but to wonder if I was about to reopen a case or was on the verge of opening Pandora's Box. After trying several search criteria, both Ed and I were surprised to see that the only results that were turning up were those associated with the Senator's death and a few cases that dated back to the nineteen-forties that involved Veterans of WWII. It was obvious that WWII cases were not relevant to what we were searching for. The fact that we came up empty in our search temporarily took the wind out of my sails. After a few seconds, I realized that something wasn't right here. Based on what Lynch just told me about his friend's son, we should have found at least two current cases in the database. With that realization, I had that feeling in the pit of my stomach that told me I had just stepped into a big pile. Could someone inside the bureau be complicit in these crimes? I could tell by the look on Ed's face that he was thinking the same thing. Maybe the reason why the investigation was closed so quickly was because there was no proof that this wasn't an isolated event. I could tell that Ed was a pro at his job, because without saying a word he knew what I was thinking.

He looked me in the eye and said "Maybe we chose the wrong place to look."

He reached for my I-pad which I handed over without any resistance. He brought up the internet browser and went into a search engine. Within minutes of entering a few words into the search criteria, pages of entries were returned.

"Welcome to the twenty-first century," he said with a grin on his face.

I guess I deserved that one for my earlier comment, but I didn't mind it one bit. We spent the next hour reviewing newspaper articles from around the country and found several cases that were suspiciously familiar. All involved the death of well-established local businessmen or local political official. In each case, a Veteran was the assailant and took his or her own life after killing their victims. No killers to interview, no clear motive that could be found, and nowhere for the case to go but into the closed case file. Although in each instance the person killed had some degree of prominence in their community, the story wasn't big enough to make it to the national stage. If not for the killing of the Senator and Lynch's close connection to the suspect in the Arizona killing—and his suspicions that they might be somehow related—these cases would have remained permanently closed.

"My gut told me there would be others," Lynch said, "I told Agent Web that there was something too coincidental about the two cases, but he didn't seem interested in listening and certainly not in sharing information with me."

"Web, Matt Web?" I blurted out.

"I believe that was his name," Lynch replied.

If that was who Lynch had met with while in Washington, then why didn't Web mention the other case to me? Why didn't he investigate the Senator's case further once Lynch made him aware of the Arizona killing? As much as I did not want to believe it, there was a strong possibility that Web might somehow be involved in these events. If he was, how could I proceed with further investigation without him knowing about it? It was clear that Lynch and I had to fly under the radar on this one. If I didn't handle this correctly, I might need Lynch to put in a good word for me with the Phoenix Police Dept. for a new job. Even if Lynch was willing to walk out on that ledge with me, it was obvious we would need the cooperation and resources of his precinct. I turned to Lynch as the plane's tires touched down and asked how much vacation time he had.

He responded, "Plenty, and welcome to Arizona, partner".

Chapter 6
Family Reunion

When I boarded the flight this morning, I thought the most difficult part of the trip was going to be spending time with my family. How quickly things had changed. As I made my way to the baggage claim with my new found friend and partner, Detective Lynch, I had a lot to think about, the least of which was my father. We had several cases that if we removed the names of the people involved and locations in which they occurred, one might think we were talking about the same event. While on the surface much of what they had in common was obvious, there was something else that tied these cases together that was still a mystery to us. There are some that might suggest that these could be copycats, but based on the lack of publicity they received outside of state line, that would be grasping at straws. There had to be something that these Vets all had in common. After a quick reunion with the family, Lynch and I were going to have our work cut out for us trying to find out what it was. It would have been a lot easier if we could draw on our combined resources for help, but any attempt to do so might jeopardize our chances of solving these cases. Lynch and I exchanged cell phone numbers while retrieving our luggage. We agreed to take a day off before starting our investigation. We both had personal business that needed attending to before we dove into the deep end.

"Do you need a lift?" he asked.

"No thanks," I replied, "I have a rental waiting for me. Besides, I have a feeling we will be spending a lot of time together over the next few days."

The car rental lines were relatively light, which was a pleasant surprise. My past experiences had not been that stellar. It wasn't long before I was on the road home.

Last time I was in town it was a nightmare. By the time I left, I wasn't speaking to my father and my mother was in tears. It took two months before my mother convinced us both to make amends. It was always about the same thing. He had built a legacy and he couldn't figure out why I didn't want to live in his shadow. This time, I was showing up without notice. I was hoping that this would give my dad less time to stew. Maybe I would catch him on a good day, yeah right. When he retired, he decided to do what he had always wanted. He bought a twenty acre horse ranch. To this day I'm still trying to figure out how taking on that kind of responsibility translates to retirement. Three months after he made the move, my mother told me that he had regretted getting involved with a business where he had to feed and clean up after his inventory. It was the first time I could remember a story about my father resulting in a good laugh. I pulled up to the entrance with the house clearly in site, paused, took a deep breath and hit the gas. As I approached the house, I saw my father unloading bales of hay off of his old Ford pickup. That old truck had to have enough mileage on it that he probably ran the odometer twice. It appeared by his side profile that he was starting to develop a gut. I guess that the work on the ranch wasn't compensating for three square meals that my mother was feeding him daily. Although age had whittled him down by a couple of inches, he still appeared to stand about six feet. My mom was just coming out the door with a glass of lemonade and my sister Carol just a few feet behind. She had moved back in after an ugly divorce. Her ex-husband was a jerk by anyone's standards. What she saw in him was probably as big a mystery as the one that Lynch and I had to solve. It wasn't long after they were married that some of his serious character flaws came out and my sister left him. I don't think my father minded having my sister move back in with them. It seemed that after we had all moved out that my mother was paying more attention to him then he wanted or needed. Having my sister around all the time helped to draw some of that attention away from him. It also gave him time to go hunting and play cards with his other retired buddies. Since my sister's ex was not a reliable source for income she went back to working at the bank that she'd been employed at before she got married. It gave her a chance to meet some people of her own age. From what my mother told me one of the men at the bank had been trying to date her, but apparently she wasn't interested. I guess she was still feeling the lingering pain of the divorce.

As I pulled in front of the barn and parked the car, they still had no idea it was me. The glare from the sun and the heavy tinting on the car window obscured their view. When I opened the door and stepped out, I could see big smiles appear on my mother and sister's face. My father's face was like stone. Not that I expected him to run up and give me a hug, but it might have been nice to see some type of positive expression to my return home. Because I didn't want my mother to suffer through another argument, I held back a pithy response to the cold reception I received. Instead I decided to be the bigger man, approaching him and shaking his hand. I then turned towards my mother and sister giving them each a long hug and kiss. Some people say that opposites attract. In my parent's case that couldn't have been more true. They had been married for forty-five years and were, by all accounts, still very happy and in love. By contrast, I'd never had forty-five minutes of conversation with my father that didn't end in a fight. Maybe that meant that we were too much alike.

While walking to the house I got the usual questions. Why are you in town? How long are you staying? I informed them that I was working a case with the local authorities and I wasn't quite sure about the length of my stay. It all depended on what I may find and where the case might take me. My father overheard and asked what type of case I was working on, knowing full well that I couldn't provide him with those details. Because of my father's high stature in the department, he was used to always being in the know regarding every high profile case. I think it must have eaten him up inside being on the outside of any case, and as bad as it might sound, it actually gave me some satisfaction.

"Well if you can't tell us about the case, can you at least tell me who you are working with?" he asked.

"Lynch," I said, "Detective Ed Lynch. He is attached to the Phoenix PD on Washington Street."

"I know where it is, and I know who he is. In fact, I know pretty much everybody on the force, trained most of them at one time or another," he replied.

My father took a lot of pride in his history with the department and his stature. That was one of the few things I understood and appreciated about him. In part, his larger than life history with the department is a big part of why I needed to make my career outside of Arizona. I didn't want to live in his shadow, never knowing if as I moved up it was because of what I did or what he did. I didn't want to be measured by a man that by many was considered one of the best cops that the state had ever known.

I took a short rest in my old bedroom. It was hard to believe that this wasn't the house I grew up in. Every piece of furniture, every article of my youth was carefully placed exactly as it was in the house of my youth. My mom was very nostalgic, and although I am sure she wanted me to feel at home when I visited, it was more for her than for me. It did bring back some fond memories of my youth and was a pleasant distraction from the investigation that I was about to embark on. I could hear the dinner bell ring. It was a tradition that my mother never departed from. I could remember hearing it as a prelude to every dinner I could recall. Strangely enough I live within a few blocks of the Washington National Cathedral and when they ring the bell from a distance it sounds like mom is calling me for dinner. It doesn't cause me to salivate like Pavlov's dog, but it does make me hungry for a home cooked meal. Most of my meals are served in cardboard or Styrofoam boxes. It was one of the things that came with being single and not being able to cook a meal without burning it.

Dinner was quiet and uneventful. When I say quiet, it means that we were all walking on eggshells as to avoid any topics that might have initiated World War III. I really expected my father to bring up the assassination of the Senator as if it was a failing on my part, but my guess is that he was warned by mom to play nice or learn how to cook for himself. Another thing my father and I had in common was that he was as dangerous in a kitchen as I was. My sister seemed much happier than she was when we had our last conversation shortly after her divorce. We used to talk every other week. But since she moved in with our folks, I had to pick times to call so that I could avoid awkward phone conversations with my father. When dinner was over I helped my mom clear the table and excused myself. It had been a long week and I needed to be well rested for what would lay ahead.

Chapter 7

Common Ground

I left the ranch shortly after eight o'clock heading for the Phoenix Police Station. Lynch felt that with all of the research ahead of us, it would be a good idea to have some hi-tech resources available. For the moment it was evident we needed to stay out of the Bureau systems. Based on the information we found, or should I say didn't find, on the plane, the accuracy of that system was under suspicion. As disconcerting as that was, what was even more disturbing was that we couldn't be sure that the inquiries we had made weren't being monitored.

I forgot how intense the heat could get during the Arizona summer. It was just after day break, and it still took about five minutes before the A/C was able to cool down the car. I'd have to remember to park under a shady tree for the remainder of my stay or I would need to change my clothes three times a day.

The family, well at least my mother and sister, were disappointed that I had to get to work so soon after my arrival. I was glad that I had surprised them with my visit and had not pre-announced my original intent to take vacation time, or that would have made these work excursions much harder to explain away. Lynch asked me to call him when I was a few minutes from the station so he could get me into the "employee" parking lot and escort me into the station. According to the arrival time displayed on my navigational system, it was time to give Lynch that call. True to his word, as soon as I made the turn into the parking lot Lynch was standing there waiting for me. He knew I wasn't there for the tour so he quickly escorted me to a conference room that he had secured for our use. What I did notice during my quick walk through the facility was the pretty hi-tech equipment. I had been in several stations around the country on official business; of all of the stations, this was probably as sophisticated a setup as I had seen.

"I have to admit," I told Lynch, "I was a little concerned that not being able to use the FBI systems would be a huge detriment in our investigation. But after seeing your setup, I feel a lot more at ease about the situation."

Lynch smiled in response to the compliment before stepping out of the room for a minute. I was just starting to get organized when he returned. He was joined by another officer. Based on the bars on the uniform, it appeared that the other man was the Chief of Police. From his stocky appearance, thinning gray hair and wrinkles, it looked like he had been sitting behind a desk for more than a few years.

"Special Agent Bennett Mills, I would like you to meet our Chief of Police, my boss, and a good friend Dan Riddle," Lynch said.

I was glad to hear the word friend, because the level of assistance we required would far exceed the typical courtesy that my FBI badge might have garnered. I shook Riddle's hand and thanked him for his cooperation. Lynch had already explained that this investigation was confidential and we needed to keep things on a need to know basis. I promised Riddle that at some point in the coming days I would provide more details. He had obviously been through this kind of thing before with the Feds and didn't appear to have his ego bruised.

Riddle responded, "If Lynch believes this case is that important, than you can look forward to the full cooperation of the Phoenix Police department."

"I appreciate it," I responded as I shook his hand. "I'm going to try and keep a low profile. The fewer people that know who I am and what I'm doing here the better".

"That won't be a problem. I've got the perfect cover story for you," he replied as he left the conference room.

Lynch closed the door and sat down in the chair next to me. He had a big smirk on his face.

"What's so amusing?" I asked.

"Dan is a great guy and an excellent Chief of Police, but he can't make up a cover story for shit!" he replied. "The whole precinct is going to know you're a Fed by noon.

"So, where do we start?" Lynch asked.

"Unfortunately, with the families of these Vets," I responded as I sat down at the end of the conference table.

We knew that both Rodney and Stone served in Iraq and Afghanistan before being sent home with honorable discharges. Upon their arrival in the states, they were both admitted to a VA medical facility for psychological review and treatment. After a couple of months, they left the VA facility, returned to their families, and what appeared to be normal lives. Neither of them—prior to committing the murders—had shown any signs of hostility towards their victims or suicidal tendencies. As a result of their actions, they both left their loved ones to have to deal with the aftermath.

We needed to review the cases we found on the plane to see how many of the check boxes match up against Rodney and Stone.

"These people have had their lives turned upside down," I said, "It might take a bit of convincing before we can gain their trust and cooperation."

We wouldn't be able to tell them that we could exonerate their loved ones, but we could tell them that we were as anxious to get answers as they were. With a computer and phone at each end of the conference table and a cup of coffee in hand we split the pile and started making calls. We didn't know what we would find, but we had a feeling that our time was being invested wisely.

Most calls went more or less the same way. They would start off with a hostile family member yelling at us. It would take all the diplomacy we could muster just to keep them from hanging up the phone. The turning point was when we were able to convince them that we're searching for the same answers that they had been desperately seeking. Listening to husbands, wives, fathers and mothers tell the story about how their loved ones turned from heroes to villains in the blink of an eye was gut-wrenching. As we went from one call to the next our determination to find answers for these families became more imperative. As each of us completed a call, we would look towards the other gesturing with a thumbs-up if we added to the tally with another similar story. Lynch and I both had a lot of experience in dealing with guilty people professing their innocence, and families lying in order to protect their own. The families we were speaking with couldn't have been any more genuine in their convictions about what happened to their loved ones was a complete and total mystery to them. We spent most of the morning on the phone. As noon rolled around, we decided it was time to review our notes. In order not to waste any time, we decided we would try to eat a fast lunch while we did our review. We found nine of the twelve assailants fit the Rodney-Stone criteria to the T. All nine, either upon completion of their tenure in the military or as a result of an honorable discharge, sought psychological help once they returned to the states. They were all holding jobs and appeared to be assimilating well into the public sector when all of a sudden, and unexpectedly, they snapped. In all cases, they took just one life besides their own, and that life was always someone of prominence in the local community—typically a local politician or a high-profile-figure in a publicly owned company. It was clear that the word coincidence no longer could be applied. Something was rotten in Denmark. Our next step was to figure out what was behind these killings. One of the questions that Lynch and I had asked the families we had spoken to was which hospital their loved ones had gone to for rehabilitation. In all but one of the cases, each veteran had been in a different facility. In the case of the vets that were in the same place, they both entered the facility the same week. Our next step was to speak to the doctors that were in charge of their cases. With our adrenalin flowing, we were anxious to continue our investigation. We sorted the facilities by time zone wanting to target from east to west coast so we could maximize the number of locations and doctors we could reach before the end of the day. We both hit the phones, but it wasn't long before yet another mystery materialized. The psychiatrists charged with the Vets treatment at each of the facilities we called were dead. Lynch was informed by the head of a facility that the supervising doctor had died in a car accident. His death occurred, just a couple of months after he started treating at that location. The facility I contacted informed me that the supervising doctor on their staff had died of a heart attack only a couple of months after he started working in that facility.

I turned to Lynch and said "Coincidence?"

Lynch responded, "Coincidence my ass!" We decided to make the remaining calls together.

Call after call yielded tragic ending after tragic ending of the psychiatrist overseeing the vets we were inquiring about. All of them died after a brief assignment at the facility. Because of their short tenure it was difficult to find out much more than the psychiatrist's name, approximate duration of their assignment at the facility, and the circumstances surrounding their demise. The information we were able to acquire was so miniscule that we had completed all of our calls in less than two hours. We had originally expected that this task would have consumed most of our day. Unfortunately, along with this unpredicted spare time came yet another mystery that required investigation. Without hesitation Lynch and I agreed that we needed to take a look further into the untimely and coincidental deaths of these doctors. We started to browse the internet, searching under each of the doctor's names looking for articles related to their deaths. We came up empty, as if they never existed. We then tried using the search engine that the Arizona Police Dept. subscribed to and still came up with nothing. Although I was hesitant to use the Bureau system, I had to take the chance to confirm my suspicions which were validated when no results were returned on any of the doctor's names. Did someone wipe out all the information on their deaths? Maybe the reports of their deaths were greatly exaggerated? Suddenly it occurred to me that not only didn't we find anything about their deaths; we didn't find anything about their lives. I turned to Lynch and asked him to read off the approximate dates that each of these doctors had worked at the facilities. As Lynch gave me the dates, I started to plot them out on a time line. It was just as I thought; there were no overlaps on the time line.

I turned to Lynch and said "We're no longer looking for several dead doctors; we are now looking for only one very busy live one."

I continued "How ingenious, it's like in boxing, he would "stick and move" not staying long enough in one place to be found out. He deliberately would avoid having any close ties with anyone else at the facility to prevent them from finding out too much about him. After a while he makes a phone call under another assumed identity and reports to the hospital supervisor his own untimely and tragic death. A couple of weeks later he shows up at another hospital under his new name.

But how is he obtaining the credentials needed to get into the VA Hospitals? How did he enlist or control these vets? What triggered their going over the edge? And the biggest question of all was for what reason? It was too late in the day to call-back all of the facilities so we decided to focus on the West Coast locations. We needed to prove our hypothesis that it was a single man impersonating several doctors and the only way to do that would be to try and get a picture, security camera video, or even a description from a co-worker. No matter how careful or clever an individual might be, it is impossible to work someplace for months and not get caught on tape. The question was how long the tape would be kept before it was erased?

We made several calls and with only two exceptions we were promised full cooperation by the hospital supervisors. Lynch took the list of the locations that we were unable to connect with due to the time difference and asked one of his fellow detectives to reach out to them in the morning. He told them with my permission to use the three letters FBI as needed to garner their cooperation. It was a long day and we both needed to take a break so we decided to make two final calls before we called it quits. The first was to Jenna Stone to see if she would allow us to meet her at her home in the morning. The second was to the Phoenix VA hospital to arrange a meeting with one of their resident psychiatrists. Stone was a patient in that facility when he returned from Iraq so we decided to visit in person rather than discussing his case by phone. After completing the calls, I took one last glance at our notes before heading out. I'm not sure how we both missed it, but there was something we had overlooked.

"It looks like the person we are looking for is Dr. H," I said.

"Dr. H.?" Lynch asked.

I pointed to the names of the dead doctors and each one of the first names started with the letter "H".

"We're looking for Dr. H," I said.

On the way out, Lynch and I walked by Dan Riddle's office. He was packing up for the day as well. I thanked him for his hospitality and Lynch reminded him that he would be unavailable for other cases for the next few days. We headed out to the parking lot; I turned to Lynch on the way and asked him what time he expected for it to cool down.

He smiled and said "Never."

I gave him the address of the ranch which was en route to Jenna Stone's house.

"Are you sure you're okay with picking me up?" I asked.

"Not a problem partner," he replied. "If we're right and this guy was involved with the deaths of these vets, I would drive off a cliff it that's what it took to nail his ass."

I nodded in agreement and then we went our separate ways.

Chapter 8

The Unwelcome Visitor

Lynch arrived early to pick me up at the ranch. I made some brief introductions to the family. When I introduced my father, Lynch's eyes lit up as if he was meeting a movie star.

"An honor," he said as he shook my father's hand.

I turned to Lynch and said "We have a busy schedule so we better get going."

Lynch tipped his hat to my family and we started walking to the car. We agreed that since we were making this visit in an unofficial capacity that it made more sense to take my rental and leave his police car at the ranch. It was about a fifteen minute ride on the local roads to Jenna Stone's home. During the drive, Lynch went into further detail about his friendship with the Stone family. He'd known them for over thirty years and played golf and cards with Dan's father on a regular basis. He described the two families as inseparable, spending almost every holiday together.

"When Dan came back," Lynch said, "he was undeniably a different man then the one that left for Iraq, but who wouldn't be? He didn't show any signs of being violent or suicidal. He was just different. Watching that security video of the day he died was the hardest thing I've ever had to do, but if I hadn't seen it for myself, I never would have believed it."

Based on the strong ties that Lynch had to the Stone family, it was clear that this case was personal. Normally that would be enough to disqualify him from being involved, but as far as I was concerned having it be personal sometimes gave you an edge. Besides, Lynch was all I had.

Jenna and Dan Stone were one of the first home buyers in a new community that was supposed to grow to one-hundred homes in total, but the builder went bust after completing their home and barely framing several others. Now instead of being in a blossoming community with her husband, Jenna found herself sitting in the equivalent of a ghost town all alone. As we pulled onto her road, we saw Jenna coming out to meet us. Considering she was the only person living in the community, when a car pulled in, it was either someone that was lost, or it was for you. As soon as we got out of the car, Jenna walked up to Lynch and gave him a big hug. Even though Lynch's connection was with her in-laws, Jenna and Lynch had become quite attached over the years.

"Jenna," he said, "this is Special Agent Bennett Mills. He's based out of DC, but his family is here in Arizona and he's taken a special interest in the circumstances surrounding Dan's death. I was hoping you would be willing to sit down with us and answer a few questions."

She nodded her head agreeing to talk to me, but it was obvious and very understandable why she would have preferred not to have this discussion. We followed her into the house which was sparsely furnished with one couch sitting in the middle of a fairly large living room.

"I'm sorry for the appearance of the house," she said in an apologetic tone. "Dan was working extra shifts so that we could properly furnish the house. Now with Dan gone, and with my minimum wage job, I'm just struggling to pay the bills. If it wasn't for Ed's help, I would probably be out on the streets."

I glanced over at Lynch for a second. He hadn't mentioned that he was helping out Jenna with her bills. I guess he wasn't one to publicize a generous deed.

Jenna couldn't sell the house considering the condition of the neighborhood, and told us that she had even given thought about walking away. However, since her last memories with Dan were here, she couldn't get herself to do it. I knew it would be painful, but I had to ask her to recall the events of that day on the remote chance that she might remember anything that might have happened that would make sense out of the senseless. She remembered that they had woken up and gone through their usual morning routine of dressing for work and having breakfast together. It was a Friday and they always rented a movie to watch as their evening's entertainment. Going to the movies was no longer in their budget after buying the house. Dan was going to pick out the movie for that night. Jenna always picked out romantic comedies on her nights and Dan would always pick out a science fiction movie. Before he went to Iraq he used to love war movies, but when he returned they would only remind him of the images that he tried so hard to forget. The images that led him to his three month stay at the VA Hospital. She told us how at first, the treatment he was receiving did not seem to be helping him.

"I was starting to lose hope," she told us, "when at the start of his second month a new doctor transferred into the facility. Within a few weeks, I started to notice a big improvement and my hope had been restored. He was actually able to sleep through the night without waking up in a cold sweat from the nightmares he had been experiencing.

I asked Jenna if Dan seemed agitated the morning of his death.

"No," she said "it just seemed like any other Friday morning. He was happy and looking forward to our movie night. He even reminded me to get his favorite popcorn from the store."

"Did Dan ever mention anything about work that would lead you to believe that he was having difficulties with anyone there?" I asked.

"Absolutely not," she replied in an emphatic tone. "Dan loved his job and had a great rapport with his co-workers and bosses."

It appeared that if he did have any issues, he hadn't shared them with Jenna. The more I heard, the more I felt like I was experiencing déjà vu from my conversation with Mrs. Rodney. He left the house that morning with intentions of enjoying a quiet evening at home with his young bride. What chain of events could have caused this tragic and incomprehensible detour? We kept coming back to the same questions and the only possible connection was our mysterious "Dr. H".

"Officer Lynch mentioned that your husband was taking medication that he was receiving from an unknown benefactor," I stated.

"When did he start having problems sleeping again?" I asked.

"It started a couple of months before he died," she responded, "he was going to stop in at the VA hospital, but then an envelope with the medication he had taken at the VA just showed up in our mailbox. We both thought it was weird since neither of us recalled mentioning to anyone that Dan was having a problem".

"Was there any name or return address on the envelope?" I asked

"No, we looked at the front and back and couldn't find anything. We even checked inside the envelope a second time hoping that we'd find a note of some sort," she responded.

"Was there a pharmacy name on the prescription bottle?" I asked having a gut feeling what the answer would be.

"No, the pills were in a plastic zip lock bag. I know we should have questioned where the pills came from, but medicine can get expensive. We were just grateful that we were able to save the money," she replied. "As soon as Dan started taking them, he started to sleep through the night again."

"Did Dan ever speak to a doctor at the hospital?" I asked.

"After a couple of weeks, I did try to convince him to go down to the VA just to talk, but he didn't want to take the chance since he was doing okay on the medicine," she responded.

"What was he worried about?" I asked in a curious tone.

"Dan knew that if he spoke to the VA doctor that it would wind up in his permanent medical records. Any sign of a relapse in his files might prevent him from future job advancement. You know, he'd hoped to one day join the Phoenix Police Department and work with Ed," she said as a tear rolled down her cheek.

Lynch mentioned during the car ride over that he started to lay the foundation for getting Dan into the academy. It was supposed to be a surprise, one that Dan fell a couple of months short of realizing.

Lynch interrupted my thoughts by clearing his throat to grab my attention. "I'm going to step outside for a smoke" he said.

He walked through the kitchen and outside with the screen door banging behind him. It was minutes after he left the house that I heard a gunshot, followed by another one which wasn't quite as loud as the first. Initially, I was a bit startled, because when you hear a gunshot in DC you duck, but then I remembered that this was Arizona and people carried guns here like politicians carried their latest poll numbers. I barely had time to settle in to ask another question when the screen door opened, I didn't see anyone come in, but heard Lynch grunting.

"Are you okay Lynch?" I yelled.

"Only if you call getting hit in the chest by a bullet okay," he yelled back.

I quickly pulled Jenna down to the ground and told her to stay put as I started to crawl my way to the kitchen. Jenna was so distraught that she probably didn't hear what I said. When I looked back she was right behind me following all the way. As I did, I reached for my gun and realized that it was back in DC in my desk drawer. I knew I should have taken the damn gun with me. I reached Lynch and saw that he was trying to apply pressure to the gunshot in the upper left side of his chest.

"Are you going to make it?" I asked.

"I think I'll survive," he responded.

"Were you hit anywhere else?"

"No," he said, "but there was a second shot".

"Yes, I know, I heard it too, but it sounded different from the first so there must be a second shooter." I replied.

"Yeah," Lynch said, "and luckily he wasn't as good a shot as the first one."

He continued, "If some nutty wasp didn't fly right at me causing me to shift to the right I might not be talking to you right now."

I reached for his revolver and asked if he minded.

"You're not carrying?" he said as he slowly pulled his gun out of its holster and handed it to me.

"No," I replied, "remember I was supposed to be on vacation."

"You've shot one of these before?" Lynch asked with a smirk on his face.

"It's nice to see that even after being shot that you still have your sense of humor," I responded.

I grabbed the gun and started moving towards one of the windows. I turned to Jenna who was still shaking and told her to stay with Lynch in the kitchen. As I passed the phone, I knocked it off the handset, slid it across the floor to Lynch and told him to call in the cavalry. He barely had time to hit the call button when a familiar voice yelled to us from outside.

"Are you okay in there?" It was my father's voice. I thought to myself, what the hell was he doing here?

I yelled "Get down! There are two shooters out there."

He yelled back "Wrong son, there was only one shooter and he's down. The second shot you heard was from my gun."

I got up off the floor just as my dad walked through the screen door.

"What kind of crap did you step into son?" my father asked.

"Can we hold off on this discussion until we can take care of Lynch?" I yelled.

Lynch stood up and started to walk over to the kitchen chair leaving drops of blood on the floor behind.

I yelled at him, "Are you crazy? Sit still so we can take a look at that thing".

Lynch yelled back; "Stop babying me, just throw me a towel so I can pack the wound".

"I'm not babying you damn it; you're dripping blood all over the floor," I responded.

While I was making sure that Lynch was keeping still I turned to my father and asked if he had killed the shooter.

"No", he replied, "but he's in cuffs and bleeding pretty bad".

"We better get him to the hospital if he is going to be of any use to us" I suggested.

"Already called the police," he responded as he stepped outside to check on the shooter.

As soon as he was out the door Lynch turned to me and said "It looks like we struck a nerve with someone".

"Yes." I said, "And whoever it is has a friend at the FBI."

The way I saw it, either this was the world's biggest coincidence or someone noticed our inquiries into the Bureau database and didn't like it. One thing I was sure about was that going forward we were going to have to be looking over our shoulders.

The ambulance came within a few minutes of the police. My father had already packed the shooter's wound to slow his bleeding. While the paramedics were loading the gunman onto the stretcher, I noticed a tattoo on his right arm. Not that I should have been surprised, but it read "Camp Navajo, Home of the Brave". The ambulance was from St. Luke's Hospital in Phoenix which was about ten minutes away. A police officer rode with the shooter. They only sent one ambulance so rather than wait for another one to arrive we piled into my father's car and followed. Lynch apologized to my father for getting blood on his seats.

My father said jokingly "No worries, I'll just forward the cleaning bill to your precinct."

Lynch started to laugh, but had to force himself to stop. It was obvious by the look on his face that he was in quite a bit of pain. We decided for her own safety that it would be best if we took Jenna with us to the hospital. Even though my father took care of the shooter; there were no guarantees that she would be safe if we left her behind. On the way to the hospital, I called my sister to ask if she could meet us at the emergency room. She was a bit alarmed at first asking if everything was okay. I told her that Lynch had been shot, but he seemed to be okay considering he had a bullet in his chest. I told her I needed her to do me a favor. She agreed to head over to the hospital right away. I didn't know what was going through Jenna's mind after all of the activity back at her house, but I knew that there were better places for her to be than at the hospital. We also couldn't be sure that Jenna wasn't the target, or at least one of the targets of the shooter. We needed to keep her away from her home until we could be sure that it was safe for her to return.

On the way to the hospital, it came to me that I never did mention to my father where I was going. "So how the hell did you know where to find us?" I asked while looking in my father's direction. I think he was a bit shocked by the question and how it came at him out of nowhere.

"Considering I just saved your lives, you would think that you might be asking that question in a more respectful manner," he quipped.

He was right; I was out of line and immediately responded with an apology.

"Not a problem," he replied, "It's probably just the adrenalin from all the activity. To answer your question, I happen to be watching as you pulled out of the ranch and hung that right onto the main road. I was just getting ready to go back inside when I noticed an old pickup truck pull out from behind that large bolder on the ranch's perimeter. I thought it a bit suspicious and hopped into the truck pursuing at a distance. He was matching your speed and every turn you made."

"I'm surprised he didn't notice you following him," I said.

"I think he was so focused on not being noticed by you, that he had no clue that I was behind him. When I saw him pull off to the side, I stopped a bit up the road and watched as he got out of the truck and moved up into the hills. I moved in after him, but lost him in the rocks. I was trying to track his location when I saw him peek out from behind a rock to take the first shot. Luckily I got a fix on him and brought him down before he could get off a second round, or there would be only three of us in the car now."

From the back seat Lynch said, "I guess I owe you and that wasp that nearly flew into me a debt of gratitude. Thanks partner, I owe you one."

"I'll add that one to my collection jar," my father said in jest.

Chapter 9
The One That Got Away

We arrived at the hospital within minutes of the ambulance, which was quite a feat considering we were traveling in a civilian vehicle without the luxury of flashing lights and sirens. As soon as we walked through the door, a young, attractive police woman started to move in our direction. She must have been about five-foot seven with dark brown hair, and soft brown eyes that stood out against her fair, unblemished skin. As unflattering as the police uniform could be for a woman, she definitely made it work. Under normal circumstances, I would have enjoyed making her acquaintance, but I was anxious to find a doctor to address Lynch's wound and to check on the whereabouts and status of the shooter. As she got closer, I noticed a pissed off look on her face. She wasn't happy about something, and I hoped that something wasn't me. I breathed a sigh of relief as she walked past me and over to Lynch.

Without hesitation, she gave him a hug that lasted several seconds before stepping back from him.

"You told me you were taking off a few days to go fishing," she said in an angry voice. "You lied to me!"

Lynch responded, "I didn't lie, I was fishing and it looks like we caught something".

"And I'm guessing you were the bait?" she responded with her voice dripping in sarcasm.

I was so distracted by her striking appearance, that I failed to put two and two together. She must have been Lynch's daughter. He had mentioned that his daughter worked at the same precinct on the flight over from DC, but she looked nothing like Lynch.

"I heard some chatter over the police radio about an officer getting shot," she told him. "You can imagine my surprise when my father, the one that was supposed to be out on a lake fishing, was named as the wounded officer."

While I couldn't blame her for being upset with Lynch, he was still standing in the middle of the emergency room with a bullet in him. I made the mistake of suggesting to her that they could continue their conversation after her father's wound was looked at.

If looks could kill, I would be dead and buried.

She turned around and gave me a stare and asked "And who the hell are you?"

Lynch quickly jumped in with an introduction. "FBI agent Bennett Mills, may I introduce my beautiful, brilliant, and overreacting daughter, Officer April Lynch."

He then turned to my father and said "I think you might be familiar with this other gentlemen who, by the way, is the reason why I am standing here talking to you instead of being escorted to the morgue."

She recognized my father immediately from his picture at the precinct and the newspaper.

"Thank you," she said giving my father a hug.

I had to admit that I was a bit jealous that he was receiving a hug, yet relieved that I was no longer receiving her angry stare. It's funny, but my father was acting like he was ten years younger. It was obvious that all of this activity suited him. The attending emergency room physician approached Lynch ordering him onto a gurney that was stationed by the wall. I think that Lynch might have objected to that mode of transportation through the hospital had April not been standing right there. In spite of his objections, we helped him up onto the gurney and then Lynch, the doctor, and April disappeared down the hall.

I saw the officer that had ridden in the ambulance with the shooter and approached him.

"How's Lynch?" He asked.

"He's in with the doctor now," I replied.

"Is the shooter in the operating room?" I asked.

"Yes," he responded. "According to the surgeon he'll be in there for at least three hours, and assuming he survives, it will be a couple of days before he can be questioned."

"You know your dad is still one hell of a marksman. He told us he was one hundred yards away when he took the shot. From the looks of it, the guy is lucky to have made it to the operating table."

The officer was heading back to the precinct. His shift was ending, but he informed me that another officer had been dispatched and would be there before the shooter came out of surgery. I thanked him for the information and started to walk back to where I had left Jenna and my father waiting. As I approached them, I could overhear them talking about Dan. I guess that since I hadn't told my father anything about the case, he figured he'd do his own informal interrogation. I was going to interrupt them to see if they wanted a cup of coffee when I noticed my sister Carol entering through the emergency room doors. She immediately saw us and started to converge on our location. I made the introductions between Carol and Jenna and then asked Carol if she could take Jenna back to the ranch and keep an eye out for anything strange.

"Why can't I go back to my house?" Jenna asked.

I did not want to scare her, but I needed for her to cooperate. "I don't know who this shooter is, and why he was trying to kill us."

"Kill us?" Jenna responded in a panicked voice with tears streaming down her face. "Why would anyone want to kill us?"

"You have to trust me and go with my sister back to the Ranch. We'll be along shortly. As soon as we feel it is safe to go back to your house, we will let you know. In the meantime, my mom is one hell of a cook. Why don't you go back and get something to eat. Carol and my mom will take good care of you".

I could tell that Jenna was upset, but did not resist our request leaving the hospital with my sister.

Carol was practically born with a gun in her hand. She was almost as good a shot as I was. One year, I took first place and she came in third in a shooting contest. With those credentials, we felt Jenna would be safe in her care while we tried to sort out the events of the day. As much as I was looking forward to a home cooked meal, I wouldn't think of leaving the hospital until I knew that Lynch was out of surgery and resting comfortably.

I told my father I was in serious need of a cup of coffee and asked if he wanted to join me. He agreed.

"If you don't mind, I want to make one stop by security. I want to browse through our gunman's personal belongings to find out who he is."

"I'm kind of curious about that myself," he replied. "I hate to shoot a man, and not even know his name".

The belongings were being held by the hospital security pending release to the Phoenix PD for review. After showing them my badge, they were
quick to cooperate handing me the box and a pair of gloves so I could go
through its contents. No wallet, no ID, just a pack of chewing gum, ciga-
rettes, and a lighter. It looked like the only way we were going to find out
his name would be by running his prints once he came out of surgery. In the
meantime, it looked like we had some time on our hands and a desperate
need for some caffeine. As my father and I walked to the cafeteria, I realized
that I had never thanked him for taking out the shooter and possibly saving
our lives.

I turned to him and said "By the way, thanks for all your help today."

Without hesitation he replied "You're welcome son".

I think this was our first father son moment in ten years. It felt weird,
but good. When I got back to the table with our coffee I felt compelled—
under the circumstances—to let my father know what we had dragged him
into. He listened without interruption, taking an occasional sip of his coffee,
as I filled him in on the details.

When I told him about our concerns regarding someone from the FBI
being involved, he laughed and said "I guess you might be rethinking a career with a local police dept."

I smiled and responded, "You might just be right."

We had been sitting around for a couple of hours talking about the case
when Lynch's daughter walked over to our table and informed us that her father was going to be fine and was resting comfortably in his room. She told us
that while she appreciated our concern for her father, that there was no point
waiting around since he was going to be out of it for at least a few hours.

My father said "Maybe I'll head home then to make sure everything is
alright at the ranch".

He then turned to me and suggested "Why don't you take Officer
Lynch out to dinner while you're waiting for her father to wake up?"

I looked at him not believing that at this moment he was trying to play
matchmaker. Up until that moment I had always thought my mother had
cornered that market.

He stared back at me and said "It's the least you can do after you got
her father shot."

I nodded my head and turned to April and said "I apologize if my father is putting you on the spot, but he is right. I guess I was in a way responsible for getting your father shot."

She hesitated for a minute. "It is dinner time, and I don't know about you, but I am starved," she said revealing her beautiful smile.

"April Lynch," she said with her hand extended, "I'm sorry about yelling at you in the emergency room earlier, and I'd love to get something to eat, but on one condition."

I was waiting for her to say that she wanted to go Dutch. "And what condition might that be?" I asked.

She responded, "I want to change out of my work clothes."

She continued "There is nothing more awkward than sitting in a restaurant in my police uniform. "

It had been a while since I was on the force, but I remember the feeling that I was being watched—and in April's case that was probably magnified ten-fold—because of her good looks.

"Not a problem," I responded. "There is one thing, do you mind driving?". I abandoned my rental at the Stone's house.

"Done!" she responded.

My father walked with us out to the parking lot and then headed for his car. I told him that I would check in later once I was able to see Lynch.

I'm one of those people that always likes to be in the driver's seat. Maybe it came from my days with the DC police. My old partner usually took the wheel, and he was one of the worst drivers I have ever seen. I always used to say that it was a good thing he was a cop, or he would have gone broke paying tickets. For some reason, I didn't find it unnerving with April doing the driving. There was something calming about her personality, that is when she wasn't giving you the stare. Maybe it was her angelic face or her soft brown eyes. At first glance, a criminal might have scoffed at her as she tried to arrest them, but after seeing how she reacted to her father when we arrived at the hospital, I could tell that she could be a force to be reckoned with when she got mad. She lived in a second floor apartment in a building on a nice quiet street on the outskirts of Phoenix. The building was actually quite respectable looking for someone living off of an Arizona cop's salary. You could tell that it was a fairly diverse building by all of the various foods that you could smell as you walked down the hall to her apartment.

As hungry as I was at the moment, it was difficult to keep from salivating, especially when I detected what appeared to be the aroma of spaghetti and meatballs as I passed one apartment. If someone was walking past my apartment assuming I cooked, the only aroma they would detect would be of something burning. I was totally inept in the kitchen turning pretty much anything I tried to prepare into an indigestible burnt mess. You would have thought that with a mother that cooked all the time I might have picked up something from her as I grew up, but unfortunately that was not the case. She swung open the door and as soon as we walked in it immediately struck me how neat everything was.

"This place is immaculate," I said, "Are you sure you live here?"

She responded, "Sometimes with all the overtime I put in I wonder the same thing."

"Actually," she said "You should see my bedroom."

She paused, laughed and said "That did not come out the way I meant it."

I smiled and told her not to worry, I understood what she meant, but appreciated the offer. She pointed to the couch and said "stay" as she walked to her bedroom to get changed. I took a seat and looked around the apartment hoping to get some insight into what made April Lynch tick. The bookshelves were full of murder mystery books and the walls were plastered with family pictures. There were college photos, pictures of her with her mom and dad on numerous vacations, and a rather large picture of a young Ed Lynch in an Arizona football uniform.

I yelled down the hall "I didn't know your dad played college football."

She yelled back "Yep and from what my mom told me he was rather good. He might have even been drafted to go pro if not for a knee injury during his senior year that ended his chances of making a career of it."

"You know," I said "one of my bosses back in DC played for Arizona."

I noticed after she had mentioned her mom that there were no current pictures of her on the wall. There were several of Lynch including a few that appeared to be taken at award ceremonies, but none included her mom. Was it possible that her mom was dead? I envisioned that as being an uncomfortable topic of conversation for a first date. Wait a minute I thought, we were just going to dinner because her dad was shot, we were both hungry, and I felt responsible. That might be a topic to be avoided even more than any questions about her mom. I was so focused on the books on the shelves, and pictures on the wall that I had initially overlooked her kitchen which was adorned by pots and pans—hanging from a ceiling rack—and a shelf which was fully stocked with a variety of herbs and spices. Could she cook too? I was so absorbed in my own thoughts, that I didn't even notice her walking out of the bedroom.

"Yes, I have been known to cook from time to time," she said.

I turned to respond, but as soon as my eyes set sight on her I became so distracted that I had forgotten what I was going to say. At that moment, the only word that came to mind was wow! I managed to break out of the trance just in time to avoid looking like a gawking idiot.

"Any place in particular that you wanted to eat?" I asked, thinking to myself; nice recovery.

"Several places I can think of." she replied "What kind of food are you in the mood for?"

"Well," I responded, "After walking past apartment 2-C, I kind of had my heart set on Italian food."

She smiled, "Mrs. Conti can make some mean meatballs, but I think I have a place that might even put her cooking to shame."

She pointed me in the direction of the door, grabbed my arm and we headed out of the apartment, down the two flights of stairs, and out into the street.

When we got outside, I was surprised that it had cooled down to a brisk eighty degrees. Thankfully the restaurant was only a few blocks away. While we walked I tried to break the ice by asking her if her dad was happy about her joining the force. April told me that her father apparently had concerns for her safety and had hoped that she would pick a safer career, but in the end, did not fight her on her career choice. She cited her mother's death as the reason why she wanted to become a police officer. She told the story of how her mother had been on the way to pick up April after a high school football game when her car was hit by a drunk driver that had run the red light.

"I sat with my friends in front of the school waiting for an hour before one of my mom's friends showed up. She didn't say much only that my mom had car trouble. After she dropped off all of my other friends, instead of taking me home she drove me to the hospital."

"When we arrived at the emergency room entrance," she said, "my father was waiting outside."

She told me how she knew by the expression on her father's face and the fact that her mom didn't show up at the school that something was terribly wrong. Her father confirmed her suspicions when he hugged her tightly and broke down in tears outside the hospital that night.

"That was the first time I had ever seen my father cry," she said. "The next and last time I saw him cry was the day of my mother's funeral. After I completed college, I immediately enrolled in the police academy."

She had explained to her father that her mother's death was her motivation for becoming a cop. I guess with a reason like that, it would have been hard for her dad to keep her from joining the force. I could tell that her recounting what had happened was upsetting her and I wondered if giving her a hug might seem a bit forward. I then decided what the hell and put my arms around her for a minute. She didn't appear to be uncomfortable with my efforts to comfort her. After releasing her from the hug, she thanked me and apologized for shedding some tears. I told her not to worry about it. I was actually a bit choked up from the story myself and I was happy to see the restaurant was directly across the street from where we had stopped. The restaurant was fairly small compared to places I frequented in DC. However, what it was missing in size it made up for in atmosphere. It reminded me of a trattoria that Hope and I had eaten in on our last date. When I considered how that evening had gone, I knew that this evening would have to be a vast improvement. The waitress that greeted us at the door gave us the option of sitting inside or outside. Considering it was still hot outside, I was relieved when April asked if I minded sitting inside.

"Not at all," I said, "I'm still melting from the walk to the restaurant." My response garnered a smile. It was the first smile I had noticed since she had told me the story about her mom and it was a welcome sight to see.

"So how did you wind up with the FBI?" she asked.

"It is a long and potentially very boring story. Are you sure you want to hear it?"

She smiled again. "Absolutely," she replied nodding her head as she pulled her chair closer to the table.

The waitress had been standing patiently two tables down waiting for us to give a sign that we were ready to order. When April nodded her head, the waitress mistook that as the sign and came over to the table. We were both hungry, so we decided that we might as well get our order in before I started telling my long and unexciting tale. April ordered a veal dish that I couldn't have pronounced had my life depended on it, and I ordered the chicken parmesan. It was not very original but I wasn't one to take chances with my menu selections. I know that to most people looking at my line of work might think it strange that I exhibited caution when choosing the meals I ordered. But for the cost of eating out these days it would kill me if I didn't at least enjoy my food. After the waitress left April took to staring at me as to say go on with the your story. I told her about how strongly my father disapproved when I told him that I wasn't planning on joining the Phoenix PD. At the time, I decided I didn't want people to point to me and say that's George Mill's son and constantly be drawing comparisons between the two of us. It's not that I didn't love my father and respect all of his accomplishments, because I did. I just wanted, maybe needed, to find my own way and know if I succeeded or failed it was because of what Bennett Mills did and not because my father was a legend. He didn't or couldn't understand the reason for my decision. Once he knew that he couldn't change my mind, it became unbearable to be within a hundred miles of him. We couldn't have a family dinner without it becoming World War III and finally one day I couldn't take it anymore, packed my bags and went to DC to join the DC police department. I was only twenty-three at the time, but DC was a place that would turn a kid into a man real fast. I was with the force for about five years. I was working my usual case load when out of nowhere I was approached by the FBI to fill an open investigative position. I remembered applying for a job with the local offices before I left Arizona, but never heard back from them. I figured either my application was lost in a pile somewhere, or they flat out rejected me. I did enjoy my job at DC PD, but let's just say something happened that gave me a good reason for moving on."

"Something?" April asked.

"That's another story for another time," I told her. "A couple of weeks later I was officially an FBI agent. I called my father with the news figuring he would be happy for me. Maybe even have him admit that the decisions I had made were vindicated. My father called me a Bureau-crat and hung up the phone. I guess the only thing that pissed him off more than my not following in his footsteps with the Phoenix PD was taking a job with the government. I had forgotten over the years how many times my father had cursed the government and its agencies for getting in the way of him doing his job.

"So that's how you wound up with the FBI," she said.

"Yes, but that's not what brought me back to Arizona," I told her. "About three years after starting with the Bureau, I received a call from my boss asking me to come to his office. It wasn't like we had regular private meetings together, so I had no idea what to expect. I was stunned when I was offered an assignment on Senator Billing's security detail. Initially, I was inclined to turn it down, but I was told that since the offer came from somewhere up above that it would be a bad career decision for me to decline. With my boss putting it that way, I took the job. I was with that detail until Billings was assassinated last week.

"Were you there when he was killed?" she asked.

"No, I had called in sick that day. I'm still not sure if it was one of those twenty-four hour bugs or a nasty hangover from drinking too much with my friends the previous night."

"I don't want to give you the wrong impression of me," I said, "I'm usually not a big drinker, but me and the other guys from the detail went out to a bar to have our own private celebration of the Senator's victory. We were all pretty happy that we were not going to be split up and reassigned. I really honestly don't recall drinking that much, but I obviously had one to many."

"I've had a few nights like that myself," she replied, "but please don't go telling my father that. He still treats me like I'm his little girl."

"My lips are sealed," I replied, "Believe it or not, I was actually planning on this being a vacation until I ran into your father on the plane ride home. Since we landed it has been more like a nightmare than a vacation."

At that moment the food arrived, and not a minute too soon. I was actually surprised that April hadn't fallen asleep while I told my story. She seemed genuinely interested, but I didn't want to push my luck. The waitress brought us complimentary glasses of wine with our dinner. We touched our glasses together and after a sip of wine started to eat our meals. The flavor was good, but different than what I had gotten used to in DC. I must have been starving because I cleared my plate in record time.

"Did you actually taste your food?" April asked with a smirk on her face.

"I guess I didn't realize how hungry I was," I said apologetically.

"I'm sorry, I didn't mean that in a bad way, you just ate fast," she replied, "But it was nice to see that you liked my choice in restaurants."

"Just don't start getting self-conscious on me," she said with a laugh.

To my surprise, April had finished her meal not too long after I did. I had thought the rule for women was to hardly touch their food when out with a new guy. I needed to remind myself that this was just two people dining out, not a date. However, I thought to myself had it been a date, it would have been a great one. Although April offered to split the check, I insisted that after getting her father shot that this was the least I could do. As much as I think we both enjoyed our meal, we were both anxious to get back to the hospital. April wanted to check on her dad, as did I, but my first stop would be to check on the shooter.

Chapter 10
No More Surprises

The roads were fairly quiet considering it was a Friday night. In DC, things would normally be hopping at this time of night and not get quiet until two o'clock Saturday morning. We arrived at the hospital just after ten pm and found a parking spot just a short distance from the main entrance. As we walked towards the door, April turned to me and gave me a surprising but much appreciated peck on the cheek and thanked me for dinner. When we got into the hospital, I suggested that April go see her father for some alone time and I would be down shortly. I wanted to check in on the shooter to see if he was conscious yet. The gunman was four floors above Lynch's room. I exited the elevator on the sixth floor and for a minute was a bit confused. I was informed by hospital security that the room was just down the hall from the nurse's station, but there was no police presence visible. There was however, one room that did have an empty chair sitting just outside its door. I thought to myself that maybe the officer needed to hit the bathroom, but in most states, protocol should require some type of security be present at all times. When I entered the room, I was still a bit distracted by the fact that the stationed officer was missing. I turned to look at the patient and he did not appear to be breathing. The flat line on the monitor confirmed that he was dead. Normally the EKG would be monitored by the nursing station on the floor, yet obviously no one but I was aware that the shooter was deceased. I thought that maybe the connections were loose and started to walk around the bed to check them when all of a sudden I noticed a pair of shiny black shoes poking out just beyond the foot of the bed. It was the officer that was stationed outside of the room. He was lying on the floor motionless. I quickly moved to him checking his pulse, but he too was dead. On the floor by his body, I noticed a rag and an empty syringe. It suddenly struck me, if someone was bold enough to come after the shooter in as public a place as a hospital then they might just try and complete the shooter's failed assignment. I bolted from the room heading down the hall towards the stairs. As I passed the nurse's station I flashed my badge.

"Call security and have them lock down the hospital then call the police," I yelled. "We have a murderer in the building".

Before I had a chance to get down the second flight of stairs the hospital alarm went off. It was four floors down and I found myself skipping steps as a I navigated the stairwell arriving on the 2nd floor in what seemed like seconds. Holding my badge in one hand and Lynch's gun in the other, I ran down the hall knocking open the door to Lynch's room to find April standing at the side of her father's bed.

"Is he...? I mean are you both okay?" I yelled.

"Yes," she responded.

"What happened?" I asked.

April was obviously shaken by the experience, but after taking a couple of deep breaths, she responded, "When I came into the room a man was trying to smother my father with a pillow, I reached for my gun and remembered I wasn't in uniform".

She continued, "When I looked-up, he was already running towards me with a look in his eyes like he was going to kill me. When the alarm went off, he changed direction and ran out of the room."

I told her to stay put and ran out the door and down the hall where I saw a security guard who had been eating his lunch at the nurses' station. As I approached him, I pointed to Lynch's room and asked if he saw anyone come out that door.

"No," he replied, "no one except you."

I borrowed his radio to confirm with his boss that all doors exiting the hospital were secured and then went back to Lynch's room. April was still standing by Lynch's side.

She quickly moved in my direction. "How did you know he would come after my father?" She asked.

"He killed the shooter and the officer that was guarding him. I had a hunch that he might try to go after your father too," I replied.

"Good hunch," she responded, "That alarm going off probably saved both of our lives."

"Did you get a good look at him?" I asked hoping to be able to get a description out to hospital security.

"He was dressed in scrubs. He caught me off guard when I came into the room," she said.

"There are probably a hundred people walking around the hospital that would fit that description. Think," I said, "there had to be something else that you noticed about him."

"Anything?" I asked.

"Yes," she replied, he was wearing thin wire frame glasses, he was very tan like he had just been on vacation, and his eyes, they were an ice blue. It was actually a bit freaky when I first saw them when he looked up at me as I entered the room."

"What about his weight and height?"

"He was leaning over my father when I came into the room and then I was looking down for my gun when he came towards me. It was all so quick," she said appearing to be upset with herself for not being able to provide those details.

"Don't worry," I told her. "I'll be right back, I want to get the description to hospital security so they can pass it along to the police when they arrive."

I stepped out of the room and walked back over to the security guard whose meal I had interrupted earlier. I asked to borrow his radio again and he handed it over to me without question. I communicated to hospital security each detail of the killer that April had provided me with. As I handed the radio back to the guard and turned to head towards Lynch's room I noticed a couple of police officers walking in my direction.

After introducing myself, I asked. "Who do I have to speak to about getting a couple of officers assigned to protect the man in that room?"

A familiar voice behind me replied "That would be me."

I turned around finding myself face to face with Dan Riddle. He looked over my shoulder to the two officers and moved his head in the direction of the door to communicate that they had just been assigned to protect Lynch.

"What the hell happened here?" he yelled with his face turning brick red as he spoke.

"We were interviewing Jena Stone and Lynch had walked outside for a minute and was shot and..."

Riddle interrupted me abruptly. "I know all that," he yelled, "after all I'm the damn police chief. I meant what just happened."

"April and I, I mean Officer Lynch and I just returned to the hospital after grabbing something to eat. She went to check on her father while I went to check on the suspect we…I mean my father had apprehended. When I got to the room both he and the officer guarding him were dead. The murderer was apparently disguised as a hospital doctor. I assume that it is protocol to have your officers accompany anyone entering the room of a suspect," I said.

"That is protocol," Riddle replied.

"My guess is that because the murderer appeared to be a doctor it allowed him to catch your officer off guard and kill him. I noticed the smell of chloroform on the rag on the floor. He probably subdued him and based on the empty syringe, he must have given him some type of lethal injection. With your officer out of the way, he was easily able to suffocate the unconscious shooter. My assumption was that he then decided to try and finish what the shooter had failed to do and kill Lynch. If April hadn't entered the room when she did, her father might be dead too".

Riddle asked if I had a description of the alleged killer.

"Yes. I responded, "It isn't much, but I just finished radioing it down to security when you and your men showed up. I was just waiting to make sure that Lynch's room was secured before heading down to security to check their cameras. I'm hoping I could get something off of the hospital surveillance tape."

"What are we waiting for?" Riddle asked as we both headed for the security office. When we arrived there was only one guard in the room. All others had been deployed to hospital exits in order to prevent anyone from leaving. I noted from the guards badge that his name was Steve.

"Steve," I said, "I'm Agent Bennett Mills with the FBI and this is Chief of Police Dan Riddle. We need to take a look at your security tapes."

The guard responded, "that might be a problem sir"

"Let me take a guess," I said, "the video system wasn't working today?"

"How did you know?" he asked with a surprised look on his face.

"Just a lucky guess," I said.

I turned to Riddle and told him that the hotel where Senator Billings was killed had similar technical difficulties the day he was killed.

"Do you think this is related?" he asked.

"Too many damn coincidences not to be," I responded. "I'm going to head back to Lynch's room."

Riddle put his arm in front of me to stop me from leaving the room and suggested I sit down so we could talk. He informed me that he had received notification from someone in DC that I was in Arizona on vacation only, and not on official FBI business.

"I was asked by one of your superiors to keep you here until they arrived," he said.

"Who, which supervisor?" I asked.

"I believe his name was Web," Riddle responded.

"Matt Web? He's on his way to Arizona?" I asked.

"Not on his way, he's already in Arizona. In fact, he should be here any minute." responded Riddle.

No sooner had he finished the sentence when the door flew opened and Web entered the room. He turned to Riddle and the security guard and asked them to leave the room for a moment. The security guard left without a problem, but you could tell that Riddle wasn't used to being asked to leave a room in his own town. I guess Web realized that Riddle was a bit disgruntled so to smooth things over promised to keep him in the loop regarding anything pertinent to the case. Riddle gave a nod yes and exited the room, closing the door behind him.

As we both sat down Web turned his focus from the door over to me saying "it looks like your making someone nervous."

"Would that someone be you?" I responded.

Web replied, "Lynch told me that you were a bit suspicious of me when you found out that I knew about the Stone case and hadn't mentioned it to you."

I was caught completely off guard hearing that Lynch had been in communication with Web after we had met. The surprised look on my face was evident to Web. The door abruptly opened and April walked into the room. Upon seeing Web sitting at the table with me a smile appeared on her face. Web stood back up when he saw her and was the recipient of a big hug from April. Of course, I thought. What an idiot I am, Arizona State football Lynch and Web must have been on the same team.

"Okay," I said, "I get it now, you are both about the same age, you both went to Arizona State and both played for the Sun Devils. So the two of you are friends, and I was being setup."

With as big of a smile as I have ever seen on Web's face, he turned to April who had a puzzled look and asked her to go check on her dad.

"Don't worry, we'll be up to the room in a few minutes," Web told her as he escorted her out the door and then closed it before sitting back down at the table.

Web explained to me that he had checked Lynch's story against the FBI database as soon as it was brought to his attention. When he couldn't find any results that included Stone's murder/suicide case, he suspected that the database might have been tampered with. He had gone the same route as I did on the plane using other search engines to find similar cases. When he came up with results, but could not find anything in the Bureau system, it confirmed his suspicions that the Bureau information had been compromised. As hard as it was for him to believe, he now had to entertain the possibility that one or more employees at the bureau might have been complicit in these murders.

"I thought that you might have been involved," Web suggested.

"Me? I asked.

"Put yourself in my shoes," he said, "We tried calling you several times and you didn't answer your phone. You called in sick, yet when you showed up that night in my office you appear to be in perfect health. Not even a sniffle."

"I see your point," I replied.

He continued to explain that he and Lynch arranged the "coincidental," plane meeting on the flight to Arizona.

"I needed to see how you reacted to Lynch on the airplane," he said.

"A test?" I asked.

"Yes, a test and based on what Lynch told me about your conversation on the plane and your actions since you landed, I was obviously wrong for suspecting you," Web responded and then proceeded to apologize for the deception.

"I guess if I was in your shoes I would probably have been suspicious of me as well." Besides, I was equally suspicious of you, so I guess I owe you an apology too."

"Now that we know we're both on the same side," Web said, "Why don't you fill me in on what's been going on. You can start with today since Lynch has been keeping me in the loop up until your meeting with Jenna this morning."

"Jenna?" I responded.

"Yes," he said, "I was at Jenna and Dan's wedding. Dan's father was also on our team and is a close friend of both of ours."

"Let's talk while we go check on Lynch," he suggested.

We barely walked through the door into the main hallway when Riddle approached us with bad news.

"The hospital has been searched," Riddle said, "Nobody fitting April's description was found."

Riddle wanted to lift the lockdown, but wanted to extend the courtesy of clearing it with Web and me prior to giving the order. Web nodded his approval and Riddle immediately passed along the order. As we walked towards Lynch's room I apprised Web of all the events that lead up to the double murder in the hospital.

We flashed our badges at the officers sitting outside of Lynch's room and walked in. April was sitting at Lynch's side. He was still a bit groggy from the anesthesia he was given, but was able to lift his hand acknowledging our presence.

After glancing at Web as he followed me through the door he said in a groggy voice "I guess the cat is out of the bag. I hope there are no hard feelings." Making an obvious reference to his complicity with Web in trying to figure out if I was involved in the Senator's assassination or not.

"No, no hard feelings at all," I replied, "I'm just glad to see you are still with us. If something happened to you, April would never forgive me".

Lynch turned to April and smiled. "It's been a long day and I think that I'm in very safe hands. Why don't you go home and get some rest."

He then looked at Web and me insisting that we go and get some rest as well.

April gave her father a kiss, got up and we all left the room together. Web and I walked April to her car. I asked if she would be okay.

She smiled and said "I'm a cop, remember?"

I nodded, but still watched as she got into her car and pulled out of the parking lot before I turned my attentions back to Web. At that moment, I realized that I had no car and no way of getting back to the Ranch.

"Do you mind if I hitch a ride?" I asked Web.

"Sure," he responded, "I'm actually staying with the Stone's and they are only a few miles from your parent's ranch."

"You know where my family lives," I said.

He quipped "We are the FBI you know".

It had been a long day and I was looking forward to getting some sleep. The clock had already passed midnight and we still had a couple of miles before we would get to the ranch. The last time I'd checked in to make sure everything was okay was just after April and I had finished dinner. Jenna had calmed down from the day's events and was sleeping in my room, which left me on the couch tonight. I was so tired from the events of the day, that I could probably fall asleep on a driveway if I had to. Out of left field, Web asked me what I thought of April. I wasn't sure what he was getting at, so I replied in jest that she was a person of extreme interest.

He responded, "I thought so." with a smile.

His cell phone rang, he picked up the call and after a few seconds, he told the caller to make sure the door was locked and to stay where they were. Web made a quick and unexpected right turn. The person on the phone was April; she had just gotten home and found her apartment door was open. She went to one of her neighbors apartments, locked the door and called from there. It looked like we were going to be starting the day a bit earlier than anticipated.

Chapter 11
The Revelation

It took us twelve minutes to arrive at April's apartment. The Phoenix PD was already on site. We ran up the steps to save time. When we got to second floor, we saw there were several officers—including April—in her apartment. Simultaneously, Web and I asked if everything was okay.

"Someone was definitely in my apartment," April answered.

I looked around the room and everything seemed to be where it was before April and I left for dinner.

"It doesn't look like anything was taken," I said.

"No," she replied, "If anything was taken, it wasn't something obvious. But something was definitely left behind".

She held out her hand in my direction. She was holding an envelope, using tweezers to keep from getting her finger prints on it. On the front of the envelope using newspaper clippings, the person that left it had spelled out "For Bennett Mills". The envelope appeared to still be sealed. As anxious as I was to open it, I knew that it needed to be examined by forensics first to see if any fingerprints could be lifted from the envelope.

We asked one of the head officers at the scene to get the letter to the forensics lab so they could start their work. We were all anxious to read the letter's contents...especially me.

I turned to April and asked "Don't take this the wrong way, but would you mind if I spent the night?"

Web quickly added "Make that, would you mind if we spent the night".

"The more the merrier," she said as she pointed down the hall. "One of you can take the spare room and the other gets the couch".

Web made his way down the hall, making it clear as to which one of us would be sleeping on the couch tonight. April went into her bedroom and came back carrying a cover sheet, a blanket and a pillow. After making up the couch, she said goodnight and headed back to her room. I could tell that she was still pondering the intrusion into her apartment. My mind, on the other hand, was focused on the letter that had been left behind with my name on it. I was getting ready to go to sleep when I remembered that my folks were expecting me to sleep at the ranch tonight. Based on the events of the day, I thought they would be worried if they woke up and I wasn't there. I decided to text my sister so she could let my parents know that I was not coming back to the ranch until the morning. They might have already gone to sleep, but my sister would definitely be awake. She was one of those people that would be up until three o'clock in the morning, and then she'd sleep until noon. Staying at the ranch with our parents since the divorce, I was surprised that she was able to keep that habit. My parents were firm believers of the "early to bed, early to rise," philosophy. As soon as my head hit the pillow, I couldn't help but notice that it was lightly scented. It appeared to be the same scent as the perfume that April had put on just before we left for dinner. It was actually very soothing and before I knew it, I was fast asleep.

It seemed like only minutes had passed before Web was nudging me awake. As I pulled myself up into a sitting position, I noticed that it was only 7 a.m. Web suggested that he drop me off at the Ranch before heading over to the Stone's house to grab a shower and some breakfast and then we would meet up later to continue the investigation. While we were waiting for the letter to be cleared by forensics, I wanted to stop by the VA hospital and speak with one of the psychiatrists currently working with Vets affected by Post Traumatic Stress Disorder. We were supposed to meet with them yesterday, but that had to be rescheduled after Lynch was shot. I also wanted to check in with Riddle. I was hoping that his people might have been able to track down the description of our phony physician at the VA hospitals where Dr. H had worked. It seemed a bit strange calling him Dr. H. It was like he was a comic book character or something. For now, it was the best we could do until we could figure out his real name. Given that his average employment at each facility was three months, you would think that somebody would be able to give us a description of what he looked like. With any luck, the descriptions would not only prove that they were all the same man, but also match the partial description that April gave us of the killer she encountered last night in Lynch's hospital room.

Before hitting the road, I made a pit stop in April's guest bathroom. As I started to walk down the hall, April's bedroom door opened and she stepped out already dressed in her police uniform. Hardly a second had passed before Web also appeared from the guest room.

"Where are we going today?" she said.

Web responded, "You are going to visit your father at the hospital, and then check in with your supervisor young lady".

She looked at me as if I was going to change Web's mind. I responded by shrugging my shoulders and smiling as we walked out the door.

I whispered to her "Try to stay out of trouble." She responded by sticking out her tongue at me.

I could tell the minute I walked out of the apartment building that it was going to be another blistering hot day. We got into Web's rental car and took off in pursuit of a nice hot shower, clean clothes, something to eat, and hopefully, a good strong cup of coffee. Web and I decided that after we took care of all of the essentials, we'd meet up at the VA facility later that morning. When I arrived at the ranch, I waited for Web to pull out of the gate and then called April on her cell phone. I wanted to make sure she had gotten to the hospital alright and to check on her father. She indicated that he was fine, but was fuzzy about the attack last night. He must have still been too sedated to remember the incident. I knew that April was anxious to help with the case, and figured that since she was heading to the station anyway, I saw no reason why I shouldn't ask her to do me a favor. I wanted her to compare the descriptions that Riddle's staff had collected from the VA facilities to see if they matched the killer she had encountered last night. I also asked her if she could push forensics on clearing the letter so we could read it. She told me that one of the guys in that department was always hitting on her and she would see if she could get him to speed things up. I suggested that maybe she shouldn't try too hard which elicited a laugh in response. It was an infectious laugh that would bring a smile to your face...and it did.

Turning to enter the front door, I found my father was standing right in front of me. "How was your night?" he asked.

"Rough," I responded, "very rough."

"Well you would never know by the smile on your face," he replied.

"Can we talk about this after I get cleaned up and something to eat?" I asked.

"Sure," he said, "your mother made a nice breakfast. I'm sure she can heat some up for you".

I walked in and headed directly for the shower. When I got out, I wrapped myself in a towel and headed for my room to get some fresh clothes.

When I opened the door, I found myself face to face with Jenna Stone. I had completely forgotten that she'd stayed at the ranch last night and was using my room. I apologized for the intrusion as I stood there wearing only a towel.

"Actually," she responded, "I'm the one staying in your room. So I'm the one that is intruding."

I told her I was just going to grab some clothes and I would be on my way. She was heading downstairs anyway and excused herself as she walked out of the room. I was dressed in no time and downstairs, joining Jenna at the breakfast table for some bacon, eggs, and pancakes. My mother always overdid things when she had company. I could smell the coffee as my mother approached with a big mug in her hand.

"This is just what I needed to get me kick started," I announced as I grabbed the cup from her hands.

A few minutes had passed when Jenna indicated that she had wanted to go back to her home. I insisted that until we had a chance to figure out who the shooter's real target was, that it would be better if she either stayed with us, or her in-laws. I didn't know the full story, but I got the feeling that things were contentious between Jenna and her in-laws after Dan's death. I think the thought that someone might be trying to kill her was sobering enough that she was convinced to stay at the ranch. She knew first hand that my father was an ex-cop and a damn good shot. I apologized to my mother for eating and running, but I had to get moving if I was going to meet up with Web.

My father drove Jenna and me back to her home so I could pick up the rental car I'd abruptly abandoned the other day. Jenna needed to pick-up some clothes and personal items for her stay at the ranch. I waited around long enough for them to check out the house, at which point my father waved me on. As soon as I got into the car, I flipped on the A/C and opened the windows. The car had been sitting all day and the air had gotten very stagnant in the sweltering heat. It took a few minutes before things finally started to cool down. Unfortunately, it would probably take most of the trip to the VA facility before my clothes dried out from when I first got into the car. I was surprised as I drove to the VA hospital that my thoughts were more focused on April than on the case. I wasn't one to be easily distracted from my work. In fact, when I was a cop in DC, they would have to turn the lights off in the office to break my concentration so they could tell me to go home. Not to pat myself on the back, but I did have a knack for solving some pretty difficult cases when I was with the DC PD, which is probably why they nicknamed me the "overachiever". I parked the car and was in the hospital with a few minutes to spare. Web had already arrived and was sitting in the lobby waiting.

"Do you have any Hawaiian print shirts packed in your bags?" he asked.

It was obvious that he was taking a cheap shot at my casual attire. I was quick to remind him that I was supposed to be on vacation, and FBI uniforms were anything but comfortable and casual. A familiar voice from behind asked when the next tour was.

I turned around to see my partner, Bill Rich, approaching. "What are you doing here?" I yelled.

"Don't ask me; ask our boss, he was the one that pulled me from my vacation at the Grand Canyon into this oven. What is it, about one-hundred and ten degrees?" he asked.

"No, just ninety-nine, but it should hit one-hundred and ten in about an hour," I said in jest. Web had called Bill just before he hopped the plane to Arizona and told him that he needed to cut his vacation short.

"Before we go inside," Web said, "I wanted to let you know that we got a match on your shooter's fingerprints. His name was Josh Reynolds, Captain Josh Reynolds. Does anybody want to take a guess where he was treated?" After a short pause with no response he continued. "Reynolds was treated at the same hospital that Stone was, right here!" pointing to the hospital as he said it.

He had arrived only a week or so after Stone. He was suffering from the same ailment as Rodney and Dan, Post-Traumatic Stress Disorder.

We checked in at the main desk, informing the receptionist of our meeting. She verified our appointment and directed us to take the elevator to the seventh floor, where we were to meet with a Dr. John Rodriguez. We had been waiting about five minutes when a tall, thin, well-groomed man approached us. As he introduced himself it was hard to see his mouth move through his thick black moustache. It appeared that he had more hair over his lip than on his entire head. When he shook my hand it was obvious that he was trying to make some type of impression by the force he was applying.

"Please feel free to call me John if you would like," he said.

On the way up the elevator, Web had requested that I take the lead on questioning the doctor. I thanked Dr. Rodriguez for taking the time to see us and then quickly proceeded with my first question.

"When I called you the other day I had asked you to pull the file on a vet named Dan Stone. His wife Jenna had mentioned that he received his treatment here. What can you tell me about Dan Stone's condition and the treatment he received?"

Dr. Rodriquez explained that Dan had suffered from Post-Traumatic Stress Disorder which is common in soldiers returning from active duty after exposure to combat situations. Before it received its clinical name, it was referred to as combat fatigue, shell shock, or war neurosis. Like most types of mental illnesses, it can be relatively mild in some cases, and yet for others, it can be quite extreme. In those cases, flashbacks could be a symptom making the person feel like they are reliving the event such as a battle they were in, nightmares of the events themselves, or of other things, that might be frightening in nature. They might also exhibit an intense physical reaction to the reminder of the event or events that had brought on the PTSD. Other symptoms would include: Difficulty falling or staying asleep, irritability or outbursts of anger, difficulty concentrating, and hyper vigilance. In the case of Private Stone, he exhibited several of these symptoms. According to the base psychiatrist's records, he and ten other members of his platoon were dispatched to secure a mosque in Tikrit that was being used as a base for Saddam loyalists. The loyalists must have seen them coming and shortly after they entered the mosque hit them with everything they had—completely wiping out all the other members of his platoon. If he had not been the last one into the mosque and within feet of the door he probably would have been killed himself. He was shot once in the arm and had shrapnel wounds in both legs. He was able to make it into a building that had been abandoned and waited there until his backup arrived. After another squad arrived and secured the building, he re-entered it to find his fellow platoon members had been mutilated by the loyalist. Although they treated him for his physical wounds, it was apparent to the base doctors that he would need psychiatric counseling, and they just weren't equipped to help him in that manner. When he arrived stateside, he entered this facility and resided here for just under four months before he was able to become an outpatient.

"What type of treatment did he receive?" I asked.

The doctor responded, "Each medical center has specialists that might prescribe any one of two-hundred specialized PTSD treatments, programs depending on the patient and the level of this disorder suffered. In the case of Private Stone, there were three treatment methods that were attempted. The first two methods of cognitive and psychodynamic treatments didn't seem to be helping. We were fortunate to have had a new doctor join our facility shortly after we decided that those treatments were not working. He specialized in a newly recognized form of treatment that seemed to be yielding miraculous results."

He continued, "I'm sure that you are familiar with the term hypnotherapy".

He had barely finished his sentence when my eyes opened wide and before I could stop myself, I blurted out "mind control, brain washing".

With a surprised expression on his face, the doctor responded, "That may be a bit extreme, but I can understand how a member of the FBI might jump to that farfetched conclusion."

"Isn't that basically what it is doctor?" I responded.

"In a sense, yes," he said, "in that the patient is induced into a state of consciousness in which they lose the power of voluntary action. At that point, they can become, susceptible to suggestion or direction by the individual initiating this state."

He must have seen the reaction on my face, because he immediately started to get defensive.

"I can assure you," he said "that we are not in the business of brain washing".

"Relax doctor, I'm not suggesting you are," I replied. "All I know is that I have several cases where ex-vets treated at this and other facilities around the country were all involved in violent killings. In each case, the unexplainable act of violence ended in the taking of their lives. Up until now, none of it made any sense to me."

"I think you have seen one too many movies Agent Mills, and I have no more time for this foolishness," he angrily responded as he started to get up from his chair.

"Sit back down!" I told him. "This is the closest I have come to making sense of these irrational and inexplicable acts of violence. If it offends you that

I am inferring that one of your associates might have stepped over the line, then that's just too damn bad."

I had turned to Web and could see by the look on his face that he was in full agreement. I think I might have even caught a glimpse of a smile. When I turned back to look at Dr. Rodriguez, I could see that his demeanor had changed. He appeared to be uncomfortable and had gone from being friendly to borderline hostile. Being the Senator's body guard for so many years, I thought I might have forgotten how to grill someone for answers. If I had, it was not apparent at the moment.

"How about an introduction to this hypnotherapist?" I asked.

"Unless you believe in the afterlife that would be impossible," he replied "He's dead."

Based on the phone conversations that Lynch and I had with other VA hospitals, I wasn't surprised to hear that. Actually, I was expecting it.

"When and how did he die?" I asked.

"A car accident about three months after he started at the facility," he responded.

"Any friends?" I asked.

"No. He was kind of a loner."

"How did you find out about his death?" I asked, as if I didn't know the answer already.

"I received a phone call from a relative in New Jersey, where he was going to be buried" he replied.

I turned to Web and Bill to see the expressions on their faces, and then turned my head back towards Rodriquez. I asked him for a list of every PTDS patient that the doctor had treated. He started to throw down the usual BS about doctor-patient confidentiality. I then told him that if he didn't cooperate, that a friend of mine at the IRS would be paying him a visit before the end of the week. It's funny how you can say FBI or CIA to someone and they barely flinch, but mention the IRS, and they turn white as a ghost. Without any hesitation, he agreed to have all the records pulled and delivered to us. I asked Bill if he would be willing to hang around and wait for the records, he agreed. I also asked if he could also try to obtain a description of the doctor from anyone that might have worked with him. Bill responded with a thumbs up.

I turned to the Doctor and said "Thanks for the cooperation," and then started walking with Web towards the elevator.

"I didn't know you had it in you," Web said in jest.

"You should have seen me in my DC PD days," I replied, "I think being with the Bureau made me a bit soft."

Although there was a sense of relief that I finally had at least one answer to this puzzle, I came to the scary realization that there were potentially hundreds of walking time bombs around the country just waiting to go off. I asked Web if he knew anyone that could start the process of getting out a bulletin to VA hospitals nationwide with the M.O. on our well-travelled doctor. We needed to locate anyone that he had treated, and for their protection get them into custody as quickly as possible. We didn't want any more of our vets being used as pawns in whatever game this lunatic was playing. Up until now, I had assumed the use of "H" as the first letter of every doctor's name that was assumed by this nut meant that his real first name started with an "H". Now, I had to wonder if the "H" stood for Hypnotist.

As uncomfortable as Web was with broadcasting this request—to the hospitals and local police departments—through the FBI systems, he saw no other choice. We needed to act fast and there was too much ground to cover to try and coordinate this effort without the sophistication of the Bureau systems. Our plan was to split up. Web would head over to the local Bureau office in Phoenix and I would head over to the Police Department to get an update from Chief Riddle. We still had someone on the inside playing with the FBI records. We needed to find out who the SOB was and stop them. We had no idea to what degree they were complicit in the murders, but they were definitely involved with the cover-up. Web wanted me to reach out to our resident geek and good friend, Bob Clayton. If anyone could figure out who had altered the records, it would be Bob. Some people are entertained by movies, some by sports, and others by the bar scene. Bob's idea of a fun evening was breaking into foreign government systems and planting viruses. He was so good at his job that they gave him one of the biggest offices in the building and did just about anything they could to keep him happy. The truth is that he just enjoyed hacking, and knowing that he could do it without being put behind bars made it that much more fun. Web wanted me to call Bob before I left the parking lot. With any luck, he would find the bastard before he or she did any more damage. Before Web headed off he handed me a piece of paper with his private cell phone number, asking me to make sure he was updated on anything new. As I started down the steps to my car, I turned to Web and told him once more that I was sorry that I had suspected him.

Web quickly responded, "Don't be, and don't trust anyone but yourself. We might just stay alive long enough to find this guy."

"They already tried to kill you once, don't bet that they won't try it again," he said.

We walked down the steps together and when we got to the parking lot we went our separate ways. I was heading to the Phoenix PD, but first I wanted to call Bob. Then check in on Lynch, and hopefully see April as well.

I called Bob, and as expected, he acted as if I had just handed him a winning lottery ticket. He just loved this cloak and dagger crap. I filled him in on the records of the other murders being deleted from our systems and told him to fetch. He laughed, and told me that I would be hearing from him real soon. If you didn't know him, you might think he was just a cocky bastard, but while others talked the talk, he walked the walk. I asked him to keep it under the radar and only contact Web or me when he had some information. We knew that there was at least one person that couldn't be trusted, but there were no guarantees that there was only one. As I hung up the phone, it felt for the first time that we were getting somewhere. Before leaving the parking lot I checked in at the ranch to make sure that every-thing was okay and to let my mom know not to hold dinner for me. I could tell that she was disappointed. But as the wife of a cop, she had gotten used to removing a plate from the dinner table when my father was involved in a case. I knew that this was different. It had been a while since I had been back home, and I'm sure that she had been preparing a special dinner. I apolo-gized, and told her that I was really looking forward to her home cooking. I told her that I would make it up to her, and promised to spend some quality time with her while I was home.

Chapter 12
The Envelope Please

I felt bad making Bill wait for the records, but asked him to track down a surveillance tape that probably didn't even exist anymore. It had been a while since either of us was involved in an active investigation. The one thing that would have sugarcoated the bitter pill of giving up his vacation would have been if he was actively helping us solve this case. Instead, he was sitting around the hospital like a messenger waiting for a package full of papers that he needed to deliver. Hopefully, at some point during the investigation, we'd be able to make it up to him. On the way to see Lynch, I called Bill to let him know that I was stopping by the hospital, and then, I would be at Phoenix PD. Once he had collected the information, I asked him to hop in the car and meet me there. He joked with me about owing him big time. I asked him if dinner would suffice. As expected, he said no, but it would be a nice start. I told him if he did a good job I might take him out to see the Hoover Dam. He didn't seem too excited, but who could blame him.

When I arrived at the hospital, I was surprised to find the parking lot was fairly empty. I figured with temperatures being as high as they were that the ER would be jam-packed with people suffering from heat stroke and heart attacks. It seemed like only a few hours had passed since I left here. I took the stairs up one flight to get to Lynch's floor. It always bothered me when someone would take the elevator to or from the first floor of a building to avoid having to walk two flights of stairs. That is probably why half the country is obese. Although my eating habits are not the best being an admitted fast food junkie, I work out every day and take the stairs when going up or down a couple of floors.

Once I got to Lynch's floor, I headed straight towards the door. After last night, it was a relief to see the two police officers standing watch. I had only a brief conversation with the officer that was assigned to guard the shooter last night. I had passed him on the way to the coffee shop with my father and stopped to chat for a couple of minutes. If only we had two officers at the door last night, he and our vet/shooter might still be alive. I knew it was silly to Monday morning quarterback ourselves like that. The purpose of having the guard was to keep the shooter under control when he came to. It never crossed our minds that someone would walk into the hospital for the purpose of killing him. If we only had the opportunity to speak to the vet, he might have been able to help us find the hypnotist and put an end to his sick games. When I thought about all of the good people that were dead or had their lives left in shambles because of this lunatic, I thought how happy it would make everyone if we didn't take him alive when we found him. It certainly would save the taxpayers some money, and based on some of the high profile scumbags that have gotten off, I would rather not leave his fate in the court's hands. In the meantime, we didn't have a clue as to who he was or why he took aim at our vets—turning our nations heroes into his own private killing machine.

I had to flash my badge to gain entry into Lynch's room. I guess my striped short sleeved shirt and khaki pants were a bit too casual to convince someone that I was an FBI Agent. As soon as I walked through the door, I saw April and couldn't help but smile. I thought I caught her returning my smile as well.

"Over here," Lynch said. I broke eye contact with April turning towards Lynch.

"Oh," I responded, "I did not realize you were in this room."

He started laughing, but by the look on his face, I could tell that he was still in pain.

"You are a federal agent," he said, "Let's stay in character by not exhibiting a sense of humor."

I could tell from the wince of pain that he regretted laughing at his own comeback line.

"Okay you two," April said, "Let's play nice boys."

Lynch and April were both interested in hearing what we found out at the VA hospital, but I didn't think either of them was prepared for what I was going to tell them.

I told them "It was just like what we found at the other VA hospitals. This guy comes in and treats several veterans, and then one day, the department head receives a call that the doctor died."

I continued "In this case it was a car accident and he was supposedly buried in Red Bank, New Jersey, but the cemetery shows no record of anyone by that name being buried there."

I paused for a minute, but Lynch could tell that I was not finished. "Okay, come clean. What else do you have?" He asked.

"We're still waiting on a description of the guy," I responded, "but I suspect that it's the same guy that has been posing under different names at the other VA hospitals. Most likely he is also the guy that attacked you. Here is the kicker, the doctor that treated Stone and the vet that shot you specialized in Hypnotherapy."

Lynch and April were speechless, just taking in what I just said with a shocked look on their faces. I told them Bill, Web, and I all had a fairly similar response.

"This is one cold hearted bastard using our servicemen like that," Lynch blurted out.

April and I both nodded in agreement.

"When we left the hospital, Web was headed to the local Bureau office to put out a nationwide bulletin to all of the VA hospitals in the country and the closest police precincts in case their assistance is required."

I explained the urgency of identifying and gathering all of his patients.

"We need to get them out of his reach and into a safe place until we could figure out who was affected and how to break whatever directive they'd been given while under hypnosis."

I told them about my friend in the DC office and how he was trying to figure out who at the office has been manipulating the FBI records.

"Whoever it is," I said, "was probably the one giving this guy a new face and identification each time he moved from hospital to hospital."

"Can we let Jenna know that her husband wasn't a killer?" April asked.

Before I could respond, Lynch told her that we had to hold off on giving her that news. She looked perplexed.

"Your father is right," I replied, "We're not even telling the local police departments why they are gathering the vets. If this was to get out to the public, it might cause some panic and possibly compel this guy to mobilize some of these vets into action before we can get them safe."

"If we don't play our cards right, it could cost our vets and other innocents their lives. Be patient, I promise we will tell her in due time. For now, it's important that this information stays amongst our small group until it is safe to tell anyone else."

I could tell by the look on Lynch's face that he was still a bit wiped out and suggested that April and I head back to the precinct. April initially wanted to stay, but Lynch convinced her that he wanted to rest and maybe even catch a college game on the tube. It was obvious that he wanted us to spend our time catching this guy. Since we both had our cars, we decided that we would drive separately meeting back at the station. We were hoping that by the time we got there that we might have some additional information from the VA hospitals. I was also hoping that forensics was ready to hand over the letter that I assumed the hypnotist aka Dr. H, had left for me. My curiosity regarding the contents of the letter had been gnawing at me since I saw my name on the envelope. When we got to the parking lot, I headed towards my car and April moved in the direction of where she had parked. I had just pulled out of my parking spot and started heading towards the exit when I noticed April waving me down through my rear view mirror. I stopped the car and backed up to where she was standing.

"My car won't start," she said, "Do you know anything about cars?"

"Just how to drive them," I said. "Why don't you drive with me. Maybe Riddle can get a mechanic out to take a look at it."

During the drive, I turned on some news radio and one of the lead stories was that Hope Billings was being considered as a replacement for her father's seat in the Senate. Even though I had heard the rumors through the grapevine as early as the day of the funeral, hearing it officially on the radio was a different story. Hope had apparently indicated that if the position was offered to her she would be honored to accept the appointment. I asked April if she would mind if we did a drive-thru for something to eat. I was starved and needed a good cheeseburger and fries to get my energy levels back up.

"You must have read my mind," April told me as she pointed to a Burger Hut on the approaching corner. "I've been craving a burger all day".

It was lunch time so the drive-thru line was ten cars long. It took us five minutes before we got our order in, and another ten minutes before they finally handed us our food. We pulled into a parking spot to eat. We were running late, so we didn't take much time to talk before starting the car and heading off to the precinct.

We arrived at the precinct about one-thirty. On the way to Riddle's office, April stopped to ask one of her fellow officers if he could dispatch a mechanic to the hospital to take a look at her patrol car.

"Just tell him that the engine wouldn't turnover," she said.

"I'll take care of it," he replied.

We proceeded down the hall, finding Riddle sitting at his desk with the door open. It appeared as if he were expecting us. We were barely seated when he told us that he had received a courtesy call from Web updating him on our visit to the VA hospital and the information we'd uncovered regarding the hypnotherapist. At Web's request, Bill had already forwarded a list of five patients that the doctor had treated at the Phoenix VA hospital. He also requested that Phoenix PD start to locate these patients and bring them in as quickly and quietly as possible. They were asked to use unmarked vehicles and to approach with caution since we had no idea what might set them off. Since Dr. H seemed to be aware of things we were doing, it made sense that he might already have planned for our intervention.

"What are your officers telling these vets when they pick them up?" I asked.

"We are only saying that we need to ask them a few questions regarding the doctor that treated them at the VA hospital." Riddle replied.

"That sounds benign enough," I replied. "Did Bill mention if he was able to obtain any video from the hospital?" I asked.

"No," Riddle replied, "They told him that they did not keep the surveillance videos for more than a few weeks before they were erased and recycled."

"We were able to get descriptions of the doctor from the hospital staff," Riddle said as he tossed a folder onto the desk in front of me.

I opened the folder and April and I both reviewed the composite drawings that were put together from the descriptions. It was as I had expected. Even though the hypnotist had tried to change his appearance in subtle ways like changes in hair color and facial hair, the other characteristics were still very much the same as we had seen in drawings from the other facilities. I turned to April to see if she recognized the picture as being man that had tried to kill her father.

"I can't be sure," she replied, "His face was covered by the doctor's mask."

She used her hands to cover up all parts of the face on the sketch except the Eyes.

"It was so fast, but the eyes do look familiar," she said.

As April started to thumb her way through the sketches again, we heard a faint knock at Riddles office door.

"Come in," Riddle said.

I could see the sleeve of a white lab coat appear as the door opened. It was the guy from the forensics that April had mentioned was interested in her.

Riddle made the introductions, "Detective Mills, this is Tom Kemp from our forensic team. He's the guy that has been checking the envelope and letter for prints, bio-agents, etc…"

I'm not sure if Kemp even heard Riddle since he was clearly distracted by April. He couldn't have been any more obvious about his interest in her. Riddle had to clear his throat a couple of times, getting progressively louder, before he was able to break Kemp's fixation on her.

"Do you have anything for us?" Riddle asked.

"Yes. I'm sorry sir," he replied.

Kemp apologized for the delay in looking at the letter but he explained that he was backed up with work because his boss was on vacation this week. He went on to reveal that there were no finger prints or bio-agents found.

"What about DNA from saliva used to close the envelope?" I asked.

"He must have used a wet cloth since the envelope was sealed with water, and trace fibers from the cloth were found on the envelope seal," he responded. "Since we found the wet cloth and the same stationary used to write the letter in the apartment, we assumed the letter was written there. We dusted everything in that area, including every pen that matched the color ink used to write the letter and came up with nothing. I'm sorry, but whoever left this letter took great care in making sure that no evidence was left to be found."

"What about the envelope?" I asked. "He used newspaper clippings to address the letter to me. I doubt he took the time to do all of that while at the apartment."

"I would guess you're right about that." Kemp said. "I guess he knew who the letter was going to, but didn't know what he was going to write until he was in the apartment."

"Can I have the letter?" I asked.

As Kemp extended his hand with the envelope in it, I reached out and took it from him. I quickly removed the letter from the opened envelope and started to read it out loud. "Today was a warning. Next time you may not be so lucky. It would be a shame to end a blossoming career, especially after I worked so hard to get you where you are today. Now you have been liberated from the tedium of standing in the shadows of a relic. Consider your Detective friend's death proof of my resolve. Do not push me into further acts of retribution. If you have not yet realized, I am watching you at all times so be mindful of your actions. A member of your family, or perhaps, your new girlfriend could be next." The letter was signed "DO AS I SAY!

Glossing over the girlfriend comment I turned to April and said "He must have written the letter before his visit to the hospital, and just assumed he would be successful in his attempt to kill your father."

Based on his signature "Do as I say", it was clear that we were correct in our assumption that the man behind these killing was the hypnotist. I wondered if we had opened the letter before our visit to Dr. Rodriguez if we would have figured that out sooner.

"What do you think he meant when he said he was working so hard to get you where you are today?" Riddle asked.

"I don't know," I replied, "but I plan on finding out".

"Could he just be trying to distract you from your investigation?" April responded, "Why would he make that kind of comment?"

I was surprised that April didn't show more concern about the threat that he'd made towards her. I couldn't imagine that the girlfriend comment in the letter could have gone unnoticed. I wanted to start to analyze the comments he had made about my career, but my focus needed to be on the safety of April and my family first. He knew where April lived, which meant that he must have followed us back to her apartment from the hospital the other night, left the note, and returned to kill the shooter and Lynch. If he was that well acquainted with my life, then he would also know that I was staying with my family. Breaking out of my momentary trance, I asked Riddle if he could supply a couple of officers to keep watch at the ranch. Without hesitation he picked up the phone and called in the request. With the concerns for my family's safety being addressed, I turned to April and told her that we needed to provide her with protection as well. She responded as I would expect any other police officer to, indicating that she could take care of herself. Since April was already in the thick of things and appeared willing to take a passive role in the investigation I asked Riddle if he would allow her to work with me on the case.

"Lynch is going to kill me for agreeing to this, but I guess under the circumstances it makes sense," he said.

I was expecting April to put in her two cents on the subject, but I guess she was good with the decision since she didn't utter a word. There couldn't have been more than a couple of seconds of silence before the officer that April had spoken to regarding her car barged into the office. Riddle appeared furious that the officer didn't even bother to knock, but before he could voice his anger the officer informed us that there had been an explosion at the hospital that Lynch was staying in.

"In the hospital?" Riddle asked as he rose out of his chair

"It was April's car," the officer said.

He turned to April. "I notified the garage that your car wouldn't start and they sent Chuck to take a look at it. A witness saw him lift the hood of the car, and then, it just blew up.

"Chuck?" April asked in a concerned voice.

"Chuck is dead." The officer responded.

We were all shocked and upset by the news, but April for obvious reasons was completely distraught. While I was trying to comfort her, I asked the officer if they could confirm the cause of the explosion. He explained that the fire department was still in the process of putting out the fire. However, it seemed clear to the explosive experts on the scene, that this was no accident. You could see in April's eyes that she knew she was the intended target, and even though she was not to blame for Chuck's death, she felt some sense of responsibility. I knew that I needed to get her out of the precinct as quickly as possible and away from all of the chaos that the news of the explosion had created.

First I needed to call my father and update him about the letter and explosion. I needed him to understand the reason for the imminent arrival of the two officers that would be stationed outside his front door. In the meantime, I needed for him to understand the urgency of watching out for anything suspicious until they arrived. As if it was not bad enough that I hardly spent any time at home, now I unwittingly had put my family in harm's way.

According to my dad, everything had been quiet and he promised me that he would keep everyone safe until the cavalry arrived. I thought he might give me some attitude about sending the officers to watch the ranch. But while he was always willing to risk his own life for the sake of the job, he knew he couldn't take chances with the rest of the family. Before I hung up, I apologized for getting him involved. I expected a lecture, but was surprised by his response.

His exact words were "Nail the bastard that's doing this".

I responded, "Will do," and hung up the phone.

I asked Riddle to call Lynch at the hospital to make sure he knew that April was okay and that she would be with me. I am sure that he would have been more comforted if she was under lock and key at the police department. But he knew his daughter well enough to know that it was unlikely that she would have agreed to that. April was still in shock over what had happened to Chuck, she didn't put up a fight when I asked her to take a drive with me. It was obvious that her encounter at the hospital last night made her a prime target for this nut. I knew it wouldn't be safe for her to go back to her apartment. I hated to ask, but it made perfect sense with two police officers, an ex-chief of police, and an FBI agent present that the ranch was probably the safest place for us to stay tonight. I guess I was just downgraded from sleeping on the couch tonight to sleeping on the floor. In the meantime, it would be up to me to keep us both alive until this lunatic was either dead or behind bars.

One of the benefits of working on a security detail for so many years is that you are able to hone your powers of observation. For both of our sakes, I was hoping that I had learned that skill well. It appeared that for some mysterious reason the hypnotist did not want me dead, well at least not yet. Since I wasn't planning on letting up on the investigation, I assumed it was just a matter of time before I would become a target as well. What complicated things the most was that if we were threatened by one of his hypnotized victims, how were we going to defend ourselves? If we had no choice but to kill the attacker, could we do it knowing that we were taking the life of an innocent man? Hopefully, Riddle would be able to have them all in custody before the end of the day and we wouldn't have to worry about it.

I wanted to engage April in conversation about something besides the case to try and distract her from what had just happened, but I was hard-pressed to find a topic that didn't appear contrived for that purpose.

Before I could think of anything to say, she turned to me and asked, "How did you get the name Bennett?"

She had presented me with the opportunity I had been looking for. When I turned to her to respond, I noticed that she appeared much more composed than she had only a few minutes earlier. Bennett was definitely not the typical name that a parent might choose to give their child. Unusual as it was, it was rarely did anyone ask me about its origin. It was equally unusual that few people over the years had attempted to shorten my name to Ben.

"My father lost his dad to cancer when he was only three years old. He had one sibling, a brother, who was fourteen at the time and helped my grandmother raise him," I told her. "He took my father everywhere with him. He taught him sports. How to hunt, and even helped him with schoolwork. Shortly after the war in Vietnam started, he was drafted into the army. After three years, when it appeared that he might make it home alive my grandmother received the customary visit by an Army officer. He informed her that her son had died bravely in action while saving the rest of his platoon."

"His name was Captain Bennett Mills. It's funny," I said, "most kids growing up with a name like Bennett would probably hate their parents for doing that to them, but I was proud to carry my Uncle's name."

I paused for a moment after finishing my story. When I did not hear anything, I glanced toward April and noticed that she had a tear rolling down her cheek, but at the same time I could see a hint of a smile as well. After a couple of minutes had passed, I handed April my cell phone and a piece of paper that I had written down Web's personal cell number on.

"Would you mind dialing Web for me?" I asked. "I want to see how the search for the vets is coming along."

"Sure," she replied.

Web picked up after a couple of rings and April handed me the phone. Even though April was neck deep involved, I did not think that Web would appreciate us talking on speaker.

"I was just going to give you a call" he said. "Is April with you?" he asked.

I acknowledged that we were in the car and that she was safe.

"If you do nothing else, you better make sure she stays safe," he said. "I already helped bury one of my best friend's sons. I don't want to repeat that unpleasant duty."

"Understood," I replied.

"What were you going to call me about?" I asked.

"Two things," he said, "first of all we reached out to every VA hospital in the country and we are starting to get some responses. It appears so far he treated anywhere from five to twelve patients at the facilities we have heard from so far".

I suggested that we try to narrow things down a bit by speaking with the heads of those hospitals and find out which of the patients treated were considered successes. My thought was that if it appeared that the patient was successfully treated for PTSD, there was a greater likelihood that they were also programmed by this nut. Web agreed to ask the hospitals to focus on those patients and to get the information out to the local precincts as soon as they were identified. Even with the priority these requests were given, it would still take some time before all of the Vets were safely detained. We both knew that with every passing moment it took to find these men, the possibility existed that Dr. H. might try to extricate the vets from their current environment.

"You told me that you had two things to tell me," I said.

"Yes," Web responded, "We think we found the person that has been manipulating our database and god only knows what else."

"What do you mean you think?" I asked.

Web responded, "We checked the archives of the database and her name was the last one attached to the records before they were deleted."

"Did you have a chance to question her?" I asked.

After a short pause he simply replied "She's dead".

"Her name was Jenny Yuen. She had been with the department for about two years," he told me, "Her record was exemplary. She was well liked by all of her co-workers and supervisors. We questioned several of her closest friends at the bureau and they saw no signs that would have made them suspicious that she would be involved in anything questionable in nature".

As I listened to the story, I couldn't help but to feel that something about this seemed eerily familiar.

"How did she die?" I asked.

"Suicide, she overdosed on sleeping pills," he replied.

"Was she a vet by any chance?" I asked.

"No, but she was a smoker," he responded.

I knew immediately where he was heading with this, "You mean an ex-smoker that had a little help kicking the habit through hypnotherapy," I suggested.

"That's what I was thinking." answered Web.

The agency had already started searching her apartment, her checking account, her personal calendar and talking to her friends and neighbors. We were trying to verify our suspicions and maybe come up with a name, or something, anything that would help us find this maniac so we could bring him to justice. At the moment, I realized that my definition of justice might not exactly match what the courts would have in mind.

"I'll get back to you once I have any new information," Web promised.

He suggested that we get together later in the evening to compare notes and to make sure we were both caught up on everything. He suggested that after I drop April off at the ranch, I meet him at the Phoenix Bureau headquarters. I asked if he would mind stopping by the ranch since it was only a couple of miles away from the Stone's house where he had been staying. He was probably as tired as I was by now. Lately, sleep had seemed like a luxury that was being rationed out like water to a desert traveler. It didn't take long for him to embrace my suggestion. He wouldn't admit to being tired. Instead he suggested that he wanted an opportunity to check in on April and Jenna. Since they were being sheltered at the ranch, it would save him from making an extra trip. I didn't really care what the excuse was, I was just happy not to be in the car a minute longer than I needed to. I was getting a bit punchy and with variety of terrains in Arizona, I was afraid I would drive into a canyon or something. As soon as I got off the phone, I planned on filling April in on what had happened; although, Web was loud enough on the other end that she'd probably overheard most of the conversation anyway.

Before I had a chance to utter my first syllable, she confirmed it by repeating Web's exact words back to me, "If you do nothing else, you better make sure she stays safe".

She seemed to have settled down a bit and it was nice to see even the smallest sliver of a smile as she mimicked Web's comments. Although, I wanted to get back to the ranch, April insisted on stopping in to see her father for a few minutes. Since we were going to pass the hospital on the way, I agreed to make this one stop. In the back of my mind I knew that even if I had not given my blessing for this detour we would have ended up there anyway. By avoiding arguing the point, I probably saved at least ten minutes of wasted discussion.

We had just turned off the exit when my cell phone rang...it was Bob Clayton. I picked up the call and told him it looked like he was too late because we already had the name of the person that had altered the database.

He indicated that he had Yuen's name five minutes after we got off the phone earlier in the day. "It wasn't her," he said. "If she had manipulated the records, she would have been careful enough to cover her tracks".

"Was she that good?" I asked.

"No," he responded, "but she wasn't stupid either.

"Are you trying to tell me that she was setup by someone to take the fall?" I asked.

"I don't know, but something just doesn't seem right," he replied.

"Have you mentioned this to Web yet?" I asked.

"No, I didn't think he would believe me," he responded.

"If anyone had suggested a week ago that we would have a hypnotherapist using his skills to turn vets into hit men, I would have taken away their car keys and offered to drive them home. I want you to call Web now," I told him, "and tell him exactly what you told me." Before hanging up the phone I asked Bob to get started proving his theory in the morning.

We arrived at the hospital, but I wasn't going to chance parking in the garage, and I certainly wasn't going to leave the car unsupervised after April's car blew up earlier today. When we got to the entrance, I flashed my badge to a security guard just inside the entrance. I explained that we needed to leave the car for about twenty minutes and needed his assurance that he wouldn't take his eye off the vehicle or let anyone else near it until we returned. As soon as we walked through the door, my eyes surveyed everyone that was sitting in the reception area. I did not know who I was looking for, but I knew what I was looking for. I was looking for anyone that took note of us or got up as we approached the elevator. For both of our sakes, we needed to avoid dark, low traffic areas like hospital staircases.

There were new officers, guarding Lynch's room when we arrived. Since April knew one of the officers they did not ask for me to show my badge before allowing us to enter the room. I had April continue in to see her father while I paused outside the door to explain to the officer that if the President of the United States were to try and gain access to the room without showing credentials that he was to arrest him. What if I was the killer and had a gun to April's back? Based on what we had already seen and learned in the past couple of days, nothing should be taken for granted.

When I walked into the room April was sitting on the right side of the bed. Lynch was sitting upright with the television tuned to a college football game. It was obvious by his demeanor that he was well on his way to recovery, but it would still be a few days before he would be released from the hospital. Lynch asked me if I still had his gun. I turned to the side and pointed to my holster. He pulled out from under his pillow a Browning High Power 9mm pistol.

"Where did you get that?" I asked.

"I have a few friends at the Bureau you know," he said with a smirk on his face.

"I'd feel a lot more comfortable with an old friend by my side, and I would think that you might be a bit more comfortable with this fellow," as he pointed to the Browning.

I opened my holster and handed him his gun as he passed me the Browning. It was orchestrated as if we were doing a prisoner exchange.

"Do you mind if I keep the holster for a while?" as I started to slip the Browning into place.

"Not a problem," he said. "I have mine holstered under my pillow," and started laughing. "It's getting dark, get her to the ranch and get some sleep".

I knew we had to get going if we were going to get the ranch before Web arrived. April leaned over and gave Lynch a kiss. As we started to walk towards the door Lynch told me to take care of April.

"I will," I replied as I left the room closing the door behind me.

Chapter 13

The Intrusion

On the way to the ranch, April had closed her eyes and fallen into a deep sleep. It had been a long day and I was pretty tired myself, but at least I hadn't had some psychopath try to blow me up today. The sun had set an hour ago, and once we left the city limits, the only illumination came from the moonlight. As it streamed through April's window, it lit up the silhouette of her face. Every feature on her face was perfect. It was hard to imagine that she wasn't involved with someone. I could only imagine that as a female police officer it might be difficult to get past the first date without scaring the guy off. The only thing worse would probably be dating someone from the IRS. If that relationship went south, you might find yourself in the middle of a tax audit. As for dating another cop, that type of relationship was frowned upon in the same precinct because of the obvious hazards of the job. I could have spent the entire drive looking at her, but then I might wind up going off the road.

With everything that had happened today, this was the first moment I had to give some thought to what the hypnotist had written in his letter about my career. How could he have helped me in my career, and what would his motive have been? As I'd mentioned to April when we had dinner last night, I had no idea how I wound up back on the FBI's radar after years of no response to my application. I was very happy with my job with the DC police at the time. The feedback from my supervisors was that I was doing a great job and had a promising future within the department.

I had a great partner for many years. Ed and I worked over a hundred cases together during our years with the DC PD. He loved playing the bad cop. Ed always knew how to apply just enough pressure to get the bad guy to slip up. My job was to bring the bad guy to the table. I've always had a gift for knowing when someone was trying to bullshit me. The harder they tried to establish their innocence, the more I would see through their thin veil of deceit. If he had not died in a car accident on the interstate just outside of Alexandria I might have never left the force.

The offer to join the FBI came in a week after his funeral and a couple of weeks before they were going to assign me a new partner. I just couldn't get myself to partner up with someone new. The chance of repeating the chemistry we had on the job was slim to none. During my short time with the DC police department, I had seen enough oddly coupled teams, and the nightmares that would ensue, that I knew I did not want to take a chance of winding up with one of those partners. I figured that I would miss some of the more unusual cases that Ed and I had come across, but could easily go without some of the more violent crimes scenes that we would occasionally encounter. There were times I would get back to my apartment and lay awake all night with the images that would make horror movies look like Disney productions. The only satisfaction you could get was when you could put away the animals that committed the crime. Sometimes, I even found it difficult to find solace in that. I knew that with the flawed court system, it was just a matter of time before they'd be put back on the streets again. Their victims had no time off for good behavior, their time was either marred by the memories of rape, and abuse, or they were buried six feet under. It was easy to understand why some of the old timers had become so cynical about the system. Sometimes they could barely make it through the day without stopping at one of the local pubs for a drink to wash down the disgust.

When I was first approached to join the Senator's security team I thought it was a joke. I had barely reached the stage where the more seasoned agents would have given me the time of day. The next thing you know, I am on security detail for one of the most prominent Senators in the country. Was it possible that the hypnotist somehow influenced my promotion by altering the records? If he did, it wouldn't have been Jenny Yuen since she wasn't even working for the FBI at the time. That would have corroborated Bob's belief that she was somehow framed, and then, murdered to prevent anyone from having a chance to interrogate her. Now I wasn't only faced with the question of who altered the records to get me into the Bureau, I had to figure out why. Maybe after good night's sleep I'd have a better chance of answering that question.

When we pulled into the ranch, I could see my father standing by the barn door with his favorite rifle sitting by his side. No other cars were in sight, so I assumed that we had beaten Web to the ranch. As my father started walking towards the car, I hurried to intercept him to prevent him from abruptly waking up April.

"She fell asleep on the way out here," I said pointing to April sitting in the front seat.

I asked if the couch was ready for her and if mom had any leftovers that she could heat up. We had not eaten since earlier in the day, and although, getting some sleep was the second thing on my mind, getting something to eat was the first. I was going to try and carry April into the house, but after giving it some thought, I wasn't sure how well that would be received if she woke up in my arms mid-way between the car and the couch. Instead, I tried nudging her a bit until she opened her eyes. She actually jerked a bit as if she had just had just woken up from a bad dream.

"We're at the ranch," I said.

She seemed a bit disoriented at first, so I repeated myself.

The first words out of her mouth were "Do you have anything to eat, I'm starved".

April appeared a bit unsteady after just waking up from her brief nap. We worked our way up the porch stairs and into the kitchen where my mom had already started heating up some dinner for us to eat. April had already met my father at the hospital, so I took this opportunity to introduce her to my mom. My sister and Jenna were already in bed, but came down when they heard the screen door slam as we walked into the house. April was at Jenna and Dan's wedding and had noticed her at the hospital, but was so preoccupied with her father getting shot that she barely had a chance to acknowledge her presence.

Jenna came running up to April, gave her a hug and asked how her father was.

"He is just about back to himself," she said, "We stopped by the hospital to see how he was doing. He acted like he wanted to get rid of us so he could watch a football game, but I think he just didn't want me doting over him."

Jenna responded, "In the case of my father-in-law, he actually would have kicked us out to watch the game."

While they continued their chatter, I sat down so I could grab a quick sandwich from the fresh turkey dinner that my mother had prepared. I knew that Web would be here any minute and if he expected for us to have a coherent conversation, then I needed to get some fuel in me.

My mother walked over to April and excused her from the conversation with Jenna, grabbing her by the hand and leading her to the table so she could eat the sandwich that she had made her. Sitting down, April thanked my mother for the sandwich and for allowing her stay at the ranch.

"You're welcome to stay as long as you would like," she said as she poured her homemade apple cider into a cup for April. She then discreetly looked at me and winked. I nearly choked on my sandwich when I saw the expression on her face. When it came to my social life, my mother was as subtle as a drunk at the opera. She knew exactly what she wanted, and that was grandchildren. With my sister recently divorced, she had decided to turn her sights on me. When I was dating Hope, she let up for a while figuring that I was headed in the right direction. Once we broke up she gave me all of a month before she started to drop those hints again about trying to meet someone new.

April must have been hungrier than I was because she had almost finished her sandwich before I had taken a second bite of mine. But then again, she wasn't being distracted by my mother's antics. I looked up at the clock, it was getting late, and Web still hadn't arrived.

At that moment, my cell phone rang, it was Web. He was probably calling to let me know that he was running late. I answered the phone but before I could make a joke about his being tardy, the sound of a gunshot rang through the headset, forcing me to take the phone away from my ear for a few seconds. Almost simultaneously, it sounded like the echo from the same shot coming from the distance. Web yelled "I'm about a mile up the road and under fire, they have me pinned down and I need some help." I asked my father to grab his rifle and told everyone else to stay in the house as we both bolted out the door. As we passed the two officers on the way out the door, I tapped one of them on the arm and ordered him to come with us. I told the other officer to call for backup. I hopped into the car with the cop and told my father to head up the hill in his truck, keeping the headlights off. My father knew the terrain like he knew the back of his hand and thanks to nature providing a full moon, he should be able to get into a good position without being detected.

As we headed up the road we could hear the gunshots getting louder. We killed our headlights about a half mile up the road, coasted about a quarter of a mile, and pulled over to the side of the road.

I glanced at the cops name plate. "Officer Dailey," I said, "I'm going to take the car from here, I need for you to follow on foot. I don't have time to explain, but if you need to shoot, aim for non-vital areas. Can you do that?" I asked.

He nodded yes. As I approached the hill where the road curved, I could see a faint headlight ahead. As I turned the corner I flipped on all of the lights on the police car and pushed the gas petal to the floor. I could see three men stationed behind a small black SUV; they were obviously caught off guard by my sudden appearance and temporally blinded by all of the lights on the police car. As they put their hands over their eyes to shield themselves from the lights, I noticed they had semi-automatic guns in their hands. As they started to point them in my direction, I plowed into the SUV forcing it to flip over on top of the men and down the embankment behind them. The deploying airbag hit me in the face causing me to become disoriented for a moment. I started to back the car up when I noticed one of the men turning in my direction with his gun in hand. Suddenly, another gunshot rang out, it wasn't from the gunmen, but at the gunmen who fell in his tracks. I hopped out of the car, still a bit dazed from the airbag, and grabbed the semi that had fallen out of the man's hand when his body hit the ground. He had been hit in the head. I slowly moved in the direction of the overturned SUV noticing a pair of feet jutting out from behind the front end of the vehicle while an arm of another man was protruding from the rear end of the SUV. If they weren't dead already, they would be before we could get the SUV off of them. I heard a noise behind me and turned around swinging the semi in that direction. It was Officer Dailey yelling don't shoot. He looked like he had just seen his life pass before his eyes.

I lowered the gun and said "Thanks for saving my life, but I thought I said shoot for non-vital areas".

He responded, "I just got here. It wasn't me".

From behind Web's car I could hear Web yell "That shot was mine, and they weren't vets, so no worries".

As Officer Dailey and I started walking towards Web, my father's pick-up truck could be seen racing up the road towards our position. We walked around the car and saw Web was sitting up.

It looked like he had taken a bullet in his left arm. "Are you okay?" I asked.

"Yep," he responded, "it's a good thing it wasn't my other arm, or you might not be to okay yourself," referring to the gunman that was within seconds of turning me into Swiss cheese.

"It looks like you were pretty fortunate yourself. With all that fire power I didn't expect to see you in one piece" I said.

"They ambushed me," Web yelled, "I was coming up the road and noticed their SUV off to the side. I slowed down to take a look when all of a sudden they started to shoot at the car, but if they wanted to kill me they could have easily taken me out."

I turned to Web's car and noticed that the tires were shot out, but the front window didn't have any bullet holes. I suddenly got a sick feeling in the pit of my stomach.

I turned to Web and said "They were waiting for you, and they didn't kill you because they wanted you to make the call. They wanted to draw us away from the house".

I yelled to my father to get back into the truck. I told Officer Dailey to stay with Web, and when backup arrived, he should tell them to haul ass to the ranch. As I got into the truck, I could hear the faint sounds of two gun shots ringing out in the distance. My father turned the key, but the truck wouldn't start. He tried a couple of more times with no success. I could see the frustration on his face. We got out of the truck, and jumped into what was left of my rental car and started the engine. I hit the gas pedal, but the car was obviously badly damaged. The front wheels had been knocked out of alignment. It would get us back to the ranch, but it was going to be a slow ride. While I drove, my father tried to call the house, but no one answered.

"No one's picking up the damn phone. "he yelled. "Can't this piece of crap move any faster?".

"I'm pushing it as hard as I can without having it run off the road," I replied trying to yell above the noise coming from the car's engine. I realized that every minute it took us to get back to the house could be the difference between life and death. As I continued to push the car as hard as I could without going off the road, the thought of what might be happening was tearing me up inside. As soon as we pulled into the main gate, we started honking the horn hoping to draw the gunmen out. When no one responded to our diversion, we pulled along the side of the house which had a limited number of windows to reduce the chance of us getting shot while exiting the car. My father with rifle in hand went around to the back of the house, and with the semi-automatic still in my hand, I slowly moved towards the front. Clouds had moved in and had muted the light of the full moon, providing us with some cover in the darkness of the night. The police officer that we had left guarding the house was noticeably absent, which led me to believe that he might have been an easy target for the approaching gunmen. I slowly turned the corner of the house and tried to peer through the front window. Everything in the house appeared as we had left it, but it was unnervingly quiet and nobody was in sight. All I could think about at that moment was the squeaky front screen door, and how opening it would announce my entry into the house. I noticed there was a broom stick that my mother always left on the porch. I grabbed it and used the handle to slowly push the screen door open. Every inch of movement was accompanied by a loud creaking. If anyone was still in the house, the noise would have certainly drawn their attention but still nothing, no response. All of a sudden, I realized that we didn't see a car when we pulled in. Could the intruders have finished what they came here for? Were we too late? I hardly had time to finish the thought before I heard my father yelling "get in here he's been shot". As the only male left at the house, it was clear he had been talking about the officer we'd left to keep watch. I was following my father's voice into the kitchen when suddenly I saw April coming down the stairs with her gun drawn. I put my hands up motioning to her to put the gun away.

"Is everyone alright?" I asked.

"Yes," she replied.

I continued on my way into the kitchen finding the officer laying on the floor. From the location of the entry point, it did not appear to be life threatening. My father was applying pressure to the wound while trying to keep him in conversation to make sure he stayed conscious. In the distance, I could hear several police cars heading in our direction. Based on how loud the sirens were, I expected they would be pulling through the gates of the ranch any minute.

April looked down at the officer. She knew him from the precinct.

My father saw the concern on her face. "He'll be fine, the bullet looks like it cleared any of his major organs". I turned to April and asked her to stay with my father.

"Sure," she replied. "Where are you going?"

"I'm going out to use the police radio to contact the other cars that are on the way. I want to make sure they know we are okay and to make sure they dispatch an ambulance."

With everything we had gone through, the last thing we wanted to risk was someone getting shot by friendly fire. As I re-entered the house after using the radio, I saw my mother, Jenna, and my sister working their way down the stairs very cautiously. They all appeared to be pretty shaken up by what had happened, but at that moment I still wasn't sure what had fully transpired. How did they had manage to evade the gunmen? On the way to the couch, my mother grabbed a bottle of my father's best scotch and three shot glasses off the den shelf. My mother wasn't a big drinker, but it was obvious that this experience warranted something stronger then lemonade.

April joined them as they sat on the den couch while my father continued to care for the wounded officer. I started to walk in the direction of the den hoping to get some answers, when two officers entered through the kitchen door. A few steps behind was Web holding his arm in a make-shift sling. Seeing that everyone was okay, he tried to break the tense mood by asking if anyone had a Band-Aid. My mother was so traumatized that she took Web seriously. She put down her glass and got up heading for the first aid kit. Web was going to stop her, but I waved him off. I thought that it might be a good diversion for her and based on the amount of blood on Web's arm, it appeared that the bullet had only grazed him anyway. I pointed to the chair next to the couch and I asked Web if he wanted to sit down.

"Don't want to bleed on anything," he said.

I asked April what had happened. She told us that shortly after we left, they saw a car pulling in through the ranch's main gate with its headlights turned off. The officer was suspicious and told everyone to go upstairs. My mother took them into my father's office. After my parents moved into the ranch my father had an access door built into the attic as a hiding place for his gun collection. To keep the location a secret, he had a bookcase built in front of it that swung away from the door on a hinge. Before the intruders entered the house, they had managed to take haven there. A couple of minutes later, they heard two gunshots followed by what sounded like three men coming up the stairs going in and out of rooms looking for us. One of the men was trying to reach someone on what sounded like a walkie talkie, and after a few failed attempts, he yelled to the other men to get out of the house. A few seconds later, they heard the car pull away. They remained hidden until they heard my father's voice yelling from the kitchen. Web asked if the men were speaking Spanish.

"The three guys that ambushed me were speaking Spanish to one another." He said as he checked his wound to see if the bleeding was slowing down.

"No," April said, "they actually sounded like they had Italian accents. They were definitely not native Arizonans".

The front screen door creaked again—a noise that I planned on remedying as soon as this nightmare was over. The medics walked in with their stretcher, followed by Dailey, who looked very concerned about the condition of his partner. I pointed them towards the kitchen. My father walked out a few seconds later having been relieved by the medics from caring for the other officer. He had blood on the sleeve of his shirt from keeping pressure on the officer's wound. I was amazed at how steady he was after everything that had just happened. I had forgotten that he had lived through many dangerous situations during his stretch on the force. I am still not sure how my mother survived all of the excitement during those years. I still remember how my father would try and downplay things to my mom to keep her from having a nervous breakdown. He would tell her that the papers and news stations were exaggerating things to make the story more exciting.

Shortly after the medics left to take the officer to the hospital and the crowd of policemen started to thin, I suggested that everyone go upstairs and try to get some rest.

Web asked one of the officers if he could hitch a ride to the hospital. "I guess I should get this thing looked at," he said. "I may just pull up a bed next to your dad in the hospital so I can finally get some rest. I'm beat".

"Me too," I responded.

We agreed to touch base in the morning…late in the morning. Jenna and April were going to share the bed in my room. I was going to sleep on the couch. Even the floor would have been fine; I just wanted to get some sleep. April told Jenna to go up to bed and she would be along in a few minutes. Since Dailey had accompanied his partner in the ambulance, we had two new officers securing the house for what was left of the night.

My mother brought down sheets, a blanket, and pillow for me. I laughed to myself when I thought just last night, it was April making up the couch for me to sleep in her apartment. I guess having a properly dressed couch for sleeping on was the "in" thing these days. I would have been fine with it just as it was, but mother would not be convinced. My mother went up to bed leaving just April and me alone in the den. She looked very comfortable and very cute in the oversized T-shirt that was on loan from my sister. She sat down on the couch next to me.

"What's up?" I asked.

"I have to get out of here in the morning," April responded.

"Why?" I asked.

"Why? She responded, "Chuck is dead, one of my fellow officers was shot and could have easily been killed. I'm jeopardizing the lives of Jenna and your entire family by being here. I think those are good enough reasons, don't you?" she asked.

I told her that we were well protected for now and we could discuss things further in the morning after we both had a good night's sleep. I knew that she was right, but there was nothing we could do and nowhere we could go at this hour. I could tell by the look on her face that there was something else bothering her.

"There's something else on your mind, what is it?" I asked.

"I should have stayed downstairs and helped my fellow officer. I shouldn't have hidden like a coward," she said as she started weeping.

"If you did, you'd be dead and that wouldn't have sat well with me," I responded.

She rested her head on my shoulder and we leaned back on the couch. April fell asleep first, and a few minute later I followed.

Chapter 14

Betrayed

I woke up to the sound of my mother's pots and pans rattling. I wasn't sure whether she was making breakfast or cleaning up afterwards. When I passed out last night, April had fallen asleep on my shoulder. While it wasn't the most comfortable way to fall asleep, I wasn't complaining. April had just come down the stairs with her hair in a towel after taking a shower. I recognized the clothes she was wearing as my sister's. She smiled as she walked by me and continued on to the kitchen. Considering how upset she was last night, it was nice to see a smile on her face. I was still a bit groggy from the late night, and taking a shower to wake myself up seemed like a pretty good idea. I walked up to my room, and to avoid another awkward encounter with Jenna, I decided to knock first.

Jenna opened the door, "Good morning, the room's all yours," she said as she walked by me.

I walked into the room and grabbed a fresh change of clothes and on the way to the shower took the only remaining towel in the linen closet. I turned on the shower and adjusted the temperature. No matter what I did, the water didn't seem to get hot. All of the hot water must have been exhausted by the other house guests. I was hoping the shower would wake me up, not put me into shock. I guess not only does the early bird get the worm, but all of the hot water too. It was one of the fastest showers I had ever taken, but when I was done, I was definitely wide awake. I got dressed and started heading down the stairs. Breakfast smelled good, but the coffee smelled even better.

As I walked into the kitchen, I saw April sitting at the table. She was looking at some family photos with my mother. April looked up just long enough to crack a joke about a high school picture of me that I wished my mom had burned. I looked like the world's biggest nerd in that photo. When the picture was taken, I had braces and the worst case of acne of my teen years. I joked back that maybe her father would share a few photos when he got out of the hospital, just to keep things fair. I had already seen several pictures of April growing up and I was pretty sure that she had nothing that compared to my high school picture in her portfolio. My mother looked up at me, smiled and commented how when she came down stairs this morning, April and I looked like nice pair of bookends leaning up against one another for support. My mother couldn't stop herself from playing the matchmaker. She clearly liked April, and I—for the first time in my life—thought that we were both hoping for the same thing.

The resiliency that everyone in the house was showing this morning was amazing. Just hours earlier we had an officer shot in our kitchen and intruders roaming the house looking to kill April. Now we were eating breakfast as if it never happened. I guess it is human nature to try and put those kinds of things behind us or we would probably lose our minds. I grabbed a biscuit and a cup of coffee to hold me over while I stepped outside to call Web. I was assuming he was awake by now since he was always in the office and at his desk by 8:00am. Many of us at the bureau thought he opened and closed the place, and a few suggested he would sleep there as well.

It occurred to me that someone had to know that Web was going to be meeting me at the ranch last night, and used that knowledge to stage the side show that lured us away from the house. I wouldn't have been surprised if Web hadn't been up all night thinking about who that someone was. I called Web's cell phone, and as expected, he answered before the second ring.

"I'm glad to hear from you. I hope you had a good night's sleep," he said.

The sarcasm related to my overdue phone call was dripping like water from a leaky faucet, but the extra sleep that I had was well worth it.

I started to say "I was thinking about the ambush last night," when Web interrupted me "I was thinking about it too. In fact, I was thinking about it a good part of the night. The three guys that ambushed me were Mexicans, probably guns for hire and considered expendable."

"Why do you say that?" I asked.

Web told me that when the Phoenix PD went back out to the site this morning to look for evidence and to recover the bodies, they noticed explosives under the SUV. One of the detonator wires must have become dislodged during impact. If it hadn't, more than likely the bodies, the car, and any evidence, would have been spread out across a mile of the Sonoran desert.

"You know that they weren't just sitting out there hoping you would come along," I told him.

After a long pause he responded, "I know. I've been thinking about who might have overheard my conversation with you and our plans to meet at the ranch, and came up empty. I was in a closed office at the time so no one could have eavesdropped. Then, I gave thought to who I might have told that I would be heading to the ranch, and came up with only two names. You're not going to like this, but the two people I told were Bill Rich and Bob Clayton."

Web told me that Bill had called him to provide an update on the effort to gather the vets. He also had something he wanted to discuss with Web and suggested that they talk over dinner. A few minutes later, Bob had called Web as per my request. He had brought up his concerns regarding the information specialist that we had suspected of tampering with the Bureau database. It was difficult to hear, and even harder to believe that either of them would have been involved in such a plot. They were both friends that I would trust with my life. Web was quick to point out that our dead information specialist probably had friends in the bureau that would say the same thing about her.

"But Bob was the one that questioned the analyst's involvement. Why would he do that if he was involved?" I asked.

"Maybe he figured we would discover something that would exonerate her, and decided to plant that very question in our minds so we would exclude him from our list of possible suspects," Web suggested. "Remember what I said about not trusting anyone."

Although I found it difficult to digest, I wasn't about to argue the point. If Web was wrong about Bob, then we would know soon enough and no real harm would have been done. We both agreed that we couldn't just approach them and ask if they had gone rogue, we would have to find some way of trapping them. Until we had a chance to figure out a plan, we agreed to keep Bill busy gathering the information on the vets. We also decided to avoid passing any critical information through Bob's area until we knew for sure who was the guilty party. We decided to meet at the Phoenix police headquarters at noon to discuss things further. Whatever the plan was, we would need Riddle to provide us with the resources necessary to pull it off. What still puzzled both of us though was why the killer continued to target

April. With his body and most of his face concealed by a surgical outfit, she couldn't make out enough detail to warrant his concern. He had taken special precautions to insure his anonymity so he had to know that she wouldn't have been able to identify him. Yet, for some unknown reason, he continued to persist in his attempts to silence her. Before we could start our brainstorming session to try to find that elusive reason, my mother called for both my father and I to come into the kitchen. I entered the kitchen through the kitchen door while my father entered from the den where he had been sitting watching the news. We converged at the kitchen table where April and my mother were sitting with one of the family photo albums still sprawled open on the table. April was pointing to a picture of my father's brother Bennett, more specifically at a tattoo on his arm.

"The killer" she said, "he had a tattoo that looked just like this one."

"When I came into the hospital room that night and he had a pillow over my father's face, his forearm was exposed. I had forgotten about the tattoo, but it was the same as this one, I am sure of it," she insisted.

My father told us that the tattoo was a symbol of the First Brigade out of Arizona. It was one of the most decorated units in the Vietnam War.

I put the phone to my ear, "Web, did you get that?" I said.

"Yes," he replied, "It looks like we have an answer on why he is so desperate to kill April and maybe our first lead on finding out the identity of this SOB".

The hypnotist must have known that if April noticed the tattoo, it could help expose his identity. It looked like he might have finally made a mistake. As happy as I was to finally get some traction in this case, I was still bothered by the notion that one of my friends could be involved with this lunatic. Before I headed into Phoenix to meet Web, I grabbed a couple of biscuits and a cup of coffee to go. I walked out onto the porch and down the steps when I heard screen door open, and then close, behind me. I turned to see April coming down the steps after me. I told her that she needed to stay at the ranch for now. I explained to her that I couldn't guarantee her safety if she accompanied me during my drive into Phoenix.

"We still have the men that were in the house last night waiting for another chance to kill you," I told her. "You shouldn't even be outside until we find them."

I walked her back inside, and told the officers at the door that they needed to keep her in the house at all times. April wasn't happy about it, but she knew that I couldn't risk bringing her with me. I'll check in on your dad and let him know what is going on and try to get back as soon as possible. As I walked back out the door it struck me that my rental car was wrecked. For the first time I was happy about the fact that I sprung for the rental insurance. With my father's truck still broken a mile up the road, the only vehicle available was my sister's nine year old red sedan. Before she handed me the keys, she asked me to promise I would return it in one piece. Based on what happened last night, I told her I could make no guarantees.

She looked at me and said "it's a piece of crap anyway." and tossed me the keys.

As soon as I got into the car I had to pop open the windows. My sister smoked like a chimney. Although my folks wouldn't let her light up in the house, it didn't stop her from smoking on the porch or in her car.

I made excellent time into Phoenix having left the ranch after rush hour. After parking the car I headed straight for Riddle's office. As I walked by the kitchen area, I noticed a couple of the officers were in the process of collecting money for Chuck's family to help offset the funeral bills. I took a minute to detour over and throw a ten spot into collection box. Fortunately, the officer that was shot last night at the ranch was expected to fully recover from his wounds or we might have had two collections being made.

I continued on my way to Riddle's office. I tapped on the closed door and heard Riddle yell "Come in".

Web was already sitting at the desk drinking a cup of coffee. You could tell that the last couple of days had been hard on Riddle. He had already lost one of his officers and a mechanic, plus another two of his men shot. As if that wasn't enough, April was now being targeted by Dr. H. Web had already gained Riddle's cooperation in a plan to try and root out our rogue agent.

I started to thank him for all of his help, and he stopped me midsentence responding "The way you will thank me is by bringing this son of a bitch to justice."

"When we catch him, it will depend on him as to whether we bring him to justice, or we bring justice to him. Either way, justice will be served," I replied.

We sat in the office for a couple of hours and when we emerged—we had a plan that if successful—would send someone that I considered a friend to jail for the rest of his life. As painful as it was to imagine, whoever had set us up the other night had betrayed not only me and the bureau, but their country. Anyone that would knowingly assist this lunatic in using our honored vets to satisfy some twisted, unknown agenda deserved what they got. Our plan was to move April out of the ranch and to a motel. Web was having Bill meet him at the bureau office to update him on "Operation Safety Net", our code name for getting the vets safely away from the hypnotist's sphere of influence. During their meeting, I would call in and while on speakerphone divulge a safe house location that April was to be moved to. Web and I refer to this location as decoy motel #1. I would then make a call to Bob—under the guise that I was checking in to see if he had any updates for me. He would be informed that I had moved April off the ranch and we were hiding out at an undisclosed location that we referred to as decoy motel #2. I knew that if Bob was guilty, he would trace my call via satellite and pass that location along to Dr. H. Once the seeds were planted, it became a waiting game. It might be a couple of days, but we were confident that someone would show up to take our bait.

Web and I were accompanied back to the ranch by three police cruisers. Web drove the a new bureau vehicle that had been loaned to him courtesy of our Phoenix office. We knew that there was a chance that we would be watched as we left the ranch so we decided to play a little shell game using the three police cars to make sure that April's real location was obscured to anyone trying to track her. When we entered the house, my mother was in the kitchen cooking, while my sister, Jenna and April were in the den watching a reality television show. It seemed like there wasn't much else on these days besides reality TV. We gestured to April to join us upstairs. She politely excused herself before following us up the stairs and into my father's office.

"This all seems very secretive," she said. "What's going on?"

"We're going to move you off the ranch to a safe house," I told her. "We have a plan that we hope will allow us to uncover and arrest Dr. H's inside man in the bureau".

We filled her in on the details, it only seemed right to fully disclose our plan since her life was the one at risk. She was relieved at any action that would remove her from the ranch and get my family out of danger. She knew that any chance of her surviving and getting back to a normal life hinged on us catching the hypnotist. Finding the rogue agent was the means to that end. We had planned on leaving straight from the ranch, but April's one stipulation was that she wanted to see her father in the hospital first. Neither Web nor I felt comfortable with that detour, but April made it clear that her terms were non-negotiable. I'm not sure that Web knew how to deal with April setting the demands. He had been divorced for several years and I don't think he had to take orders from anyone since. Even after we left the ranch with April, I knew that we would still need some police presence to keep my family safe. It was clear that this guy would use every tool in his arsenal in order to keep us from catching him. I wanted to make damn sure that my family didn't end up as a bargaining chip.

On the way out, April said her goodbyes, giving everyone a hug. She thanked my folks for taking the risk of keeping her at the ranch. My mother actually started to cry and gave April and extra hug and squeeze. My mother hugged her with such strength that I surprised that April didn't start to turn blue.

Before we left for the hospital, my father asked me to take a walk into the kitchen with him. I figured he would try to offer some words of wisdom regarding his experiences in similar situations.

Instead he caught me completely off guard with his words.

"Son," he said, "I just wanted to let you know that I was wrong about you taking the job in DC and with the FBI. If it wasn't for your instincts and perseverance, this guy probably wouldn't have even been on the radar. We can't bring back these vets, but we can bring back their honor and prevent any other families from suffering like the Stones did. I'm proud of you and I'll be even prouder when you deliver this SOB's head on a platter."

As I left the kitchen, I patted my dad on the back and told him I planned on making him very proud. On the way to the door, I saw Jenna standing by the window looking out. She looked like a lost soul. Her husband was gone; she had been yanked from her home and was without any family around to give her support. From the bits and pieces I was able to put together from conversations with Web and Lynch, it appeared that Dan's parents held Jenna partially responsible for what had happened to Dan. They thought that Jenna should have noticed the signs that Dan was in trouble and gotten him to the VA hospital. Even though Lynch and Web were very close to the Stones, they did not seem to share those beliefs. They saw Jenna as an innocent victim of a terrible tragedy, and as far as I was concerned, they were right. I knew I shouldn't say anything. But she had been living with this guilt for over a year now and I had to say something to help her find peace. I walked over to her and put my hand on her shoulder.

"Jenna," I said, "I'm going to tell you something, something that you are going to have to take my word for right now with no questions asked. Hopefully, I will be able to tell you more someday soon, but in the meantime you have to promise me to keep this between us."

"I promise," she replied.

"I wanted you to know that Dan wasn't responsible for his actions that day. I also need for you to believe me when I say that there was nothing you could have done that would have saved him."

She started crying and gave me a big hug. "Thank you," she said as the tears cascaded down her cheeks. "Thank you," I held her hand in mine for a minute, and then released it as I headed for the door.

As our convoy pulled out of the ranch, I could see my parents standing on the porch. At a glance it appeared that they both had concerned looks on their faces. I couldn't blame them since with any plan—no matter how well thought out you think it might be—there is always the risk that your opponent might be one move ahead of you. Our adversary was depraved, but he was not stupid. He had proven himself to be a master of manipulation and a man without conscience. Underestimating a man like this would be a mistake, and I had no plans of falling into that trap.

With the lead car flashing its lights and sirens, we made it to the hospital in just over twenty minutes. Our escort brought us into the hospital's service entrance just below the main floor. We secured a service elevator and took it straight up to Lynch's room. He was moved last night to the seventh floor into a room with two beds. I guess Web wasn't kidding when he said he might stay the night with Lynch after he had gotten shot. We followed our police escort right to his door. When April walked into the room, Lynch's eyes lit up. He heard the bomb go off in the hospital parking lot, and was made aware that April was its intended target. Web had also informed him of the second attempt on her life last night. Lynch was well aware of the inherent risks of the job when his daughter became a cop, but he never imagined that she would be the target of a psychopath. We filled him in on our plan, and although he was justifiably concerned, he knew that we had no choice. April couldn't stay in protective custody for the rest of her life.

Lynch turned to Web and asked "Who is assigned to protect her at the motel?"

Before Web could respond, April said "That would be Bennett."

By the look on Lynch's face, it was obvious that he wasn't too thrilled with the idea that his daughter would be sharing a motel room with a guy for a few days.

"Don't worry Dad," April said, "we've already slept together once".

Web and Lynch both turned their heads to look at me. "We fell asleep sitting up on the couch," I blurted out.

Lynch responded, "Just remember two things son. I will be out of the hospital in a couple of days, and I sleep with a gun under my pillow".

April had a good laugh at her dad's response, but I wasn't so sure he was joking. Lynch looked at Web and he could tell that we were getting a bit antsy sitting in the hospital room. He turned to April and told her that she better be on her way.

He then turned to me and said "keep her safe son, she's all I've got".

"I would never let a man who sleeps with a gun under his pillow down," I replied.

Lynch was a tough old bird, but I could see the concern in his face, and hear the emotion in his voice. April with a tear running down her cheek leaned over, gave her father a kiss and promised to see him soon. I put my hand on her shoulder and Web and I escorted her out of the room. I reached into my pocket and pulled out a handkerchief and handed it to her. She laughed a bit as another tear ran down her cheek.

"What so amusing?" I asked.

"A handkerchief," she said with a giggle.

"My mother handed it to me as I walked out the door this morning figuring it might come in handy," I responded.

We followed our police entourage into the service elevator and back down to the garage. The three police cars had tinted windows so our presence would be concealed to anyone trying to get a visual on which car we were in. The cars rolled out of the underground garage and we headed down West Thomas Road on our way to Interstate Seventeen. One car would take the Interstate 17 North, one the Interstate 17 South, and the third car would exit Interstate 17 onto Interstate Ten. None of the drivers knew their final destination until we were in the cars and ready to leave the hospital. Even though two of the locations were the decoys, April and I would be staying at the third location, and for her safety, we needed to make sure that we kept that location anonymous to everyone but Web, April and myself. For that reason, Web was driving the car we were in. In order to mask his identity he was dressed from the waist up in a police uniform. I joked with him that he looked good in the uniform and asked him if he had ever considered being a cop. He didn't find much humor in it. After driving around the city and suburbs for about a half hour making sure they weren't being followed—the other cars would then station themselves within close proximity to one of the decoy motels. They were to sit, watch, wait, and hope that someone would take the bait. In the meantime, April and I would make ourselves visible at the front desk of each of the decoy motels as we pretended to check in. Web would keep the police car within sight of the desk clerk to make sure he was seen. If anyone came looking for us, they were bound to go to the front desk to get a room number. We wanted to make sure that the clerk made the connection. When we arrived at the second decoy motel, we checked in and then while April went back to the car, I went to the room and called Bob Clayton. As we had planned, I asked him if he found out anything new about the Information Specialist that killed herself. He informed me that there was nothing yet, but he would let me know if anything changed. I told him I was protecting a witness at a motel in Phoenix and that any new information should go to Web while I was unavailable. After hanging up the phone, I plugged it in, placed it on the desk and left the room, locking the door behind me. I then hopped into the car and we took off for the real safe-house. I had hoped that it would be nicer then the first two motels we stopped at, but no such luck. When we pulled into the lot, I thought that Web was joking.

I told him "By the looks of this place, I'm not sure what scares me more, the hypnotists zombie squad, or the size of the roaches that we would probably be sharing the room with."

Web pulled off to the side of the motel so the patrol car wouldn't be visible, removed the police jacket and cap he had worn, and went to check us in while we waited in the car. This time inconspicuous was what we wanted. Web came back and got into the car. He threw me a key and a cell phone with two numbers written on it. He told me the first number was the cell phone he would be using so we'd know it was him calling, and the second number was for the cell phone he had issued for me to use while we waited. As we got out of the car, April asked how she was going to get changes of clothes and personal items. Web popped the trunk which contained two pieces of luggage.

"We couldn't risk going back to your apartment so we had a few items picked up for you," Web told April. "Bennett had to guess your size so if they don't fit, blame him."

"Why didn't you just ask?" she said.

"I thought it would be more fun this way," I quipped.

"Not if you guessed wrong" she responded.

We brought the bags into the room.

"You rented a room with only one queen bed?" April asked.

"It would have looked a bit suspicious my checking in as the only oc-cupant and asking for two single beds wouldn't it?" Web replied.

Web moved towards the door. "I have to go and bait the trap for Bill with the address for the first decoy motel, let's hope I'm wrong."

He told us that there were two cops staked out at the motel across the street.

"If they see anything suspicious they'll be at your door in a flash," he told us before walking out of the motel room.

Chapter 15
Killing Time

April and I sat on the edge of the bed for about ten minutes after Web left just examining our dreary surroundings. I could only hope that whatever happened, it would happen quickly so we could get out of this dump. In the meantime, we decided to settle in not knowing how long we would be here. I started to unpack my bag. It's a good thing my mother had taken care of my laundry, since with all the activity, I didn't have much time to deal with such mundane issues. April opened her bag and started to laugh.

"What's so funny?" I asked.

"Who did you have shop for these clothes?" she asked. "They're a bit on the bright side".

As she started to pull out one article of clothing after another I could see her point.

"I guess they wanted to make sure that you didn't try to leave the motel," I quipped.

She acknowledged that they had succeeded. She had a great laugh and a smile that could brighten up even this dreary place, but seemed subdued in comparison to her newly acquired wardrobe.

We hadn't eaten since early morning, so we grabbed a phone book and ordered a pizza and a couple of diet sodas. It wasn't up to the same standard as our first meal together at the restaurant, but I was sure that the company would make the meal. April had given what I thought were subtle hints that she was interested in me. I was hoping that it was not just my active imagination running wild. With our focus on trying to catch our rogue agent, I hadn't much of a chance to contemplate the letter that the hypnotist left for me. What did he mean about helping me with my career? Could it be possible that I had been a pawn in his game all along? Maybe being locked up in this roach motel for a while would give me a chance to try and figure out the cryptic meaning behind his comments. April was still putting away her clothes when she pulled out a fairly scant nightie.

"Who did you pay to pick this out?" she said with a smile.

"I didn't, but I'm starting to change my opinion of their taste," I responded.

She walked over to the garbage, paused for a second and then dropped it in the pail.

"I guess I'll just have to borrow one of your shirts to sleep in," she said as she walked to my closet pulling out the only one I had that didn't have pinstripes on it.

When she was done unpacking she turned on the television and propped herself up on the bed. Why was I not surprised that she flipped to a channel with a police show? The phone rang, it was Web. He informed me that he had been in contact with Bill and that both of our suspects were now in the game. He had spoken to Bill about twenty minutes ago, noting that he had picked up a little stress in Bill's voice. He wondered if Bill was onto us. Both decoy motels were being watched and at the first sign of activity Web would give us a call. In the meantime, while we waited for our pizza to arrive, I started reviewing the latest information Web had provided regarding Operation Safety Net. With everything that had been going on it was no surprise that I hadn't had a chance to review the files myself. I was just finishing the latest update when I felt a tap on my shoulder.

"What are you looking at?" she asked.

I told her it was the latest report on the number of Vets currently in protective custody, and how many were still unaccounted for. We were fortunate that the VA hospitals—understanding the urgency of the situation—were quick to get the local police departments the information they needed. The good news was that they were able to bring in thirty vets. The bad news was that there were still at least seven unaccounted for from the twelve hospitals the hypnotist had worked at. That meant there were at least seven ticking time bombs ready to blow up at any time at the command of this maniac. That meant seven more families that could be on the brink of having their lives ripped apart. In an effort to prevent any further communications between the hypnotist and the vets, we used our clout with the cell phone companies to have their cells temporarily deactivated. We were also having the records of both their incoming and outgoing home and cell phone calls scrutinized hoping to find one number that they all had in common. It seemed like a long shot that Dr. H. would be that sloppy, but beggars couldn't be choosers. At this point we had to track down any possible leads and hope that sooner or later he would make a mistake. If our suspicions were correct, and one of my colleagues and friends was the inside man, we might have a lot more information once, or should I say if, our trap worked.

April tapped me on the shoulder again "You seem to be pretty focused on that report," she said.

"Why would you say that?" I responded.

She replied, "Because I just got undressed and changed into my new nightshirt and you didn't even notice".

I turned my head so quickly that I almost snapped my neck. To my dismay, she was still fully clothed. It appeared that April was just exhibiting the same unusual sense of humor that almost got me killed by her father back at the hospital.

"Very funny," I said.

April continued to surprise me with her ability to keep her sense of humor at a time when her life was in jeopardy. I think she knew that she had me wrapped around her little finger, and played into it whenever the opportunity presented itself. April was startled by a sudden knock at the door, but she quickly settled down after realizing it was the delivery guy with our dinner. With everything that had been happening over the past few days, I didn't want to take any chances. I handed April her gun that she had left in her holster that was draped over a chair and pointed to the bathroom. As she moved out of site as I started heading for the door.

Before I could get to the door, there was another knock. "Hang on," I said. "I'll be right there."

I took a glance through the peep hole in the door. There was a tall well groomed man standing there with a pizza bag in one hand and a six-pack of soda's in the other. I opened the door and asked what the bill was as he carried the bags into the room placing them down on the dresser by the door.

"That will be seventeen dollars," he said.

"That is one expensive pizza," I replied as I reached into my wallet for a twenty.

He responded, "You've never had a pizza like this one, it's to die for".

As he reached into the warming bag to pull out the pie April stepped out of the bathroom with her gun pointed at the man. Before I could ask her what she was doing, the man pulled a gun from the bag and started to point it in my direction. April responded by firing off two rounds into his chest. As the guy hit the floor, I kicked the door closed and pushed the dresser down in front of it to create a blockade. I couldn't take a chance that this guy had a backup waiting outside. April and I jumped back behind the bed, keeping as close to the floor as possible. With our heads jutting out on one side of the bed. April had her gun pointed at the door and mine was aimed at the window waiting for another gunman to possibly try and gain entry to the room.

"How the hell did they find us?" I said and then turned to April and asked "How the hell did you know he had a gun?"

"The voice, I recognized it from the other night at the Ranch. He had the same Italian accent," she said.

I told her that it's a good thing he had a gun in that bag because a pizza guy with an Italian accent wasn't that unusual.

"Couldn't you have just wounded him?" I asked.

April gave me the same daunting stare that she had given me when we first met at the hospital after her father was shot.

"Never mind," I responded.

There was another knock at the door.

A voice yelled "Are you all right in there?" I recognized the voice as one of the patrolmen stationed in the motel across the street.

"Yes," I replied, "but we have a dead guy lying on our pizza." I pushed the dresser away from the door and slowly opened it. The two officers came in. They were apologetic for not catching the guy before he got into the room.

"How could you have known? I asked "Other than the fact that he was a bit overdressed, he was delivering a pizza."

"We saw the pizza guy pull in," they responded, "but then we got a check-in call from the precinct. While we were on the phone this guy must have knocked out the delivery kid and taken his place. We didn't even see him pull up. After we heard the gunshots, we ran outside and noticed a Black Mercedes sitting a couple of hundred feet up the road, but as soon as they saw us they took off."

"Did you get the plate number?" I asked.

"No," he responded, "they were too far up the road to get a clear read on it and by the time we made it down the stairs they were gone. We did call for backup immediately, but none of the units that were close by reported seeing a black Mercedes."

When the officers stepped out of the room to use the radio I turned around to see April sitting on the edge of the bed. She appeared to be in shock.

"Do you think he was one of the missing Vet's?" she asked.

"No," I replied "That gun costs more than we probably make in a month. Not something your typical vet would be carrying around".

It's never easy for a cop when they kill someone, even if that someone was intending to kill you. I sat next to her on the bed and tried to comfort her for a few minutes, but now that they knew where we were, a few minutes was all we had. We needed to get out of this place, but this time we couldn't let anyone know where we were going. I went outside and broke into a white sports utility that was parked in front of our room and hotwired it. I told the officers that we were borrowing the car and to keep the report of the vehicle being stolen off the records. I quickly checked our dead friend's pockets.

"He's got no ID on him, you better run his prints," I said. "Give Agent Web a call and tell him what happened here. When you get the results on the prints, get them to him. I'll call him as soon as I can."

We quickly stuffed our clothes into our bags, put them into the trunk of the SUV, and took off for a destination still unknown. We were a few miles away when it came to me that Jenna Stone's house was temporarily abandoned. The likelihood that anyone would think to look for us there was remote. We would also be within a few miles of the ranch if help was required. On the way we decided to hit, let me reword that, stop at a drive-thru to pick up some burgers and drinks. There was no telling if Jenna would have anything that we would be able to eat once we got to her house. I had my heart set on pizza, but after having our shooter bleed all over the one we ordered, I kind of lost my interest in replacing that pie. One positive note was that I managed to lift the nightie from the garbage pail before we left the motel.

We ate our meal while we drove through the city. I was so distracted trying to figure out how they had found us, that I don't think I took notice of the taste of the food I was ingesting. We took every precaution imaginable and within hours they were at our doorstep with pizza, soda, and gun in hand. My call to Web was way overdue. If my phone was used to trace us to the motel, then I'd need to make that call prior to heading on to our final destination. I had turned my phone off before we left the motel room just in case. Once I completed my call to Web, I would shut it off and leave it off until circumstances required me to make another call. I reached into my pocket to pull it out, but realized that I had thrown it into my bag when we hastily packed and my bag was in the trunk.

April reached into her pocket and pulled out her cell phone. "Do you want to use mine?" she asked.

It was one of those smart phones, and as soon as I saw it, I knew who the culprit was for giving away our location.

"Do you have the GPS Tracker set on your phone?" I asked.

You would think April had just seen a ghost. "Oh my god, it's my fault. I almost got us killed" she responded.

While waiting at a light, I noticed that a car carrier with four pickup trucks in tow had pulled up to us on the driver side.

"Do you have a replacement policy if this thing gets lost?" I asked.

She replied "Yes". I extended my hand as far out the window as I could and tossed the phone into one of the pickup trucks on the lower level. The truck carrying the pickup was about to get onto interstate seventeen headed north, while we were heading east out of town.

"Why couldn't you have just asked me to turn it off?" she asked.

"Because I wanted to get good night's sleep, and whoever was tracing this phone will be going on a wild goose chase until they catch up to that truck," I told her.

"Got it. You're not only cute, but smart too," she said with a smile on her face.

I pulled over to the side of the road and quickly retrieved my phone from the trunk and dialed Web.

He answered immediately, "Where the hell are you? I've been trying to reach you for the past hour!"

I told him that for the moment we needed for that to be April's and my secret. I couldn't take any chances. I told him that they had been tracking April's phone, but we took care of that situation and were now on our way to find a safe haven for the night.

I told Web "I think Bob is our guy. I don't think that Bill is technical enough to have pulled this off."

Web responded, "I'll make arrangements to have him taken into custody. If it's him, then we just killed this guy's information source. If it's someone else, we will know it soon enough".

"I still wouldn't mention anything to Bill at this time," I said and Web concurred.

I informed Web that I was going to turn off the phone for the evening, but I would call him first thing in the morning. They were running the pizza guy's prints and Web had hoped to have a name to go with the corpse we hastily left on the motel room floor. He and his friends had intercepted the real delivery guy leaving him unconscious in the stairwell of an adjacent motel. All things considered, I thought he was pretty fortunate that they had left him alive. I turned off the phone and stuffed it back into my pocket. We would be at the Jenna's house in about twenty minutes. I kept checking the rear view mirror just in case someone might be tailing us. But it seemed more than likely that our friends in the Mercedes were just figuring out that they had been duped. I wish I knew how long it took before they realized we had turned the tables on them.

We pulled into the one house development of Jenna Stone. We parked the car in the driveway leaving the car running and the lights on just long enough for me to pick the lock and get inside. It was a typical builder's grade lock, and didn't require much finesse in order to gain entry. April appeared impressed that I was able to pick it so easily.

"Is there something you want to tell me?" She asked.

"A trick that a friend on the DC police force taught me a few years ago," I told her.

We parked the SUV into the garage and turned on the house lights just long enough to find a couple of flashlights and candles in the pantry. It was easy to find the items we needed since Jenna obviously did not have a large stash of food. While we were in the pantry, we were able to identify a few items that would make for a quick breakfast in the morning. Before we headed up the stairs, I grabbed a couple of light bulbs from the lamps that sat on either side of the lone couch in the family room.

"What are those for?" April asked.

I had April follow me to the landing at the top of the staircase. I then threw the bulbs down the stairs and watched as they exploded leaving glass all over the bottom steps and floor around the entranceway to the house.

"Our burglar alarm," I said.

"Cute, smart, and resourceful," she responded.

I had glossed over the cute comment in the car, but this time I couldn't keep from smiling.

I walked April into the master bedroom, put down her bag and told her to get some sleep. As I started heading towards the adjacent room to sleep on the floor, April called my name.

"Would you mind staying here tonight?" she asked.

I couldn't blame her for being scared. It's not every day you have to shoot a pizza delivery guy before he tries to shoot you.

"I'll be right back," I said, "I'm just going to see if I can find a spare pillow and blanket".

April pointed to the bed and said "If you promise to be a good boy, you can share the bed. After all we already shared the couch last night".

I came back into the room dropping my bag on the floor replying "I'll do my best."

After changing into my t-shirt and shorts, I came back into the master bedroom. My eyes nearly darted out of my head when I caught sight of April. She was standing by the edge of the bed in the scant nightie that I had salvaged from the motel garbage.

"I don't want you to get the wrong idea," she said, but in our rush to get away from the motel I left the shirt I had borrowed in the bathroom."

"Not that I'm complaining, but I do have a few more shirts," I responded.

"I know, I was going to borrow one when I came across the nightie in your suitcase. I figured it was either this, or one of your striped shirts. There's only one thing I'm less fond of then this nightie," she said, "and that's a striped shirt. Stripes are not flattering on me at all"

It was hard to imagine that there was anything that wouldn't look good on April.

Before getting into bed she gave me one last reminder that I'd better be nice or I would find myself sleeping on the floor for the duration of our stay. I considered myself warned and climbed into the bed. It felt weird sleeping in Jenna and Dan's bed knowing that instead of sleeping with Dan every night, now Jenna slept alone with only a broken heart for company. It was a strong reminder to me that we had to bring this lunatic to justice.

We had to leave the lights off in the house to avoid drawing attention to the house. Fortunately, the full moon beaming through the windows provided all the light we would need. Before putting her head down on the pillow April surprised me with a thank you and a long sensual kiss. As if it wasn't going to be hard enough trying to get to sleep after the excitement of the evening, now I had the image of April standing there in that low cut nightie engrained in my mind. Just in case that wasn't enough I thought, she decides to plant that kiss on my lips.

With her head still on her pillow, she whispered "Are you still thinking about the dead pizza guy?"

"Definitely not now," I replied.

"Good!" she responded.

I put my head down on the pillow and spent several minutes trying to go to sleep. As tired as I was, the combination of thinking of April sleeping in her nightie only inches away and the scent of her perfume was too distracting. I finally grabbed my pillow, got out of bed, laid on the floor, and finally fell asleep.

Chapter 16
A Dose of Reality

The night slipped away as the moonlight gave way to sunlight. April was still sleeping when I woke, so I slowly eased my way out of bed and walked softly towards the window. I was shocked when I looked out to see a car sitting in the driveway with a familiar figure leaning on the hood of the car reading a newspaper. It was Lynch. He wasn't supposed to be out of the hospital for at least couple of more days. My first thought after wondering why he was here, was how the hell he found us. I started to head out of the room to go down the stairs to get that question answered when I remembered the broken glass at the bottom of the stairs. I walked over to my stuff, retrieved my shoes, and put them on. Before proceeding down, I moved my bag to block the stairs, just as a reminder to April in case she woke up and tried to follow me down. While I did my best to navigate and minimize making even smaller pieces out of the glass, there were still numerous crunches as I made my way down to the main floor. I guess I did too good a job of breaking the bulbs last night. As I opened the door ready to walk out of the house, Lynch walked in. He walked by me without saying a word and headed directly towards the kitchen that he'd been bleeding in just a few days ago. I quickly and quietly followed him, stopping just inside the room. There was dried blood on the floor and coffee mugs on the table that were abandoned in our haste to get Lynch to the hospital.

"What are you doing out of the hospital and how did you find us?" I asked.

Lynch responded, "Web called me about the incident at the motel. I decided it was time to stop lying on my back and to start helping to bring this bastard to justice. As for finding you, it was an educated guess. I figured an abandoned house in an abandoned community would have been my first choice as a hiding spot".

He barely finished answering my questions when I heard the sound of crunching glass. It was a telltale sign that April was on her way down the stairs. I could only hope that she had changed into a little more clothing than the nightie she had worn to bed, but no such luck. Lynch's jaw dropped, and although April was initially surprised to see her father, the surprise quickly turned into embarrassment as she moved the coffee mugs off the kitchen table and wrap herself in the tablecloth.

"Please tell me you don't have a gun," I said to Lynch.

He responded, "Don't worry; I'm not going to kill you. I haven't ruled out shooting you in the kneecap though. You kept my girl alive. That's all that matters to me at the moment."

Technically speaking, April had actually kept me alive by shooting the pizza guy. But then again, it was her phone that led him to us so I had no problem taking the credit.

"I have two pieces of bad news that your boss wanted me to relay if I found you. He said when they went to arrest that Bob fellow, he was nowhere to be found."

"And what's the other piece of bad news you have for me?" I asked.

Your Phoenix office received a phone call from the hotel your partner Bill was staying at. Apparently, the maid found him dead when she came to clean the room. According to the first responders, it sounded like he over-dosed."

April saw me step back towards the chair to sit down, and quickly moved it closer to make sure it was under me by the time I finished dropping. I wasn't sure if it was that I didn't know what to say, or just couldn't get the words out. April stood behind me with her hands on my shoulders.

Finally, I found enough clarity to ask "Where is Web now?"

Lynch responded in a sympathetic tone "He was on his way to the hotel son".

I turned to Lynch "Can you hold down the fort for a few hours?"

"Get going, we'll be fine," he replied without hesitation.

I ran up the stairs and quickly changed before stopping in the kitchen on the way out. Lynch and April were sitting at the table waiting for a pot of coffee to brew. As I moved to the door, I asked Lynch if I could borrow his car. I didn't know if the SUV had been reported as stolen yet and didn't want to get arrested on the way to the hotel.

"Are you going to be okay to drive?" April asked.

I was still numb from the news, but nodded yes as I headed out the door.

It was probably a fifty minute drive to the hotel, but it felt like hours. I kept envisioning Bill's face when we left him at the hospital the other day. I tried to search my mind for reasons why he might have taken his own life, but only one came to mind…guilt. Was he the rogue agent? Was Bob innocent? Or did they conspire together? Based on how quickly they were able to locate us using April's phone signal last night, I was now leaning towards them both being guilty. I pulled in front of the hotel and threw the keys to the valet. I wasn't going to take the time to find a parking spot. I was getting ready to flash my badge to the desk clerk to find out the room Bill was in when I saw Web exit the elevator with two police officers and a gurney that held the body of someone that I once considered to be a friend. Now not only did I have to deal with his death, but also the fact that he had crossed the line to the wrong side of the law. Web walked over to me and patted me on the back.

"I guess Lynch found you. Are you alright?" he asked.

"Yes, Lynch found us, but I'm not exactly sure how I feel right now," I responded.

Web moved his head in the direction of the elevator and we went up to the room. The forensic team was still dusting for fingerprints, taking pictures, and bagging evidence. Pills were found scattered across the desk where Bill's head was resting when he had succumbed to the cocktail of drugs that he ingested. From the looks of things, he had his last meal delivered to his room. Considering he was planning to take his life, it did not appear to be a particularly extravagant last meal, but Bill was a lot like me. We both had simple tastes.

"Any notes? I asked.

"Nothing that we could find, and no signs of a struggle," Web responded. "It looks like either the guilt got to him or he knew we were suspicious. Either way, I guess he figured the easiest way out was to take his own life".

Web had mentioned that Bill had sounded a bit stressed when they spoke yesterday night. I guess that made sense since no one planning on suicide is going to do it without some trepidation. Web informed me that they were taking the body down to the coroner for an autopsy.

"Someone from the bureau forensic team will be present while the autopsy is performed." Web continued "I'm sure Lynch told you that they checked Bob's apartment. It appeared that he had packed up some of his belongings and was on the run. I want to get a few policemen to protect April. Where is she?"

"At Jenna's house," I whispered.

I told Web that I wanted to head over to the ranch to check in on my parents, and then, I would meet him there later. Web was waiting to see if the bureau's database had come up with a match on the pizza guy's finger-prints. As I started walking out of the hotel, Web called me back. He had forgotten to give me the test results on the Vet that shot Lynch. He told me the autopsy showed he was on a drug called Imovane.

"Isn't that the same drug they found in Rodney's blood?" he asked.

"Yes, and according to Jenna, Dan was taking it as well," I replied, "There has to be something more to this drug than just being a glorified sleeping pill. I think I'll check in with our Doctor friend at the VA Hospital".

By that I meant Dr. Rodriguez. I was just hoping that he got over the threat of the IRS audit. I walked out of the hotel, handing the valet my claim check. When he pulled the car up in front of the hotel, I stood there for a minute before I realized that I had driven Lynch's car here. I would have liked to attribute my momentary lapse to the fact that I had been in so many different cars during the past few days, but I knew the real reason was something else. I kept thinking about Bill being dead. As much disdain as I had for the traitor Bill turned out to be, I felt the loss of a good friend he had once been. I had given some thought to calling Mike and Fred to let them know that Bill was dead, but they would ask details that I wasn't in the position to release. How do you begin to explain to them that our friend and associate of so many years was a traitor? I tried to isolate the two people in my mind. Bill, the friend that I would work out with, get drinks with, and share laughs with. And then, there was the other side of the coin. This was also the Bill that was involved in my boss's assassination, and possibly the murder of innocent vets, and the attempted murder of Web, April, and my-self. It was all too confusing. It was obvious that for the moment, that I was not going to make any sense from what had happened. At first, I thought his suicide was his way of taking the coward's way out—allowing him to avoid facing those he betrayed and paying for his wrong doings—but maybe, I was wrong. Maybe, Bill couldn't reconcile these two sides of himself, and in the end he couldn't live with the guilt that had been inflicted on him by the Bill that betrayed us.

Before getting into the car, I pulled out Dr. Rodriguez's card, turned on the phone and dialed his number. When I got his voice message, I hung up realizing that I would probably have better luck getting the information I needed from a search engine on my dad's computer than from him. I pulled out of the hotel parking lot heading for the Ranch. I wanted to make sure that everything was okay before returning to the Stone's house. It felt a bit strange not having April with me. We had been pretty much joined at the hip since we met. As I drove, I thought about how when Hope and I were dating there was always something that kept our relationship from moving forward. I could tell you her favorite movies, food, music, sports team and dozens of her other likes and dislikes. Still, it always felt that the more intimate aspects of her personality, which drew you closer to a person were missing. I was never able to explain to my friends what our relationship was missing. I guess I wasn't sure what it was myself, until I met April. It just seemed that I couldn't break down this wall that she built around herself. I remember when she ended the relationship. I was surprised, but it didn't hurt. There was no moping around the apartment, no hollow feelings in the pit of my stomach, and no regrets. With April, I felt as if there was no pretense. April was just April, and I felt very comfortable about it. I'm not sure if that type of reassurance came from her good looks, being a cop, her upbringing, or a combination of all of the above. In that one moment—when we were walking to the restaurant—when she told me about her mom dying and her reasons for becoming a cop, she shared more of herself than Hope revealed during the entire time we had dated. In retrospect, I think she might have been doing me a favor when she broke up, knowing that she could never share that part of her. Hopefully, one day she'd find the right person to help her break down the walls that she'd erected around herself. In the meantime, while I was driving, I had turned on the news to distract myself. By some strange coincidence they were talking about Hope. Apparently, her confirmation to take her father's place in the Senate was moving forward. Although there were many things that Hope and the Senator disagreed about, she had never publicly been at odds with her father. Hope was expected to be in Arizona sometime tomorrow. It might be difficult with everything going on with this case, but if time permitted, I wanted to see her and wish her well.

As I pulled into the ranch, the first thing I noticed was that my father's pickup truck was back in the driveway. Riddle had volunteered one of his mechanics to get the truck started and have it delivered back to the ranch. He had also made arrangements to get my rental car towed back to the rental facility. I was sure that there would be a few messages waiting for me to retrieve on my cell phone after the car was delivered back to the rental company. Unfortunately, my personal cell phone was still sitting at one of the decoy motels waiting to be retrieved. Hopefully, there are no exclusions on the rental policy regarding damages resulting from an ambush. The minute I walked into the house, my father could tell that something was wrong.

"What happened son?" he asked.

"My friend Bill," I said, and then paused for a couple of seconds, trying to get the words out. "He killed himself".

My parents had never met Bill, but they knew from our conversations that I considered him to be very good friend.

"It looks like he was somehow involved with the hypnotist," I said, "I'm guessing that he either killed himself out of guilt, or maybe he knew we were on to him and just didn't want to do the time."

My father walked over to the coffee table in the den, extracting an envelope from a pile of mail that had been sitting there.

"This came for you son. It was in today's mail."

I reached for the envelope and as I pulled it closer I saw no return address, only the name "Bill Rich". It was postmarked yesterday, before we set our plan in motion. I stared at the letter for a minute before I opened it. It was a letter from the dead. My parents sat back on the couch, eyeing me, as I read it silently.

"To my friend Bennett, I'm guessing that by the time you read this letter, I will be dead. I do not expect redemption in anyone's eyes after I betrayed you and the bureau, but I needed to explain what happened. And hopefully, in some small way, try to make things right between us and with our maker. Several years ago, I applied to the FBI for an investigator's position. I thought the job was mine, but then, I received a phone call from the bureau telling me I had failed my psych profile. I always wanted to join the Bureau, and after that news, it seemed unlikely that it would happen. After the call I headed over to the local bar to get drunk...it seemed like a good idea at the time. I just finished my third drink when a guy sat down at the bar and started talking to me. He had noticed that I was upset. He introduced himself as a psychiatrist and offered a listening ear. I wasn't as drunk as I intended to be, but I'd already consumed enough Tequila to start spilling my guts to him.

After listening for about fifteen minutes, he told me he had connections at the bureau and that he might be able to help me out with my psych test results. I told him I would be indebted to him for life if he could help me. We shared a drink. He told me to give him a week and then got up and walked out of the bar. One week later, I received a call from the Bureau telling me that I was hired. I wanted to thank the guy for helping me, but I never heard back from him. I didn't even have a name or number to reach him.

A couple of days before the Senator's lunch, I got a call from him. After thanking him, he asked me how things were going with the Bureau and asked me if I meant what I had said in the bar that night about being indebted to him for helping me out. I confirmed that I meant what I said. He asked me if I could do him a small favor. I told him I was happy to repay the debt. He had some friends that were members of a war protest group. They wanted to hang some protests signs from the balcony of the hotel facing the property adjacent to the back of the hotel. They thought they'd get some good publicity if the press noticed the signs at the Senator's event. Based on past history, I knew the hotel had always tightened security during high profile events that they hosted. All he needed me to do was to use my credentials to get past hotel security and discreetly take the camera system down. I didn't think it was a big deal since the press and Senator were supposed to be in the banquet room for the event, and the protestors would have probably gone completely unnoticed anyway.

There was one problem I told him. I was not scheduled to be at the event and that I was only a fill-in for the detail if one of the regular guys got sick. He told me he would leave some pills in my mailbox. When mixed with alcohol, they would give the person flu like symptoms, but the effects were very short term. I was asked to slip it into the drink of one of the regular guys the night before the event. I was also told that the effects would be far less extreme for a younger person. I knew we were going out for drinks to celebrate the night before. Since you were by far the youngest person on the detail, I put the pills in your drink. At the last minute I was going to back out, but I was concerned that the guy might notify the Bureau of my indiscretion. It wasn't until Billings was shot that I realized that I'd unknowingly made the leap from cheating to get into the FBI, to an accomplice to murder.

I know what they say about the slippery slope, but I never figured the fall would be so steep and so fast. As much as I hoped that I would never hear from him again, I knew that I was probably kidding myself and was proven right only a few days later. Once he realized that you started looking into the Billing's killing again, he told me to figure out an excuse for showing up in Arizona. He made himself clear that he wanted me to keep an eye on what you were doing. Web made that easy by calling me in to assist with the investigation. As soon as I learned that he used my information about Web's meeting with you at the ranch to try and kill April, I knew that I could no longer be a part of this insanity.

The next time he called for information about April and your hideout, I told him I was through helping him and he would have to get his information from someone else. He tried to assure me that the only person he planned on killing was April and you wouldn't be hurt. I asked him why only April and not you. He wouldn't tell me why he wanted to kill April, but did say that he wouldn't kill you. It had something to do with repaying a debt to your Uncle. I didn't get it, but maybe this information will mean something to you. He also mentioned that he had briefly met you when you were with the DC Police Department, but wouldn't say anything more about that. I told him that I had paid back my debt and that he shouldn't call anymore. He threatened to turn me in, and I told him to go to hell. Based on the way he has treated his other victims, I knew that refusing him was a death sentence and now sit here waiting for his appointed executioner. It's what I deserve for my part in this. Just as I will pay for my indiscretion, I hope and pray that you'll catch this SOB and make him pay for his crimes. Above all, I'm hoping that someday, you will find it in your heart to forgive me for my transgressions. You were a good friend to me, and you deserved better." It was signed "With deepest regrets, Bill".

I dropped my hand that had been holding the letter to my lap. I must have been sitting there for a few minutes trying to absorb what I just read, when my father called my name trying to break me out of the trance I was in.

"Is everything okay?" he asked.

"Yes," I replied, "How many men did Uncle Bennett save in his platoon when he died that day?"

My father responded, "I believe there were seventeen".

I called Web on his cell phone to make sure he was at the Stone's. I asked him to find the names of the surviving platoon members that served with Captain Bennett Mills on the day he was killed. I thought to myself, he was a hero that won the Medal of Honor posthumously. There had to be some record of the men he saved. Web asked if I could tell him the reason I had him searching for information on one of my deceased family members. I told him to trust me and that I would fill him in when I got there. Before I left, I had to search the internet for some information on the drug Imovane. I asked my sister if I could use her laptop that was sitting on the kitchen table. With a big grin, she asked me if I promised to give it back to her in one piece. I'm sure she was just trying to lighten things up a bit, but she could tell by my face that I wasn't in a joking mood. She put up her hands and just told me to go ahead. I did a search on the word "Imovane," and the results that came back were what I'd expected. Not only was Imovane used as a sleeping aid, it was also used to help assist in the process of putting people into a hypnotic state. It was starting to make sense to me now. Prior to putting the vets under his hypnotic control, Dr. H would somehow get the vet to start taking the imovane, which he generously delivered right to their mailbox. This would make his victims more receptive to suggestions when he needed to use them to do his bidding. It looked like I was going to be making a stop by the VA hospital to speak to Dr. Rodriguez after all. With all that was going on, I realized that I hadn't eaten all morning. I got up from the table, grabbed a couple of freshly baked muffins and a bottle of water as I headed for the door. On the way out, I apologized to my parents for the abbreviated visit. My father told me to get going. It was clear to me that my father and I had hit a turning point in our relationship. I realized that coming home no longer seemed like a stressful event in my life and it felt good to have that tension lifted from my shoulders. I'm sure my father felt the same way.

It was only a few minutes from the ranch to the Stone's house. All I could think about was how easy it would be for anyone to fall into the clutches of this manipulative bastard. I had to wonder if the whole psych test failure and bar meeting wasn't just a big setup to lure Bill into his web. Until now, we thought his only power was his ability to put his prey into a deadly hypnotic trance. Now, it appeared that his power to control extended to blackmail as well. We were also under the false pretense that he was only using our veterans, and then we expanded it to people trying to stop smoking, maybe even someone trying to lose weight. Now—as we saw with Bill—it could be anyone that was willing to sell their souls to this devil. The hypnotist appeared to have a great deal of patience making his connection to his victim, and then waiting sometimes years before calling them into action. I knew Web would be more than a little intrigued by the information in Bill's letter. He told me he also had some new information he needed to share with me, but hesitated to tell me until I arrived. It sounded like we were going to be engaged in a game of show and tell.

Chapter 17
Checkout Time

I pulled into the driveway of Jenna's house and showed my badge to the officers stationed at the base of the steps. As I entered the front door, I noted that April had changed into her day clothes and was cleaning the broken glass off the floor and staircase.

"Hey Bennett, next time you break it….you clean it up." She said in jest as she pointed me in the direction of the family room where Web and Lynch were sitting.

As I started walking in that direction, she asked "Do you mind if I join you?"

I responded, "I would have been disappointed if you didn't".

The corners of her mouth turned up in an playful grin. She put the sweeper down by the side of the staircase and stood up. I could not take my eyes off of her as she stood up. April must have noticed that I was watching her.

"Were you having flashbacks of me wearing that nightie?" She asked.

Caught red handed, I just nodded my head yes.

She responded, "Good," as the playful smile reappeared on her face.

I was completely taken off guard by her response, making me unable to acknowledge Web or Lynch's presence in the room. I moved to the chair as April sat down on the couch between Web and Lynch.

I began our meeting by reading Bill's letter out loud. Periodically, I would look up to take note of their facial expressions as I read.

"Now I understand why you requested that search of surviving platoon members of your uncle's squad," Web said after I finished reading the letter.

"Based on the description that April had given us," I said, "the hypnotist would be too young to have fought in that battle. My guess is that it must have been his father or another close relative, maybe even an uncle. If we could find the name of that relative, we might be able to identity this maniac."

Web brought up how astonished he was that a man with no qualms about killing vets and ruining so many lives would feel an obligation to keep me alive in order to repay a debt. I made it clear to everyone that I had a debt to repay as well, but it was to all of his innocent victims. If we took him alive it was okay, if we took him dead it would be better. I just wanted to get to him before he got to anyone else.

I realized that so far I'd been the only one sharing information during our get-together. I turned to Web and asked him what information he was planning on telling me when I got here.

Web responded, "We got the fingerprints back on your pizza guy, his name was Anthony Barone, he was a hit man for the local mob. You're both lucky to be alive considering his reputation."

I could see by the look on April's face that she was thinking the same thing I was. Why would a mob hit man be trying to kill us? Did Dr. H's sphere of influence now extend to the mob? Before I could say anything the phone rang. Outside of solicitors, it would be odd for anyone to be calling the Stone's house. Jenna's parents were both dead and she told her friends that she would be away for a couple of weeks. As for her in-laws, they hadn't spoken to her in months. More than likely it was a solicitor, but my curiosity led me to the kitchen phone to take a peek at the caller ID. No name was displayed, but strangely enough the phone number began with the DC area code. Who from DC would know to reach us at Jenna's house? I paused for a second before I decided to hit the talk button.

"Hello," I said.

The voice on the other end responded, "Bennett, Bennett is that you?"

I knew that voice. It was Bob Clayton. "Where the hell are you?" I asked in a demanding tone.

"I'll tell you in a minute, but first I need to clear something up," he responded.

During the next five minutes, Bob not only persuaded me that he wasn't our rogue agent, he had also convinced me to give him a chance to find whoever was. We finished our conversation and I was just about to hang up when it struck me...how the hell did he know where to reach me? I gave serious thought about asking that question, when it occurred to me that Bob would just give me some Hi-Tech explanation that I wasn't going to understand anyway. I decided not to waste the time by asking and just said goodbye and hung up the phone. As I put the phone back on in its base, I breathed a sigh of relief knowing that Bob was still one of the good guys. We needed someone of his caliber on our team to combat whoever had been helping Dr. H.

As I walked back into the family room, Lynch said "This is ridiculous, I can't let April continue to be a target for this guy. Somehow, we need to make this nut aware that we already know about the tattoo on his arm and his connection to Bennett's uncle. Maybe if he knows that the cat is out of the bag, he won't feel that he has a reason to kill her."

"I don't think that will be necessary," I responded.

"My daughter's life is in jeopardy and you don't think it's necessary? Are you nuts?" Lynch asked while looking at me like I had just lost my mind.

"The reason why it's not necessary, is because he already knows," I replied.

"And how the hell did you come to that conclusion?" Web asked.

"Because Bob wasn't the inside guy. When Bob disappeared, we thought Bill and he were both rogue agents. With Bill and Jenny Yuen dead, and Bob on the run, we made the mistake of getting comfortable with using the Bureau systems again. In the meantime, the real inside guy was watching our activity on the system. As soon as we started researching the members of my uncle's platoon, the hypnotist had to know that we made the connection between the tattoo and my uncle."

"Maybe I missed something, but when did you deduce that Bob wasn't our inside guy?" Web asked.

"About five minutes ago," I replied.

"And what happened five minutes ago?" Lynch asked.

I told them that Bob was the one that had just called, and after listening to him for a few minutes I was convinced that he was on our side.

"If he's not guilty then why the hell would he go into hiding?" Web asked.

"He didn't exactly go into hiding," I responded, "Bob wanted it to appear that he was on the run."

"And why the hell would he want to do that?" Lynch asked. "If he's not guilty, it sure made him look that way."

"Think about it," I said, "Bill and Jenny Yuen are dead. Bob pulls a disappearing act. We think we have all of our conspirators accounted for."

"And?" Web asked in an impatient tone.

"So we relax and start using the Bureau systems again, convincing the real rogue agent that he was safe. Then we wait," I said.

"Wait for what?" April asked.

"For the conspirator to get comfortable and hopefully sloppy enough to make a mistake," Web responded.

"Exactly! A mistake that with Bob's help will lead us right to him," I replied.

I looked down at my watch realizing that I needed to get going. I turned to Web and asked him if he wanted to take the ride with me to the airport. When he asked me why we were going to the airport, I told him to pick up Bob of course.

"When did you become such a smartass?" Web said in jest.

"About ten minutes ago," I replied. "Are you coming along, or not?"

As we started out the door, I turned around and asked Lynch and April to stay at the house until we returned. I knew that the pantry was pretty empty. I told them that we would bring something back for everyone to eat, and under no circumstances were they to order pizza. In response to my admittedly lame joke, April picked up a pillow from the couch and threw it at me.

"Bennett," she said "Be careful".

"You too," I replied.

"What about me?" Web asked.

April responded with a smile.

While in the car, I filled Web in on the details of the plan that Bob and I discussed while we were on the phone. Once we picked-up Bob, we'd sneak him back to the Stone's house. He told me that he had created a special algorithm that would allow him full monitoring access of the Bureau systems without anyone knowing he was connected. Web didn't seem comforted by the thought that someone would be able break into our systems that easily. I reminded him that Bob wasn't your ordinary hacker. With Dr. H. knowing that we were getting closer to discovering his identity, he'd be relying that much more on his inside person to help keep him informed and to cover his tracks. Bob's assignment would be to set a few traps for our conspirator to get caught in. Once we stopped his information source, he would be as much in the dark as we had been until now.

Chapter 18

Turning the Tide

We made good time to the airport. Web waited outside keeping an eye open for anyone suspicious while I went inside looking for Bob. We were supposed to meet in front of the Stanton Gift shop, just outside of airport security. Even though Bob had used his talents to book his flight under an assumed name, I figured if by chance someone did follow him, he would be much safer being within arm's length of airport police than waiting around baggage claim for me to collect him. As I approached the gift shop, I couldn't help but to start laughing to myself. Bob had obviously seen one too many spy flicks. He had tried to obscure his identity by wearing a fake mustache, beard, and a pair of what looked like two inch thick glasses, which made his brown eyes look like they were popping out of his head. As if that didn't make him look ridiculous enough, he was also sporting a hat that most people wouldn't be caught dead in. It was so oversized that every lock of his curly brown hair was covered. The absurd thing was, he stood out so much, that nobody would ever consider that he was actually trying to disguise himself. People probably just thought he was eccentric. When our mild mannered Bob wasn't dressed for Halloween, his baby face and slender build grabbed the attention of many of the female analyst in his department.

I walked right up to him and asked "Why no nose ring? It probably would have completed the look."

"Can we get the hell out of here?" he asked, "This beard and mustache are making me break out in a rash".

I walked a few feet in front of him as he followed me out to the car. It wasn't as much for security reasons as to just avoid being seen walking with him in that ridiculous outfit. He hopped into the backseat and as we pulled away from the terminal heading back to the house he started to peel off his disguise. As hard as Web tried to restrain himself, he broke out into raucous laugh.

"What were you thinking wearing that outfit?" Web asked.

"I'm here aren't I?" Bob responded.

On the way back, we pulled into a drive-thru and picked up an assortment of burgers and chicken sandwiches. I wanted to hit the food store for provisions, but I figured that we were way past lunch time. Everyone at the house had to be getting pretty hungry by now. During the remainder of the trip Bob went into a detailed explanation of how he planned to trap the conspirator. Web and I were not the most technically savvy guys on the face of the earth, and I think the only thing we got from Bob's elucidations was a giant headache. When he shut up long enough for me to get a word in edgewise, I apologized for doubting where his loyalties lied.

"If Bill could have gone down the wrong path, then it was possible that any of us could have," he responded as he leaned forward from the rear seat and patted me on the back.

As we pulled onto Jenna's block, I noticed another car in the driveway. I was surprised when I realized it was my father's. I hadn't even told him we were staying at the house which led me to the question of what was he doing here? April met us as we walked through the front door. After giving me a quick kiss on the cheek, she quickly grabbed the food out of my hands and started laying it out on the kitchen counter. After the officers grabbed their food, April and Lynch took a sandwich and sat down at the kitchen table. Bob followed suit, introducing himself as he sat down to join them. Web and I continued on into the family room, where both Jenna and my dad had been sitting and waiting for us to return.

"What are you doing here?" I asked my father.

"That's funny son. I think that Jenna had the same question for you," responded my dad.

I guess I could see her point. My father explained that he offered to run her by the house to make sure everything was okay. I could imagine her surprise as she pulled up to see that we had moved in without permission during her absence. I told them the story about what happened at the motel and our run in with the mob hit man.

"We needed to relocate to a more secluded place" I told her, "and your house was the first, and only thing, that came to mind."

"I wasn't really upset." Jenna responded, "I was just surprised. This house hasn't had this many people in it since Dan and I first moved in."

While we were speaking, Web grabbed a sandwich from the kitchen and went upstairs to take a phone call. When he returned, he gave us some good news that we had been waiting for.

"I just got off the phone with Phoenix office," he told us. "they have the list of the sixteen men that had fought alongside Captain Mills the day he died."

"That's strange," my father said, "I was pretty sure that there were seventeen other men."

If my father was correct, then the possibility existed that the records had already been tampered with by Dr. H's conspirator. Since this was the closest thing we had to a lead at this point, we needed to start cross referencing the names on the list with younger relatives that had served on the same base as these men. Hopefully, my father was wrong and we would be able to find a match that would deliver us the name of this madman. Bob's second job would be to start researching the list, his first was to deploy the traps he had created.

After introducing himself to Jenna, Bob asked if she had a computer that he could use. In haste to avoid being taken into custody, he abandoned his own laptop at his apartment in DC. For Bob that must have been like a trapped animal chewing off an appendage to escape the trap.

"I have a desktop computer upstairs," she said as she led him to a small room situated just to the left at the top of the steps.

After taking a fast glance at her antiquated computer, Bob headed back down the stairs and into the den where we had all congregated for a quick meeting. "Web" he interrupted, "I think I need to do some equipment shopping."

"How much is this going to cost us?" Web responded.

"A lot less than if we don't catch the guy. Think about it, if he's willing to help a murderer, who knows what he might be doing with our intelligence information," Bob replied.

"Get whatever you need, but ask Riddle to authorize the purchase. We don't want to alert anyone at the bureau that you are working with us," Web responded.

It was agreed that Lynch and Bob would make the trip to a local computer store for the equipment Bob needed. Web was going to follow-up on the status of the remaining missing vets with Riddle, and then deal with some of his other work that had been piling up. April and I were heading to the police precinct to review some of my old DC police case files. Bill had mentioned in his letter that Dr. H. revealed that we'd met while I was still on the force in DC. Since I hadn't crossed paths with many shrinks either socially or personally while in DC, it was more likely our meeting would have been the result of a case I'd worked on during that time. With April's help, and a lot of luck, maybe we could find out when that meeting took place.

Lynch and Bob left first, followed shortly after by Web. April and I were on our way out when my father pulled me aside. He suggested that it might be good for Jenna to spend a couple of hours at home.

"I don't mind hanging around waiting for her," he said.

"If you don't mind, I think that would be fine," I replied.

"I'm retired, what else do I have to do?" he said with a smile.

I patted him on the shoulder, and then headed for the door. Once I was outside, I noticed that the only vehicle that was left in the driveway was a police car, and April was already buckled in the driver's seat. I walked up to the window and suggested that it might be better if I drove.

"I'd like to oblige, but I don't think you are authorized to drive this vehicle," she said with a wink and a mischievous smirk.

I walked around the front of the car, and reluctantly, got into the front passenger seat.

"Are you a good driver?" I asked as I buckled myself in.

She responded, "That's for me to know and for you to find out".

That wasn't the reassurance I was hoping for. With April behind the wheel, we pulled out of the driveway and headed for the precinct. Just as Jenna was content to be back in her own home, April seemed equally content to be anywhere outside of the house. She did not strike me as the type of person that liked to sit still for too long.

"If I'm not being too nosey, what did your father pull you aside for?" April asked.

"He thought it would be good for Jenna to be in her own house for a while. I guess she was homesick," I said.

"Having been away from my apartment for a few days, I can completely relate to how she must be feeling," she responded.

"Speaking of my apartment, would you mind if we made a quick excursion there so I can make sure everything is okay and pick up a few things?"

April asked. "It would be nice to be able to wear clothes that don't make me look like a circus clown."

I guess it was the last time she would be wearing that nightie, but the memory would live on.

"You know," April said, "as bad as the past few days have been being hunted by killers, having my father shot, being driven from my apartment, and having to wear those god awful clothes that you gave me, there are a couple of good things that have happened".

I stared at April, waiting to be enlightened. After a small pause and a flash of her beautiful smile she continued.

"First of all, it seemed to help you mend fences with your father, I got to spend time with your family and they are really nice. And," she paused again turning briefly to look in my direction.

"And?" I asked.

"You're a smart guy and an FBI agent," she said, "I'm sure you can figure it out."

We were about fifteen miles out of the city. I was hoping to press her for an answer to my question before we got into town when I noticed a change in April's demeanor. The smile that had adorned her face during most of our drive changed to one of concern.

"What's wrong?" I said.

"I just noticed that we are being followed and they're coming up on us fast," she replied.

It didn't take much to persuade me that she was right. As beautiful as she was, I couldn't forget that April was also a cop. And if I needed any more convincing, all I needed to do was look into my rearview mirror. The car that April noticed pursuing us just happened to be a black Mercedes.

"I thought you said I'd be safe?" she yelled.

"Either I'm wrong and the hypnotist still is unaware that you already informed us about his tattoo," I replied, "Or these guys aren't happy with us killing their pizza delivering buddy. In either case, let's not hang around to find out which it is."

April hit the accelerator as I tried to radio for help. I was pretty sure that unless there were some cops close by we were going to be dealing with these guys on our own. Even though April now had the gas pedal down to the floor, the Mercedes continued to gain on us.

"Can't this car go any faster?" I asked.

"Bennett," she replied. "This may be a suped-up Chevy, but they're driving a Mercedes CLS Class with a twin turbo V8. By the way, did I forget to mention that I'm a car enthusiast?".

"You're kidding me?" I yelled back.

"You're right, I only knew that because I pulled over a drunk in the same kind of Mercedes about a month ago. I had as much luck getting him to shut up about the car as we're having out running one," she responded.

April continued to push the Chevy's engine to its max, but it was no match for the Mercedes which was practically on top of us by now. I looked out the rear window and noticed they were making an effort to pull along-side. The passenger had what appeared to be a semi-automatic that he was now pointing out the window. I pulled out my gun, hoping I could get off a couple of rounds and take him out before he had the chance to riddle us with bullets from the semi. I was not liking our odds against that kind of fire-power. April tried to sway the Chevy back and forth to impede their forward motion to no avail.

They were just about to pull alongside when April yelled "Hold onto your seats and get ready to fire."

I had no idea what she was planning, but I had a bad feeling. I barely finished the thought when April slammed on the brakes causing the car wheels to screech. Smoke rose off of the hot Arizona pavement as the Chevy shimmied from side to side before coming to a full stop. The driver of the Mercedes was caught completely off guard, darting by us at what must have been one-hundred and thirty miles per hour. In an effort to one-up our ma-neuver, the driver slammed on his brakes while simultaneously trying to turn the car back in our direction. The driver lost complete control of the vehicle as it flipped over several times, flying off the road and finally coming to rest in a ravine. April hit the gas again pulling the Chevy to within one-hundred feet of the Mercedes. As our car came to a stop I hopped out with my gun in hand. I anticipated little resistance by its occupants after the aerial acrobat-ics that the car had just performed. I hadn't taken five steps towards the car before it burst into flames. The smoke was thick and air was noxious forcing me to return to the car. As soon as I got in the car, I closed the door and then turned towards April to see how she was doing. Without warning, she leaned over into the passenger seat and stunned me with a long passionate kiss. When her lips parted from mine I asked "Not that I minded, but what was that for?"

Her response was classic April "For not complaining about my driving".

I started leaning toward her in hopes of garnering at least one more kiss. I was just shy of our lips touching when April stopped me, directing my face with her hands to the look out the rear view mirror. It appeared that while we were both distracted by the first kiss, another car had pull up behind us. I saw Lynch step out of the driver's side with a perturbed look on his face. As he slammed the car door closed, Bob stepped out of the passenger side with a big smirk on his face. They had left shortly before us heading in the other direction, but must of heard my call for back-up on the radio. Before they had a chance to start walking in our direction, another police vehicle pulled in just ahead of us. It stopped adjacent to where the Mercedes had landed and was still burning in the ravine. I was relieved to see them arrive, knowing that Lynch wouldn't be able to shoot me after bearing witness to April's and my kiss, well at least, not at the moment. We must have looked like two frightened teenagers caught making out in the family car. Lynch walked over to April to make sure she was okay. Bob came over and slapped me on the back. He proceeded to make an off handed comment about the kiss, which earned both of us a death stare from Lynch.

"I thought you said that April would be safe now," Lynch growled.

"If it makes you feel any better, I think these guys were looking for a little revenge for the death of their friend. I don't think the hypnotist had anything to do with this one" I replied.

"And what makes you think that?" he asked.

"The driver was pulling up on my side of the car, leading me to believe that they were intent on killing either me, or both of us. If they only wanted to kill April, they would have approached us from the driver's side not the passenger side. This, of course, assumes that Dr. H. hadn't changed his mind about not wanting to kill me," I replied.

"Why don't you get April out of here," Lynch suggested. "I'll take care of things here before Bob and I head over to the computer store."

April and I were to continue our trip to the Precinct. I noticed that April hesitated getting into the squad car after opening the driver's door.

She looked at me and asked "Are you sure you want me to drive?"

"After the driving exhibition you just gave, you can take me anywhere," I replied.

"Are you saying that because of my driving? Or was it the kiss?" she asked in a suggestive tone.

Her response was meant to be funny, but Lynch was still in earshot and didn't seem to find it particularly amusing. Up until now, I was mystified as to why April wasn't already in a relationship. After seeing how Lynch responded to men that April showed interest in, it suddenly became crystal clear. Most suitors probably avoided courting April knowing that it would draw Lynch's ire. I was determined to wear him down, or die trying.

April started the car and we were back in route to Phoenix. I was happy to be moving again since the air was filled with the stench of burning brakes, burning rubber, and as sickening as it was to think about, burning mobsters. I was reluctant to make a detour to April's apartment after this last incident, but with the steering wheel in her hands, I did not seem to have much of a choice. As a precaution, I was able to convince Riddle to dispatch a couple of his officers to the apartment to check things out before we arrived. When we pulled up to the front of the building we were met by two officers, one male and the other female. They informed us that they had checked out everything upstairs and it appeared to be safe.

The male officer ribbed her about all of the cooking gear she had in her apartment. In response, his female partner whacked him across the head and directed him to their patrol car. They were going to wait outside until we were done collecting April's things and then follow us back to the precinct.

After entering the apartment, I took my familiar position of laying on the couch while April went to her bedroom to gather her things. While I was sprawled out, I gave the family photos on the wall a second look, but this time it was different. When I first came to the apartment April was a stranger, a beautiful one, but still a stranger. Now, April was...April. It seemed strange how things had progressed in only a couple of days. If our relationship went anywhere, would I find myself indebted to a lunatic for bringing us together? I thought about it and figured if anyone asked, I would just tell them it was fate.

April came out of the room with a duffel bag on her shoulders.

"If I offered to carry your bag, would you be offended?" I asked.

"No," she replied, "I may be a cop, but I do not mind being treated like a lady".

She handed me the duffel bag, and led me down the stairs to the car. As we pulled away from the curb, we were followed closely by our escort on the way to the precinct.

Chapter 19
Memory Lane

We arrived at the precinct in just under twenty minutes. We were met at the door by Riddle. He couldn't help but to comment on our recent encounter with the mob.

"You two sure know how to pick your enemies. The guy in the morgue and the two guys you left roasting like marshmallows worked for Joseph Beninni."

The name didn't ring a bell, but then again, I hadn't lived in Arizona for many years. However, I could tell by looking at the expression on April's face that he wasn't someone that you wanted as a friend, and definitely not someone you wanted as an enemy. April explained that Beninni was the Arizona mob boss. It was more than a rumor that he was in tight with the Mexican drug cartels, helping them smuggle and distribute a variety of drugs into our country.

"Why haven't you been able to put him away yet?" I asked.

"He's too smart to be involved in any of the deals himself. And he is too dangerous to a person's health for anyone to rat him out," Riddle replied.

No sooner did we unravel one mystery before we found ourselves faced with another. I couldn't help but to wonder how Dr. H. and Beninni might be connected. If not for the two attempts on our lives, I might consider putting that one on the back burner. For now, it appeared that April and I would have to split up in order to continue the investigations into both Beninni and the hypnotist. We could only hope that when we were both done, we would be able to somehow connect the dots between them.

Riddle walked us down the hall to the same room Lynch and I started our investigation in only a few days earlier. We'd come a long way since then, but not far enough. Riddle had a computer setup on either end of the conference table that filled most of the room. April and I each walked to opposite ends of the table preparing for a long afternoon. On the way out, Riddle informed us that the initial autopsy results on Bill were expected by the end of the day. He promised to stop by as soon as he received them. It was hard to believe that it was only this morning that he was found dead in the hotel room. Since arriving back in Arizona, it seemed that the days were so long they felt like weeks instead. It was clear that our extensive effort to find our killer was wearing us all down. I was sure that a pot or two of coffee would be needed to keep us from falling asleep at the table before the day was done. Thanks to Web's connections at the DC Police Department, he was able to obtain a computer access code for their system. With the hypnotist not being aware of the contents of Bill's letter, I felt comfortable that we would be able to do our research of my old cases without it being detected by the turncoat.

It had been a few years since I'd worked within this system, but fortunately—due to budget cuts—it didn't seem to have changed much. It wasn't very long before I had full access to all of my old case files. There was a lot of information to review, but I guess I was fortunate that I'd only been a detective for a few years, or we could be here for weeks. I started by searching for all cases that involved a physician. Considering that almost every crime above a misdemeanor involves some psychological or medical testimony, filtering using that criteria did not do much to reduce the number of cases to be reviewed. I was hoping I'd get lucky by changing my search criteria to hypnotist or hypnotherapy. I closed my eyes and hit the enter button. When I reopened my eyes, I was disappointed by a "Zero Results Returned" message flashing on the screen. That would have been too easy, and so far nothing about this case was easy. I shouldn't have been surprised. Let's try psychiatrist and psychologist I thought and typed in "Psych%" which returned just under one hundred results. That was an improvement over my earlier attempt cutting almost two hundred and twenty cases from my list. Yep, it is going to be a long evening. April walked over to my side of the conference table.

"Do you have something?" I asked.

"Yes," she replied, "a headache. I need some caffeine, can I get you some?"

I told her yes as I proceeded to drop my head into my hands. While I was waiting for April to return, I started reviewing the cases. I hadn't made it half way through the highlight reel of the first case before she came back with our coffee.

"Anything?" she asked.

I looked at her and raised my eyebrows. She took the hint and headed back to her end of the table.

Two hours passed and I had just completed reviewing the tenth case. At this rate, I wouldn't be finished until this time tomorrow unless I got lucky... I wasn't going to bet on that. I'd noted that April had put her head on the table about twenty minutes earlier, and although I couldn't be one hundred percent sure, it appeared that she was napping. If I didn't have another ninety cases to review, I could have watched that angelic face for hours, but there wasn't any time for distractions. I'd just finished that thought when Riddle entered the room. The sound of the door closing behind him startled April, triggering her to quickly lift her head off the table. Based on her reaction she must have been sleeping. He dropped a folder on the desk in front me.

"I have the autopsy results on Bill Rich," he said.

I could tell by the look on his face that he had something that he wanted to share with us.

"You look like the cat that just swallowed the mouse," I said "What did they find?"

Riddle responded, "Your friend died of a drug overdose," he said.

"That's it?" I said, "I didn't need an autopsy to tell me that".

Riddle saw the look on my face and decided to expand on his report. He informed me that the overdose of sleeping pills killed him, but it turned out that the pills were a chaser for something else he had drunk earlier that evening.

"The autopsy showed a toxin in his system." Riddle said. "If he hadn't taken the sleeping pills, the toxin would have eventually killed him, but it would have been an excruciating death."

It did not make sense. Why would someone deliberately ingest a poison before killing themselves by over dosing on sleeping pills...unless he didn't knowingly or willingly ingest the poison.

"Bill had indicated that he was expecting someone to try and kill him in the letter he mailed me. What if he was poisoned by someone, and then, given the choice of taking his own life by ingesting sleeping pills or suffering a slower more painful death by poison? It could be a perfect cover-up for a murder. Based on the evidence of sleeping pills strewn across the desk and in Bill's system, an overworked coroner looking to clear another case might easily shortcut and overlook the toxin. The hypnotist knew we were looking for his inside person, and he obviously knew that Bill had stopped cooperating with him. By killing Bill, he eliminates any chance that he might spill his guts to us, and at the same time puts an end to our search for the rogue agent. If not for Bill's letter, He might have been able to pull it off. I asked Riddle if he could setup a conference call with Web. He was apparently as technologically challenged as I was. April extended her hand to get Web's cell phone number from me, and in under a minute, he was conferenced in. He asked us to give him a minute until he could get into a private office. The sound of a door closing was my signal to start filling everyone in on my theory. I made the case that Bill didn't overdose, but in fact, was murdered. I cited Bill's letter to me and the findings of the autopsy. It was only a theory, but I did not hear anyone attempting to counter it.

"You have a few high level friends on the DC police department, don't you?" I asked Web.

"As a matter of fact, yes," he responded. "Why do you ask?"

"I'd bet good money that if we autopsied our overdosed analyst Jenny Yeun, we'd find the same toxin in her body," I replied.

If I was correct, she was killed in order to draw our attention away from somebody else in the intelligence area. I started to wonder if she was even involved with the hypnotist, or was she just another victim of this deranged lunatic? It was too late to get an autopsy done today, but Web promised to make the request first thing in the morning. After ending the conference call, Riddle left the room and April and I got back to our research.

It was like taking a walk down memory lane, or should I say nightmare lane. Not only was DC known for its corrupt politicians, it was also known for its high crime rate. We had a wide variety of crimes that would come across our desk. In any given week, we'd have rapists, murderers, robbers, pedophiles, drug dealers, and the occasional embezzler. The embezzlers would always bring in the best lawyers that other people's money could buy. When the case was over—even if they lost—the lawyers would have consumed all of the victim's funds leaving them nothing. Thinking about it, this was true of our justice system as well. Criminals victimized innocent citizens. Then those victims—as taxpayers—paid for the public defenders trying to keep the criminal out of jail. In essence, the victim was getting screwed twice. God bless the criminal justice system.

While reviewing the cases, I couldn't help but reminisce how good it felt to put away that scum, and I wasn't talking about the politicians either. That was one of the things I remembered about my father when I was growing up. You could always tell when he'd put away one of the more notorious crooks by the way he acted when he got home. If it was a good day he would grab a beer when he walked through the door, give my mother a hug and a kiss and sit down to eat dinner with the family. If the courts allowed one of the crooks to go free—by some technicality—it would eat him up inside. He would walk through the door, grab the beer and sit in the living room staring at the walls for a couple of hours while cursing under his breath. We all knew that on those days it was best to stay clear of him. No one could ever question his passion and dedication to his job. That's probably why he is considered a living legend in the state. When I was younger, he would never give me the details of his cases to avoid scaring the crap out of me. As I got older, he would water things down a bit, but would tell me enough to make sure I knew that the world could be a nasty place. It was my father's way of keeping me safe, and perhaps grooming me to be a cop. He was right about the world being a nasty place. This case was solid proof of that. There were nights after investigating particularly brutal crimes that I wouldn't be able to fall sleep. One of the many advantages of transferring to the Bureau was that it allowed me to get away from those types of cases. I paused for a minute and tried to rewind that thought.... "One of the advantages of transferring to the Bureau was it allowed me to get away from those types of cases."

At that moment, a wild thought crossed my mind. What if the hypnotist wasn't trying to help me get into the bureau, but instead was trying to get me away from a case I was working on? Maybe a case that we were both working on and I was getting too close to solving it? That would leave him with two options. He could either kill me using one of his patients, or get me away from the case by expediting my move to the Bureau. Because of this debt he felt he needed to repay to my uncle, it would make sense that he'd opt to get me out of the way rather than killing me. Maybe I was a bit punchy from all of the reading I had been doing, and so desperate for an answer that my mind was playing tricks on me. Or maybe, I'd just hit the nail on the head. I needed to share this epiphany with someone. I turned to look at April and was surprised to see that she was already looking at me with a huge smile on her face.

"What?" I asked.

She got up and walked towards me sitting down in the seat next to mine.

"I know that look. My dad gets that same look whenever he has a break through on one of his cases. Enlighten me!" She said.

I started to fill her in on my revelation, and I could see by the expression on her face that she was impressed by the dots I had just connected.

"So, what case was it?" she inquired.

"I have no idea," I responded, "but it would have been one of the last cases I was working on before I left. It had to be a case that I left open for my replacements to take over."

It was starting to look like we might make it out of the station before the end of the week. It was past my dinner time and it looked like a home cooked meal was not in the cards. I turned to April and asked if she knew any good delivery places that we could order up some dinner.

"I know a great pizza place," she said with a smile.

"Very funny," I responded.

She left the room and when she returned, she had a couple of menu's to choose from. She held them behind her back and asked me to pick a hand. It was a bit juvenile, but was also very cute.

"Left hand," I said.

"Deli it is," she responded.

At least, it wasn't pizza or burgers. It had actually been a while since I had a good corned beef and pastrami sandwich so I was pretty happy with my choice. April called in our order then sat back down at her computer and continued in her efforts to find the connection between the hypnotist and Bennini, I sifted through the cases that were left open at the time when I left the DC police department. I was hoping that I'd be able to substantiate my theory, or it would be back to the drawing board. About forty minutes had gone by with no luck when all of a sudden April jumped up from her seat pumping her hand in the air shouting "Yes, yes, yes!". I lifted my head up in response to her obvious excitement.

"What did you find?" I asked. At that moment the phone rang and April answered.

"The food is here. I'll be right back," she said.

I was amazed at the bad timing of the delivery. It had to arrive just as April was about to tell me about her exciting discovery. I didn't want to go back to my review knowing that at any minute she would be returning. It was only a few moments, but it felt like ages before she came back...empty handed.

"Where's our dinner?" I asked.

"I gave it away," she responded.

"What?" I said.

"I decided that we should go out of dinner instead of eating in this dingy office. In fact, I know the perfect place for us to go!" she said cheerfully.

"Aren't you going to tell me what you found out first?" I asked.

She leaned towards me, gave me a kiss on the cheek and whispered in my ear "I'll tell you at dinner".

On the way out, we passed the front desk where two officers were enjoying our meal. I started to salivate a bit as I walked past them smelling the corned beef and pastrami sandwiches that I'd looked forward to eating myself. Once outside, we glanced around quickly mindful that someone might still be trying to kill April, or possibly both of us. All appeared to be clear. We moved quickly to the car and started on our way. We were several blocks from the station when I broke the silence asking April where we were going and more importantly what did she find out. She informed me of her findings at the station. After hearing it, I understood her excitement over her discovery. I asked her again where we were headed for dinner, but she insisted that our destination remain a secret until we arrived.

Chapter 20
Guess Who's Coming to Dinner

We drove about fifteen blocks before pulling into the parking lot of an Italian restaurant. As soon as I walked through the front door and had a chance to survey some of the restaurants clientele, it became obvious why April wanted to keep our destination a secret. Had I known she was bringing us into a mob run restaurant, I wouldn't have let April out of the station. Before I knew it, April had marched past the maître d into the main eating area of the restaurant. The maître d started off in pursuit of April to stop her. Before he got too far, I grabbed his shoulder to get his attention. After showing him my badge, I hastened my pace, catching up with April just as she approached a secluded table in the back left corner of the restaurant. I wasn't familiar with the men sitting at the table, but I'd be willing to bet a year's salary that one of them was the mob boss, Joseph Beninni. As April and I approached, I could see that the men stationed at either side of the table conspicuously moved their hands inside their jackets. It must have been their less than subtle way of announcing that they were packing guns. They were obviously not deterred by my Bureau badge, or April's police uniform. "I want to speak with your boss," April insisted. The men stood their ground not giving an inch to April. At the center of the table sat a well-manicured, well-groomed, and well-dressed man. He appeared to be in his mid-fifties. His black hair was swept towards the back of his head and his upper lip adorned by a pencil thin mustache. Based on his features, there was little doubt of his Italian descent and even less doubt regarding his identity.

"Mr. Beninni" I said in a tone that demanded his attention, "we would like a moment of your time to discuss something that you might find of great interest. It's something that you might want to hear in private."

I noticed one of the henchmen reaching towards me and my martial arts training kicked into gear. Grabbing his arm I put him into an arm bar, kneed him in the gut, and propelled him head first into the wall. As I turned, I caught a glimpse of the other body guard moving towards me and was ready to throw a back fist to his head when he was stopped dead in his tracks by one-hundred and fifty thousand volts discharged by April's stun gun.

"I love these things," she said with a big grin on her face. She then turned and pointed it in the direction of the men that were seated.

As they stood up and started to move towards us, I yelled out "Hypnotist". It obviously struck a nerve with Beninni. He quickly motioned his henchmen to stand down. He then quickly dispatched them from the area, allowing both April and I to approach the table without any further resistance.

"Sit down," he said pointing to the chairs directly across from where he was sitting. "So what's the reason for this intrusion of my dinner?"

April was chomping at the bit to respond, but I motioned to her to let me handle the conversation.

"Allow me to introduce ourselves," I said as I held my badge up. "My name is Detective Bennett Mills of the FBI, and this is Officer April Lynch of the Phoenix Police Department".

I watched for a reaction, but as I expected it was clear that he already knew who we were.

"And what's so important that you would keep me from my Veal Marsala?" he replied as he gestured towards his plate.

"Three of your men tried to kill myself and Officer Lynch. One is in the morgue with two bullets in his chest, and the other two are still having their charred remains collected off the desert floor by the Phoenix police forensic team. Oh, and I'd be remiss if I didn't mention the three Mexican goons that tried to ambush my friend and wound up with an SUV parked on top of them." I continued on in an elevated voice "We want you to call off your gorillas now!"

He swallowed a piece of veal he had put in his mouth while I was speaking and followed up with a sip from his wine glass.

"And why would I be involved in such a thing?" he retorted with a contrived look of bewilderment on his face.

"Save us the theatrics," I said, "This is what you're going to do."

"You're going to call off the hit on us before we leave the restaurant. If you don't, Officer Lynch and I are going to make a little visit to the DA's office and have a talk with him. I have a feeling that after our conversation, he might decide to initiate an investigation into the murder of your old boss by one of his trusted associates."

Beninni started to open his mouth, but before he could say a word I continued. "It was very clever of you having the hypnotist use one of your old boss's inside men to pull the trigger on him, and then conveniently put a bullet in his own mouth. How did you get him to the hypnotist? To stop his smoking or drinking, or maybe to deal with the little weight problem I heard he had".

Beninni tried to bluff me, but I could tell that I had unnerved him a bit.

"This is a very imaginative story that you've concocted, but I can assure you that I had nothing to do with the killing of my old boss, may he rest in peace. Nor was I involved in the attack on you and this beautiful young lady. So, why don't you leave my establishment before I have you escorted out," he said in a stern tone.

I could tell that April wanted to dive across the table and start hitting him after the "beautiful young lady" comment, but she managed to restrain herself.

"Okay," I responded, "let's try this one. I plan on spreading the word to all of your fellow goons that you had your old boss and his sidekick murdered. I'm sure they would be interested in hearing about the deal you made with our hypnotist friend to help him out in return for the favor. I think the three bodies of the men you sent to kill Officer Lynch and me should help lend credibility to the story. Once the word gets out, it won't be too be long before some of your very pissed off friends put together a plan to replace you." I observed the smug look on his face disappear as I continued. "Unless of course, you are willing to listen to reason and call off the hit".

Beninni in an inquisitive tone responded, "Not that I would be involved in anything you've accused me of, but if someone was, how would they know that you would keep your word?"

"If I put you away, there is just going to be another low life standing in line to take your place. I personally don't give a damn if you kill each other off. But this lunatic is killing innocent people, and I'm going bring him to justice dead or alive, with or without your help." I replied.

Beninni put down his wine class and nodded his head. It was clear that we had come to an agreement that was in both of our best interests. As April and I got up from the table, Beninni got up as well and extended his hand to seal the deal. I had no desire to shake his hand, so I didn't.

"Just to make sure you don't have a change of heart, keep in mind that I've documented this information. If anything should happen to either of us, the information will make it into the hands of several of your associates." I said as we walked toward the door.

We weren't more than fifty feet outside of the restaurant when April gave me a big hug.

"You were great!" she said.

"Thanks," I responded.

Why do you look so depressed?" April asked.

"I didn't get to eat anything and I'm starved," I replied.

April said, "Now that it looks like it is safe to go back to my apartment, how about stopping at the store. I can pick up a few items and I'll cook up some dinner for the two of us?"

As hungry as I was, the offer of a home cooked meal at April's apartment was tempting enough to fend off my hunger a bit longer. We stopped at a food market just off of Interstate-10. April wanted the meal to be a surprise, so she had me stay in the car while she shopped. While I was waiting, I reflected on the progress we had made with the case. Although it appeared that we had made some headway, with Dr. H's identity still unknown, we were far from being able to pat ourselves on the backs. It had been a few hours since I had heard from either Bob or Web. I assumed that they had nothing new to tell me and more than likely called it a day. As tired as you can get when working a case like this, at times you have to force yourself to take a break, remembering that this is a marathon and not a sprint. With that said, it isn't always easy to do when you consider that several vets are still out there wandering the streets under the influence of this lunatic. It's difficult for me to imagine what is going through the minds of their families right now. It's not like these vets are thousands of miles away in Iraq or Afghanistan anymore. They came back from the war alive. Their family's worries about them being in danger should be something of the past, Yet their loved ones have disappeared without a trace or explanation.

April got back into the car, putting the bag temporarily between our two seats. When I leaned over in an effort to sneak a peek into the bag, she quickly closed the bag.

"I told you it was a surprise," she said as she gave me a gentle tap on the head.

"Police brutality," I said with a smile.

April leaned over and gave me a long kiss. "Are you going to report me now?" she asked playfully.

Suddenly dinner was the last thing on my mind.

"Report what?" I asked.

We pulled out of the parking lot of the shopping center heading for April's apartment. Even though she did not say it, I could tell by her demeanor that she was relieved not to be looking over her shoulder for someone trying to kill her. Slightly dazed and perhaps distracted by our last kiss, it seemed like only a minute before we arrived at April's apartment. We navigated the steps leading up to her floor, opened the door, and she carried the groceries into the kitchen.

"Do you need any help in there?" I inquired.

"I thought you said you can't cook," April replied.

"I figured maybe I could pick up a few tips on how to not burn my food," I quipped. "Besides, I need something to get my mind off of that last kiss".

"I think there's a cosmetic surgery reality show on at this time," she suggested.

"Thanks, but no thanks," I responded in a sarcastic tone as I proceeded to sit down on the couch.

While the couch was comfy for sitting on, it was not as comfortable for sleeping on as I discovered a couple of nights ago. I was hoping that I wouldn't be sleeping there tonight. Although the aromas emanating from the kitchen were fantastic, I still couldn't figure out what April was preparing for dinner. All I could discern was that it involved a lot of clanking of pans, dishes and silverware. About fifteen minutes after the process had started, April announced that dinner was served. She directed me to sit at a small bistro table situated in the corner of her small eat-in kitchen. A few minutes later April set two plates on the table, one in front of me and one on the opposite side of the table. It looked like a Mexican omelet served with a side of wheat toast.

"I knew you were hungry, so I wanted to make something that was quick," she said. "I hope you're not disappointed."

"Looks great!" I said as I waited to dig in.

She smiled as she sat down and cut the omelet with the edge of her fork. I cut into mine and took a bite.

"Wow, this is amazing!" I said.

She seemed relieved that I liked it. As hungry as I was, I took my time eating to show her I was enjoying it rather than just woofing it down.

I was down to the last bite of my omelet and reaching for a drink, when out of nowhere April asked me a an unexpected question. "Why did you join the FBI?"

"Because the Hypnotist didn't want me on the DC Police anymore?" I replied have jokingly.

She gave me a serious look, and asked with even more determination "No. Really, why did you leave the DC Police Department? It sounds like you really enjoyed your job and trying to solve the tough cases. From what I've seen over the past few days, you're really good at it".

I thought for a second before I answered. I wasn't sure that at this point in our relationship it would be wise to let my guard down and give her the real reason. Then, I figured what the hell. I told her that after I was promoted to detective, I was determined to prove to my father that I was every bit as good a cop as he was. I wanted to show him that I could build a reputation on my own rather than living in his shadow by joining the force in Phoenix. I found myself spending more and more time at work solving cases, until one day it seemed like work had become my life rather than just being a part of it."

"Is that why you left?" she inquired.

"Partly," I said, "but even when the offer came through for the FBI, I was still considering turning it down. Then, my partner was killed in a freak car accident a couple of days before I had to give the Bureau my answer. He was a great partner and a good friend. I still miss him. After that, I guess I just re-evaluated what I wanted in life. It didn't seem that important anymore that I prove myself to my father. I waited until after my partner's funeral, and then turned in my badge and gun. I started with the Bureau two weeks later never looking back."

April reached across the table and took my hand into hers. She stood up drawing me out of my chair and then led me by the hand down the hall to her bedroom. I didn't have to be a detective to know where this was going.

"Are you sure about this?" I asked knowing what I wanted the answer to be.

"Yes," she replied as we entered the bedroom and she closed the door behind her.

Chapter 21

The Morning After

I woke up and looked towards the windows to see the bright sunlight peeking around the sides of the drawn shades. I leaned over to look at the time on my phone and realized that I had turned it off. April had an alarm clock sitting on her night stand. It was only eight o'clock, but I felt compelled to get up and start the day. I had to get my bag out of the car, grab a shower, and get back to working on the case. April was still sound asleep. I laid in bed for a few minutes wondering if things would be awkward between us after last night, but I had a feeling that it wouldn't be. I hung my legs over the bed. Before standing up I turned to glance at April as she slept. I realized that my glance became a long gaze. What would she think if she woke up to find me staring at her? Would she like it? Or would it creep her out? I decided that rather than risk that potentially uncomfortable moment, I would quietly get out of bed and move into the den. It was still pretty dark in the room so I stumbled about for a couple of minutes until I was able to locate my clothes. I quickly put on my pants and grabbed my shirt, socks and shoes as I quietly crept out of the bedroom. Closing the door behind me, I headed down the hall towards the den buttoning my shirt on the way. As I approached the end of the hall, I looked to my left and was startled to see Lynch sitting on the couch. Startled might have been an understatement. It was probably more like how Beninni's henchman felt last night after April had zapped him with one-hundred & fifty thousand volts.

"What are you doing here?" I asked in a surprised tone as I quickly started to tuck my shirt into my pants.

Lynch replied in an annoyed tone "That's exactly the same question I was planning on asking you. But, by the looks of things, I guess I don't need to ask it."

He continued, "And if your next question happened to be how did I find you. The answer is if you don't want to be found, don't drive a police car with a built-in tracking device."

"I'll try to keep that in mind in the future," I replied trying to introduce some poorly received levity into the situation.

Lynch snubbed my comment and continued "When you didn't come back to the ranch or Jenna's house last night, I got worried that you ran into some more trouble. I had a friend of mine track the car back to the apartment."

"Being April's father," he said emphasizing each word as he spoke them, "naturally I have a set of keys to the apartment. I hope that that covers all of your questions, and by the way you might want to zipper your pants."

Before I finished zippering my pants, I heard the bedroom door open followed by the tapping of April's feet racing down the hall "Bennett, FYI. My dad texted me around 2am asking where we were. He might come by the apartment looking..."

"Too late," I said gesturing for April to look at the couch. I was grateful that April had put on a robe before running out, or that would have been an even more awkward moment than when she came down the stairs the other day in her nightie.

"Hi dad," she said. Her mortified expression spoke volumes. She was obviously grasping for what she would say next, but nothing appeared to be coming to mind.

"I think I'm going to go down to the car and get my bag so I can get some fresh clothes. I'll leave the two of you alone to talk," I said.

April looked over to me and mouthed what appeared to be the word "coward". As I started for the door, Lynch held up an envelope.

"It looks like I wasn't the only one that figured out where you were. I found this note from your friend, the hypnotist, tucked under the apartment door".

He was obviously using the word friend sarcastically. His disclosure of the new note however stopped me dead in my tracks.

"What did he say?" I asked as I reached for the envelope that Lynch held in his hand.

"I don't know", Lynch said, "the letter was addressed to you and I'm not one to invade a person's privacy."

That seemed funny coming from Lynch, considering he had done just that, by entering April's apartment unannounced this morning. He could have knocked on the door before entering the apartment. But after getting to know Lynch over the past few days, I realized it just wasn't his style. Lynch placed the letter into my outreached hand. Considering the care that the hypnotist had taken with the first letter to obscure his identity, I knew that it wasn't worth the effort of having it fingerprinted or checked for DNA again. This time, I just tore open the envelope and pulled out the letter without giving it a second thought.

"To my dear friend Bennett," I had to pause to force down the bile that rose in my throat. It was sickening to have him refer to me as his dear friend. "I have underestimated you thus far in your ability to track me down, but you haven't found me yet. Be forewarned that many of my patients are still at large, and like a time bomb that has been activated, if not deactivated will eventually go off. If you persist in trying to capture me, you may have more blood on your hands than you can live with. Remember, I'm always watching you." The letter was signed like the first "Do as I say."

I could see April was a bit shaken to know that while we were in the bedroom that this son of a bitch was just twenty feet away from us.

"How did he know we were in the apartment? " She asked.

"I'll let your father fill you in on that one while I get my clothes from the car," I replied as I started moving towards the door. "It looks like we need to push even harder to get those missing vets into custody, and to find that case that I was working on when I crossed paths with Dr. H," I said.

I stepped out of the apartment and walked down the stairs leaving April and her dad to have a father-daughter conversation that I wanted no part in. I got down to the car and was ready to unlock the trunk when I decided it might be a wise precaution to move back a hundred feet or so and use the remote release button instead. Maybe I was getting paranoid, but I had no idea when or if this nut was going to consider the debt he spoke of as repaid. Maybe I'd end up being blown up like Chuck the mechanic was. Fortunately, the trunk opened and the car was still in one piece. I flipped the trunk open the rest of the way, grabbed my bag, and walked back up to the apartment. April was in the kitchen making a fresh pot of coffee when I walked back into the apartment. I was starting to head for the guest bathroom to take a shower and get dressed when Lynch called me over to the couch. I was cautious as I approached him, not knowing if he had any plans to punch me in the face when I got to within reach or not.

"You're not going to punch me are you?" I asked partly in jest.

"No, not for now at least," he responded, showing no signs that he meant it jokingly.

I wasn't particularly comforted by his response, but I sat down on couch next to him anyway.

"What were you doing at Beninni's restaurant last night?" he asked.

"How did you know about that?" I asked, and immediately answered my own question. "The GPS in the car."

I explained to Lynch that April tricked me into thinking that we were just going to get something to eat. It wasn't until we were inside the restaurant and April was charging towards Beninni's table that I realized where we were.

"That sounds like my daughter alright. Just like her mother," he whispered, "when she had her mind set on something, there was no way of stopping her."

I told him about what we discovered regarding the link between the hypnotist and Beninni. And that even though we had no hard evidence to prove Beninni's involvement in his boss's murder, it was enough to scare him into backing off from any further attempts to kill us.

"The first two attempts to kill April were at the request of the hypnotist to cover-up his identity. After that, it was all about Beninni avenging the death of the hit man that we killed at the motel," I said.

Lynch's demeanor changed from anger over what he perceived as a reckless visit to the restaurant to one of relief, knowing that for the moment his daughter was no longer being targeted by either Dr. H., or Beninni.

"We have a lot to do today. I better get showered and dressed," I said.

"Have you heard from Web yet today?" I asked.

"No, but he told me he would call us when he had some information," Lynch responded.

I got up off the couch and headed for the shower with a change of clothes in hand. I knew that it was going to be another long day. Hopefully, with any luck if we could find his relative in that list of sixteen platoon members that served with my uncle, we might have his name before the end of the day. I was getting real tired of calling him the hypnotist, Dr. H., not to mention several other colorful metaphors.

I got out of the shower and dressed. It felt good to be able to take a shower with hot water. The other day all of the hot water had been depleted by our houseguests at the ranch. Now, all I needed was a cup of coffee before I would be ready to take on the world, or at least this maniac. April followed my lead and had jumped into the shower while the coffee was peculating. She was still getting dressed for the day when I walked into the kitchen. I grabbed a cup off the counter and filled it to the rim with coffee. I took a big swig, nearly burning my mouth, as I headed for the couch where Lynch was still sitting with the letter in his hand. He seemed to be in a bit of a trance himself. I wasn't sure if he was thinking about the case, or the fact that April and I slept together. "What's up?" I asked as I sat down taking another swallow of my coffee. "Web just called," he said, "They have one of the missing vets in custody".

"That's great," I replied, "How did they find him?" I asked.

"They didn't," Lynch said, "he found us. He just walked into the Phoenix VA hospital in a somewhat confused state looking for a doctor.

"Where was he all this time?" I asked.

"According to Web, the last thing the vet remembered was the phone ringing at his house and going to pick-up the call. The next thing he knew, he was sitting in a theatre watching a movie. He had no idea where he was or what he was doing there," Lynch said, "and one more thing. When he showed up at the VA hospital, he surrendered a semi-automatic fully loaded."

"Was it his? I asked.

"He had no idea how he came into procession of it, and no idea what he was supposed to do with it. My guess is that his being in a movie theatre wasn't a coincidence," Lynch replied.

"It looks like our hypnotist wasn't kidding when he equated the missing vets to time bombs waiting to go off." I said. "We have to find the remaining missing vets before any more innocent people are hurt."

I had planned to meet Web downtown at the precinct around 11am so we could debrief each other on the details of the case. Based on what Lynch had just told me, I wanted to, scratch that, I needed to make an excursion to the VA hospital. This would be the first chance we had to speak with one of Dr. H's patients and I wasn't going to let that opportunity pass. I placed a call to the hospital. After a few minutes of being passed around from one office to the next, I finally was able to track down Dr. Rodriguez. He told me that he had a late morning meeting, but if I could get there right-away he would make time for me. I thanked him for agreeing to meet on such short notice and told him I would be heading over now.

I told Lynch I needed to get going now if I was going to make the appointment.

"Can you and April meet me at the station in a two hours?" I asked.

"Can do," he responded.

I started to head towards the door with the keys to the police car in hand when Lynch stopped me.

"You know you're not authorized to drive that vehicle," Lynch said.

"So I've been told," I responded.

Lynch took his car keys out of his pocket and tossed them to me.

"Take my car," he said.

In exchange, I threw him the keys to the police car. As I started down the steps to the car, I thought about how much I hated running out on April like this. I wanted to talk to her about last night, but with her father's heart stopping surprise visit, there just wasn't the opportunity. If she had been dressed, I would have taken her with me to the hospital. With the small window of opportunity to meet with Rodriguez, I couldn't take the chance of waiting. I had the feeling that things were copasetic between us. However, it would have been nice to hear her say it. I just hoped she didn't take my running out on her as an indication that I was running from her. Because nothing would have been further from the truth. I realized after I was outside that Lynch had neglected to tell me where the car was parked. I ran up and down the street a couple of times before I finally found the car. It had been obscured by a double parked delivery truck which I quickly dispatched with a wave of my badge. I then hopped into the car and pulled away from the curb heading for the hospital.

It took about fifteen minutes to arrive at my destination, giving me plenty of time to meet with the good doctor before his meeting. I stopped at the reception desk to announce my arrival and to get a visitors pass. The receptionist directed me to Dr. Rodriguez office on the seventh floor. During the brief elevator ride it had occurred to me that Rodriguez was being considerably more cooperative than during our last encounter when I threatened to feed him to the IRS. I wondered if that reflected a better understanding of why we were so desperate to solve this mystery, or if he was just trying to avoid that IRS audit. After exiting the elevator, I checked in at the 7th floor reception area where I was guided to an office at the end of the corridor. It wasn't a particularly impressive office, but I guess as a public servant you seldom live the life of luxury that you might in the equivalent private sector job.

Dr. Rodriguez stood up as I entered the room and reached over the desk to shake my hand. We both started to talk at the same time. It appeared we were both interested in apologizing for the less then cordial ending of our last encounter. We kept the apologies brief realizing that we had more important things to worry about at the moment.

"So, what do you think happened to our vet?" I asked as I shifted my chair closer to the desk.

"I interviewed the patient for a couple of hours," he said as he flipped open a folder on his desk. "Based on his responses, it was pretty evident that he had been under hypnotic suggestion. He had no recollection from the moment he answered the phone in his house until when he came out of it in the movie theatre. He could have done anything during that time and he would have been oblivious to it."

"Anything else?" I asked.

"Yes," he replied, "He told me that a couple of months ago he started having bouts with insomnia. Shortly after the onset of the insomnia, he had a ninety day supply of Imovane delivered to his mailbox. There was a note in with the pills that said from a friend."

"Like the other vets," I said.

Rodriguez explained that it was not uncommon for the drug to be prescribed for people suffering from sleep disorders. However, another use of the drug was to assist in the process of hypnotism.

"How did he get the vets to blindly take a prescription that they received in the mail?" I asked.

Rodriquez theorized that the vets took it because they were told to by the hypnotist.

"He must have been using a low level of hypnotic suggestion that did not require them to be on the drug," he suggested.

"But for more significant suggestions like doing harm to themselves and other people..." I started saying when I was cut off by Rodriguez. "For more significant suggestions, he needed them to be under prolonged use of the drug."

"So, if he was that deeply under hypnotic suggestion, why did he all of a sudden snap out of it in the middle of a movie?" I asked.

"It's simple," he replied. "just like a hypnotherapist might use a phrase to put a patient under hypnosis, another phrase would be used to bring him out of hypnosis."

"A phrase?" I asked as I shifted forward in my seat.

"Yes," he responded, "We wouldn't want to use a word, or for that matter a common phrase that a patient may come across in their daily lives. If we did, then we might risk them being accidentally put under hypnosis. If that happened, the results could be disastrous."

"So the phrase could've been a line in the movie?" Or maybe something said by someone sitting nearby him in the theatre?" I suggested.

"Yes, yes!" Rodriguez said, nearly jumping out of his seat.

"Do you know what movie he was seeing?" I asked with a great sense of urgency.

"I don't know. But he did say the theatre was on West 3rd and the movie was some type of documentary," he replied.

I thanked Dr. Rodriguez for the information and was heading for the door when he called my name.

"Agent Mills, do you really have a friend at the IRS?"

I replied with a smirk on my face, "Does anyone have a friend at the IRS?" I could see the beginning of a smile appear on his face before turning to head towards the door.

"Didn't you want to talk to the Vet?" he called out.

"Maybe later," I responded. "I have a movie to catch."

I called April's apartment to see if she'd left for the precinct yet. When she answered the phone, I wanted to tell her what a great time I had last night, but there was no time for that. Instead, I asked her to have her father inform Web that we might be a couple of hours late for our meeting at the precinct. When she asked why, I told her I'd explain during the ride to the movie theater.

"Have you left the apartment yet?" I asked.

"No, we were just getting ready to leave," she replied.

"Don't leave, I'll be there in ten minutes to pick you up if you're ready," I said trying to catch my breath after running all the way to the car.

"Isn't this a strange time to be catching a movie?" she asked in an inquisitive tone.

"I'll explain in the car, just look out for me and if you can bring something to eat that would be great," I said, "I'm starving and I don't want to have popcorn for breakfast".

I hung up the phone and started heading for the apartment. I pulled up in front of the building's entrance. Within a minute April came out of the front door with a brown bag in her hand hopping into the passenger seat.

"I grabbed a muffin and a cup of coffee for you," she said.

"You are the best" I said as I leaned over and gave her a peck on the cheek.

"We didn't really get a chance to talk this morning about last night. Any regrets?" she asked in an noticeably uneasy tone.

"No, none whatsoever," I responded without any hesitation.

"You?" I asked.

She smiled "Nope." And without skipping a beat asked "What movie are we going to see and why?"

During the twenty minute ride to the theatre, I filled her in on my meeting with Rodriguez and told her that we were looking for a phrase that could be used to release Dr. H.'s victims from their hypnotic trance. We had no clue what the phrase might be, but if we figured it out, we might be able to defuse his human time bombs before they went off.

We arrived at the theatre two hours prior to its normal opening time. I called Riddle on my way to pick up April. I asked him to arrange for the manager to meet us in the theatre parking lot, and to make sure he would give us his full cooperation. If he resisted, Riddle was to tell him it was a matter of life and death. If that didn't work, he should just threaten an IRS audit. It was like the gift that just kept giving.

We parked in the lot behind the movie theater and within ten minutes of our arrival, the manager pulled up.

"Thank you for helping us out," I said.

"You threaten me with an IRS audit, and now your thanking me?" He replied.

"Didn't they tell you it was a matter of life and death?" I asked.

By the blank look on his face, it was obvious that Riddle had jumped the gun with the IRS threat. The manager opened the side door for us and asked us what movie we needed him to setup for a showing. According to the marquis, there was only one documentary playing in the theater. When we requested it, he responded by informing us that they were planning on pulling it at the end of the week due to its poor attendance. He led us to the theatre and told us he would setup the projector. I thanked him for private viewing, and he started to laugh.

"Even if you came during its regular playing you would probably have been watching it yourself," he said. "Last night, there was a guy that about a half hour into the second reel got up and walked out of the theatre. He didn't even know how he wound up here. That probably explains why he paid for a ticket to see this piece of junk".

I asked the manager if he saw the guy walk out, but he hadn't. He only knew about the incident because one of the ushers told him that the guy looked a bit disoriented and wanted to make sure he is okay. It sounded like it could have been our vet. Seeing how time was of the essence, I took a gamble by asking the manager if he could start the movie at the second reel.

While April and I sat waiting for the movie to start, she turned to me and said "I think my father likes you."

"How did you come to that conclusion?" I asked.

"You're still alive aren't you?" She said with a big smile, and then leaned over and gave me a kiss.

The lights in the theatre went out at that precise moment. I wasn't sure if the owner was trying to give us some privacy, or he was about to start the reel. A few seconds, later I had my answer when the movie began. After a few minutes of watching, it became apparent why the movie was doing so poorly. The only question I had was how anyone could have made it to the second reel in the first place, but then I realized our vet was in a trance. April and I tried to keep alert to any subtle phrases that might have woken him from his trance. When the phrase we had been waiting for was finally enunciated by the actor, there was no doubt in my mind that we'd discovered the magic phrase. "Do as I say, not as I do." Within seconds of hearing it, I yelled up to the manager that we had what we needed. He stopped the movie and turned on the lights before meeting us in the lobby. We thanked him again for his help, apologized for the miscommunications regarding the IRS audit, and promptly left the theatre heading for the precinct. April took the wheel while I placed a call to Dr. Rodriguez, providing him the phrase. He explained that in order to test our theory, we'd need to find a vet that was currently under the hypnotic trance. The vets we had in protective custody were taken prior to the hypnotist being able to put them under his influence. For them to be of any use, we would have needed the phrase that put them into the trance first.

"I have an idea on how we can test the phrase to take them out of the trance," I told him. "In the meantime, you might want to try just "Do as I say" as the phrase on one of your patients, but have a couple of guards standing by, just in case. I have a hunch that it is the expression to put them under."

Rodriguez told me he would give it a shot and call me back to confirm if it worked.

As soon as I hung up the phone with Rodriguez, I dialed Web. I told him I believed the phrase "Do as I say, not as I do" will bring the vets out of their hypnotic trance.

"We need to activate the cell phones for the remaining missing vets and have every agent available keep calling those cells until all the vets have been contacted. If the phrase works, instruct the vets to head right over to the VA hospital. Then turn off the phone again so that Dr. H. can't slip in a call before we get them into safe hands."

"I'll get right on it," Web replied.

"April and I should be at precinct in about ten minutes," I responded. "April's driving so I'll be keeping my fingers crossed that this works all the way there."

We arrived at the precinct and immediately headed for Riddles office. On our way, we passed the room we had been working in the night before and noticed Lynch and Web already sitting and waiting for our arrival. We stopped in our tracks and went into the conference room sitting on the opposite side of the conference table.

"I have one man assigned for each missing vet making the calls." Web told me. "Hopefully, we will know within the next hour if this is going to work or not. Lynch gave me a general update, but I'd like a complete update while we are waiting."

With the obvious omission of my romantic interlude with April, I proceeded to give Web a complete briefing on all of the events of last night that led up to our unplanned meeting with Beninni.

Although we had made some serious progress in the last twelve hours, it wasn't time to open the champagne yet. We still had to identify this madman and bring him to justice. As I finished my report, I sat anxiously waiting for any information that Web might be ready to divulge.

Web informed us that he still didn't have any results from the autopsy of the dead female analyst, but was hoping to hear from the coroner's office by early afternoon.

"Anything on the sixteen men that served with my uncle?" I asked.

"Yes, I spoke to Bob about an hour ago. So far they've only come up with two of the men that had relatives serving on the same base," he responded.

"And?" I said interrupting Web in mid-sentence.

"Relax, neither of them could be our man," he replied. "One was killed by a road side bomber in Iraq a couple of years ago, and the other ironically was one of the men in Dan Stone's platoon that had been ambushed, and killed in that mosque in Tikrit."

"How many names does that leave us with?" I asked.

"Only five names are still in play," he replied in a less than enthusiastic tone. "We should know if any of them had relatives serving on that base by the end of the day."

He didn't have to say it, we all knew that if none of those men turned out to be related to Dr. H., we were back to square one.

"Any good news?" I asked facetiously as I walked to the water cooler to get a drink.

"Actually, there is one piece of decent news," Web replied. "Bob's monitoring looks like it is starting to pay off."

I stopped in my tracks, turned around, and waited for Web expand on that comment.

"The inside guy helping the hypnotist," he said, "is not one of ours, he's CIA."

Bob told Web how he was able to figure out where the hack came from, but Web was quick to admit that the technical jargon Bob used, as usual, went way over his head.

"Are you bringing him in for questioning?" Lynch asked after a long moment of silence.

"No," Web responded. "Bob swore that he would be able to control the information flow. The only information that this CIA guy is going to see from us is what we want him to see".

"You mean misinformation?" Lynch responded.

"Exactly," Web replied as he stood up. "I'm going to check in with the office to see how we're doing on reaching out to the unaccounted for vets. Let's just hope they still have their phones on and that the phrase you gave us works.

Dr. H. was clearly planning to use the missing vets as leverage against us. Possibly even as bargaining chips, if we started to close in on him. Getting these men safely into custody would take those chips away, and allow us all to breath a lot easier. In the meantime, I needed to get back to reviewing my old cases. Although April and I did not get much sleep last night, I still felt like I was ready to take on the world. I was hoping that this new found energy might lead me to some success in finding the case that Dr. H. didn't want me to solve. Riddle was supposed to join us during our debriefing, but was held up on another case away from the precinct. He had called in to let us know that he was running late and not to wait for him. When he arrived back at the station, he stopped by and asked Lynch and April to come to his office so he could be filled in on our meeting, leaving Web and me alone in the conference room. Web made it clear that once he was informed that Beninni might be involved in the death of his old boss, that he became obligated to share that information with the local authorities. With April's and my safety hinging on Beninni thinking that we had a deal, I implored Web to sit on the information for a little while longer.

"At the moment all we have is a theory." I told Web, "If we can bring in the hypnotist alive, we might be able to squeeze the evidence we need out of him and put these dirt bags in adjoining cells."

"I'll see what I can do to get Riddle to sit on it for a few days," Web said.

I hadn't given thought to the fact that as we sat in the room talking, that Lynch and April were updating Riddle about what we had found on Beninni.

"I'm sure he will go along with it. As you said, all we have is a theory. Beninni is too smart of a character to take down without hard evidence," Web said as he rose from his chair.

Web started heading towards the door when he paused, turned around, and said "I think Lynch likes you".

I wasn't sure if he was talking about April or her father. "April?" I asked.

"No," he replied "Ed. If he didn't, you'd be walking around on crutches right now".

I assumed he was talking about my spending last night with April.

"I'll stop by Riddle's office and ask him to hold off on doing anything until he speaks to one of us," Web said, and then walked out of the conference room closing the door behind him.

It just struck me that I hadn't called my folks since early yesterday. I grabbed an outside line and dialed the number. My father picked up the phone. I explained that it had been a late night, and with everything going on I had forgotten to call in. It seemed weird having to check in with my family since when I was in DC I could go a week or more without calling the house. But things had certainly changed in the past week. Speaking to my dad was no longer something I had dreaded. My father asked me if we had any luck tracking down the hypnotist using the names of my uncle's old platoon members. I told him that of the sixteen names, there were only a handful that we still needed to check on, but so far we were coming up empty. My father repeated his assertion that he was sure there were seventeen names. He might be right, but if the hypnotist was one step ahead of us and had the name removed from the database, then we'd hit a dead end. I promised my father that I'd stop by the ranch sometime later that day and asked him to apologize to my mother and sister for not being around as much. He told me not to worry about them and to just focus on catching the SOB. I said goodbye and turned toward the computer screen. It was time to get back to reviewing my old cases.

About twenty minutes passed, when April entered the conference room carrying two cups of coffee. "I love you," I said referring to her timely arrival with the coffee. As soon as the words left my mouth I realized that after last night that it might be misconstrued. April saw the panic in my eyes and started laughing.

"Don't worry," she said, "I knew what you meant".

I smiled in response feeling a sense of relief as I did. It wasn't that I didn't have strong feelings for April, but I wasn't one to use those words in a cavalier fashion.

"Anything yet?" she asked.

"No," I replied. "I'm just hoping that the case is still in the system."

April excused herself so that she could take care of some paperwork that built up over the last few days. I told her I'd let her know if anything turned up. She leaned over, gave me a kiss and started walking towards the door.

"You know," I said, "after that kiss, it is going to take me a few minutes before I can start working again".

She turned, smiled and said "Only a few?" and continued out the door.

Chapter 22

An Awkward Situation

An hour had passed before April returned to the conference room. "Bennett, do you want to get lunch?"

"Are you asking me out on a date?" I asked.

"Only if you're paying," she responded. "Remember, I got the last meal."

I agreed that lunch would be on me, but only if she was willing to let me get through one last case before we left to eat. April agreed, and without hesitation plunked herself down in the seat to the left of me.

I opened the next file on the screen and began reviewing the case. A few minutes later, I turned to April and said "This is very strange."

"What?" April asked.

I responded, "This case was marked as closed, but there's no record of anybody being arrested or prosecuted."

As I started reviewing the details, I wanted to kick myself for not remembering it earlier. It was definitely one of the strangest cases I had come across during my time on the force. April, seeing the intensity in my eyes, pulled her chair up alongside mine and began reading the case file while I re-familiarized myself with the details. A woman called in a shooting that she'd observed from the window of her second floor apartment. Her view was of an alley behind a singles bar. She observed a blonde woman and two men talking in the alley. At the time, she assumed the blonde and her male friend were looking to purchase drugs. Having observed similar transactions in that alley on several other occasions, it seemed like a reasonable conclusion. Based on the her account, it appeared that after a few minutes of discussion between the two men, an argument broke out and each man drew a gun. The man that appeared to have been in the company of the blonde had his gun knocked from his hands by the other man. The two men struggled, falling to the ground. Within a matter of seconds, the other gun went off. As the presumed dealer pushed the other man's body off of him and started to get up from the ground, the women retrieved her friend's gun and pointed it at the alleged dealer. According to the witness, the dealer started walking towards the woman and she discharged two shots into his chest. The man fell to the ground, and the blonde took off into the shadows of the alley taking the gun with her. The woman observing the crime was badly shaken by what she had witnessed, but managed to run to her phone and dial 911. At a cursory view, nothing seemed particularly unusual about this crime. During my time with the DC Police Department I must have come across a dozen of cases where a drug deal went wrong. In most cases, the buyer was dead, stripped of his money and other valuables and the dealer would hit the road. This case was anything but typical. The first odd thing about it was when the woman returned to the window after calling the police, the bodies of the two men were in different positions than when she had left to make the call. She also mentioned that strangely enough she did not notice much blood around the bodies when she went to make the call. However, when she returned her window the two men were lying in pools of blood. When the police arrived on the scene and talked to the woman, they asked if she would submit to a sobriety test. Her account of what happened seemed inconsistent with what the police had observed. We wanted to make sure she wasn't impaired in anyway. She indicated that both men were shot at close range and were facing the person that pulled the trigger. Yet the autopsy showed that one man was shot in the back and the other in the chest. According to the autopsy, neither man was shot at close range. The ballistics report showed that both men were killed by rifle shots. Based on the angle of entry and the location where the shells were recovered, it was clear that the shots were fired from an elevated position, most likely the roof of the brownstone adjacent to the witness's apartment building. As if this wasn't strange enough, blanks were recovered from the area that the woman had initially indicated the men had fallen. Gunpowder residue was found across the shirt of the first victim, as if a blank was fired across the body of that victim and not into him. When the victim's clothes were removed for the autopsy, plastic capsules were found with what appeared to be remnants of fake blood. I stopped reading, turned to April, and told her that when I first read the file, all I could think of was a movie I had seen on TV. In the film, two men setup a gangster by making it appear that one of the men shot and killed the other for helping the gangster win a bet. The gangster is forced to abandon his money to avoid being implicated in the killing. After the gangster flees the scene the two men walk away with the loot. The men had used blanks and fake blood in their ruse.

When I started investigating the two dead men, I was shocked at how close I had come to hitting the mark. Both men turned out to be part time actors that were attending the same acting school. Neither one of them had been able to make much of a living as actors, yet they each had approximately a thousand dollars—in hundred dollar bills—on their bodies. Based on how the blonde reacted by running away with the gun, it seemed clear that she was supposed to be the patsy. But the question is, what did they want from her? And who really killed the two men with the rifle, and why? It appeared that there might have been three people setup that night and two of them paid with their lives. But what was the woman's part in all this? April seemed as intrigued by the peculiarity of the case as I had been several years ago. Then in a sudden flash, it came back to me. One of the victims had a card on him from the office of a local hypnotherapist. I remember going to his home on the fringes of Southeastern University to question him and having him indicate that he didn't have a clue who the victim was, or why he was in possession of one of his business cards.

"My God, that must have been Dr. H," I yelled, as I banged my fist on the table.

I started feverishly looking through the photos and other evidence, but I couldn't find any images of the business card. Just when I thought I was going to come up empty again, I saw something in the file that caused me to stop dead in my tracks. It was an image from an ATM camera that captured the side profile of a blonde woman that matched the description we got from our witness. She was obviously aware of the camera because as she approached it, she put her arm up to help obstruct the view of her face. What had caught my interest was what she was wearing around her lower arm. It was a huge gold bracelet in the shape of a snake. When I saw the bracelet when I first viewed the photo years ago, it meant nothing to me. But now, it seemed so familiar. I had seen a bracelet just like that it, or was it the same bracelet? Even though I was unable to see the women's face, her other features were as familiar as the bracelet itself.

I turned to April, "Would you mind taking a rain check on our lunch?" I asked.

"Sure. You look like you've seen a ghost, is everything alright?" she responded.

"Perhaps the ghost of Christmas past," I said. "I can't explain right now, but can you do me a favor," I asked.

"Sure," April responded, "What do you need?"

"Can you work with Riddle to see if DC police can find the evidence box on this case?" I asked. "I'm looking for a business card of a hypnotherapist".

"Our hypnotist?" April asked.

"Yes, Bill indicated in his letter that the hypnotist had mentioned to him that we'd met when I was with the DC police department. Now, I know when we met, and I think I know why he wanted me away from this case. I'll try to get back as soon as possible. Would you mind having dinner with me at the ranch tonight?"

April responded, "Sure, but that doesn't get you off the hook. I'm still expecting you to take me out. Where are you going anyway?"

"Can't tell you at the moment, but if anything comes from this you will be the first, or maybe the second to know," I replied as I left the conference room.

I passed Lynch in the hall and asked if I could borrow his car. He asked me if I was taking April with me, I responded no. He reached into his pocket and tossed me the keys that I had returned to him only a few hours ago. I really had to talk to Web about getting a company vehicle, this borrowing cars stuff was getting really old.

I headed into the parking lot and got into the car. It had been a few years, but I was pretty sure I still knew my way to her Phoenix home. Would she be there? If she was, would she want to see Bennett Mills, or would Agent Mills of the FBI have to insist on a conversation with her? The bracelet in the picture was the same one that I had seen her wear on several occasions when we were dating. The bracelet in that photo belonged to Hope.

I had a feeling that I wouldn't receive a warm welcome after the way our relationship ended. Even if the conversation was cordial at first, it would not remain that way for long. Once I start to insinuate the possibility of her involvement in a double homicide, I knew it was going to get ugly.

I remembered what Fred and Mike had told me at the bar about how Hope had gone through a rough period just before my joining the FBI. Apparently, she was always getting into some type of trouble, then she turned on a dime and straightened herself out. Was it coincidental, or did the events of that night behind the bar scare her straight?

Web called me while en route to Hope's home to deliver the bad news to me. We'd come up empty once again. They finished checking the remaining five names on the list, and none of the men had relatives serving on my uncle's base. Web also confirmed my suspicions regarding the analyst's death. It wasn't suicide, the coroner found the same poison in her system that was found in Bill's. Another death to be attributed to this lunatic.

"Where are you heading?" Web asked.

"What do you mean?" I responded.

"I thought the question was pretty clear," Web replied sounding a bit annoyed that I had evaded answering the question the first time.

I knew he wasn't going to be happy, but I had to risk his wrath. I wasn't ready to implicate Hope until I had some concrete proof.

"I know you're not going to like this," I said, "but I can't answer that question at the moment."

I was surprised by his response. He told me that I'd earned a free pass for the moment, but I better be ready to provide him with some answers when we spoke later this afternoon.

I felt guilty withholding information from him, but I expected some absolution for the information I was about to tell him.

"Web," I said, "I found the case where I had met the hypnotist."

There was silence on the phone, "Web?"

"I heard you kid." he responded, "Go ahead."

"It was a homicide case I had worked on just before I came over to the FBI. One of the victims had a business card of a doctor that specialized in hypnotism. Can you believe that I actually interviewed this maniac in his home?"

"Do you remember where he lived?" Web asked.

"No, just the general area," I replied. "I have April reaching out to the DC police department to see if they can track down the business card in the evidence room. She's supposed to call me as soon as she hears back from them. Keep your fingers crossed that the card is still in with the rest of the evidence".

Web responded, "Based on what I've seen so far, it will take a lot more than crossing my fingers for that evidence to still be there."

"Got to go," I replied, "I'll call you in a couple of hours, and hopefully, I'll have something to tell you then."

I hung up the phone as I turned onto Hope's street. I'd forgotten how ritzy the neighborhood was and how big the homes were. This neighborhood boasted some of the most affluent and influential residents in the city of Phoenix. I could tell by the activity around her house that Hope was in the residence. I drove by the house and parked across the street. Lynch's car stuck out like a sore thumb in this neighborhood. My guess was that every car on the block would cost me a year's salary. As I approached the house, a couple of body guards walked to the end of the driveway to intercept me. Knowing that most body guards were prone to overreacting, I placed my badge hanging out of my front pocket before getting out of the car. I figured that if I tried to pull it out of my pocket after getting out of the car that I might wind up getting shot or bludgeoned before I had a chance to say anything.

"What can we do for you officer?" said the larger of the two guards.

"I'm here to see Ms. Billings" I responded.

"Do you have an appointment?" he replied.

I told him that I was here on official business, and asked him to let Hope know that I was waiting to see her. As the guard turned around and headed for the house, I heard a familiar voice from behind me. I turned around, and to my surprise, I was standing face to face with Fred and Mike.

"What are you doing here?" I asked as I extended my arm to shake their hands.

"Hopefully getting a private security job. Hope called us shortly after she was offered her father's seat in the senate and asked us if we were interested in coming to work for her." Fred responded.

"What are you doing here?" Fred asked, "I thought you were on vacation, but by the expression on your face and that big beautiful badge dangling from your pocket this looks official."

I responded, "Even if it was, you know that I couldn't be giving out information to a couple of civilians. Let's just say that I'm here to pay my respects and leave it at that."

I didn't want to mention Bill's death to them, although it was difficult to withhold that information seeing how we were all friends. I asked them where they were staying and gave them my cell number and wished them luck. The guard returned and directed me to follow him into the house. As soon as I walked through the door I had flashbacks of my first visit to the Billing's home. Not much had changed. The guard escorted me into the study just off of the entranceway. The guard informed me that Hope would be with me shortly and to take a seat. The study was the most impressive room of the house. The furnishings were all antique, and the walls were adorned with historic photos depicting the best and worst times that our country had seen. It was where the Senator had spent most of his time when he was away from his offices on Capitol Hill. I was so captivated by my surroundings that I didn't notice that Hope had entered the room until she cleared her throat to announce her presence.

I turned around and tried to break the ice by bringing up my encounter with Mike and Fred in the driveway. Before I could finish my first sentence, Hope interrupted me using a punitive tone I'd encountered many times throughout our relationship. It was clear that this was going to be an encounter of the hostile kind.

"If you're here to pay your condolences, it isn't necessary," she said, "you did that at the funeral."

I responded, "I did try reaching you after your father was killed, but I assumed that you were either avoiding all calls, or possibly just mine. Since I did nothing wrong outside of being sick the day your father was shot, and you're the one that broke up with me, I assumed you just didn't want to talk to anyone. So I respected your privacy and left you alone."

I continued, "While I do want to tell you how sorry I am about your father's death, and I also wanted to congratulate you on your imminent confirmation to the Senate, I am not here for either of those reasons."

"Then, why are you here?" She asked.

"I am actually here on official FBI business."

Her tone changed momentarily as she asked me "Is this related to my father's case?"

"In part," I responded, "but I can't give you too many details at the moment since it's an active investigation."

Hope seemed confused by my comment since she had been informed that the case was closed. Since the purpose of my meeting was to question Hope, I had to be cautious about what I told her. I paused for a minute before continuing so I might chose my words more carefully.

"I'm actually not here to discuss your father's murder, but a case that I worked on when I was still with the DC police department," I said.

"So why would you be talking to me about it?" she asked.

"It was a homicide," I said, "actually a double homicide. Two men were shot in an alley behind a singles bar."

"And how does this involve me?" Hope responded without hesitation.

"There was a witness that saw a blonde running from the scene of the crime and although we couldn't identify her from an ATM camera, I noticed that she had a bracelet that looked just like the one that your father had made for your mother. The one he gave you when she died," I said.

"My father was just murdered and now you come into my house when I am still in mourning and accuse me of being involved in a murder? Get out of my house!" she demanded.

I told her that I was here in an official capacity, and as much as I wished I did not have to do this, especially based on our past relationship and how much I respected her father, I had no choice.

"I don't think you killed anyone, and whoever that blonde woman was, she didn't kill anybody either. It was some type of elaborate setup. I don't know why, but I'm going to assume it was to make her think that she killed one of those men, and possibly to use it against her, or maybe her father. Hope, I need to look at that bracelet," I said.

"I lost that bracelet a year ago. Now get out before I have you thrown out," she yelled.

Her body guard must have heard her and came into the room to make sure that everything was all right. I told her that if she was that blonde, she may be protecting the man that murdered her father. After I said it, I wished I could take it back.

"The man that murdered my father is dead," she shouted.

"I'll be at the Phoenix police precinct if you want to reach me. I'm sorry again for your loss," I said.

As I started walking out the door, she yelled "The only person you will be hearing from is the governor."

I walked out of the room and out of the house. Mike and Fred where still waiting outside. It was clear from the look on their faces that they heard some of the yelling from the study and appeared to keep their distance, waving to me as I walked down the driveway towards the car. On a scale of one to ten with ten being the worst, the conversation between Hope and I was a solid ten. While we talked, I covertly watched her facial expressions trying to pick up on anything that would show signs of her involvement. But Hope loved playing cards and she had one hell of a poker face. I couldn't tell if her anger over my accusations were genuine, or if it was just an act like her threat to have the governor call me. With her Senate seat within her grasp, it wouldn't be a wise move to bring the governor into this, and she knew it. It was just an idle threat that she probably hoped I wouldn't see through.

I hopped into my car, turned around in the cul-de-sac and drove slowly by the house on my way out of the block. I was pretty sure that I saw a silhouette at the study window. I would have preferred to leave with Hope's cooperation, and hopefully, be one step closer to solving this case and finding the hypnotist. But I knew that it was wishful thinking at best. If she was the blonde in the alley, then she had truly made the transition into politics by putting her own political future ahead of the people she would represent.

Although I had no hard evidence to prove my theory, there were two things that my gut was telling me. The first was that Hope was the blonde in the alley. She told me she lost her bracelet a year ago. I'd be the first to admit that I don't pay particular attention to how a woman accessorized, but I was sure that I had seen her wearing that bracelet in the past six months. It's not like it was some flimsy piece of jewelry that could easily be overlooked. The snake, when wrapped around a woman's arm, would be a good three inches wide. If I was correct about seeing it in the past year, then she was lying to me, in which case she was hiding something. I was sure that after I left she realized her mistake and was probably beating herself up over it. The second thing my gut was telling me was that Dr. H. was probably blackmailing her. My guess was that as soon as it was announced that the governor selected her to fill her father's senate seat, she received a call from him with a list of demands. Although I expected her to become hostile once I insinuated her involvement in the alley incident, she seemed to enter the room with a chip on her shoulder. I'm assuming that her bad mood was the result of her being contacted by Dr. H. The last person you want to see besides your ex-boyfriend, is an ex-boyfriend that happens to be an FBI agent when you are being blackmailed.

I was hoping that April was having some success in obtaining Dr. H.'s business card from the evidence file. If we could find him, then the information that Hope appeared to be withholding wouldn't be important anymore. After all, if she was setup and didn't kill either of the men, what was she really guilty of? I leaned over and turned on the radio, flipping through the stations until I found some classic rock. It was the first music I had listened to since I arrived in Arizona, and I was in desperate need of a distraction. To block the road noise in Lynch's car, I had to pump the volume up a bit. Thank God for rock n' roll I thought as I jumped onto the parkway and headed east.

Chapter 23
The Man Behind the Mask

When I arrived at the station I was still so distracted by my encounter with Hope, that I actually walked by the conference room. As I passed the door, I heard April calling my name. I stopped in my tracks realizing that I had overshot the room and walked back a few steps. The first thing I saw was April's face and it made me smile, but then, as I entered I saw Web and Lynch sitting in the room and the smile disappeared from my face. I was just sitting down in the chair when Web asked me how my visit with Hope went.

"Why do you think I went to see Hope?" I asked.

"Take a guess," he responded.

"Because we're the FBI," I answered.

"Actually, it was because Lynch has a tracking device on his car," He replied.

"Is there a car in this state that doesn't have a tracking device in it?" I asked in a sarcastic tone.

Web explained that after I spoke to him he headed over to the precinct asking April to show him the case I found. Apparently, Web also recognized the bracelet in the ATM photo. He recalled seeing it on Hope about five months ago at a party hosted by the Senator and his daughter.

"What did she tell you?" Web asked.

"You mean besides her threatening to call the Governor for questioning her about the case?" I responded.

"Yes, besides that," He replied.

I told Web that if he was sure about seeing the Bracelet only five months ago, then there was no doubt she'd lied to me. Web confirmed she had lied to me. I filled him in on the full conversation, the good, the bad, but mostly the ugly. Based on her pending confirmation, I could understand her concern over any information leaking out with regards to the case. Even if we could prove that she had been setup and didn't kill anyone, it wouldn't excuse her running from the scene of a crime or for that matter, the circumstances that placed her there to begin with. The press would have a field day with it, putting an end to Hope's political future.

I also started to wonder about the anxiety the Senator exhibited during the weeks leading up to his re-election bid. Was it a case of Pre-Election Day jitters, or could Dr. H. have attempted to blackmail him over that night in the alley? Was it possible that Dr. H. had killed the Senator because he wouldn't capitulate, gambling on the fact that Hope would take his seat so he could blackmail her instead? Did Hope suspect the possibility that Dr. H. had something to do with her father's murder? That would certainly explain why she didn't react to my insinuation that her father's killer was still out there.

It was becoming more and more obvious that the manipulative skills of this lunatic went beyond hypnotism. He setup Bill, and now it appeared he had setup Hope as well. Who knows how many others he has under his thumb that are yet to be uncovered? If his original intent was to use Hope's involvement against the Senator, he had exhibited a great deal of patience in playing those cards. With all of the effort we were putting into trying to track him down, we were still lacking motive. Up until now, we were assuming he was just a psychopath trying to kill innocent people for his own vile amusement. If we now added blackmail to his resume, we have to assume that he wanted something from his victims. The question was what?

The conference room phone rang. April reached for it answering "Officer Lynch". It was the evidence department for the DC police. April put in the request to the Captain at my old precinct to have the case evidence pulled and inspected for the hypnotist's business card. The news wasn't good...no card was found. I could see by the look on everyone's faces that there was a feeling of defeat amongst us. At every turn, Dr. H. seemed to be one step ahead of us. I don't know about anyone else, but there was a moment of doubt in my mind as to whether we'd ever catch him. The only thing I was sure about at the moment was that we all needed to take a break and call it a day.

My cell phone rang, breaking the silence that had shrouded the room. It was my father checking to see if we were going to be coming to the ranch for dinner. He told me that my mother was preparing dinner for everyone, and that she wouldn't take no for an answer. Considering we had nothing better to do at the moment, I told him I would extend the invitation, but based on the bad news we had just received, I wasn't sure any of us would have much of an appetite. To my astonishment, everyone accepted the invitation, even Web. I guess the prevailing thought was anywhere away from the precinct would be a welcome change. After gathering all of the paperwork we had accumulated from the case, one by one we filed out of the conference room, down the hall, and out the door into the parking lot. April and I were designated to take Lynch's car. While we were going to head straight to the ranch, Web and Lynch were going to swing by the Stone's house to pick up Bob. Hopefully, they would be able to conjure up some pleasant memories from their football days to take their minds off of the case. It seemed that for all of our efforts and ingenuity, for the moment, the only leads we had left were the conspirator at the CIA and Hope. From my conversation with Hope, I considered that avenue a "hopeless" one. Maybe Bob will surprise us all by bringing some good news to dinner along with his appetite.

April and I had barely gone a block before she asked me if meeting with Hope was strange, considering our past relationship. I wasn't sure if she was asking because she was genuinely interested, or if she was curious if I still had feelings for Hope.

"If you're asking if I still have feelings for her," I said "the answer is absolutely not."

April responded, "I had a hunch that if Web didn't confront you about your meeting with Hope, that you wouldn't have brought it up."

"Believe me," I said, "the thought did cross my mind, but only for a moment. If I didn't, it wouldn't have been for her sake, but for her father's. He was a good man and I wouldn't want to be the one that caused his family name to be dragged through the mud."

"I'm glad to hear that," she said, "You're a good man Charlie Brown."

"Thanks," I replied.

I tried to change the topic by asking April if any conversation had come up between her and her father regarding last night.

"He was concerned that I might get hurt," she answered.

"Hurt?" I asked "Why would you get hurt?"

She explained that Lynch thought that once the case was over, I'd be on my way back to DC.

"You know," I said, "we do have a Phoenix office. If you wouldn't mind, I might just stick around for a while."

April reached her hand out putting it on top of mine and squeezing it. "I'd like that," she said.

I warned April that having everyone over for dinner was probably a guise.

"The truth is that my mother probably planned all of this just to see the two of us together. You already know subtlety is not one of her strong points."

April laughed and told me she already knew that. Actually she got a kick out of my mom paying so much attention to her when she was staying at the ranch.

"I think my mom would have been the same way," she said, as a tear ran down her cheek.

"I'm sorry," I said.

"She would have liked you because you are a lot like my father" she responded.

"Well, I'm not sure your father would share her sentiment," I responded.

"My father does like you, he just has an odd way of showing it," she insisted.

My knee jerk reaction was an uncontrollable laugh. April gave me a few seconds to get myself under control before responding with a light punch to my arm. We arrived at the ranch and walked hand in hand up the steps to the porch. Then, we unintentionally announced our arrival by opening that squeaky kitchen door. My mother must have been staked out waiting for us. We had barely made it into the living room when she intercepted us, taking April's hand and asking her to help her in the kitchen.

"I hear you're an amazing cook," she told April as they disappeared into the kitchen.

My father walked over to me "You know she can't help herself son. But for what it's worth, I like her too."

Web, Lynch and Bob Clayton walked through the door just as my father finished offering his two cents about April.

"From the looks on your faces," my father said, "I'm guessing you've all had a crappy day".

"The two leads we had on this guy both went down in flames," I said.

"What about that list of men that served with your uncle?" he asked.

"Nothing came from it." I responded, "None of the sixteen names checked out."

"You mean seventeen names?" my father asked.

"There were only sixteen names on the list we found," I replied.

My father walked over to the coffee table, picking up what appeared to be an envelope yellowed by time. He returned to where Lynch, Web, and I were standing holding it firmly in his right hand.

My father went on to explain the origin of the envelope. "In this envelope are letters that were sent by all of the members of your uncle's platoon that he saved. They wanted to send their condolences and express their appreciation for your uncle giving his life to save theirs."

"Count them." he said, "There are seventeen letters with seventeen signatures in it".

I took the envelope in my hand and did as he suggested. I thumbed my way through each letter, reviewing each signature as I did. When I hit the seventeenth signed letter, my jaw nearly dropped to the floor. I turned towards Web and Lynch and in a gleeful tone yelled "we're back in business boys". I started off towards the den where Bob and Jenna were speaking. My father put his hand on my shoulder to get my attention. I stopped and turned towards him.

"If anyone is planning on leaving before dinner, your mom isn't going to be happy," he said in a concerned voice.

I think we could arrange to stay through dinner if you don't mind letting Bob use your computer," I replied.

"No problem," he said as he walked with me towards the couch.

"Bob," I said as I put my hand on his shoulder, "we need you to do a little research for us. My father is going to show you where his computer is located. Can you covertly tap into the bureau's system and bring up the sixteen names on that list we were working with?"

"Sure, but I have my laptop in the car. I never leave home without it," he responded, "What are we looking for?"

"First, we want to compare the names on our list against the signatures on these letters. I need you to locate the name missing from our list." I told him.

"I don't think I need a computer to do that. What do you want me to do when I find the missing name?" he asked.

"We need to see if that veteran had any relatives that served with the First Brigade in Arizona," I responded.

"What about dinner?" Bob asked.

"You get to work on this, and I'll bring you the biggest plate of food that you've ever seen," I responded.

My father took Bob into his private office so he could work without any distractions. I walked into the den, and suggested that we all sit down and eat. If I was correct and this was the lead we were waiting for, it was going to be a long night. I saw that April had temporarily escaped the kitchen and my mother. I pulled her aside and brought her up to date concerning the seventeenth man. I had expected for her to jump out of her shoes with excitement hearing that we were back in the game, but after all of the twists and turns in the case, I could understand why she was being guarded in her response. I think that of all of us, I was the only one that felt that we were on the verge of putting a name to this lunatic.

My first task after being summoned to the kitchen to eat, was to keep my promise to Bob. I grabbed a plate and filled it from edge to edge with food and started walking out of the kitchen.

"Where are you going with that plate?" my mother asked.

"I'm taking it to Bob," I responded.

"Won't he be joining us for dinner?" Jenna asked in what seemed like a disappointed tone. Bob and Jenna were sitting together in the den talking when I pulled him away to research the names in the envelope. It was the first time since I had met Jenna several days ago that I saw a smile on her face.

"Bob is working on something for us in my father's office," I told her.

"I'll bring him his food and if you don't mind, I might just keep him company as well," she said, causing a few raised eyebrows.

"Jenna," I said, "Bob is in the middle of a very important project and we need him to stay focused on what he is doing"

She responded, "I promise not to disturb him, but I just don't think it is right for us to all be sitting together and have him eat alone".

I looked at Web and he gave an approving nod. "Okay," I responded, "but make sure he stays focused on what he is doing".

Jenna removed herself from the table carrying her plate and Bob's plate down the hall to office. I followed with drinks and returned to the table. It seemed apparent that Jenna was showing an interest in Bob. I wasn't sure how that sat with Web and Lynch, as they are friends of Dan's family. Jenna's existence since Dan's death over a year ago had been difficult at best. I think for the most part, we were all happy to see her happy if even for a short time. When I returned to the table I sat down next to April. She immediately reached under the table and squeezed my hand. It appeared that I wasn't the only hopeless romantic sitting at the table. My mother had prepared several of my favorite foods for dinner. I think she was trying to make up for the fact that I had been unable to find more time to eat at the ranch since I'd been home. Over the past week, I doubt that any of us had enjoyed a good sit down meal since we started with this investigation. You could tell while we ate that everyone was finding it difficult to muster up conversation knowing that at any minute we might be chasing down another lead. The rare banter that we did have was about my father and his illustrious career as a Phoenix cop. He wasn't someone who liked being bragged about. As much as he tried to divert the conversation to other topics, my mother would keep bringing up stories that would take us right back to talking about him.

We had just finished dinner. As my mother and April started clearing the plates Bob and Jenna appeared. I could tell from the smile on Bob's face that he had found something and was chomping at the bit to tell us what it was.

"What did you find?" I asked as we all moved towards him.

"You were right on the money," he responded. "The seventeenth soldier's name was George Fein. You know what I found when I researched relatives that had active duty with the first Brigade?"

"What?" I demanded.

"Nothing," he responded.

"Then why the hell, are you smiling?" Web yelled.

"Relax boss," he replied "the reason why I am smiling is because I decided to broaden my search to anyone that had tried to join the first brigade. That's where I found him."

"I have a gun, and if you don't tell me something soon, I might just be using it tonight" snapped Web. It had been one of those days where we had all been on a roller coast ride and patience was running thin. "Sorry," Web said apologetically. "What did you find?"

"Gregory Fein. That's his name, Dr. Gregory Fein," Bob blurted out.

Bob went on to tell us that Fein had tried to enlist with the First Brigade in the same Arizona base as his father had served so he could follow in his father's footsteps. The only problem was that he was rejected for both physical and psychological reasons. According to the doctor that performed the psychological review, Fein was incredibly agitated—bordering on enraged—when he was rejected. It looked like we might have found his motive for using vets as his personal assassins. I asked Bob if he could track down a current residence. He responded by flashing me a wide smile.

"You already know where he is staying?" I asked.

"It looks like he has moved around quite a bit. He's rented several apartments around the country over the past few years, but he only has one house." Bob responded.

"And?" I asked after Bob paused for what appeared to be a theatrical moment.

"You will not believe this when I tell you." Bob asserted. Web's irritated expression prompted him to continue. "He lives about thirty five minutes from here."

Bob barely finished his sentence before Web started dialing his cell phone. I wanted to give Bob a big hug, but Jenna and April beat me to it. Web called the precinct looking for Riddle's cell number. The officer at the desk informed him that he would need to contact Riddle and have him return the call. Before ending the call, Web made sure that the officer understood the urgency of the situation. He promised to make the call right away and convey the urgency to Riddle. Web got off the phone and thanked my mother for dinner, apologizing for leaving before dessert. We decided that we would wait ten minutes to hear back from Riddle before heading out. Not knowing how things might unfold, we decided that it would be best for us to take two cars. Always thinking ahead, Bob had already printed out two sets of directions and a map of the neighborhood. After a brief review of the neighborhood, we picked a street corner two blocks away from Fein's home. If we got separated en-route, that would be our meeting place. While we were making our plans and anticipating Riddle's call, my mother had been in the kitchen preparing two bags of fresh baked cookies to send along with us.

Considering how the day had gone thus far, it was hard to believe that we might actually be on the verge of bringing this lunatic to justice. Web's cell phone rang and he picked up before the second ring.

"Hello," he said, "Riddle, we have an address on the hypnotist. I need you to grab as many men as you can spare to meet me at the corner of Biltmore Road and Calloway Crossing. Have them come in from the east side in unmarked cars. I want to setup a net around this guy's house that this bastard won't be able to slip through."

Riddle must have requested the exact address of the house because Web reached his hand out to Bob and asked for the directions he had printed.

"The address of Fein's house is 213 Rose Down Trace," Web responded.

Riddle must have said something that didn't agree with Web because the color drained from his face. It was a disconcerting site not knowing what had just transpired.

Web paused for about ten seconds before responding "We're on our way now." And then hung up the phone.

"What's the matter?" I asked.

"Riddle just told me that he is standing in front of what's left of Fein's house now," he said.

"He's where?" I asked as if my ears had deceived me the first time I heard it.

"There was an explosion there about two hours ago. They're still trying to put out the fire". He responded.

We all stood there in complete shock for a moment. "Why are we all still sitting around staring into space?" He barked. "Let's get going." As we headed for the door, my mother was there waiting with to-go bags in hand. Based on what had just happened, none of us were particularly interested in desert, but out of respect, Web took one bag and April the other. On the way to the car, in my mother's defense my father repeated what he had said earlier in the evening. "She can't help herself son, she's a mom." I gave him a hug and thanked him for finding the letter. He patted me on the back and simply said "You're welcome son".

When I got to the car I found April already ensconced in the passenger seat.

"Do you want to drive?" She asked.

"I thought you said that only members of the Phoenix PD could drive the car," I responded.

"I know," She replied, "but to hell with the rules, you earned it".

As I opened the driver's side door I heard Lynch call my name. I turned to see him sitting in his car with the window open.

"Hey, are you forgetting something?" he asked.

"You mean that I am not supposed to be driving this car?" I responded.

"No," he replied, "you left your bag of cookies on the roof the car". I ran back around to grab the bag off the roof, got into the car, and followed Lynch out of the ranch on our way to Fein's house.

Chapter 24
Well Done

The car ride was so quiet that we might as well been driving in separate cars. This case, this day, had been like riding a roller coaster in the dark not knowing what twists and turns lay ahead of us. Every time we thought the ride was coming to an end, we would have another drop followed by even more twists and turns. It seemed for the first time since we started this investigation that we were finally in the driver's seat, yet only minutes before we turned the car on; things blew up in our faces.

It was only a thirty-five minute drive, but it felt like two hours. I'm not sure if April was in the same frame of mind as I was, or just wanted to avoid saying anything to avoid the possibility of saying the wrong thing. As we pulled onto the street, she reached over to grab my hand and squeezed it. I returned the sentiment by putting her hand to my lips and kissing it. Regardless of everything that went wrong this week, I knew that there was one thing that had gone right for me, and that was meeting April.

Police barricades were already setup two blocks away forcing us to park the car a street over from our original rendezvous point. As we continued on foot, we noticed that the fire lit up the night sky like a beacon drawing us to it. Since April was still in uniform, we were able to effortlessly navigate our way past the police barricades. We made it within three hundred feet of the house before a fireman warned us not to move any closer. Glass had been thrown everywhere by the explosion. Several of the neighboring homes had their windows broken as the result of either the force of the explosion or the flying debris. It was fortunate that it was a still night. Had there been any kind of wind blowing, the fire would have easily spread to the neighboring homes. Even with the fire department out in full force, there were still many neighbors out spraying water on their homes in an effort to ensure a stray piece of airborne debris would not ignite a nearby tree or possibly their roofs.

We initially lost Lynch and Web in the chaos as we approached the neighborhood. It was only a few minutes before we located them approaching our position from the opposite side of the block. A fireman that appeared to have recently come out of the house was drinking a bottle of Gatorade and wiping the soot from his face. I called out to him waving my badge to try and get his attention. Noticing my efforts, he put down his drink and started walking towards our location. By the time he arrived, Lynch and Web had joined us.

"What happened?" I asked the fireman.

"The only thing we know for sure is that there was an explosion," he responded. "We're not going to be able to tell much more than that until we get this thing put out. Once it cools down, we can get our investigators in and get some answers".

"Do you know if anyone was in the house?" I asked.

"We found one body in what appeared to be the study, but to the best of our knowledge there wasn't anybody else in the house," he replied.

"Did you get the body out?" I inquired.

"No," replied the fireman, "Whoever he or she was, the poor bastard was burnt beyond recognition. We didn't want to risk any lives trying to transport the body until the fire was under control. It's a mess in there. Things were thrown all over the place. It was like an obstacle course."

I asked the fireman what he meant by that. It seemed to me that after an explosion any house would be a mess. Wouldn't it? He suggested that based on where the explosion emanated from, the mess in the study wasn't caused entirely by the explosion.

"What do you mean?" I asked.

"It looked like that room had been ransacked by someone before the explosion occurred," he explained.

"Why would you think that?" I inquired.

"There were papers and folders scattered about the floor," he responded.

"Couldn't that have been from the explosion?" I suggested.

"The explosion looks like it occurred in the kitchen two rooms away from the study. I'm no expert, but the mess in the study does not look like it was caused by the explosion. The furniture was still in an upright position," he responded.

It was the fireman's turn to relieve one of his co-workers, so he politely excused himself. Before he walked away, I made note of his name and station number in case we had any further questions.

If the fireman was correct about the house being ransacked prior to the explosion and the body they found was Fein's, then it appeared that someone else had beaten us to him and delivered their own form of justice. The only thing we could do at the moment was go door to door speaking to the neighbors in hopes that someone took note of Fein's last visitors. We decided to split up with each of us taking two of the neighboring homes.

As I approached the first house, I noticed that there was a man on the front porch with a broom in his hand. He was sweeping up the glass from the windows that had broken from the force of the explosion.

"It looks pretty bad," I said as I stepped up onto the porch.

"If you think it looks bad out here, you should see the inside. The glass flew halfway across the living room. You see this cut?" he asked pointing to his head. "I was sitting in my chair watching the television when the house blew up. A six inch piece of glass cut into my chair like a knife, but a smaller fragment scratched my head. Pretty damn lucky that that bigger piece didn't hit six inches higher, or I wouldn't be here talking to you right now," he said. "By the way, who are you?" he asked.

I took out my badge and holding it towards him so he could read it in the fire lit night.

"Agent Bennett Mills," I said. "I'd like to ask you some questions if you have a moment".

"FBI," the man said, "I'm Jim Easton. I knew something was strange about that guy."

"What do you mean strange?" I asked.

"The guy was hardly home. When he was you hardly ever saw a soul come in or out of that house. Actually, I think tonight was the first time I saw anyone visit him in months. Not that I want to give the impression that I'm a nosey neighbor, but I'm retired. I do spend a lot of time sitting in that chair watching the television. With that window being next to the television, it's hard not to take notice of people coming and going through the neighborhood."

"So he had visitors tonight. Did you happen to notice anything about them, or the car they drove?" I asked.

The man told me that he noticed a black Mercedes pull in front of the house, but his wife called him into the kitchen to eat dinner so he had no idea when they left. He did describe one of the men as being a well-dressed middle age man that appeared to be of Italian descent. It seemed that I hit pay dirt with the first house. I started walking towards the second house, but noted the lights were out and assumed that the owners weren't home. I turned around and headed towards our original location when I noticed that Lynch, April and Web were already there.

"We all came up empty," Web said. "Did you have any better luck".

"You might say that," I replied. "Actually, I think I hit the mother-load. The retired man across the street was telling me that Fein was hardly home, but when he was he didn't get many visitors," I continued, "Tonight, he had visitors about an hour before the explosion."

"Was he able to give you any descriptions?" Lynch asked.

"Yes, he did. He described one of the men as a well-dressed middle age man that appeared to be of Italian descent."

Before I could say another word, April burst out "Beninni?"

"Based on the description, it sounded like it could have been him," I responded. "Maybe our visit to the restaurant and our insinuations that he was linked to Fein put a scare into him. Beninni had to figure that if we were able to track down Fein first, he could turn evidence on Beninni to reduce his own sentence. It sure sounds like a good enough motive for Beninni to kill Fein and try covering it up with an accidental gas explosion."

It was pretty late, and it appeared that there was nothing to be gained by prolonging the evening. We decided to get some sleep and meet back at the precinct at 10am. It seemed clear that, our first order of business would be to push the coroner to confirm Fein as the victim. To do that it would be necessary to track down some type of medical or dental records for comparison. Since Fein, surprisingly, had the house registered under his real name, there was no reason to believe that we wouldn't be able to find his dental records. Based on how clever Fein had been I didn't think any of us were going to assume it was his body lying in the house. We also wanted to go into the house with the fire inspectors. We needed to see if anything could be found that might have been overlooked by whoever ransacked the house prior to the explosion. Finally, I wanted to see if Fein's neighbor could ID a photo of Beninni as the man he saw walking up to Fein's front door. If he was able to ID him, I would have him brought in for questioning.

April and I said goodnight and started walking away when Lynch called us back.

"April," Lynch said, "How about I drive you home tonight?" he asked. I was pretty sure that it was Lynch's effort to avoid a repeat of the previous night.

April smiled at me and shrugged her shoulders. She took her father's hand and they started walking to the car. They stopped about twenty feet or so up the road, and April came running back.

"I forgot that you drove here. I need the keys," she said.

I reached into my pocket and pulled them out handing them to her. She leaned towards me and gave me a kiss on the cheek. After the kiss, she whispered in my ear that I still owed her dinner before walking back to where Lynch was standing. I turned for a brief moment to look for Web, and when I looked back, they had disappeared behind a fire truck that was parked on the corner.

"Sorry Romeo," Web said, "I guess you'll be sleeping at the ranch tonight. Come on, I'll drop you off on my way to the Stone's."

"Thanks. Thanks a lot," I replied.

It was a two block walk to where Web and Lynch had parked their car. There was still a lot of activity going on, even though the majority of the fire appeared to be extinguished. I was guessing the fire department would be here into the early morning hours making sure that everything was out. Hopefully, we could then get the body out of the house to be delivered to the coroner's office for an autopsy. On the ride back, Web and I talked about what a strange case this was, especially for a couple of guys that worked for the Bureau. We talked about Hope and her reaction when I met with her earlier in the day. If the body in the house turned out to be Fein's, Beninni wouldn't be the only one that would be breathing a sigh of relief. With Fein's death, the truth about what happened that night in the alley would probably die along with him. We would never be able to prove that Hope was the blonde woman that the witness saw. We would never know if Fein had tried to blackmail Hope or the Senator, or if Fein and Hope had any communications after that night.

We drove through the entrance gate into the ranch. Web pulled up to the front door to let me out.

"Bennett," he said, "I don't want to get personal, but obviously you have a lot of people that care about you out here. When this case is over, do you really want to come back to Washington?"

"Are you trying to get rid of me?" I asked.

"Not after I did such a great job of breaking you in," Web said in jest. "I think you have something special going on here. Take some advice from a man that put his work ahead of his family, and as a result has been living alone now for more years than I want to count. If I met someone like April and had a family like yours here, I might give some thought to staying."

"Thanks, I can't say that the thought hasn't crossed my mind in the past few days. If there is anything good that has come from this case, it is that every reason I had for leaving no longer exists. Honestly, the thought of leaving April just doesn't sit right with me. I need to see where this relationship is going, but I can't do that from DC," I replied.

"Assuming that was Fein's body in the house, we probably have a few days before this case will be wrapped up. You might want to take some vacation time and try to figure things out before you make a decision one way or another". Web suggested.

"Thanks, I appreciate it. I'll see you in the morning. Have a good night," I said.

I walked through the front door and the house seemed quiet. My mother and father were sitting watching the television with my sister, but nobody else was in sight. My father jumped up as soon as he saw me, clearly interested in knowing what happened. As an ex-cop, I'm sure that being on the outside of all of the activity must have been difficult.

"So," he said "what happened? That fire was all over the news you know".

"They found a body in the house. We think it's our guy, but we won't know for sure until the autopsy," I responded.

"Did you see the body?" he asked.

"No," I responded, "we couldn't even get near the house and things were still too hot
for them to remove the body. By the way," I asked, "where is everyone else?"

My father told me that he drove Bob and Jenna back to her house, figuring that it was safe enough for her to go home. My father handed me an envelope.

"What's this?" I asked.

"Bob wanted me to give it to you," he replied. "He thought you might want some light reading if you came back."

I took the envelope from my father's hands and walked into the den sitting down on the couch by my mother.

"Don't you want to read that?" my father asked.

"Later," I responded. "For the moment, I only want to know two things. What are we watching and do we have any more of those cookies? April took the car with my bag in it. I'll have to keep an eye on her".

My mother responded, "That's funny. It looked like your biggest problem was keeping your eyes off of her."

My sister and father got a good chuckle from that one. My mother got up and headed to the kitchen to get me some cookies. Web was right; I had a lot to think about. We watched a couple of my parents' favorite television shows—that of course were of the crime genre—before they got tired and went up to sleep. It was already way past their bedtime, but I guess since we hadn't much time together they delayed their bed time to spend an hour sitting with me. After they excused themselves, I found myself sitting with my sister, Carol. I decided that while she watched the entertainment channel, my time would be better spent reading through the information that Bob had left on Fein. It's funny how we knew so little about him when the day started. Now I had a good part of his life story sitting at my fingertips. My sister was still watching the television, but knowing that Web would be by to pick me up in several hours I decided to catch some sleep. I was pretty tired and was grateful to be back in my own bed. Too bad Lynch made my preferred option of spending another night with April impossible.

Chapter 25
Bait and Switch

My cell phone rang. Where's the damn phone, I said to myself as I felt around the nightstand by my bed. I forgot that I left it in my pants pocket. I jumped out of bed and stumbled around the room trying to find my pants. They were lying on the floor just inside the door of the bedroom. I got to the phone just seconds before it went to voice mail.

"Bennett," I said.

"Did I wake you sleeping beauty?" Web said in a sarcastic tone.

"Funny," I replied, "but actually you did. What time is it?"

"It's time for you to get ready," he responded, "I'll be there in about thirty minutes."

"I'll be ready," I replied. I hung up the phone and tossed it on the bed. Thirty minutes isn't a lot of time, so I grabbed some fresh clothes and jumped into the shower. When I got out the cell phone was ringing again. I had thrown the phone onto the bed and now I was having trouble locating it in the twisted bedding. Once again, I found it just before the call went to voice mail.

"I thought you said thirty minutes," I said.

"Is Web trying to rush you this morning?" It was April's voice on the other end. "How did you sleep?" she asked.

"I slept much better the night before lying next to you," I responded.

"So did I," she responded with a laugh. "When are you going to be at the precinct?" She asked.

"I should be there in about an hour," I told her.

"Okay, I'll meet you there. And Bennett, don't forget our dinner plans," she replied.

Forget them I thought, I was looking forward to them. With the case winding down, I needed to give some serious thought to what Web and I discussed in the car. Considering Web's imminent arrival I decided that the first order of business was to grab something quick to eat. The aroma of bacon, eggs, and homemade biscuits permeated the house. I grabbed my gun, badge and the papers Bob left for me, and headed down the stairs. My folks were sitting at the table having a cup of coffee waiting for me to come down. My mother had prepared a plate for me and left it on the table covered in foil to keep it hot.

"I'm sorry," I said, "but Web is going to be here any minute. I'm going to have to eat and run".

"That's okay," my mom replied. "We've gotten used to it."

"As soon as things are wrapped up, I promise I'll be spending more time at home. I am planning on extending my stay for a bit, so I am not heading right back to DC."

That announcement put a big smile on my mom's face. While I ate she put a couple of biscuits in a to-go pack and poured some coffee into traveling cups to take with me. I barely got to finish with breakfast before the horn honked outside. I grabbed the bag and the coffee cups and headed out the door.

"I'll call you to let you know what's going on. I told April I would be taking her out tonight for dinner, but I'll see you before we go out," I said.

The horn honked again. I opened the screen door and ran out. Web had conveniently pulled up to the kitchen door.

"I have a couple of biscuits and coffee," I told Web.

"I had a big meal before I left the Stone's," Web responded, "but I didn't sleep very well, so I'll take you up on the coffee."

I handed him one of the cups and he took a sip from it and then put the cup in the car's cup holder.

"That's good coffee," he said, "You know, it was probably a good idea that you moved to DC. With the way your mom cooks, you might have become the fattest cop on the Phoenix Police Dept."

"You're probably right," I replied.

I asked Web if he had heard anything regarding the body found in the house. He informed me that he called the coroner's office before he picked me up and confirmed that the body had been delivered. Now, we were just waiting for the coroner to arrive and get started on the autopsy. Web voiced his concern that without dental records or some other method of identification, we might be unable to prove whether it was Fein's body or not.

"I was on the phone this morning as well," I told Web. "I already spoke to Riddle and asked him if he could have one of his men pick up the dental records from Fein's dentist."

"How the hell did you get his dentist's name?" he asked.

"After we left to go to the house last night, Bob did some research and put together a little bed time reading packet for me to read when I returned to the ranch last night. I think I know more about Fein right now, than I know about you," I replied. "I also asked Riddle about bringing Beninni in for questioning. He agreed under the condition that I could have Fein's nosey neighbor confirm it was him. He's going to get me an old surveillance photo to show the neighbor."

Lynch arranged a meeting with the fire investigators this morning. Web suggested I tag along so I could talk to the neighbor following the inspection. If he did identify Beninni from the photo, he wanted to be there when he was interrogated.

"What's on your agenda until then?" I asked.

"Since it appears that we have a few hours to spare, I thought it might be a good idea to head over to the bureau office and try to catch up on all the work I have been neglecting for the past week," he said.

"I'll let you know as soon as we hear anything," I replied. "By the way, I don't think we should take any action against this traitorous bastard at the CIA until we are sure Fein is dead."

Web nodded his head in agreement. We pulled into the parking lot at the precinct and Web drove straight through the parking lot, pulling right up to the front door.

"You're not coming in?" I asked.

"No, I think you have things covered," he replied, "I might as well head over to the bureau now. Just keep me informed. I can be back at the precinct in about ten minutes if anything changes."

"Will do," I responded.

I got out of the car and entered the precinct. April was waiting for me in the hallway.

"Before you go in to see Riddle, I have a question for you," she said. "Once this case is solved, are you heading right back to DC?"

"Actually, I have some vacation time I wanted to take. I thought that maybe I could spend it here, with you," I replied. "If you don't mind of course."

"That's a funny coincidence, I have some vacation time built up myself. I've been waiting for the right person to spend it with," she replied with a smile.

I asked April if I should consider this a date. She leaned over and whispered in my ear, "Yes," and gave me a kiss on the cheek. We started walking towards Riddle's office. Lynch and Riddle were sitting talking about another case when we walked in.

"Have you two already closed this case?" I asked sarcastically.

"No, but we do have other crimes that need to be solved besides this one," he replied in a mocking tone.

Riddle reached to the side of his desk pulling a folder off the top of a pile of paperwork and handed it to me. Inside was a picture of Beninni.

"Hey Lynch. What time are we meeting the fire inspector at the house?" I asked.

"We have an appointment at ten-thirty," he replied.

I looked at my watch and noticed it was already nine-twenty. It was about a half hour's drive from the precinct.

"We better get going if we're going to make it on time," I suggested.

"I reckon so," he responded and got up from the chair.

On the way out, I turned to Riddle to confirm that one of his officers was arranging to get the dental records to the coroner. He informed me that the officer was sitting in the dental office as we spoke. The dentist had an early round of golf, but was expected in around 10am. He assured me that as soon as the dentist got in, they'd get him to pull the records and take them over to the coroner.

"Thanks," I said. "I bet you will be glad to get rid of me when this case is over."

"Actually, I'm betting that you will be sad to head back to that boring job at the bureau. You know, I have a lot of unsolved cases just waiting for the right person to crack them," he replied.

"Don't tempt me" I said, "or you might just wind up seeing more of me that you care to."

Riddle smiled just enough that I thought I could see his teeth through that bushy moustache he sported. I headed out the door where Lynch stood waiting for me. As we walked down the hall towards the door, April joined us.

"So where are we headed?" she asked.

"We're headed to the house," Lynch said, "but I think it might be a good idea for you to stay here and wait to hear from the coroner".

"We're not going to have any news for at least a few hours," she replied.

"Okay, let me put this another way. I want to have a chance to talk to your boyfriend here in private," Lynch responded.

"Well, why didn't you say so in the first place. I'm sure I can find something to do while you're gone," she said.

Lynch caught me off guard with his response to April. Now, I wasn't sure if I wanted to go or not. Lynch started walking towards the door while I continued to contemplate what had just happened.

"Agent Mills," he said in a very official sounding voice, "are you planning on joining me?"

I walked towards him and we both exited the precinct heading for his car. We were about ten minutes into the drive before we exchanged a word. Then, Lynch started going down the path that I was hoping not to travel.

"You know April lost her mom when she was very young. Because of that loss, she missed out on all of those mother-daughter discussions that she should have had. I tried my best, but if you haven't figured it out yet, I'm not the type of dad that she could open up to in that way. April really seems to like you a lot. By the look on your face when you're around her, you seem to feel the same way. She is all I have, and I don't want to see her heading half way across the country. The thought of only seeing her a few times a year doesn't sit well with me," he said.

Lynch was a tough cookie, but I could see when it came to April, he was very emotional. I guess if I was in his shoes, I would be feeling the same way.

"Lynch," I said, "I do like April a lot. You raised an amazing daughter and she is a remarkable woman. To be honest with you, although it's only been about a week since we met, it feels like I have known her forever. I'm not sure where things go from here, but I'd like to give our relationship a chance. I'd like to find out if we have a future or not. If it does turn out we can make a future together, I'd like it to be here in Arizona, so we'd be close to our families."

Lynch responded, "I knew I was going to like you after that flight from DC. For the record, if you upset my daughter, I might have to kill you".

I knew that he didn't really mean it—at least I was hoping he didn't. As we pulled onto Fein's block, I was surprised by how calm things seemed in contrast to the turmoil that existed only several hours ago. As we approached the house, the acrid smell of smoke was still evident in the still Arizona air. The fire inspector's truck was sitting in front of the house. I was actually surprised, based on its appearance, that anyone would take the chance of walking through the house. But here we were getting ready to do just that. The fire inspector saw us pull up and got out of his truck. We met him at the side of the vehicle, where he had started removing several items from a hidden compartment in the truck. After a brief introduction, he quickly sized us up and issued each of us a yellow set of coveralls, a mask, and an oxygen tank.

"Do we really need to wear all of this?" I asked.

"Only if you want to be able to breathe and keep your clothes from getting covered in ash. It's still pretty noxious in there," he replied.

Lynch and I grabbed the equipment and put the coveralls on over our clothes. The investigator suggested that since the structure of the house was still in question we follow him closely and make sure not to lean against any of the remaining walls or we might cause the structure to collapse. It wasn't the kind of thing I wanted to hear. The mask gave me a claustrophobic feeling, but after a several minutes I started to adjust. As we walked to the house, we noticed a variety of kitchen items strewn about the front lawn. Once inside the house, it was fairly evident that the explosion came from the kitchen. The adjoining wall between the kitchen and the dining room had been destroyed by the explosion. Most of the furnishings in that room, along with a dishwasher, were in a pile of rubble that had been thrown across the room. Smaller items were flung through the window coming to rest on the front lawn. The fire investigator pointed in the direction of the oven.

"It looks like it was a gas explosion. Based on the trajectory of the debris and the condition of the gas stove, it appears that the owner might have left the gas on and somehow it was ignited," he said.

"Are you sure of that?" I asked.

"No, I'm just speculating, it's not official," he replied, "I'm just making an educated guess based on my previous experience. It wouldn't be the first time I've seen it happen. Considering that I am being accompanied by the Phoenix PD and FBI, I am going to assume that you suspect foul play."

It wasn't necessary to confirm his suspicions, our presence was confirmation enough. It was clear that this wasn't the first time he'd been involved in this type of investigation. We walked into the kitchen. The first thing that struck me as odd was considering that all of cabinetry that had been blown pieces, I didn't see any remnants of broken dishware. I could see how boxed goods wouldn't have survived the fire, but that didn't explain why there weren't cans, pots, or pans. Since we were guests of the fire department, I asked the investigator if I could open what remained of the refrigerator. He said it wasn't a problem but to be careful. When I was finally was able to pry open the door, the only things I found inside were broken glass from the refrigerator shelving, and what appeared to be some melted plastic soda bottles.

"What are you thinking?" Lynch asked.

"For someone that lived here for five years, it doesn't appear he did much, if any cooking. If he'd been cooking and left the gas turned on, wouldn't you think that he would need something to cook with or some food to cook?"

Playing devil's advocate, the fire investigator suggested that if food was on the stove when it blew, it could be sitting on someone's roof or in a neighbors backyard.

"While possible," I said, "based on the lack of canned goods and the empty refrigerator it seemed highly unlikely."

We continued to walk through the house which appeared to have been sparsely furnished. Fortunately, it was a ranch layout with no basement so there weren't any concerns that we might fall through the floor during the investigation. Walking down the hallway, we came upon a room which appeared to be the study. This was where the fireman had stated the body was found. This room appeared to be more heavily damaged by the fire than any of the other rooms.

Lynch turned to the investigator and asked "If the explosion started in the kitchen, why does this room have more fire damage than other areas of the house?"

The investigator responded, "There are a couple of explanations that come to mind. First, it could be related to the furnishings in the room. Some furniture, depending on what wood it is made of, could ignite easier and burn hotter than other types of wood. But based on the charred floor and where the furniture most likely sat in the room, I would guess an accelerant was used.

"An accelerant?" I asked, "So you think this might not have been an accident?"

"That is what I am here to determine," he replied.

"I had a brief conversation with one of the fireman last night after he had come out of the house," I told the investigator. "He indicated that the room that he classified as an office appeared to have been ransacked prior to the explosion."

"Yes, I did see that mentioned in the report," he responded.

"If the fireman's assessment was correct, then it was likely that someone else had been in the house prior to the explosion looking for something," I suggested.

"I know the kid that reported that, and he is pretty astute." The investigator announced.

"Are you agreeing with him then?" I asked.

"I'm not disagreeing with him," he replied. He continued "There's no doubt that the explosion was centered in the kitchen. But to cause this amount of damage, the gas must have been leaking for a long period of time before the blast. It's my guess that the victim was probably dead from the gas long before the detonation."

"But if he died from the gas," I suggested, "then, he couldn't have ignited the gas."

Lynch added, "If he didn't ignite the explosion and no other bodies were found, then what happened?"

The investigator explained "A timed mechanism could have been used to ignite the gas. This would have given the perpetrators an opportunity to safely distance themselves from the explosion."

"It's possible that he came to the house to find the evidence against him," I told Lynch. "After he found it, he kills Fein, and then sets the explosion to make it appear as if it was an accident. The accelerant would insure that everything in the room including any evidence would have been incinerated."

"Who would have set the explosion?" the fire investigator inquired.

"I'm sorry," Lynch said, "but this is part of an ongoing investigation, and at the moment, we cannot share that information with you".

"No need to apologize. I've been around long enough that I shouldn't have even asked" he said with a smile. "For what it is worth, it does appear that there were a lot of papers in the vicinity of the body when the explosion ignited the accelerant."

It appeared that any documents that we might have been looking for, were either gone, or destroyed. We decided it was time to move on to the neighbor across the street. We thanked the investigator and I handed him my card. I asked him to give me a call if he found anything else that would prove our theory that this was a homicide and not an accident.

After leaving the house, our first stop was to drop off the equipment and coveralls we'd borrowed. We placed them into the storage compartment on the side of the investigator's truck. We then proceeded on our way to visit Fein's nosey neighbor Mr. Easton. As we started crossing the street, I noticed the sun glinting off something just below the second floor of the house to the right of Mr. Easton's. We changed directions moving towards that object. As we approached the front door, we were able to identify the reflection as coming from a camera. It was mounted just under the easement at the remote corner of the front porch. It was obviously placed in such a manner to obscure its existence from the other neighbors, or anyone that might be passing by on the street. If not for the reflection of the sun on the lens, I might not have even noticed it.

"It looks like a security camera," Lynch said.

"Yes, I'm guessing that Mr. Easton wasn't the only person on this block that was keeping track on what happened in the neighborhood.

"Hello," a voice called from behind us. "You have the wrong house. I'm over here".

It was Mr. Easton. I didn't think I was going out on a limb by assuming he'd been monitoring our activities from the moment we pulled in front of the house this morning.

"So did you find anything in the house?" he asked.

"I'm sorry sir," I replied, "but we cannot discuss the details of an active investigation."

"So, I see you noticed the camera," he said.

"Yes, we were about to speak to the owners," I replied.

"They're not home. They went on vacation, I'm assuming they'll be gone for a while," he responded. "Some people accuse me of being a bit nosey, if you can believe that, but at least I don't have a camera recording everything that goes on in the neighborhood."

I took out the picture of Beninni and showed it to Easton, asking him if this was the man that had shown up at the house in the black Mercedes.

"Yes, that's definitely the guy, no doubt about it. I would recognize him anywhere," he said.

"Thank you for your help Mr. Easton. If we need any further information, we will let you know," I told him.

"Are you going to break into the house to get the recorder?" he asked.

Lynch replied "No, we are definitely not going to break into the house. We are going to investigate the house to make sure that nothing was stolen during the night since the windows were broken."

"Oh," he said, "I get it," he replied with a snicker, as he turned and headed back to his house.

If the camera was working up until the time of the explosion, it might have recorded any visitors that came and left Fein's house yesterday evening. If this security camera was like others I had seen, it would have timestamp overlays on the video.

"We might have just struck gold," I told Lynch.

"That's an understatement," he responded.

Since the windows were almost completely blown out by the explosion it made no sense to try and pick the lock to the front door. We carefully reached into the house to unlock the window and slid it open. Lynch climbed in first and I followed. As we stepped into the house the broken glass crunched beneath our feet. It reminded me of the glass bulbs I broke on the stairs at Jenna's house. Not surprisingly, it had also triggered the memory of April wearing the nightie.

"You seem distracted," Lynch said.

"Who me? I asked, "No, not at all."

We started looking around the down stairs for televisions, figuring that the recorder would be close to a set for easy play back. After checking three different televisions, we decided to trace the wiring and found it led to a recorder that was hidden behind a set of encyclopedias. We should have realized it—since nobody used encyclopedias anymore, except to hide things behind them. We removed the books and hit the rewind switch. At first, it was moving backwards in slow motion. It took a couple of minutes before we figured out how to increase the rewind speed. Since we were able to see the events up to our approaching the house and speaking with Mr. Easton, it was clear that the camera was still functioning. We went backwards past the explosion and there it was, the Mercedes pulling away.

"Hit the stop button," Lynch said.

I pressed the stop on the machine, and then the play button. We watched as the Mercedes pulled up to Fein's house and the car door opened.

"It's Beninni, we got him," Lynch said.

It was definitely Beninni. We watched as he walked up to the front door with a couple of his goons.

"Did he just ring the doorbell?" I asked. "Why the hell would he announce himself if he was coming after Fein?"

As if ringing the bell several times wasn't enough, he followed-up by knocking on the door several times. If he was planning or even considering trying to kill Fein, why would he be so blatant? After waiting for several minutes and looking noticeably uncomfortable he walked back down the steps, hopped back into the Mercedes and drove away. Five minutes later the house blew up. If Beninni wasn't there to kill Fein, then who did? And for that matter, why and what was Beninni doing at the Fein's house? The only way that we were going to get those questions answered was to confront Beninni himself. I rewound the video and used my phone to record the segment where Beninni pulled up and was walking towards the front door. Lynch then disconnected the recorder from the television so we could take it with us. I left a note telling the owner that we had impounded the recorder for an important case and it would be returned or replaced.

We called Riddle to let him know that we wanted to interrogate Beninni. Lynch needed Riddle's permission to go to Beninni's restaurant and pick him up. Riddle was reluctant at first, but once we told him about of the video, and our plan, he reluctantly agreed to let us bring him in. I decided to check in with Web since we had a good twenty minutes before we reached our destination. He told me that the coroner had received the dental records and already started the autopsy. It would only be a couple of hours before we'd know if it was Fein's body or not. I told Web what we learned from our walk through the house and about our questionable entry into his neighbor's home. He didn't seem too pleased about it, but under the circumstances, approved our actions retroactively to prevent either of us from taking any heat. He was going to leave for the precinct in twenty minutes so he would be there when we brought Beninni in.

We arrived at the restaurant and walked through the front door with our badges clearly visible. We walked through the restaurant unobstructed. As we were about to enter the kitchen area, the two goons I'd met the other night walked out the kitchen door. The guy I'd thrown into the wall had a lump on his head. The other guy appeared to have an odd twitch. I'm not sure whether he twitched before April hit him with the stun gun, but he certainly had one now.

"We're here to see your boss," I said. "Hopefully, we can avoid the unpleasantries of our previous encounter."

At that point the kitchen door opened, and Beninni walked out. Motioning with his hands, he directed his men to walk away and like well-trained animals they obeyed.

"What can I do for you gentlemen?" he asked.

"We'd like you to accompany us downtown for some questioning," Lynch said.

Beninni laughed in response. "I don't think that would be possible," he replied, "I have a very busy schedule today".

"I have something I want to show you," I replied as I took out my phone.

"What's this?" he asked, "your Facebook page?"

I started playing back the video. "This is you pulling up to Fein's house and approaching his front door" I said.

"Who's house?" he replied. It was obvious that the video caught him off guard.

"Our hypnotist's house. We can discuss this here, but I would think it would be better to discuss this further at the precinct," I suggested.

He extended his hands for us to put cuffs on him.

"I don't think that will be necessary," I said.

"Actually," Lynch said, "it is very necessary. We need to make it appear that he is going against his will, or his gangster buddies might start to get ideas that might be dangerous for him."

Beninni put his hands out again. This time, I cuffed him. As we headed towards the door his boys started to approach us, but Beninni stopped their advance with the nod of his head. We exited the restaurant, and got into the car and started heading for the precinct. After a couple of minutes of silence, Beninni asked "Do I need to have my attorney meet me at the precinct?"

"You might want to hear what we have to say before making that call," I said.

With the exception of that one exchange, not another word was spoken. Lynch and I didn't speak to each other hoping that it might provide for a psychological advantage. As soon as we arrived at the precinct, I walked Beninni into an interrogation room, sat him down, and left the room. It wasn't long before Web arrived. Web, Lynch, and Riddle watched from the video camera in Riddle's office. I had the pleasure of interrogating Beninni. I walked into the room and sat down. I looked Beninni in the eye for a minute before I spoke.

"What were you doing at Fein's house yesterday evening?" I asked.

"I have no idea who this Fein guy is," he responded. "Me and my guys got lost and we stopped at a house to ask directions, but nobody was home."

"Is that the way you want to play things Beninni?" I asked. "We have the video of you showing up at his house. Less than thirty minutes later, there's an explosion at the house and Fein's body is found torched. It all seems a bit suspicious if you ask me. I wonder what a judge might think."

"I didn't even go into the house. If you have the video, you'll see I left when nobody answered the door," he replied.

"Unfortunately for you, the recorder must have run out of space because we didn't get that part," I told him. I needed to convince him that we had a case against him if I was going to get to the bottom of what happened. I figured if it took a little lie to do it, then so be it.

"Okay," he said. "Hypothetically speaking, if I were to receive a phone call from some guy that tells me that he wanted to meet with me at an address to discuss a very lucrative financial deal with me. And let's say that I tell that individual I'll meet with him, only to show up at the address and the guy is a no show. My boys and I hop back into the car and head back to the restaurant where I have witnesses that can testify that I was nowhere near the house when it blows."

"Is that the story you plan on sticking with?" I asked.

"If you are going to insist otherwise, I think I will phone my lawyer now," he responded.

I got up from my chair and walked out into the hall headed for Riddles office. I barely closed the door before Web asked "Do you believe him?"

"The video backs up his story," I said. "If he was planning on killing Fein, I doubt he would walk up to his front door and ring the doorbell. He's obviously lying about the reason for the meeting. It's possible he did receive a phone call from Fein, but we'll never know for sure. As far as I know, you can't arrest a guy for ringing a door bell and knocking on a door."

At that moment Riddle's phone rang. It was the coroner's office calling to let us know that the autopsy was complete. I didn't want to hear this one over the phone. The coroner was only a few minutes up the road. I suggested we head over there to hear the report in person. It had been a long week, and if it was Fein's body, I wanted the satisfaction of seeing it to help bring closure to this case. It was unanimous that we all go. I asked them to page April. After all, she'd been involved with this case from the beginning, and she'd risked her life to solve it. I just couldn't imagine going there without her. Asking her along wasn't personal, it was purely professional courtesy. As I passed the officer guarding Beninni, I said "Hold him for about thirty minutes, and then let him go."

The officer acknowledged my instructions, and we continued to the front desk where April had just arrived. We decided to take two cars. Lynch surprised me by suggesting that I drive with April and that he would drive with Riddle and Web. Had I been sitting down, I would have fallen off my seat. I think April was just as surprised as I was. April and I got into the car. Since Riddle was in the car ahead us, April took the wheel this time. After closing the car door, April started the car then turned to me.

"Looks like the old man is warming up to you," she said.

"I guess my charm is finally wearing him down," I responded.

"Let's not push it," she replied with a smile. She gently squeezed my hand then started the car rolling out of the precinct parking lot on the way to the coroner.

There wasn't much conversation since the coroner's office was only a couple of miles away. We did manage to come to an agreement on where we would eat dinner that night to hopefully celebrate the end of the case. We pulled into the parking lot at the Maricopa County Medical Examiner on West Jefferson. Lynch, Web, and Riddle pulled in just ahead of us and had already parked. We pulled up into the spot right next to them and got out of the car. I wasn't sure how everyone else was feeling at that moment, but I felt like I had just walked seven miles through the desert without a drink of water and thought I saw a lake just ahead. Was it a real lake, or just another mirage? The person who would answer that question was just through the set of double doors directly in front of us. We walked in through the main entrance, sitting down in the waiting room for a few minutes before the coroner's assistant came for us. He escorted us down a long well lit hallway into the office of the Chief Medical Examiner. Sitting behind the desk was short, stocky bald man who appeared to be in his late sixties.

"This is my boss, Dr. Rodgers," the assistant said.

We each in turn introduced ourselves.

"Please sit down," he said.

It was obvious that he was pressed for time because he didn't engage in any superfluous conversation.

"The victim appears to have died from asphyxiation from the gas in the house. Based on what I found during the autopsy, I would say he died within an hour or so of the the explosion. This explains why his body although badly burnt was still intact," he said.

"Pardon me for interrupting you Dr. Rodgers," Web said, "but if what you are saying is true, our victim couldn't have been the one to ignite the gas."

"There is no doubt in my mind," he replied, "if he had been alive we would have found shrapnel from flying debris in his body and he would probably be missing some of his extremities."

"I'm sorry to interrupt, but can we cut to the chase? We can come back to the details later." I said. "We want to know if the dental records we sent over for Fein matched the body you autopsied."

"Yes," he emphatically responded, "they were a perfect match".

I think that at that moment, we all breathed a sigh of relief. Web reached over and gave me a pat on the back as a congratulatory gesture.

"Do you mind if we see the body?" I asked. I figured it would give us all some closure.

"It's not a pretty sight and I wouldn't suggest it if you have a weak stomach. But, you are welcome to if you would like," Dr. Rodgers responded.

Looking at my companions I asked "Does anyone else want to join me?" The bevy of nodding heads signified that we all wanted to see tangible proof that the man that had inflicted misery on so many lives was indeed dead and gone. Dr. Rodgers got up out of his chair and walked to the door. We each rose from our chairs and followed him out the door and down the hallway to what the coroners nick named the "freezer room." This room was where all of the bodies were stored, either awaiting their turn on the autopsy table, or waiting to be dispatched to their final resting place. Rodgers opened one of the doors and slid the body out of the unit. He then lifted back the veil that was used to cover the body. I didn't know about anyone else, but I was glad that I hadn't eaten a big breakfast. I looked at April and she had turned her head after a quick peek.

"I think we have seen enough," I said.

Everyone else seemed to be in agreement. Rodgers put the cover back over the body and started to slide it back into its drawer.

"Stop!" I yelled.

Rodgers paused.

"That's not Fein," I said.

Rodgers responded, "According to the dental records it most certainly is."

"Then, the dental records are not Fein's," I responded.

"If you have something, how about sharing it with the rest of us?" Web said in a demanding tone.

"Remember when I told you that Bob had pulled the information on Fein and left it for me to read the night of the fire," I said.

"Yes," Web replied.

"If you recall, the reason why Fein couldn't join the military was stated as for both psychological and physical reasons?"

"Yes, go ahead, Web responded.

I continued "The reason noted by the doctor performing the physical was that he had a left club foot. Please correct me if I'm wrong Dr. Rodgers, but the left foot on this body appears to be perfectly normal."

"I would definitely agree with you that this man does not have a club foot," responded Rodgers.

At that moment, I realized that Fein as a master manipulator had struck again. I asked Rodgers not to divulge what we discovered to anyone. I told him that this madman was still at large, somewhere, thinking he had just gotten away with murder. I told everyone that we needed for him to keep believing that. Rodgers agreed to go along with the charade by leaving his records as stating that the victim was in fact Fein. I thanked him for his help and cooperation, and suggested that we all reconvene our conversation back at the precinct. We exited the building with a much different feeling then when we entered it. We thought we would leave the building with a feeling of closure; instead, we left feeling like we'd been duped.

Chapter 26

The Trail Goes Cold

The drive back to the station was a quiet one. April and I hardly exchanged a word between us, but if we had the word would have been "defeated". That is how I think we both felt after our latest setback in the case. We arrived back at the station and from the look on everyone's faces, you would have thought we'd just attended a friend or family member's funeral. We all piled into the conference room and grabbed a seat. Web was the first to break the silence.

"What the hell just happened?" he said, "and what the hell can we do about it?"

"It appears that Fein had an emergency exit plan if he was discovered, and this was it," I said. "My guess is that he had a client that worked at the dentist's office and arranged for our victim's records to be switched with his. Our victim was probably someone he had met at the dentist that resembled him physically. Either he was also a client or knowing Fein, he probably just offered the guy a free consultation. When the poor bastard gets to Fein's house, he hypnotizes or drugs him. Then, he pours an accelerant on his body and leaves him to be asphyxiated by the gas. The explosion is tripped by some type of timing device, creating the fire which then engulfs our victim. With the body burnt beyond recognition, he knew that the coroner would have to rely on the dental records to identify the corpse."

"How does Beninni's appearance at the house figure into all of this?" Lynch asked.

"Fein must have known that we made the connection between himself and Beninni. That gave Beninni cause to want to see Fein dead, which would make him our prime suspect. The motive was simple; he wanted to make sure any evidence in Fein's house was destroyed along with the man that could send him away for life as part of a plea bargain, if we ever caught him. All Fein had to do, at that point, was to bait Beninni into showing up at the house. Fein knew his nosey neighbor would see Beninni and his boys at the house, and be able to identify him once we started questioning his neighbors.

If Beninni and his men happen to go into the house they would probably have succumbed to the gas, and either died by asphyxiation or been killed in the explosion. It would have looked like a murder gone wrong. If he didn't go into the house, the evidence implicating him in the murder might be enough to put him in jail for life. As far as we're concerned, we start patting ourselves on the back for a job well done. In the meanwhile, Fein disappears, spending the rest of his life laughing about how he got away with murder while making us look like a bunch of idiots. The first mistake he made was not knowing that he had a second nosey neighbor with a hidden camera, pointing in the direction of his house. If we didn't have that video, Beninni would be sitting in jail with his goon squad awaiting trial for murder."

"And the second mistake, I assume, was not being able to find a victim with a club foot," Lynch said.

"Yes," I replied. "If our morbid curiosity didn't take us to the coroner's office, we would have never picked up on it."

After I stopped talking, I noticed that silence had once again taken control of the room.

"How do we find him now?" Riddle finally asked breaking the silence.

"I think the question is, will we ever find him?" Web replied. "As of this moment, we are starting from scratch with no leads to go on. I'm going to guess that if he hasn't left the country already, he probably will try. Without knowing what identity he is going by, we won't have a chance in hell to stop him. All in all, this has been a huge failure."

Web was right. The odds of finding Fein at this point were highly unlikely.

In an effort to cheer us up, April pointed out that thanks to our efforts, vets like Stone would now have their names cleared giving their grieving families some comfort.

"And think about how many other vets and families might have been destroyed had we not discovered what Fein was doing?" April asked.

While she was right that we did make a difference, there wasn't a cop or agent that would walk away from this case without feeling sick to their stomach.

"I think we should all take the rest of the day off to clear our minds and meet tomorrow to see if we can come up with any options. If not, we are going to have to walk away from this one," Web said.

I didn't even want to think about walking away. But if we couldn't come up with some new ideas or leads, we might have to leave the case in the open case file hoping that Fein would show up on our radar in the future. Riddle and Lynch left the room. I was guessing that Riddle was planning on getting Lynch back into a normal case schedule. April waited for a minute until Web asked to talk to me alone for a minute, and then walked out the door, telling me she would be at the front desk when I was done.

Web walked over and closed the door. "I know how this must be eating you up inside, because it is doing the same to me right now," he said. "I just wanted to let you know that if it wasn't for your hard work we wouldn't have gotten anywhere close to this guy. April was right about one thing, you closed down this operation. There are a lot of people out there that are indebted to you, and even more that don't even realize the impact you just made on their lives. This is the unfortunate part of life. Sometimes you win, and sometimes you lose. We both have to learn to live with the latter of the two, or we won't be worth a damn to the bureau or anyone else for that matter."

"Is that all?" I asked.

"Yes," he responded, "get some rest and we will talk tomorrow."

As I walked toward the door, Web sat down in the chair and was reaching for the phone. I left the room and continued down the hall to the front desk. April was standing there talking to one of the other officers. She turned to see me coming down the hall and walked towards me.

"Are you going to be okay?" she asked.

"I'm not sure," I responded, "but I do know that there was one more positive thing that came from this investigation that you forgot."

"What's that?" She said.

"You," I replied, "you".

"I don't want to start crying my eyes out in front of my fellow officers. It's hard enough trying to get some respect from you men. If we leave now, I'll let you buy me lunch instead of dinner and it doesn't even have to be a fancy place."

I put out my arm and April wrapped her arm around mine as we left the precinct.

"Which car are we going in?" I asked.

"Yours," she replied.

"I haven't had a car since the rental got destroyed a few days back," I responded.

"While I was at the front desk," she said, "someone dropped off keys for a bureau car that Web had sent for your use".

We walked out the door arm in arm towards the car.

"Do you want to stop at your apartment to get changed before we go for lunch?" I asked.

"If you're talking about my discomfort with being stared at while I eat, let them stare. If you are just trying to get me back to my apartment, there is plenty of time left in the day," she replied with a smile.

Chapter 27
It's About the Money

April and I just finished lunch when we received a call from Bob. He'd been staying at Jenna's house monitoring the CIA informant's actions. He reported that there'd been so little activity in the past couple of days that most of his time was being spent watching the television with Jenna. While I knew it was a long shot, I'd hoped that Fein might have reached out to his informant for a new identity, or for something that might have given us a new lead. I guess the elaborate hoax he'd put on to fake his own death was not only meant to fool us, but his informant as well. I'd asked Bob to keep monitoring, although I held out little hope that he'd come up with any new information. I told him that April and I picked up some lunch for Jenna and him and would be stopping by on my way to the ranch to see my folks.

"Do you mind making a stop at Jenna's house?" I asked April.

"No, it will give me some time to digest lunch before your mom tries to feed me again," she said with a smile.

"We hopped onto I-10 heading towards Jenna's house. On the way, April and I tried to figure out a way to tell Jenna that the man responsible for her husband's death had gotten away. We hoped that she would be able to take some solace in knowing that Dan's name was going to be cleared. I remember sitting down with Jenna the day we met. She told me how she took full responsibility for not picking up on the signs that Dan was in trouble. The more I thought about it, I came to realize that the guilt she felt wasn't something she'd contrived, but something that had been thrust upon her by Dan's parents. By holding her responsible, they'd severed any remaining connection they might have had to Dan.

When we pulled into Jenna's neighborhood, I was surprised to see several well-dressed men and what appeared to be a couple of contractors. They were inspecting the vacant lots and shells of houses that had been previously abandoned mid-construction. It looked like there might be some renewed interest in developing Jenna's community. While we were both surprised by the sudden activity, we were happy for Jenna. It appeared that she might have some new neighbors, and a real community to look forward to in the near future. Jenna must have been watching the activity as well from her windows. We hadn't made it up the stairs before Jenna opened the door for us. I'd asked April to keep Jenna busy and to avoid discussing the case until I had a chance to talk to Bob alone.

"We brought lunch for the two of you," April said. "Let's set it up in the kitchen."

As soon as they walked away, I quickly stepped into the living room to speak with Bob. He was so fixated on something he was watching on the business channel that he didn't even turn his head when he spoke to me.

"They're reviewing the big winners and losers for the trading day," he said.

I sat down on the couch close to him so I could fill him in without Jenna over hearing us.

"Damn," he yelled."

"What's wrong?" I asked.

"Belzair Industries." he replied, "I would have killed to have had a short on that stock. It lost over a hundred points today because of a government contract they lost. I could have made some serious money on that trade."

"Sorry," Bob said. "Did you have something you wanted to talk about?"

My brain just went into high gear. I felt like I just got a brain-freeze.

"Are you alright? Bob asked.

"Alright!" I yelled, "I think I just had another epiphany, thanks to you". I leaned over and gave Bob a kiss on his cheek.

"Don't be getting weird on me." Bob responded as he wiped his face. "I think Jenna might like me and I don't want her getting the wrong idea."

"Sorry," I replied. "I just got caught up in the moment. I need for you do some research for me in a hurry."

"Does this mean I don't get to eat lunch?" he asked.

"You'll have to eat while you work," I replied. "I need you to get started on this immediately."

Within five minutes, I had filled him in on what information I needed. I reminded Bob that we still had to keep this under the radar.

"Any questions?" I asked.

"It shouldn't be a problem to get that information," he replied.

"Do you think you can have it for me by tomorrow morning?" I asked.

"Tomorrow, are you kidding me?" he asked. "If you're right, I should have something for you within a couple of hours."

"You are the man!" I yelled as I headed to the kitchen to get April.

"We have to go," I told her.

I then turned towards Jenna and apologized for our abrupt departure.

"I hope you enjoy the lunch," I said.

"Don't you want to have a certain conversation?" April asked.

Jenna interrupted, "With me?"

I told Jenna that we were still on the trail of Dan's murderer and would let her know if there were any new developments. I grabbed April by the hand and rushed her out the door and into the car.

As soon as the car doors shut, April asked in an excited tone, "What are you doing? Why did you say that? How? How?...."

I stopped April mid stammer. "To answer your question, what I am doing is heading over to my parents so I can introduce them to my now official girlfriend April Lynch.

I continued, "While we are there, you will have your second lunch of the day, and have my mother tell you all my good points, which should take about three minutes. While that is all going on I will be sitting on the couch with my father praying that my hunch is right, or Jenna is going to be very upset with me".

"I'm guessing I missed a few things while I was keeping Jenna busy in the kitchen," she said. "For example, official girlfriend?"

"I'm sorry, I didn't mean to be presumptuous," I said.

"No, I'm okay with that one," She responded.

She stared at me for a few minutes while we were driving before asking. "Are you going to fill me in on the other item I missed, like how you are on the trail of Dan's murderer?"

I told April that at the moment, I was travelling with my girlfriend and not with Officer Lynch. "Sharing that type of information with my girlfriend might be in violation of Bureau policy," I said in jest.

"You know I have a gun," she responded.

"Just be patient, I don't want to raise your hopes anymore in case I'm wrong. There is no sense in both of us being miserable."

"Once I hear back from Bob and I know I have something worth sharing, I will get everyone to meet us back at the precinct and I'll spill my guts.

Just keep your fingers crossed for now that your boyfriend is as smart as he thinks he is."

"Being full of yourself isn't one of those good qualities that your mother is planning on telling me about is it?" She asked. "Because if it is, this might be the shortest relationship on record".

"Actually, no," I responded, "that one probably would not be on her list."

As I was finishing my response, we passed the gates leading up to the ranch. I thought to myself, not a moment too soon. We pulled in front of the house, parked the car, and started walking up the porch steps. I opened the screen door. Something was missing...the creaking noise was gone. I looked on the floor and to the right of the door sat an oil can. My father finally had gotten around to oiling the door hinges. When we walked into the house, the den and kitchen were empty. It was a bit unusual not seeing my mother standing over the oven cooking. Under the circumstances, I was starting to get a bit alarmed when all of sudden my mother appeared walking out of my father's study.

"You had me worried there for a minute when I didn't see you in the kitchen," I said.

My father was a few steps behind "I told you that we shouldn't have fixed the damn door. Now, we could have anyone walk into this house and not even know it."

"You sound like you are in a cantankerous mood," I told him.

"He was just paying the bills." My mother replied. "Has it been that long that you forgot how pleasant your father can be on those days?"

"I just finished baking a fresh apple pie do you want some?" she asked. We all followed my mother into the kitchen and took a seat at the table.

I informed them that April and I were now officially an item. That brought a huge smile to my mother's face at which point, she nearly suffocated April with a hug. My father even managed a big grin at hearing the news. As I expected, my mother sent my father and I into the den so she could have April all to herself. As we started walking to the couch, I heard my mother start telling April what a great guy I was. April turned towards me for second as if she was looking to be rescued. In response, I put up a big grin on my face. April responded by moving her hand down towards her gun, immediately wiping that grin off my face. While we were waiting, I started talking to my father about the case. I knew that he was chomping at the bit to find out what transpired since our last conversation. When I told him about the body not being Fein's his face went limp of expression. Although I couldn't give him all of the particulars at the moment, I did tell him a bit more than I had divulged to April. I asked him to please keep a lid on it, or I might be in the doghouse if she found out.

"That was some good detective work," he said.

"We don't have him yet, and there is still a good chance that I could be wrong. If that's the case, we may never find him," I replied.

My father told me that the toughest part of the job is when one of the bad guys gets away. But whenever that happens, you need to focus on all of the ones that didn't.

"It's funny," I responded, "I don't remember that ever working for you."

"It didn't, but it sure does sound good in theory," he said with a short chuckle.

He told me almost to the word what Web had said earlier in the day. "Even if Fein is never caught, think about all of the people's lives you saved from the misery he would have inflicted on them."

My cell phone rang and I fumbled it for a second after retrieving it from my pocket. I could tell immediately by caller ID that it was Bob. He'd regularly alter his phone number to show up on caller ID with the area code "666". He had a strange sense of humor, but that was one of things that made him so endearing.

I answered the phone, "Please tell me that you have something for me."

The voice on the other end replied, "I'm still running two of my search comparison algorithms, but I think it is safe to say that you were right."

"Yes!" I responded not realizing that I had said it so loud that it startled my father and drew my mother and April to the kitchen door.

"Email me everything you have so far, and keep it coming as you get more. I owe you big time. Thanks," I said in an excited voice.

I told my father I had to get back to the precinct, and then proceeded to save April from her second slice of apple pie, and even worse, my mother telling childhood stories about me.

We got out to the car and I headed immediately for the passenger seat. "What are you doing?" she asked. "This is an official FBI vehicle and you should be doing the driving."

I responded, "You let me drive yours, I'm going to let you drive mine. Besides, I need to review the information that Bob just sent me and get everyone back to the precinct."

"You're not going to give me a hint of what Bob is sending you?" April asked.

"I'll do better than that, I'll tell you everything. But only when we are all back at the precinct," I replied.

April punched me in the arm almost knocking the phone out of my hand as I dialed her father.

"Detective Lynch," he answered.

"Surprised to hear from me so soon?" I asked. "Can you call Web and Riddle and ask them to meet us in the conference room in about thirty minutes?"

"Can you give me a good reason to pass along for this impromptu gathering?" he asked.

"Tell them I promise it will be worth the trip."

I had just under thirty minutes to review what Bob had sent me on my smart phone, while April navigated us through downtown Phoenix. I didn't have to read far into what Bob sent before I was convinced that we were back on Fein's trail. It looked like Christmas came early this year and Bob Clayton was playing the role of Santa Claus. We arrived at the station with a couple of minutes to spare. We parked the car and headed directly to the conference room. We'd spent so much time here over the past week that it was starting to feel like a second home. When we walked in, Lynch was sitting at the table rummaging through some papers related to another case.

"Anyone else here?" I asked.

"Riddle was finishing a call, and I expect that Web should be here any minute," Lynch replied.

Lynch asked, "So, April do you know why we're here?"

"No, he wouldn't tell me until we were all together," she replied.

Web and Riddle were coming from different directions of the hall and had converged in front of the conference room. Web yielded to Riddle, allowing him to enter the room first.

"Don't you know what take the rest of the day off means?" Web asked directing the question to me.

"When you hear what I have to say, you will be glad that I didn't."

"Well," Web replied. "you have a captive audience, let the show begin."

"Up until now, we all thought that Fein's actions were all motivated by revenge," I said, "but in fact, while revenge might have been a part of it, I came to realize that the primary motive was money."

I told them about Bob's comment regarding the stock he had been watching.

"It dropped a hundred points today."

Riddle asked, "What the hell does a stock dropping have to do with this case?"

I explained to Riddle that when you short a stock, you are betting that within a short period of time, the stock is going to drop in value.

He responded with a blank stare.

"Think about it," I said. "Let's say you know that a key figure in a publically held company is going to be murdered. All you would have to do is bet the stock is going to drop by shorting it. Then, you just have to wait a couple of weeks before you pull the trigger on your victim."

"And?" Riddle inquired.

"Then, you just sit back and wait for the stockholders to panic. The more important the victim was to the company, the more the stock falls."

"And the more the stock falls, the more money you'd make," Web said.

"What about the local politicians and the Senator that he had killed? The state and federal governments don't have shareholders," Lynch said.

"If it was a key political figure like the Senator," Web suggested, "Any pending appropriation decisions for or against a particular company such as giving or taking away a government contract could manipulate the stock as well".

"Yes, exactly," I replied. "In the case of the Senator, Fein might have been trying to blackmail him to make certain decisions that would hurt or favor companies so that Fein could buy stock or short those companies as well."

"So do we go to the FCC and investigate anyone that had huge windfalls from shorting the stocks of these companies?" Lynch asked.

"No, that would take too long and might tip Fein off. That's where Bob comes in. I'm having him look at any company that might have had its stock influenced by the murders that were perpetrated by Vets under Fein's control. He's already found one name that's shown up as shorting stocks on

David A Sterling

three of the companies from that list. Millions were made just in these three transactions alone," I said.

"Was the name Fein?" Riddle asked.

"No, that would have been too obvious and too boring," I said, "This cocky bastard used the name Ben Mills."

"You're kidding me," Web said. "What a set of balls on this guy!"

After saying it, Web turned to April and apologized.

"I'm a police officer, not a nun," April responded.

"He probably figured that with the way he had been playing us so far, even if we figured out the body wasn't his, we would never be able to figure out his end game."

The phone rang and April picked it up. "It's Bob," she said. She then put him on speaker phone.

"Hi Bob, I'm sitting in the room with Riddle, Lynch, Web, and April. Since you're the one that set this idea into motion, why don't you fill everyone in on what you've got."

"Fein had made several trades that I have found so far involving the vet killings. All of the trades were made by Ben Mills," he said. There are at least a dozen more trades under the same name that I am still trying to connect to vet killings. But I haven't been able to come up with anything yet."

"So, where do we find him?" Web asked.

Bob responded, "Didn't Bennett tell you?"

"I haven't gotten to that point yet," I replied. "Why don't you tell them?"

Bob continued "All the money was wired to several bank accounts set-up in the Cayman Islands. It looks like Fein was planning for the worse and purchased a ten million dollar beach front home just three weeks ago in an all cash transaction".

"Thanks Bob," I said, and then picked up the phone. "Did you take care of that thing I asked you about?"

"All is good," Bob replied.

"Great, I think you should get going now," I responded and then hung up the phone.

"Do we have an extradition treaty with the Cayman Islands?" Lynch asked.

"This might be our last chance to nail this bastard, and I'll be damned if I'm going to trust the Cayman Island police to bring Fein in!" I shouted. "According to Bob's totals on the accounts we know about, his combined net worth exceeds one hundred million dollars. That kind of money can buy you a lot of friends in Grand Cayman."

"So, what are you suggesting?" Web asked.

"I've always wanted to take a vacation in the Cayman Islands and I do have six weeks of vacation time accrued," I replied.

"Are you suggesting that you go as an FBI Agent to an island that we have no jurisdiction in, apprehend a criminal, and bring him back to the States to be tried?" Web asked.

"It sounds like fun to me," April said.

Both Lynch and I, in unison yelled "You're not going!"

"Neither of you are going!" Riddle yelled, "Our jurisdiction ends at the Phoenix city limits."

"I'm sorry Bennett," Web said, "I know we all want to see this dirt bag brought to justice, but I can't approve a Federal agent under my command entering a foreign country knowing that he's going to violate that country's sovereignty. We're going to have to handle this through diplomatic channels and hope for the best."

I pulled out my badge and gun and put them on the table. "It's been a pleasure serving with all of you, but a man's got to do what a man's got to do. How long do you think it will take to start the diplomatic process?" I asked.

"It's a Friday. You know those diplomats, they like to start their week-ends early. I doubt that anything will get done until sometime Monday afternoon," Web responded.

Web shook my hand and wished me luck. I walked out the door, down the hall and out of the precinct as an unemployed civilian. I heard a voice calling my name. It was April, she had followed me into the parking lot.

"If you do find him, you'll never get him off the island and back to the States to stand trial!" she yelled.

"I'll cross that bridge when I come to it," I replied.

"You're not planning on bringing him back, are you?" she asked.

"As I said, I'll cross that bridge when I come to it."

"I guess that we just took the first prize for the world's shortest relationship," she said with a tear running from her eye. She started to turn around to walk away. I grabbed her arm and gently pulled her towards me. At first, she hesitated to look me in the eye, but when she finally did I could see that she didn't mean it. I held her in my arms for a few minutes then followed up with a long kiss. April then turned and walked back into the station. Before she walked through the doors she turned around and yelled "Remember you owe me a dinner!"

"I thought I took care of that the other day," I yelled back.

"That was lunch, you're not getting away that easy," she replied.

I turned and looked at the car that Web had just gotten for me to drive, reached into my pocket and pulled out the keys. I stared at them for a minute and then said to myself, "I guess I can't drive you now," I tossed the keys onto the hood of the car, and then walked to the end of the parking lot.

A few minutes later my ride appeared. "Where to Bennett?" Bob asked.

"Do you have everything I need?" I asked.

"Everything is in your bag," he responded.

"To the airport then," I said.

As Bob started to pull away, I looked back at the precinct. I wasn't sure, maybe it was just my imagination, but I could have sworn I saw a familiar blonde haired silhouette on the other side of the door. As we drove to the airport, I realized that I better come up with a good story to tell my parents, or I might not want to come back. We arrived at the airport and Bob pulled up to the curb of the passenger drop-off zone.

"Are you sure you want to go through with this?" he asked.

"Go back to Jenna. When this is all over you might find you have a future together," I responded.

Bob smiled and wished me luck as I got out of the car closing the door behind me. I watched as he pulled away, wondering if I'd be coming back. I reached into my bag and pulled out the tickets that Bob had purchased for me. I laughed when I saw that he had purchased roundtrip First class tickets to Grand Cayman and thought to myself, roundtrip, that's a vote of confidence. I knew that Web couldn't let me go in an official capacity, I just hoped that the rest of my plan would be executed as flawlessly.

My timing couldn't have been much better, by the time I got through security and to the gate, I had an hour before the plane boarded. As many times as I'd been on a plane, this was the first time that I'd flown first class. I was hoping it wouldn't be my last. The plane ride was a bit turbulent shortly after takeoff, but settled down once we hit higher altitudes. It was a nine hour flight. Normally in coach I wouldn't have been able to sleep, but thanks to the comforts of first class, I closed my eyes and was unconscious within minutes.

Chapter 28
Till Death Do Us Part

I woke up to the sound of the flight attendant asking me to put my seat back into the upright position. I must have been pretty tired to have slept through the entire flight, but I was happy I did. It would be early Saturday morning. There wouldn't be time for sleep once I got off the plane. I needed to check into my hotel and start reviewing the satellite images that Bob had printed of the house and the roads leading up to it. The next stop would be at a gun store somewhere in town. In Grand Cayman money talked. I made a substantial withdrawal from my savings to make sure that it talked loud enough to avoid any unnecessary questions. Then I needed to do a test run of the area and carefully plot out my next steps. Sunday would be the day. That is when I would confront Fein, and if I made any mistakes, it might be the last day of my life. I got off the plane, and grabbed my luggage off the conveyor. After clearing customs and immigration, I headed to the car rental service.

It was a five minute ride from the airport to the rental depot. If I survived this trip and wanted to go on a real vacation, Bob would be the guy I'd have plan it. The car he'd rented for me was a black Porsche. If I was going out, at least I'd be going out in style. Based on my last rental experience, I made damn sure I took out every insurance option that was available to me. Thanks to the GPS system I made it to my hotel in good time. As I drove around the island, I wished that I had more of an opportunity to enjoy it before confronting Fein. I knew that with Web initiating diplomatic efforts on Monday, time was a luxury I did not have.

I checked into my suite, which was almost as big as my apartment in DC. I pulled out my paperwork and laid it out across the King size bed so I could start my review. While in DC, I spent most of my off time alone, but after the past seven days of having someone with me all of the time, being alone now felt very strange.

I spent a few hours studying all of the documents including road maps, aerial photos, and the original plans for the house. Considering the cost of

Fein's home, I was surprised at how little privacy it had. I guess that's what you get for ten million when you buy on the beach in Grand Cayman. As far as I was concerned, the close proximity to the busy beach gave me a tactical advantage. With all of the people travelling up and down the shoreline, I should be able to get within fifty feet of his front door without being noticed. After being locked in the room all morning, I was in desperate need of some fresh air and food. While I was out taking care of those basic necessities, I figured I'd do my drive by of the house to get a better take on the lay of the land. Pictures and satellite imagery will only get you so far. To avoid the risk of a chance meeting with Fein, I knew I'd have to stick to the local fast food drive-thru windows for my meals. I always found those coincidental meetings tended to happen most when you wanted them to happen the least. I laughed to myself as I had flashbacks of the disguise that Bob had worn at the airport. If only I had that moustache and beard, I might be on my way to fine dining instead of having fast food as potentially one of my last meals.

I left the hotel and hopped into the Porsche, taking the roof down before going in search of my lunch. About a mile up the road from the hotel, I found a seafood joint and ordered some fish and chips. I pulled into a parking spot just long enough to finish eating before driving by the house a couple of quick times. I kept the baseball cap I'd been wearing tilted down to obscure as much of my face as possible. After each pass, I'd pull off the road, pick-up my notepad, and jot down the landmarks that were discernible on the beach directly behind the house. After three passes, I pulled over a couple of miles past the house and tried to relax my mind for a few minutes while I took in a view of the waves and a few bikini's, mostly the bikinis of course. Twenty minutes later, I pulled back onto the main road and used my GPS to direct me to a Gun Shop that I'd found on the internet. I was amazed at the selection they carried, even more amazed at how easy it was to pick-up a gun. All it took was plunking down the cash, no questions asked. They had a shooting range setup in the back. I took three guns into the range for testing, and decided to purchase two of them. I figured it never hurt to have a second weapon concealed and available, just in case. I realized that there wasn't much else to do at the moment, except go back to my hotel, and review the documents and my plan one more time. First thing I did when I got back to the room was to check my personal emails. I hoped I'd see something in my inbox from April, but surprisingly, nothing was there. It made we wonder what she might be doing back home. I spent the next hour doing my final review before deciding to watch a movie hoping to keep my mind distracted from the day that was ahead. It was closing in on eleven o'clock when I finally put my head down on the pillow.

I woke up at nine in the morning feeling refreshed, and unexpectedly, relaxed. I didn't know if that reflected confidence, or stupidity on my part. The hotel had advertised a continental breakfast that was included with the room. I went down to the restaurant had some eggs, toast, and two of the best cups of coffee I ever had. If I knew for sure that I would make it through the day, I might have bought a couple of bags to take home with me.

I made a quick trip up to my room, grabbing everything I needed before heading down to the parking lot. I sat in the car for a minute with the engine running, took a deep breath, and pulled away from the hotel. The island wasn't as confusing as I thought it would be, but it was still nice to have the GPS. At the moment, that often stuttering digitized voice was the only traveling companion I had.

After a short three-mile drive, I'd reached my first checkpoint. I turned off the main road pulling into a parking lot that was within a quarter of a mile of what I hoped would be Fein's last safe haven. The house was located on a stretch along Seven Mile Beach. My casual touristy attire seemed to work in my favor, allowing me to blend in with the rest of the beach crowd. I wore a wide brimmed straw hat, keeping it tilted down to obscure my face. As I approached the house from the beach, I took extra precautions to avoid making eye contact with anyone. My first face to face with Fein needed to be in the house and not on a public beach. At the moment, he had one noteworthy advantage over me, he knew exactly what I looked like. Although Bob was able to scrounge up a couple of twenty-year old photos, anything current had been wiped out of existence by his friend at the CIA. The only thing that I had in my favor was the element of surprise, or so I hoped. With any luck, the detailed floor plans that Bob had supplied me with would allow me to navigate Fein's home as easily as he would. As I walked the beach, I paid special attention to the approaching landmarks looking for the ones I had noted yesterday during my surveillance. Each home I passed was more palatial then the next. I wouldn't have been surprised if half of them were purchased by embezzlers, and the other half by Wall Street brokers. Some might argue that they are one and the same. If my memory served me correctly based on the landmarks just in front of me, I was within two homes of my second checkpoint, Fein's house.

I figured that carrying around a pair of binoculars on the beach would have made me stick out like a sore thumb. Instead, I decided to bring a digital camera with a compact telephoto lens to help me get a better view of what was going on in and around the house. I needed to be sure that no one would see me once I started making my approach. The one thing that seemed to be a standard feature on all of these homes were big windows. I guess if you're going to pay that big price tag for oceanfront property, you want to have big views to go with it. After taking several quick pictures, I moved into the shadows of a portable gazebo erected on the beach to review them. All the images seemed to indicate that there was no activity in or around the house. As I got closer I was able to peer into the garage window finding it to be empty. The car that the satellite image had shown in the driveway was nowhere to be found. For the moment, lady luck smiled on me, it appeared that no one was home.

I wasn't sure how long I might be waiting, but getting inside the house while it was empty would give me a strategic advantage that would be well worth the wait for Fein to return. Before entering the main house, I looked through the kitchen window and with the help of my telephoto could see that the alarm had not been activated. I took that as a possible sign that wherever he went, he would not be gone for long. I quickly picked the side door lock and entered the house. Not knowing when Fein might return, I didn't waste any time surveying the house. From the floor plans that Bob had given me, I was easily able to navigate my way into the study. It was the most insulated room in the house from the view of the beach crowd. The last thing I needed was to have someone calling the police while I was pointing a gun at Fein. I didn't know if the ten million Fein paid for the house included the furnishings, but I could tell that whoever did the decorating wasn't short on cash. The furnishings in the study alone probably cost more than I took home in two years. I'd purchased a pay as you go phone which I placed in clear view on the desk which was located at one end of the den. I situated myself in a leather recliner that was in the opposite corner of the room. If I could draw him into the room, he wouldn't be conscious of my presence until he was standing behind the desk. By the time he took note of me, he would be in the open and I would have the drop on him. While I waited, I thought about how nice it would be if April was here with me. I didn't mean in the house, but on the island. I was looking forward to getting to know her better and hoped that if everything went as planned, I would be on a plane flying back to her tomorrow.

My wait was not as long as I expected. It couldn't have been more than twenty minutes before I heard the car pull into the driveway, and the garage door open and then close. The moment I had been waiting for was quickly approaching. Finally, I would have the chance to come face to face with this psychopath. Seconds later, the door leading from the garage opened and then shut. I could hear the sounds of footsteps in the kitchen and the faint whistling of a tune that was unfamiliar to me. Up until now, the execution of my plans had been flawless. I was now about to enter into uncharted territory. It wasn't just about how Fein would react once he was staring at the end of my gun, but how I would react once I was facing Fein. It was an unsettling feeling not knowing how far I was willing to go if necessary.

He had illustrated too many times how clever and resourceful he could be. Even with the element of surprise and a gun in hand, I could not allow myself to become overconfident. I opened my cell phone and hit the speed dial to the phone I had left on the desk. As soon as it started ringing, I could hear the footsteps getting closer and closer trying to get a fix on where the noise was coming from. Finally, I saw Fein walk into the study from the kitchen. Based on the angle at which he was approaching the desk, all I could see was the back of his head. It wasn't until he walked around it to pick-up the phone that I had my first look at his face. It was the tan face and ice blue eyes that April had described to me that night at the hospital. What she couldn't see under the surgical mask he was wearing that night were his sunken cheeks and hooked nose. His hair was jet black and had receded from the time the pictures I had seen were taken. Not to sound overdramatic, but it was the face of a madman. He examined the phone for a few seconds with an uneasy look appearing on his face before flipping it open.

"Hello, hello," he said as he spoke into the cell phone appearing puzzled by its presence.

I hit the end call button on my phone and while still sitting in the recliner I said "Dr. Fein I presume".

He turned in the direction of where I was sitting, looking startled at first. When I stood up even though I had a gun pointed directly at him he seemed to relax once he saw it was me.

"Agent Bennett," he replied, "what an unpleasant surprise. I realize now that I made a mistake not killing you at the same time that I had your old DC police partner killed."

At that moment, I realized that the accident that killed him wasn't an accident at all. I guess moving me to the FBI wasn't enough, he needed to make sure that my partner wasn't going to carry-on with the investigation of the alley case once I was gone. I must have worn the shock on my face because Fein immediately commented.

"By the look on your face, it appears you hadn't figured that one out yet, but obviously you did figure out enough to allow for this little reunion," he replied.

"Reunion," I said, "You mean when I came to your home during the case to ask you questions. Based on my recollection of that house, you have substantially upgraded since then."

"Thank you, it just goes to show if you work hard what you can achieve," he replied.

At that moment it took every ounce of willpower in my body to keep from putting a bullet in his head and ending this conversation right now.

"I'm really surprised that your boss allowed you to come after me here. As a Federal agent I am sure your government is taking quite a risk. I'm honored that they are holding me in such high regard," he said with a laugh.

"Don't flatter yourself," I said. "I handed over my badge to have the pleasure of either killing you or bringing you in. For the record, I'm leaning towards killing you."

"That's not very nice, after all because of your uncle saving my father's life that day, I reciprocated and allowed you to live. I would think you would at least be a little grateful. If I had killed you, you never would have met your blonde girlfriend," he replied.

"If my uncle knew the slime that your father was going to spawn, he might have given saving his life a second thought," I said. "I do have to give you credit though for your effort to frame Beninni. If it wasn't for one minor oversight on your part, you might have gotten away with it."

"With everything I have accomplished, that is the only thing you can think of giving me credit for?" he asked in an agitated tone.

It was obvious that I had just bruised his ego with my comments. He started to reach towards a drawer in his desk and I cautioned him that I would shoot.

"I just want to get something from my drawer. I'm sure that you would be able to kill me long before I could pull out a gun anyway," he asserted.

I told him that if I saw anything that looked like a gun coming out of the desk, it would be the last thing he did. He slowly reached down retrieving an incredibly thick leather bound book from the drawer.

"You see this book?" he said. "This is my diary where I have recorded all my accomplishments. I have manipulated hundreds of people from mechanics making brakes fail to Senators passing legislation to suit my financial needs. I've even manipulated a few mobsters, but you already knew that didn't you. All of them doing my bidding whenever needed."

Seeing that he was in the mood to talk, I decided to egg him on in order to find out as much as possible about his operation.

"I guess I underestimated you. Who would have believed that you were actually able to hypnotize all those people," I said.

"No, not all. As I am sure you are already aware, my abilities to control are not limited to hypnotic suggestion. In some cases, I just needed to make myself available through some not by chance encounters. I would be there to offer my services to help them out of an occasional indiscretion," he said. "They were more than willing to accept my help to save their own asses".

I interrupted him "And in return, you had them tied around your finger to do as you say."

"Yes, to have them do as I say," he replied. "Let's take your friend Bill for instance. All I had to do was alter his records on his Bureau psych exam. It was easy to tell from his answers that he was desperate to work for the FBI. That made him an easy mark. I didn't even need to break a sweat on that one."

"You know what surprises me most," I said.

"What is that?" he asked.

"That you're so chatty," I responded, "If I decided to take you into custody instead of killing you, everything you're telling me can, and would, be used against you in a court of law. I would think that you would be a little bit more careful about what you were saying."

"I might be concerned about that," he said, "if I was the only one that had a gun pointed at their heads".

I heard the click of a of a gun being cocked behind me. I turned around slowly as to not startle whoever it was into pulling the trigger prematurely. No one was directly behind me, but when I looked up towards the loft overlooking the study there was a man pointing a gun directly at me. By the tattoo on his arm, I could tell he was a vet.

"Do as I say, not as I do," I said hoping that if he was hypnotized that he would snap out of it. In response, both he and Fein just started laughing.

"Allow me to introduce my partner in crime, this is John Alverez, formerly Private John Alverez before he was dishonorably discharged from the military. I met him at one of the VA hospitals. It seemed clear at the time that his training in explosives and his self-acquired knowledge of poisons would come in handy from time to time."

"So it was your friend that blew up April's car at the hospital. I'm assuming he was responsible for serving my friend Bill his last meal at the hotel and killing Jenny Yuen."

"Yes, he replied. "John does do nice work. I am sure that your friend Bill could have come in very handy, but he said he would rather die than continue to betray you. So in a sense, I guess we did him a favor by poisoning his dinner that night. John was actually quite compassionate towards your friend. When he came into the room Bill was on the floor dying a painful death. John offered him the sleeping pills to put him out of his misery before it got any worse."

"You sick bastard," I replied.

"Now, now. Sticks and stones Bennett. I'm growing tired of this dialogue. It's time to do what I probably should have done a long time ago." he said as he was getting ready to signal his friend to shoot me.

"So your friend here isn't hypnotized?" I blurted out.

Alverez responded, "No, I was just in it for the money."

"That's all I wanted to hear!" I yelled.

A shot rang out. I looked up into the loft just in time to see Alverez with a bullet in his head falling backwards to the ground. Then, out of the corner of my eye I saw Fein reach into the already open drawer. He was reaching for a gun. He barely got it out of the drawer when I gave him a matching tattoo on his forehead. He stood standing for a few seconds with blood streaming from his forehead before falling forward crashing his head into the desk and lights out.

"What took you so long?" I asked.

"He still seemed very chatty as you put it, I wasn't sure if you wanted to get any more information recorded before I took out Alverez," Web responded.

"Thanks for showing up, but how did you find me?" I asked.

"You have April and Bob to thank for that. April saw Bob pick you up outside the precinct. We both convinced him that you were going to need a little help," Web said.

"Remind me to give him a big kiss next time I see him," I responded.

"Actually, April gave him a big kiss and he said he preferred her kiss to yours. I didn't even want to ask what that was about," Web replied. "I have a question for you, how did you know I was even here?"

"Hasn't anybody ever told you that you use a bit too much aftershave?" I replied.

"Not until know," he replied with a twisted smile on his face.

"I'm sure that someone heard the shots and the police will probably be here any minute. You better get going". I told Web.

"What about you?" he asked.

"Don't worry about me," I said. "I've got this covered."

"If you say so," he replied.

I handed Web the keys to the car and directed him to where it was parked. I asked him to take it back to the hotel. I would meet him there.

"How are you getting back, assuming you don't land in the local jail?" He asked.

I told him to trust me. He nodded his head and exited the house through the back door disappearing into the crowd on the beach. I had a few things that I needed to get done before the police arrived. When I completed my list and the police still had not arrived, I decided to sit and wait for them on the front porch.

I greeted the officers as they pulled up. I told them that I came home from shopping and found two men robbing my house.

"I was fortunate that I had my gun with me and I was able to kill them before they killed me."

"Sir, may I see your identification?" the officer in charge asked.

I pulled out my passport, "I'm Bennett Mills, but my friends call me Ben, Ben Mills. If you check the registration you will find that this house belongs to me."

The officer called into the station and after a few minutes hung up. "I apologize Mr. Mills, but I needed to be sure. Have you ever seen these men before?" he asked.

"No, not until today," I responded.

One of the policeman carried over paperwork that he found on the bodies.

"I found a wallet in the pocket of the man by the desk," the policeman said. "According to his identification his name was Gregory Fein. The other guy didn't have any ID on him, but had a map of this house in his pocket."

I asked the head officer to walk into the other room with me. I told him that I was a very private man and didn't like a lot of attention. I voiced my concern that if this was publicized the men might have friends that could try to avenge their deaths. I offered him a significant cash donation for his favorite charity if he could take care of this matter for me. I could tell by the look in his eyes that he believed in the old saying that charity begins at home.

"There are five thousand dollars US in this bag," I said as I exposed the money that was obscured by my camera.

"Don't worry Mr. Mills," he said as he closed the camera bag putting the strap across his shoulder, "My men and I will take care of this matter for you." The officer went outside for a minute, and then backed his police car into the garage. He laid down some plastic drop clothes in the trunk and then placed the bodies onto them. Within twenty minutes of their arrival, they were gone. My only hope was that Fein and Alverez wound up at the bottom of the ocean. That was the only burial they deserved.

Before I left, I picked up the diary that Fein had revealed to me. I figured it would make for some good reading on the nine hour flight home. I decided to tour the house to see if there was any other useful information lying around. As tempting as it would have been to have kept the house, since it was in my name anyway, I figured Web would never give me back my badge if I did.

After an hour of looking around and throwing everything I thought might be useful into Fein's car, I locked the door to the house and drove back to the hotel. I thought the Porsche was nice, but it was nothing compared to Fein's red Lamborghini. As I pulled out of the driveway and onto the main road, I wondered if Web would at least let me keep the car.

Driving the Lamborghini was something I could definitely get used to. Since it was highly unlikely that I would ever drive one again, I decided before heading back to the hotel that I would take a short spin. After a nice drive along the coast, I headed back to the hotel. I pulled into the spot adjacent to where Web had parked the Porsche and ran up the stairs to the room. I had to knock a couple of times before Web finally opened the door.

"I was starting to get worried that I might have to break you out of jail tonight," he said.

"I'm sorry but I figured after what I'd gone through the past couple of days, I deserved to cruise for a while in the Lamborghini," I responded.

"You drove a Lamborghini?" a familiar voice from the bathroom yelled out. It was April. She opened the door, stepped out of the bathroom. "I was just changing after a swim," she said. "Once Web told me you were okay, I needed to relieve some stress."

I turned to Web "Are you out of your mind bringing her here?" I asked.

Web replied "You know that I am still your boss, right?".

"Actually, since I handed in my badge and gun, you're technically not my boss at the moment," I responded.

Web suggested that one more comment like that and my civilian status might be more permanent.

"If you boys are done fighting over me, I think that Bennett owes me a night out."

Web told April that before I went anywhere he wanted to find out how I managed to avoid winding up in jail.

"Why would they arrest Ben Mills?" I asked. "After all, the house and all of the bank accounts are in my name."

"What happened to the bodies?" Web asked.

"If I know my friends at the Cayman Police department, they're either buried in a ditch, or swimming with the fish," I responded.

I told Web how Bob and I figured that once Fein was killed the Cayman government would lay claim to the money that he had in his accounts.

As long as they think Ben Mills is still alive, the money stays in our control and we can get it back to the states.

"Makes sense, I guess we can talk about the rest later," Web said, "How about some dinner on me?"

"Actually, why don't I treat," I said as I pulled out Fein's wallet which was stacked with credit cards in my name.

"Then let's make it someplace nice," Web replied.

"Let's," April responded.

I put Fein's Diary into my bag, tucking it under my clothes, and we all walked out of the room closing the door behind us.

Chapter 29

The Layover

April and I drove Web to the airport. We had arranged for an upgrade to a first class ticket for his return flight to DC, courtesy of Ben Mills. I figured that was the least I could do considering he stuck his neck out by flying here, not to mention that he saved my life. We were up almost all night reviewing and copying Fein's diary. At least, it would be a comfortable flight back and he would hopefully get some sleep.

"Are you sure you don't want to stay for a while?" I asked. "I'm picking up the expenses."

"Thanks, but no thanks. I've got to get back and get the ball rolling on what we discussed," he said. "When should I expect you back?" he asked. "I'm assuming that you'll want to be around for the festivities."

I told Web that my plan was to stay for a couple of days with April before returning.

"After all, she did fly all this way to take a little vacation and see the island," I told him. "It wouldn't be fair to put her right back on the plane. As far as the festivities go, we'll fly directly into DC on Thursday. As soon as we land, I'll let you know."

"That was some fine investigative work you did. I'm assuming you won't be requesting a security detail assignment ever again," Web said.

"Probably not," I replied. "I think my father would shoot me if I did. I'll see you in a couple of days. Have a safe flight, and thanks for saving my ass. I probably would have been in an unmarked grave by now if you didn't show up."

"A man's got to do, what a man's go to do," Web replied with a smile on his face.

Web walked into the terminal. April and I drove off to enjoy some well-deserved time by ourselves. We spent two more glorious days roaming the beaches and bars in Grand Cayman before getting on the plane to DC. I promised April that when we returned, I would show her the town before she headed back to Arizona. The day prior to our leaving, April followed me

in the rented Porsche to a small church in one of the poorer villages of Grand
Cayman. It was called Bhatta-Parsaul. We walked into the rundown church
in the center of the town and located one of the priests. We proceeded to
make one of the biggest donations that the church had ever received. When
we handed the elderly priest the keys and title to the Lamborghini, I thought
he was going to faint. I wasn't sure what the going rate on a hardly used
Lamborghini might be, but I was sure it would be put to good use. Then we
hopped into the Porsche and drove to the airport to catch our flight. Once
we were on the plane, we talked for a while about our little adventure. Later
April rested her head on my shoulder and fell asleep. I put my head back and
breathed a sigh of relief, knowing that I was heading home. I leaned over and
gave April a soft kiss on the head then closed my eyes, and fell asleep.

We arrived back in DC Thursday at ten in the morning and took a cab
back to my apartment. I was dropping April off so she could freshen up while
I met with Web. It seemed funny to me that for several years I called the
apartment my home. After being back in Arizona with my family, it didn't
feel like home anymore. As soon as we walked into the apartment, I could
tell that April was giving it the once over. I can't blame her for wanting to
see how I lived. I did the same thing the first time I was in her apartment.

"So this is your bachelor pad?" she said.

"Yes," I replied. "You are free to look around as much as you want
while I'm gone."

"Hmmm," She replied. "I might just take you up on that."

"Would you like to show me where the bedroom is?" she said with a
smirk on her face.

"I would love to," I replied. "But I have some business to take care of
with Web and he'll be waiting for me. When I get back, I'll take you anywhere you want to go in DC, including the bedroom."

"I'll take that rain check," she responded. "Do you want me to make
you something to eat for later?"

"You might want to make reservations. The pickings in the fridge are
pretty lean." I replied. "If you get hungry, I have about twenty menus in the
top left drawer."

"Okay," she responded. "Remember you promised to show me all of the
sights in DC. I love history."

On the way out, I gave April a long kiss goodbye. There was a point that I had to break it off or I might have never been able to leave. I could only imagine the look on Web's face if I didn't show up on time. We had plans to meet at the Senate building where Hope was to be sworn in as the new Senator from Arizona. As soon as I walked into the rotunda I saw Web sitting on a bench.

"Are you ready?" he said.

"Do I have a choice?" I responded.

As we walked, we were joined by several DC police officers, creating what appeared to be a blockade in front of Hope and her entourage.

"What's this all about?" Hope asked in an annoyed tone, "I'm running late for my swearing in ceremony."

"I'm afraid you are going to be much later than you think," I replied. "Two of the conspirators in your father's death were killed last week in the Cayman Islands."

"What do you mean two of the conspirators?" she asked.

"How could you do it?" I asked.

Hope might have been a good bluffer when it came to playing cards, but she didn't see this one coming and had no time to prepare for it. Her initial expression and the color draining from her face said it all. Before she could regain her composure, I handed her a copy of the notes and photos from Fein's diary. He might have been a psychopath, but he was a meticulous psychopath. His diary contained recorded phone conversations and photos on DVD's along with explicit notes. The dates and times of every meeting and conversation were recorded. He always made sure that when he reeled in his victims that he had them hook, line, and sinker.

"You were the blonde in the alley that night. Fein paid those men to set you up. He told them that he was doing it to straighten you out. The man you met in the bar was supposed to take you to the alley so you could both buy drugs. The plan was to fake an argument between the two men. Then using a gun with blanks the guy acting as the drug dealer would make be- lieve he shot and killed the other man. He would then coerce you into shoot- ing him in self-defense. After you panicked and ran off that night, Fein had his friend Alverez kill both of the men."

Hope interrupted, "I was setup, you said it yourself!"

I continued, "Fein waited patiently for years until he needed some help on capitol hill that required a level of influence that only your father could provide. He then tried to blackmail your father, using you for leverage. The only problem with Fein's plan was that unlike his other victims, your father had the fortitude to refuse his cooperation. As much as he loved you, he knew that once he gave in, the demands would never end. He decided to inform you of his plans to make the incident public. He agreed to hold off until after the election was over to give you time to prepare. You knew that once this came out, it would put an end to your chances of having a political career, and one day, taking your father's place in the Senate. With your father unwilling to cooperate, Fein turned to you offering a possible way of saving your future political career. He asked you to book the hotel for your fathers brunch, knowing that it would be the ideal time and place for an assassination. Once your father was dead, you knew the outpour of sympathy would make you a shoe in for his vacated seat."

"I'll repeat my earlier question," I said in an angry voice. "How could you do it Hope?"

In a defensive tone, Hope responded, "All my father had to do was to award a couple of insignificant military contracts to companies that Fein had a financial interest in. These kinds of things are done all the time in Washington, but not my father. He would rather see his daughter's life ruined then to step off of that high horse of his. Every day he would try to figure out how to help people he had never even met. You would think that for once he would put his own daughter ahead of his constituents!"

"For the sake of a future in politics, you conspired in the taking of your father's life. I didn't think it was possible, but you just brought politics to a new low." I responded.

"So what happens now?" she asked in a uncharacteristically meek voice.

"I'm sorry Hope, but you are under arrest as an accessory to the murder of your father," I replied.

She pointed at the policemen that were standing behind Web and I, "Did you really need all of these men just to arrest me?" She asked.

"No, only one. After you are read your rights and taken into custody, we have some house cleaning to do."

I turned to the officer standing to my left and asked him to read Ms. Billings her rights. As the officer finished mirandizing Hope and started to cuff her, Fred and Mike came running up to me. They had been waiting in the room for Hope to show up so she could be sworn in. "What's going on here?" Mike asked with a confused look on his face.

"Hope is being placed under arrest as an accessory to murder." I told them.

While Mike stood there with a shocked look on his face, Fred stepped in front of him and said, "What the hell are you talking about Bennett, she just hired us back as part of her private security detail."

"I'm sorry guys, but it looks like you were just sent back into retirement."

I then turned to Web and asked him if he needed me anymore, "I need to get some fresh air. Are you okay here?"

Web replied "I can take care of the others. Why don't you get out of here and take April sightseeing? You can read about the rest in the morning papers." Web then gave the signal to the remaining policemen to enter the Senate chamber.

"Go clean house guys," he said with a chuckle.

I starting working my way through the rotunda just in time. A herd of reporters must have gotten wind of Hope's arrest and started to barrage Web with questions. I continued walking undetected by the press out through the main doors. As I walked down the stairs to grab a cab, all I could think about was that the air seemed a lot cleaner in Arizona.

April and I spent a week travelling around DC, taking in all the sights, while Web handled the press. I had to admit that he looked pretty good on television. With all the attention he was getting, maybe he would wind up in office. There were going to be plenty of vacated spots. As for me, aside from having my ex-girlfriend arrested, it was otherwise a pretty good week.

When I called my folks to check in, my father told me that Lynch had arrested Beninni for the murder of his old boss. Web had forwarded Riddle a few pages from the diary the day he arrived back. He called it a thank you present for all their help. The next day, Beninni was out on bail driving back to his restaurant, when his car blew up. The poor bastard was so smug that he probably didn't even see it coming. Riddle told my father that the car was still smoldering when his successor was chosen.

The money from the Grand Cayman accounts was transferred back to the US and taken control of by the commerce department to be pissed away on God knows what. Before the transfer was made, Bob had covertly transferred, from an undisclosed account, two million dollars to each of Fein's victim's bank accounts courtesy of the Grand Cayman Lottery. We figured it was the least we could do for all of the suffering that they had endured. As for Bob, he arranged a transfer so he could be based out of the Phoenix office of the Bureau. The DC office wasn't happy about it, but he told them that if they didn't let him go, the CIA had an opening. Apparently, one of their top Information Specialists was just arrested for collusion in Fein's criminal activities. I'm guessing that being close to Jenna had something to do with Bob's request. It looked like Jenna's life was taking a turn for the better. She met Bob and it looked like she was finally going to have some neighbors. It seemed that word of a possible military contract in her town had slipped out, and developers were tripping over themselves trying to get the homes completed to handle the influx of the new residents. I didn't ask, but I would bet a Lamborghini that Bob had something to do with it.

All the way to the Dulles Airport, April kept asking me when I would be in Arizona the next time. I kept replying with the same cryptic answer "Soon." When we arrived at the airport, I walked with her to the gate and we sat down while waiting for her flight to board. On the airport television we noticed that a local news station was reporting on the seven congressmen and senators that were arrested on the same day as Hope. They reported that the exact details of their arrest had not yet been made public, but involved ethics violations. The follow-up story was about Hope being arraigned for the murder of her father. They mentioned that she was within thirty minutes of being confirmed to take over her father's vacated senate seat. Now, the only seat she would be filling would be in a prison cell at a Federal Penitentiary. When it came time to board, April gave me a big hug and a kiss before entering the jet way to the plane. I waited about ten minutes before following her on board. The look on her face when I asked her if I could pass through to the window seat was priceless.

"You're coming with me?" she asked with a big smile on her face.

"Why are you so surprised? I told you I would see you soon," I replied.

"How long will you be in Arizona?" she asked.

"That depends," I said.

"On what?" she asked.

"On how long you want me there. Web arranged for a transfer to the Phoenix branch. He felt that with everything going on in DC, it might be a good idea for me to get out of town for a while." I told April that I planned on taking a few weeks of vacation time before I started my new job as a lead investigator.

"Does my dad know?" she asked.

"Yes, and so does Riddle. Do you know what Riddle wants me to do during my vacation?"

"No, what?" April asked.

"He wants me to help him out with some of his unsolved case files," I said.

"On your vacation?" April asked with a surprised look on her face.

"Actually, it sounds like fun," I responded.

April leaned over and gave me a kiss, and then whispered in my ear, "Not on my time mister!"

I returned the kiss and whispered back, "I'll take you out to your favorite restaurant."

"Okay, maybe just one case," she replied, before giving me another kiss and then resting her head on my shoulder.

While we sat on the runway waiting to take off, I thought back to the day I arrested Hope. When I returned to the apartment, April had asked me if I was okay. I told her I was fine, but she knew that I was lying. I kept thinking back to Bill's letter where he mentioned that slippery slope. It's ironic how one bad decision can affect so many. Bill was dead, Hope's life irrevocably ruined, and here I was, for the second time in three weeks, on a plane sitting next to a Lynch. No offense to Ed, but I considered this a huge upgrade.

-The End-